MYSTERY WRITERS OF AMERICA *Presents*

DEATH
do us
PART

ALSO BY HARLAN COBEN

The Innocent

Just One Look

No Second Chance

Gone for Good

Tell No One

Darkest Fear

The Final Detail

One False Move

Back Spin

Fade Away

Drop Shot

Deal Breaker

MYSTERY WRITERS OF AMERICA *Presents*

DEATH
do us
PART

NEW STORIES ABOUT LOVE, LUST, AND MURDER

edited by
HARLAN COBEN

LITTLE, BROWN AND COMPANY
NEW YORK • BOSTON • LONDON

Little, Brown and Company
Hachette Book Group USA
1271 Avenue of the Americas, New York, NY 10020
Visit our Web site at www.HachetteBookGroupUSA.com

First Edition: August 2006

Library of Congress Cataloging-in-Publication Data

Mystery Writers of America presents death do us part : new stories about
love, lust, and murder / edited by Harlan Coben.—1st ed.
   p. cm.
ISBN-10: 0-316-01250-5 / ISBN-13: 978-0-316-01250-8 (hc)
ISBN-10: 0-316-01263-7 / ISBN-13: 978-0-316-01263-8 (pb)
1. Detective and mystery stories, American. 2. Interpersonal relations—
Fiction. I. Coben, Harlan, 1962– II. Mystery Writers of America. III. Title:
Death do us part.
PS648.D4M95 2006
813'.0872083552—dc22   2006001926

10 9 8 7 6 5 4 3 2 1

Q-FF

Printed in the United States of America

CONTENTS

Introduction   vii

QUEENY, *by Ridley Pearson*   3

SAFE ENOUGH, *by Lee Child*   12

THE HOME FRONT, *by Charles Ardai*   27

THE LAST FLIGHT, *by Brendan DuBois*   55

PART LIGHT, PART MEMORY, *by Bonnie Hearn Hill*   70

BLARNEY, *by Steve Hockensmith*   83

HEAT LIGHTNING, *by William Kent Krueger*   104

TILL DEATH DO US PART, *by Tim Maleeny*   115

THE COLD, HARD TRUTH, *by Rick McMahan*   125

ONE SHOT, *by P. J. Parrish*   144

CYBERDATE.COM, *by Tom Savage*   168

HOME COMING, *by Charles Todd*   184

THE MASSEUSE, *by Tim Wohlforth*   197

A FEW SMALL REPAIRS, *by Jeff Abbott*   212

CHELLINI'S SOLUTION, *by Jim Fusilli*   231

ONE TRUE LOVE, *by Laura Lippman*   247

WIFEY, *by R. L. Stine*   268

PUSHED OR WAS FELL, *by Jay Brandon*   288

ENTRAPPED, *by Harlan Coben*   313

About the Authors   331

Copyright Information   339

INTRODUCTION

I'M ABOUT TO give away the ending.

Crimes involving money don't interest me all that much. Oh, sure, as a red herring, they're pretty cool and, hey, now that I'm talking about this, maybe I'll do it in my next story just to fool you. But between us, it's just not what I'm into.

I'm also not big on serial killers hacking people up for no reason. Or conspiracies reaching the White House. There are people who write them well. But they don't really grab your heart, do they?

You want something bigger, more complex, more driven. You want something that you can relate to. You want to read about the crime that you can almost ALMOST see yourself committing. You want the story to explore a place as small as your fist and as vast as the universe. You want the story to trek through a land you know so well and yet you'll never really understand.

In short, you want the story set in the human heart.

You want it personal. You want it to be about you and that special someone who is lying beside you. You love your partner, don't you? The way she sleeps peacefully. The way she tosses and turns. You could stare at her all night.

Or maybe . . . ?

Those are exactly the kinds of stories that have been assembled for your reading pleasure within the pages of this anthology. With the assistance of the Mystery Writers of America, nineteen of today's top mystery authors, from established bestselling pros to new writers, have provided a collection of masterful mystery and suspense stories that all delve into the pulsating heart of relationships most foul or, worse, most splendid. They will, I think, give new meaning to the ultimate expression of "till death do us part."

Lest you think that mystery writers are all cynical curmudgeons, there are also several stories in here that celebrate the power of a loving relationship as it pertains to crime and punishment (which is possible). But at least half of these stories end badly for one spouse or both. Come to think of it, according to statistics, that's about the percentage of marriages that end in real life, although usually by not so permanent means.

So give your spouse or special other a big kiss and a hug before settling down to read these stories of domestic discord and marital malice (if you're single, then you don't have anything to worry about, unless this introduction has made you think about keeping a closer eye on your significant other, but that's another anthology altogether) as we present all-new crimes of the heart in *Death Do Us Part*.

—Harlan Coben

MYSTERY WRITERS OF AMERICA *Presents*

DEATH
do us
PART

QUEENY

RIDLEY PEARSON

I LAST SAW her at breakfast.

I work alone, in a room above the garage where a carpenter once told me the wood in the floor dated back pre–American Revolution. He could tell by the tightness of the grain, and the history of the building. People know that stuff. A friend of mine makes guitars. He once saw an instrument at a trade show and knew it had been made out of the same piece of African mahogany that he'd built a guitar out of. He exchanged stories with the luthier responsible, and sure enough he was right: same wood. People know weird stuff.

She'd mentioned it in passing, when I was furiously cooking pancakes for one of our daughters and scrambling eggs for the other; cooking oatmeal for my wife and me. It's the one real spoil I give our daughters: any breakfast you want, anything you name. But I'm a stickler with them in every other way. We get along well because the boundaries are set. There's respect and love now, not testing and challenges. There's harmony, real harmony, and that's a cherished commodity in a family.

"Some guy turned around running at Queeny Park and caught up to me, and ran with me."

"Seriously?"

"Yeah."

I think she told me to impress me, to remind me nine years into our marriage that other men still look. It wasn't news to me—I knew they looked—but I sensed that this was one of those moments in a marriage when you don't want to say the stupid thing. But she wasn't asking me if I liked her haircut.

"He say anything?" I ask.

"Yeah, we talked. He asked questions like how often I run. Stuff like that."

"You talked to him." I try not to make it sound accusatory, but my concern gets the better of me, and I blow it.

"I can't talk to a guy?" She goes back to the dishes. I have a pancake I'm burning. I flip it. The color of shoe leather.

She soaps up, runs the water a little louder than necessary.

"It isn't like that," I say, when I get a chance.

"No, it isn't," she replies.

"I mean . . . I'm not trying to tell you what you can and can't do. But it's a park, sweetie. You're a single woman, or at least a woman running alone, as far as he's concerned."

"You write too many of those books."

She often blames my occupation on my tendency to see criminal behavior in everyone. She's right, of course. She knows she'll always win this one, and she does.

A day passes. Two. It's breakfast again. It's crepes this time, and soft-boiled eggs for the youngest, a dish we call Fishies in the Brook—why, I have no idea. Soft-boiled eggs on pieces of torn bread in a bowl. No brook. No fishies. But the girls love it and eat it down to a yellow smear on the walls of the bowl.

"He was there again. Yesterday. He was running in my direction this time. Caught up to me and . . . and we ran together."

"I wish I could say something positive." But I can't. It's not that I care about the contact, the attention. Lord knows we can all use it. I get it too, the flattering comments out on book tour, the looks that go beyond a normal look. I don't act on them, and neither will she. That's not my worry at all. And if she does act on it, then that's dealt with then. But there's not a grain of jealousy spilling out of my shaker. This is straight concern, and I try to disguise it just enough so that I don't scare her. I'm good at scaring people. I've scared millions of readers for a very long time. I know the effect I can have, even when I don't mean to. I work hard not to scare my family, the kids especially.

"It's a dark park is all," I continue. "Long stretches in the woods. A long way from anywhere. Some guy pulls up to you out on Adams and runs along with you, you can at least scream. You scream in Queeny Park and you'll be lucky to scare off a few birds."

There's a hidden message here I'm not sure she gets. She stopped running for about five months—over a year ago now—because a car stalked her at five in the morning. It scared the pee out of her, literally. Slowed down and cruised alongside her before the sun was up, before the neighbors were up. When she hid behind a tree, the guy from the passenger window threw a can of soda at her and nearly hit her. We called the cops. I had the opening of *Mystic River* running through my head. She had laundry to do. The cop was pleasant and genuinely concerned. He took it around the block to the Bread Company, no doubt, and warmed up his cup and went on with his day. Bottom line: she stopped running. For five months.

Now she's back at it, and this time the guy's on foot and she doesn't see the parallels.

"If he was in a car 'running' alongside of you, how would you feel?"

"It's not the same thing," she says.

"What's his name?"

"I don't know."

"Where's he live?"

"I don't know."

"What's he drive?"

She goes back to the dishes because she can hear me say: "It *is* the same thing."

"How much does he know about you?" I ask.

She shakes her head. I sense she's blown it out on the trail and knows it, and doesn't have an answer.

We've been watching a movie on PBS where the husband is a jealous, controlling freak—it's Trollope—and I use that as my reference. "I'm not trying to be the guy in the movie. You know that, right? You want to run? Run. You want to talk? Talk. But maybe run with a friend so it's two against one. Maybe choose a park that isn't so completely isolated and dark. Queeny Park is so wrong for a woman running alone. It's totally wrong. You can see that, right?"

She shrugs.

I know that shrug. I've come to hate that shrug. It's the blow-off shrug. We're done here, and it's on her terms, and that burns me.

Another day or two. Three, maybe. She comes home that afternoon for lunch and lists the friends she ran with this morning. She doesn't do it in a way to sting me. She could, but she doesn't, and I love her for it.

"Thanks," I say between bites.

A couple days later it's the same: Laurel and Tracy, four-mile loop at Queeny, Starbucks afterward and a good talk. No mention of Him.

So today when the call comes from school, my first reaction is to be pissed off. Our eldest, at all of seven, wasn't picked up. Missed the bus and wasn't picked up. Missed the bus because her mother told her not to take it. Makes sense because it's Thursday and that's ballet. I'm on the way there when the BlackBerry rings and it's the private school. The youngest wasn't picked up.

Now, for the first time, the tick goes off in my brain. It's like a Tourette's misfire of a synapse: a burst of cursing aloud followed by near blindness and the inability to keep any one part of my body still. My seven-year-old is freaking out in the back-seat. She's come out of the shoulder strap, and that really frosts me because she's been doing this *a lot* lately, and it isn't safe, and she knows it. So I brake to a stop rather dangerously, and get a bunch of car horns as my prize.

"PUT YOUR STRAP BACK ON, YOUNG LADY!" She's the nearest target and she gets both barrels. My mind is racing now and I'm wondering how much of this is me the writer and how much the husband. I can see it all in my mind's eye, and I erase it just as quickly. *Do not go there!* I tell myself. *Steady keel.*

⤜◈⤛

IT HAS BEEN six days. There's no such thing as adjustment. I jump every time the phone rings. I hear cars on the street and am convinced she's pulling into the drive. But her car is down with the police. They found it at Queeny Park. Locked. Parked where she always parks, according to Laurel and Tracy. They never saw the guy. She'd never mentioned him to them. Embarrassed, maybe. Or private. Or a little bit of both.

No evidence. Dogs. Crime scene guys. Nothing. The TV shows are all liars. When they're gone, there's nothing left. They're just gone. No hairs and fibers. Not even a scent.

DAY TEN AND a crew of five guys and one woman enters my office above the garage with a search warrant. Their arrival hits me like a fist in my chest. They confiscate my computer, all my bills, my BlackBerry, my car.

I can't focus on the questions they fire at me. Mainly because it's *at* me. The tone is adversarial. There's no mistaking it. Accusatory. I'm dumbfounded. And I'm pissed, the way they're dealing with my gear. I'm a freak about my gear. I treat it like most people treat their pets. They're dragging the server downstairs, wires trailing. I'm burning mad about everything. Just the *thought* that they would dare do this to me . . . I've written books about it; I've interviewed cops who are twice the cop of these guys about it: when all else fails, look pretty hard at the husband.

And now it's me squarely in the sights.

DAY TEN AND a half. My attorney, a woman with a brain bigger than Texas. I've known her five minutes, but she comes as the choice of my New York entertainment lawyer, also a woman, and so well connected that I know this is the right one even before we meet. But now we've met and I even like her as well.

There's four of us in the small room. The cop looks tired, but it feels like an act. I've written better characters than this guy will ever be. He's K-Mart to my Bergdorf. But I don't, I won't, challenge him. I won't out-cop him. I'm just alive enough somewhere in my brain to know not to do this. I tell myself to listen. Let the attorney do the talking.

I say, "What's this all about?" wondering how my mouth can be so disconnected from my brain.

The attorney's head swivels like an owl's. She could have me for breakfast right now.

"When was the last time you visited Queeny Park?" the cop asks.

I look to the attorney. She nods.

"With you guys," I answer.

"Before that," he says. "The last time before that?"

I know where this is going. I'm mortified. I nod. "Okay," I say. "Okay, I see where this is going."

"Just answer the question, please."

I lean in to my attorney. She smells nice. I whisper my explanation.

She looks the cop in the eye and says, "Next question."

The cop's brow furrows. He's pissed. I don't blame him.

My car must have been seen by someone. It was *one morning*. Only one. I went out there to see if I could see the guy, see the car he climbed into, get something more on what she'd been telling me. Shouldn't have done it. Never saw a thing. But there it is. And I never mentioned it to them because I thought how stupid it sounded. How *bad* it sounded. And now it does. It goes unanswered.

"Can you tell me about Magic Movies?" he asks.

I feel my face go red. A home movie Web site. Voyeurs. All adult stuff. Amateur videos. Soft stuff for the most part. Some of it graphic. They'll use it to imply a dissatisfaction with our sex life—not true. They'll use it to suggest something troubled underneath the surface—not true. They'll spin it into violent acts, and not one of them showed any such thing. They're building a case. It's their job. K-Mart is having a sale, a banner day. Blue Light Special.

DAY NINETY-FIVE. A jury of my peers. I don't think so. Their case is all oblong shapes made to fit a square box. The twelve morons in the real box are nodding and looking at me like I'm Manson. I'm still in grief, still can't sleep or wrap my mind around her doing the dishes and me cooking crepes and never bothering to get one stitch of factual information. My one act of covert surveillance meant to protect her is used against me, and used effectively. What's amazing are the looks from Laurel and Tracy. Their trust in me is gone. Shot. They've bought the story. And if they've bought it, then what about the twelve morons? I tell my attorney it's a twofer: he got her and he got me all in the same act. He's out there ready to do it again. I'm going down as his surrogate. Mainly because I write this stuff. People know weird stuff; I'm one of the weirdest. Their case keeps heading back there, looping around. Who knows how to pull something like this off better than someone like me? If I decided to do this, would they expect to find much physical evidence? Of course not. Who better than me to make up a story about some guy? It's all me—but they don't know me.

They convict.

It's all me.

Down for the count.

❧

DAY SIX HUNDRED and ninety-seven. Cell block C. My girls are nine and seven. I've seen them once a month for the past two years. They look at me like they want to love me but can't figure out how to do it.

They found the body. Sixty-three miles out of town, buried alongside an interstate. Two others within fifty yards of it. There's semen in the remains. DNA. Day eight hundred and seventy-four and a hearing, and I'm given my walking papers—

DNA wasn't mine. I tried to tell them that. They say they're giving me my life back. Not true.

Two girls who don't want to be with me. They're living with Grandma. I'm told the transition will be difficult. No shit.

I go home and sit down and write.

It's all I know how to do.

The next Saturday I'm making crepes and Fishies in the Brook. They're looking at me with empty plates. Empty eyes. I catch myself holding my breath. I laugh. But they just stare.

I think I scare them.

SAFE ENOUGH

LEE CHILD

WOLFE WAS A city boy. From birth his world had been iron and concrete, first one city block, then two, then four, then eight. Trees had been visible only from the roof of his building, far away across the East River, as remote as legends. Until he was twenty-eight years old the only mown grass he had ever seen was the outfield at Yankee Stadium. He was oblivious to the chlorine taste of city water, and to him the roar of traffic was the same thing as absolute tranquil silence.

Now he lived in the country.

Anyone else would have called it the suburbs, but there were broad spaces between dwellings, and no way of knowing what your neighbor was cooking other than getting invited to dinner, and there was insect life in the yards, and wild deer, and the possibility of mice in the basement, and drifts of leaves in the fall, and electricity came through wires slung on poles and water came from wells.

To Wolfe, that was the country.

That was the wild frontier.

That was the end of a long and winding road.

The road had started winding twenty-three years earlier in a Bronx public elementary school. Back in those rudimentary days a boy was marked early. Hooligan, wastrel, artisan, genius—the label was slapped firmly in place and it stuck forever. Wolfe had been reasonably well behaved and had managed shop and arithmetic pretty well, so he was stuck in the artisan category and expected to grow up to be a plumber or an electrician or an air-conditioning guy. He was expected to find a sponsor in the appropriate local and get admitted to an apprenticeship and then work for forty-five years. Which is precisely how it turned out for Wolfe. He went the electrician route and was ten years into his allotted forty-five when it happened.

What happened was that the construction boom in the suburbs finally overwhelmed the indigenous supply of father-and-son electrical contractors. That was all they had up there. Small guys, family firms, one-truck operations, Mom doing the invoices. Same for the local roofers and plumbers and drywall people. Demand outran supply. But the developers had bucks to make and couldn't tolerate delay. So they swallowed their pride and sent flyers down to the city union halls, and followed them with minivans: pickup at seven in the morning, back in time for dinner. They found it easy to compete on wages. City budgets were stalled.

Wolfe was not the first to sign up, but he wasn't the last. Every morning at seven o'clock he would climb into a Dodge Caravan full of stuff belonging to some suburban foreman's kids. A bunch of other city guys would climb in behind him. They would stay silent and morose through the one-hour trip, but they watched out the windows with a degree of curiosity. Some of them were turned out early in a manicured town full of quarter-acre lots. Some of them stayed in until the trees thickened up and they hit the north of the county.

Wolfe was put to work on the last stop of the line.

Anyone who had seen a little more geography than Wolfe would have pegged the place correctly as mildly undulating terrain covered with hundred-year-old second-growth forestation and a few glacial boulders, with some minor streams and some small ponds. Wolfe thought it was the Rocky Mountains. To him, it was unbelievably dramatic. Birds sang and chipmunks darted and there was gray lichen on the rocks and tangled riots of vines everywhere.

His work site was a stick-built wooden house going up on a nine-acre lot. Every conceivable thing was different from the city. There was raw mud under his feet. Power came in on a cable as thick as his wrist that was spliced off another looping between two tarred poles on the shoulder of the road. The new feed was terminated at a meter and a breaker box screwed to a ply board that was set upright in the earth like a gravestone. It was a two-hundred-amp supply. It ran underground in a graveled trench the length of the future driveway, which was about as long as the Grand Concourse. Then it came out in the future basement, through a patched wound in the concrete foundation.

Then it was Wolfe's to deal with.

He worked alone most of the time. Drywall crews were scarce. Nobody was slated to show up until he was finished. Then they would blitz the Sheetrock job and move on. So Wolfe was a small cog in a big dispersed machine. He was happy enough about that. It was easy work. And pleasant. He liked the smell of the raw lumber. He liked the ease of drilling wooden studs with an augur instead of fighting through brick or concrete with a hammer. He liked the way he could stand up most of the time, instead of crawling. He liked the fresh cleanliness of the site. Better than poking around in piles of old rat shit.

He grew to like the area too.

Every day he brought a bag lunch from a deli at home. At first he ate in what was going to be the garage, sitting on a plank. Then he took to venturing out and sitting on a rock. Then he found a better rock, near a stream. Then he found a place across the stream with two rocks, one like a table and the other like a chair.

Then he found a woman.

She was walking through the woods, fast. Vines whipped at her legs. He saw her, but she didn't see him. She was preoccupied. Angry, or upset. She looked like a spirit of the countryside. A goddess of the forest. She was tall, she was straight, she had untamed straw-blond hair, she wore no makeup. She had what magazines call bone structure. She had blue eyes and pale, delicate hands.

Later, from the foreman, Wolfe learned that the lot he was working on had been her land. She had sold nine of thirty acres for development. Wolfe also learned that her marriage was in trouble. Local scuttlebutt said that her husband was an asshole. He was a Wall Street guy who commuted on Metro North. Never home, and when he was he gave her a hard time. Story was, he had tried to stop her from selling the nine acres, but the land was hers. Story was, they fought all the time, in that tight-ass, half-concealed way that respectable people use. The husband had been heard to say *I'll f-ing kill you* to her. She was a little more buttoned-up, but the story was she had said it right back.

Suburban gossip was amazingly extensive. Where Wolfe was from, you didn't need gossip. You heard everything through the walls.

They gave Wolfe time and a half to work Saturdays and slipped him big bills to run phone lines and cable. Being a union man, he shouldn't have done it. But there were going to be modems, and a media room, and five-bedroom phone extensions sharing three lines. Plus fax. Plus a DSL option. So he took the money and did the work.

He saw the woman most days.

She didn't see him.

He learned her routine. She had a green Volvo wagon, and he would see it pass the bottom of the new driveway when she went to the store. One day he saw it go by and he downed tools and walked through the woods and stepped over the property line onto her land. Walked where she had walked. The trees were dense, but after about twenty yards he came out on a broad lawn that led up to her house. The first time, he stopped there, right on the edge.

The second time, he went a little farther.

By the fifth time, he had been all over her property. He had explored everything. He had taken his shoes off and padded through her kitchen. She didn't lock her door. Nobody did, in the suburbs. It was a badge of distinction. "We never lock our doors," they all said, with a little laugh.

More fool, them.

Wolfe finished the furnace line in the new basement and started on the first floor. Every day he took his lunch to the twin rocks. One time-and-a-half Saturday he saw the woman and her husband together. They were on their lawn, fighting. Not physically. Verbally. They were striding up and down the grass in the hot sunlight, and Wolfe saw them between tree branches like they were on a stage under a flashing strobe light. Like disco. Fast, sequential poses of anger and hurt. The guy was an asshole, for sure. Completely unreasonable, in Wolfe's estimation. The more he railed, the lovelier the woman looked. Like a martyr in a church window. Wounded, vulnerable, noble.

Then the asshole hit her.

It was a kind of girly roundhouse slap. Try that where Wolfe was from and your opponent would laugh for a minute before beating you to a pulp. But it worked well enough on the woman. The asshole was tall and fleshy and he got enough of his dumb bulk behind the blow to lift her off her feet and dump her on her back onto the grass. She sat up, stunned. Disbelieving. There was a livid red mark on her cheek. She started to cry. Not tears of pain. Not even tears of rage. Just tears of sheer heartbroken sadness that whatever great things her life had promised, it had all come down to being dumped on her ass on her own back lawn, with four fingers and a thumb printed backwards on her face.

Soon after that it was the Fourth of July weekend and Wolfe stayed at home for four days.

❧

WHEN THE DODGE Caravan brought him back again he saw a bunch of local cop cars coming down the road. From the woman's house, probably. No flashing lights. He glanced at them twice and started work. Second floor, three lighting circuits. Switched outlets and ceiling fixtures. Wall sconces in the bathrooms. But the whine of his augur must have told the woman he was there, because she came over to see him. First time she had actually laid eyes on him. As far as he knew. Certainly it was the first time they had talked.

She crunched her way over the driveway grit and leaned in past the plywood sheet that was standing in for the front door and called, "Hello?"

Wolfe heard her over the noise of the drill and clattered down the stairs. She had stepped inside the hallway. The light was behind her. It made a halo of her hair. She was wearing old jeans and a T-shirt. She was a vision of loveliness.

"I'm sorry to bother you," she said.

Her voice was like an angel's caress.

Wolfe said, "No bother."

"My husband has disappeared," she said.

"Disappeared?" Wolfe said.

"He wasn't home over the weekend and he isn't at work today."

Wolfe said nothing.

The woman said, "The police will come to see you. I'm here to apologize for that in advance. That's all, really."

But Wolfe could tell it wasn't.

"Why would the police come to see me?" he asked.

"I think they'll have to. I think that's how they do things. They'll probably want to know if you saw anything. Or heard any . . . disturbances."

The way she said *disturbances* was really a question, in real time, from her to him, not just a future prediction of what the cops might ask. As in, *Did you hear the disturbances? Did you? Or not?*

Wolfe said, "My name is Wolfe. I'm pleased to meet you."

The woman said, "I'm Mary. Mary Lovell."

Lovell. Like *love,* with two extra letters.

"Did you hear anything, Mr. Wolfe?"

"No," Wolfe said. "I'm just working here. Making a bit of noise myself."

"It's just that the police are being a bit . . . distant. I know that if a wife disappears, the police always suspect the husband. Until something is proven otherwise. I'm wondering if they're wondering the same kind of thing, but in reverse."

Wolfe said nothing.

"Especially if there have been disturbances," Mary Lovell said.

"I didn't hear anything," Wolfe said.

"Especially if the wife isn't very upset."

"Aren't you upset?"

"I'm a little sad. Sad that I'm happy."

❧

SURE ENOUGH, THE police came by about two hours later. Two of them. Town cops, in uniform. Wolfe guessed the department wasn't big enough to carry detectives. The cops approached him politely and told him a long and rambling story that basically recapped the local gossip. Husband and wife on the outs, always fighting, famous for it. They said up front and man-to-man that if the wife had disappeared they'd have some serious questions for the husband. The other way around was unusual but not unknown, and, frankly, the town was full of rumors. So, they asked, could Mr. Wolfe shed any light?

No, Mr. Wolfe said, he couldn't.

"Never seen them?" the first cop asked.

"I guess I've seen her," Wolfe said. "In her car, time to time. Leastways, I'm guessing it was her. Right direction."

"Green Volvo?"

"That was it."

"Never seen him?" the second cop asked.

"Never," Wolfe said. "I'm just here working."

"Ever heard anything?"

"Like what?"

"Like fights, or altercations."

"Not a thing."

The first cop said, "This is a guy who apparently walked away from a big career in the city. And guys don't do that. They get lawyers instead."

"What can I tell you?"

"We're just saying."

"Saying what?"

"The load bed on that Volvo is seven feet long, you put the seats down."

"So?"

"It would help us to hear that you didn't happen to look out the window and see that Volvo drive past with something maybe six-three long, maybe wrapped up in a rug or a sheet of plastic."

"I didn't."

"She's known to have uttered threats. Him too. I'm telling you, if she was gone, we'd be looking at him for sure."

Wolfe said nothing.

The cop said, "Therefore we have to look at her. We have to be sensitive about equality. It's forced on us."

The cop looked at Wolfe one last time, working man to working man, appealing for class solidarity, hoping for a break.

But Wolfe just said, "I'm working here. I don't see things."

WOLFE SAW COP cars up and down the road all day long. He didn't go home that night. He let the Dodge Caravan leave without him and went over to Mary Lovell's house.

He said, "I came by to see how you're doing."

She said, "They think I killed him."

She led him inside to the kitchen he had visited before.

She said, "They have witnesses who heard me make threats. But they were meaningless. Just things you say in fights."

"Everyone says those things," Wolfe said.

"But it's really his job they're worried about. They say nobody just walks away from a job like his. And they're right. And if somebody did, they'd use a credit card for a plane or a hotel. And he hasn't. So what's he doing? Using cash in a fleabag motel somewhere? Why would he do that? That's what they're harping on."

Wolfe said nothing.

Mary Lovell said, "He's just disappeared. It's impossible to explain."

Wolfe said nothing.

Mary Lovell said, "I would suspect myself too. I really would."

"Is there a gun in the house?" Wolfe asked.

"No," Mary said.

"Kitchen knives all accounted for?"

"Yes."

"So how do they think you did it?"

"They haven't said."

"They've got nothing," Wolfe said.

Then he went quiet.

Mary said, "What?"

Wolfe said, "I saw him hit you."

"When?"

"Before the holidays. I was in the woods, you were on the lawn."

"You *watched* us?"

"I saw you. There's a difference."

"Did you tell the police?"

"No."

"Why not?"

"I wanted to talk to you first."

"About what?"

"I wanted to ask you a question."

"What question?"

"Did you kill him?"

There was a tiny pause, hardly there at all, and then Mary Lovell said, "No."

⁓

IT STARTED THAT night. They felt like conspirators. Mary Lovell was the kind of suburban avant-garde bohemian that didn't let herself dismiss an electrician from the Bronx out of hand. And Wolfe had nothing against upscale women. Nothing at all.

⁓

WOLFE NEVER WENT home again. The first three months were tough. Taking a new lover five days after her husband was last seen alive made things worse for Mary Lovell. Obviously. Much worse. The rumor mill started up full blast and the cops never left her alone. But she got through it. At night, with Wolfe, she was fine. The tiny seed of doubt that she knew had to be in his mind bound her to him. He never mentioned it. He was always unfailingly loyal. It made her feel committed to him, unquestioningly, like a fact of life. Like she was a princess and had been promised to someone at birth. That she liked him just made it better.

⁓

AFTER THREE MONTHS the cops moved on, mentally. The Lovell husband's file gathered dust as an unsolved case. The rumor mill quieted. In a year it was ancient history. Mary and Wolfe got along fine. Life was good. Wolfe set up as a one-man contractor. Worked for the local developers out of a truck that Mary bought for him. She did the invoices.

⁓

IT SOURED BEFORE their third Christmas. Finally Mary admitted to herself that beyond the bohemian attraction, her electrician from the Bronx was a little . . . boring. He didn't *know* anything. And his family was a pack of wild animals. And the fact that she was bound to him by the tiny seed of doubt that had to be in his mind became a source of resentment, not charm. She felt that far from being clandestine co-conspirators they were now cell mates in a prison constructed by her long-forgotten husband.

For his part Wolfe was getting progressively more and more irritated by her. She was so damn snooty about everything. So smug, so superior. She didn't like baseball. And she said that even if she did she wouldn't root for the Yankees. They just bought everything. Like she didn't?

He began to sympathize vaguely with the long-forgotten husband. One time he replayed the slap on the lawn in his mind. The long sweep of the guy's arm, the arc of his hand. He imagined the rush of air on his own palm and the sharp sting that would come as contact was made.

Maybe she had deserved it.

One time, face-to-face with her in the kitchen, he found his own arm moving in the same way. He checked it inside a quarter inch. Mary never noticed. Maybe she was shaping up to hit him. It seemed only a matter of time.

The third Christmas was when it fell apart. Or to be accurate, the aftermath of the third Christmas. The holiday itself was okay. Just. Afterward she was prissy. As usual. In the Bronx you had fun and then you threw the tree on the sidewalk. But she always waited until January sixth and planted the tree in the yard.

"Shame to waste a living thing," she would say.

The trees she made him buy had roots. He had never before seen a Christmas tree with roots. To him, it was all wrong. It spoke of foresight, and concern for the long term, and some kind of guilt-ridden self-justification. Like you were permitted to have fun only if you did the right thing afterward. It wasn't like that in Wolfe's world. In Wolfe's world, fun was fun. No before, and no after.

Planting a tree to her was cutesy. To him it was a backbreaking hour of digging in the freezing cold.

They fought about it, of course. Long, loud, and hard. Within seconds it was all about class and background and culture. Furious insults were thrown. The air grew thick with them. They kept on until they were physically too tired to continue. Wolfe was shaken. She had reached in and touched a nerve. Touched his core: *No woman should speak to a man like that.* He knew it was an ignoble feeling. He knew it was wrong, out of date, too traditional for words.

But he was what he was.

He looked at her and in that moment he knew he hated her.

He found his gloves and wrapped himself up in his down coat and seized the tree by a branch and hurled it out the back door. Detoured via the garage and seized a shovel. Dragged the tree behind him to a spot at the edge of the lawn, under the shade of a giant maple, where the snow was thin and the damn Christmas tree would be sure to die. He kicked leaf litter and snow out of his way and plunged the shovel into the earth. Hurled clods deep into the woods. Cut maple roots with vicious stabs. After ten minutes sweat was rolling down his back. After fifteen minutes the hole was two feet deep.

After twenty minutes he saw the first bone.

He fell to his knees. Swept dirt away with his hands. The thing was dirty white, long, shaped like the kind of thing you gave a dog in a cartoon show. There were stringy dried ligaments attached to it and rotted cotton cloth surrounding it.

Wolfe stood up. Turned slowly and stared at the house. Walked toward it. Stopped in the kitchen. Opened his mouth.

"Come to apologize?" Mary said.

Wolfe turned away. Picked up the phone.
Dialed 911.

THE LOCALS CALLED the state troopers. Mary was kept
under some kind of unofficial house arrest in the kitchen until
the excavation was completed. A state lieutenant showed up
with a search warrant. One of his men pulled an old credenza
away from the garage wall and found a hammer behind it. A
carpentry tool. Dried blood and old hair were still clearly visible
on it. It was bagged up and carried out to the yard. The profile
of its head exactly matched the hole punched through the skull
they had found in the ground.

At that point Mary Lovell was arrested for the murder of her
husband.

THEN SCIENCE TOOK over. Dental, blood, and DNA tests
proved the remains to be those of the husband. No question
about that. It was the husband's blood and hair on the hammer
too. No question about that either. Mary's fingerprints were on
the hammer's handle. Twenty-three points of similarity, more
than enough for the locals, the state police, and the FBI all put
together.

THEN LAWYERS TOOK over. The county DA loved the case to
bits. To put a middle-class white woman away would prove his
impartial evenhandedness. Mary got a lawyer, the friend of a
friend. He was good, but overmatched. Not by the DA. By the
weight of evidence. Mary wanted to plead not guilty, but he persuaded her to say yes to manslaughter. Emotional turmoil, tem-

porary loss of reason, everlasting regret and remorse. So one day in late spring Wolfe sat in the courtroom and watched her go down for a minimum of ten years. She looked at him only once during the whole proceeding.

Then Wolfe went back to her house.

HE LIVED THERE alone for many years. He kept on working and did his own invoices. He grew to really love the solitude and the silence. Sometimes he drove down to the stadium, but when parking hit twenty bucks he figured his Bronx days were over. He bought a big-screen TV. Did his own cable work, of course. Watched the games at home. Sometimes after the last out he would sit in the dark and review the case in his head. Cops, lawyers, dozens of them. They had done a pretty thorough job between them.

But they had missed two vital questions.

One: With her pale, delicate hands, how was Mary Lovell accustomed to handling hammers and shovels? Why did the local cops right at the beginning not see angry red blisters all over her palms?

And two: How did Wolfe know exactly where to start digging the hole for that damn Christmas tree? Right after the fight? Aren't cops supposed to hate coincidences?

But all in all, Wolfe figured he was safe enough.

THE HOME FRONT

CHARLES ARDAI

I PULLED UP to the pump, stubbed out my Victory cigarette in the ashtray, and waited for the kid in the overalls to come over. He was wiping grease around on a gear shaft with a cloth that had seen better days. Looking at him, you couldn't say what had gotten him out of the service. Flat feet, maybe. But he was about twenty years old, big as an ape, and I couldn't see any reason that he wasn't using those big arms of his to bayonet Nazis instead of to pump gas.

I pressed the horn. "Hey! Max Baer!"

The kid looked up, half a grin on his face. He put the gear shaft down on a shelf and came over.

I showed him an A coupon. "Give me my four gallons, kid. I've got money."

The kid wiped, wiped, wiped his hands, but the rag only made them greasier. "Ration's been reduced," he said. "An A gets you two gallons now."

"You think I don't know that?" I held the coupon out the window. "Give me four. I've got enough to pay for it."

"Have you got another one of those?"

"No."

"Then you don't get four gallons." The kid looped the rag under his belt and shrugged. *What can I do?* the shrug said. *Don't blame me, blame Hitler.*

"I'll pay double," I said.

"You could pay triple. I don't have the gas."

"So what's in the tanks? Sand?"

"Air. And two gallons of gas if you want them."

"I want four."

"Two is as much—"

"That I heard already." I pulled a five-dollar bill out of my pocket and held it out to the kid. "I'll pay a dollar a gallon."

The kid's eyes got wide, and as round as dinner plates. "That's a lot of money."

"Yeah. It's a lot of money."

"I've got some that I've . . . wait here." The kid ran off behind the garage.

He came back carrying two metal gas cans, one in each hand. He uncapped the nozzle on one and upended it into the car's tank. When it was empty, he started the second can.

I put the bill back in my wallet.

"Four gallons." The kid came back around to the window. "That'll be four dollars, mister." He said it as though this were a legitimate transaction.

I unfolded my wallet and held it up, showing the kid a badge that said "Office of Price Administration" in small letters. He didn't have time to read the words, but he knew what the badge meant.

"Hold on," he said. "You asked me—"

"And you agreed."

"Please—my family—"

"Should've thought of that sooner," I said. "Get in."

I GOT TO keep the gas. Everyone else in the country had to wait in gas lines for just enough gas to get to the next line. I may not have had three meals every day, but, by God, I could drive where I wanted.

It was a job—a war job like everybody else's, more respectable than some, less than others. When the OPA had held the recruitment meeting in their office in Times Square, more ratty guys than you'd think existed showed up to get on the gravy train. Mr. Bowles himself walked down the line, threw the bums out, and took the rest of us out of our civilian togs and made us agents of the federal government.

Then he explained the special arrangement: Ours wasn't a factory job and they couldn't pay us a factory man's wages. But to even things up, they'd let us keep part of what we scored. With gasoline, we could keep all of it as long as it was less than five gallons.

The guy standing next to me when he told us this, a sweaty, bald-headed grifter named Tom Doyle, leaned over when Bowles wasn't looking and whispered in my ear, "What you do is, you always ask for four." Doyle was probably the worst, but every one of them was always figuring an angle.

You'd think there wouldn't be work for guys like us, shutting down the black market operator by operator, not with the war on and posters up on every block telling you that each black market bite you ate or mile you drove was taken off a soldier's plate or out of his plane's fuel tank. But the fact of the matter was that there was plenty of work, enough for the OPA to deputize three thousand starving PIs around the country to do it. You couldn't turn around without catching someone selling something under the table: meat, shoes, nylons, cheddar cheese, you name it. And most of the time these were the same people who were growing victory gardens on their fire escapes for Uncle Sam.

On the other side were mugs like Doyle, collecting a paycheck from the government to sniff out profiteers and getting cash under the table from the profiteers to look the other way. The worst of it, depending on how you looked at it, was that Doyle would take the dirty money week after week and then, when he needed to show he was doing his job, would turn them in anyway.

I wasn't lily-white myself, driving around on illegal gas, eating illegal steak whenever I could corner some. The difference between the profiteers on one hand and the PIs on the other was that they were cheating their country and we were serving ours. It may not seem like much, but it was the reason that I was driving while the boy next to me was in handcuffs, and not the other way around.

His name was Matt Kelly. He looked it too, Irish coming out his ears. He had hair like carrot shavings and a big Irish jaw and when he spoke you could butter your bread with his *r*'s. He told me his life story as I drove him in, how he'd come over with his mother in '38 and worked for an uncle in the garage, how he'd saved out the gas he'd given me for his own personal use and would never have sold it on the black market if I hadn't made the offer so sweet.

"You're digging your grave deeper, Kelly," I said. "All you're telling me is that you wouldn't have sold it to me if I hadn't offered to pay through the nose."

"You're twisting it around, mister. I'm telling you, I wouldn't have sold it at all, but you kept asking for it—"

"You didn't have to say yes," I told him. "I didn't hold a gun on you. All I held on you was a lousy fiver, and you jumped at it."

"You know how bad things are. I could have fed my ma and her brother for a month with that money."

"You mean you would have used it to buy on the black market too," I said. "Oh, you're a pip."

"Have a heart, mister."

"I should have a heart?" I floored the brake right there in the middle of the highway, let his gas burn away as we idled. "You're not dying at the front, you're not blowing up in an airplane, you're not putting your life on the line. You're a big boy, you could be out there fighting, but you're not. You're sitting at home, listening to it on the radio. And while they're dying for your freedom, you're worried whether you can get some roast beef for your dinner. And I should have a heart."

I started forward again, floored the gas, steered the car into a turn. I was really steaming now. "And another thing—"

But the other thing never came out.

I went into the curve at forty miles an hour and ran head-on into a car coming the other way in the wrong lane. The front of my car crumpled and Kelly, who couldn't use his hands because of the cuffs, went smashing through the windshield and onto the hood of the other car. I threw my arms up in front of my face and caught the steering wheel in my chest. But at least I lived.

Kelly was shredded, bloody, screaming. He had gone through the windshield face-first. The driver of the other car, a white-haired man with glasses, had a broken neck, if you went by the mismatched angle of his head and his body. He had fallen against his horn and the damn thing was blaring like an air raid siren.

I had some cracked ribs. I could feel them grate in my chest as I dislodged myself from under the wheel. I shouldered my door open and fell onto the side of the road.

Did the explosion start from the other car or from mine? I

don't know. In an instant, the frozen scene of the two wrecked cars and the two bodies erupted into flame. Kelly died somewhere in the middle of that first explosion. I know because he stopped screaming. The horn stopped too, as the other man's corpse shifted in his car.

I lay flat on the side of the road and let the wave of heat from the blast pass over me. Then I sat up and watched my goddamn four gallons go up in smoke.

IT WAS THE war and I was a federal agent. The cops didn't want any part of me and the feds had bigger items on their docket than the death of a black marketer who had tried to wrestle control of the car away from me, which was the way I told the story.

They had a nearsighted stateside doctor tape my chest up, which he did so badly that it ached every time I tried to lie down. And then, with so little fanfare that I didn't know what was happening until it was over, they gave me a week's pay and my papers and told me to disappear. They didn't say it just like that, but it was what they meant. My name and picture had made the papers, so I was useless to them.

But disappear to where? I was too old to enlist, I had no car, the government didn't want to know me, and my private practice, such as it ever had been, had had fourteen months in which to dry up.

I sat in my office waiting for the phone to ring, but it didn't. So I had a lot of time to sit by myself while my ribs healed, listening to the floor creak in the hall outside when people visited the eye doctor one flight up from me. I thought about Matt Kelly—I thought about him plenty. I remembered having a hard time cinching the cuffs on him, his wrists had been so big and meaty. I remembered the look he'd had when he'd spoken of his ma and uncle. He'd been trying to provide for his family. He'd broken the law, but nowhere was it written that you had to die for hoarding two cans of gasoline.

I hadn't seen Kelly's face when he died, but in my dreams I saw it and it was the face of a boy burning up in the worst pain you can imagine. And I remembered how sanctimonious I had been, how cocky, how red-white-and-blue. *You're not dying at the front,* I'd told him, and I'd been right. He hadn't died at the front, for his country. He'd died at home, for nothing.

When the end of the month came, my bank account was dry, my refrigerator had nothing in it but a few bottles of beer, and if I didn't mind when the phone company turned off my service it was only because I couldn't remember the last time the phone had rung. I woke up each morning afraid to shave after I caught myself, once, fingering the edge of my razor a little too thoughtfully.

My beard grew in. My lease ran out. The day my cash finally dropped into the single digits, I took a long shower, toweled off, packed my things into a traveling bag, and started walking. I wasn't coming back, so I took everything I had with me, even the wet towel.

I walked down Broadway, forty blocks or more, walked clear out of the city, walked on the shoulders of roads and through patches of forest, walked until I was too tired to walk anymore. Then I sat in the shade of a tree, took my shoes off, massaged my insoles until the ache dulled, shouldered my bag, and started walking again.

I had five dollars and change in my pocket, a wristwatch I could pawn if I had to, a hand-tooled leather belt I could sell if I got desperate enough. I had tired feet and a chest that had never healed properly and no idea where I was going. I passed houses and roadside taverns; I was passed by cars. I almost thumbed a ride once but embarrassment took hold and I lowered my hand before any driver saw it.

When the sun passed overhead and started blinding me from the right, I started thinking about where I would spend the night. It was warm, so sleeping outdoors wouldn't be too bad—unless I ended up in the stir for vagrancy. I passed a restaurant that had a sign advertising rooms, but I didn't want to spend the little money I had renting one of them. I passed a house with an open window, and through it I saw a family sitting down to dinner. I thought about stopping, ringing the bell, asking them to take me in for the night, but I couldn't do it.

Then I came to a gas station that was shutting down for the day. A woman was wrestling with the garage door. It kept sticking and she kept pulling at it, inching it toward the ground. I was walking slowly and in the time it took me to get to her she wasn't able to get it more than halfway down. Her denim shirt was stained under the arms and across one forearm where she kept wiping the sweat from her forehead. Her hair was tied behind her and her hands were red from the effort.

The house attached to the garage looked bigger than one person needed for herself alone and the thought crossed my mind that there might be room there for me. But this wasn't the reason I stopped, not really. I just couldn't stand to see her fight with that door anymore.

I walked onto the lot, slid my bag to the ground, approached the garage. The woman stepped back. I took a firm grip and put my weight into it, forcing the door down. It clattered the last two feet and hit bottom with a bang. I held my chest and took deep breaths. It hurt like hell, like my ribs were still broken.

"You okay?" she said.

I nodded. "Just an old injury. Comes back to hurt me now and then."

"I appreciate your help. You saw the sign, I suppose."

"The sign?"

She pointed to a square of cardboard wedged on top of one of the pumps, hand lettered to say MAN WANTED TO HELP IN GARAGE. FOOD, LODGING.

"No, I didn't see that," I said.

"In that case I'm doubly grateful." She bent over to close the padlock on the door.

I lifted my bag, waited for her to straighten up. "Listen—"

"Yes?"

"I hadn't seen that sign, that's the truth," I said, "but I had thought about asking if I could stay here for the night." I felt her eyes on me. I looked down at my feet. "Now that I have seen it . . . well, you probably want a younger man to do the work and that's fine. But I'd be grateful if you'd give me the job till someone better comes along. Even if it's only for a day, that's a day's more food and lodging than I have reason to expect now."

She watched me for a second or two more, then wiped her hands on her apron, untied the strings in back, and lifted it over her head. She held it out to me. "Why would I want a younger man? You dealt with that door just fine. Fold this up and come with me. You can wash up before supper." I took the apron from her and she kept her hand extended.

"I'm Moira Kelly," she said.

Her words hung in the air between us. It took a moment. I looked at her, looked at her hand, looked at the pumps and the house behind them, looked at her red hair and her tired eyes, and I suddenly realized where I was. Where I had walked. Who I had helped. I started to cry then. She thought it was from gratitude; this made it worse.

Now that I looked for it, I could see him in her features, in her prominent jaw and in the tight curls of her hair. Even in her size: she was half a foot taller than I was, and broad-shouldered. Thoughts collided in my head. *Of course she needs help, now that he's dead.* And: *How could I not have known where I was? How could I not have remembered?*

"Come along," she said, "Mister . . . ?"

I wanted to walk away, but I couldn't. Not after offering my help, not when she needed help and I could give it. But I couldn't speak either. I shook my head. I forced out the first name that came to mind. It came out in a hoarse whisper. "Doyle. Tom Doyle."

"Okay, Mr. Doyle. You come in, wash your hands, and put some food in you. Right through here, up the stairs, on your left. I'll be up after you."

I SPLASHED WATER on my face, scrubbed my hands free of road dust, combed my hair, straightened my beard. I looked at myself in the mirror and tried to compare what I saw with the pictures that had run in the papers two months before. The beard made a difference, but how much? My hair was longer and had a little more gray in it, I thought. But it was still me under there.

Still, she and I had never seen each other, and a picture in the paper is just a picture in the paper. She didn't know who I was.

I took my bag back out into the hall and waited for her. My hands were shaking a little. I stuck them in my pockets, played with the change I found there.

Moira came up the stairs and pointed me toward a room at the end of the hall. I went in ahead of her. The room had a bed in it covered with a gray blanket, and a dresser with a radio and a photograph on it. The picture showed Matt Kelly at about eighteen years old, maybe two years younger than when I had killed him. She saw me looking at the photo and took it off the dresser.

"That's my son. This used to be his room."

The silence between us was unbearable. I had to say something. "What happened?"

"He died in an accident. Few months back, a man picked him up for selling more gas than he should have, drove him into an accident."

"I'm sorry," I said.

"Don't be; you didn't do it." She slid the photo into the side pocket of her dress. "His name was Matthew, Mr. Doyle. You'll see some of his things around. I'll get them out of your way tomorrow. You can use the radio if you like. Anything else of his gets in your way—"

"No, it's fine."

"Well, if it does, you just move it out of your way and I'll take it downstairs tomorrow. Give me ten minutes to get supper ready and you can join us in the kitchen." She paused. "There's my brother living here too. It's he that owns the station, though he's not able to work it anymore. I think I've told you everything now. Have I?"

"I think so."

"No, I haven't—there's the work." She shook her head. "We'll talk about that tomorrow, if it's all right with you."

"It's fine, thank you."

We looked at each other. She'd taken the tie out and her hair hung down over her shoulders, a rusty red streaked with gray. She had to be forty or more, and a life like hers usually makes you look your age, but she didn't. She had a handsome face, though I didn't especially like having to look up to see it, and a nice figure. Her palms were callused and her forehead creased, but the effect on her was not a bad one. She was a strong woman who looked like she had been through a lot, but the point was that she looked like she had been through it. It hadn't beaten her.

"I hope I don't have to tell you this," she said, "but while you're working for me you're not going to drink and there'll be no violence between you and anybody around or you can take your bag back on the road."

"No, you don't have to tell me that," I said. "I don't drink more than the average man. I'll even stop that if you want. And I don't remember the last time I was in a fight."

"How did you get your injury, then?"

"Accident," I said, without thinking. Again I spat out the first lie that filled my mouth. "A ladder collapsed under me while I was working on a roof. Caught a toolbox in my chest."

"I hope you'll be more careful here."

"I will," I said. "I won't make the same mistake twice."

Before I followed her downstairs, I changed my shirt and stowed the rest of my clothing in the top dresser drawer. The drawer was empty except for a pullover cardigan and two pairs of socks. She had told me to move them out of the way, but I couldn't bring myself to touch them. They had every right to be here. I was the one who didn't.

The kitchen was plain, a square room with a stove and an icebox along one wall and a bare wooden table in the middle. A man sat at the head of the table in a wheelchair, his hands curled tightly around its arms. He had deep-set eyes that darted left and right constantly and a throaty baritone that sounded like an engine turning over. "You're Mr. Doyle," he said. "You'll be helping Moira out."

"Yes."

"Have you done this kind of work before?"

"No."

"What kind of work you done, then?"

"I don't know," I said. "You name it."

"No, *you* name it."

"Drove a delivery truck with my father out in California."

"Recently?"

"No. Years ago."

"So what have you been doing recently?"

Working for the government. Catching black marketers. Killing your nephew. "I had a job with a . . ." I took a drink from the glass of water Moira had put out in front of me. I wasn't used to inventing so many lies in one day. "With a printer. We did print jobs for shops."

"How did you lose it?"

"Lose it?"

"The job," he said. "You don't have the job anymore."

"The shop went out of business. The man who owned it closed it down."

He nodded, either satisfied or just tired of the conversation. Maybe he assumed that there was something in my past that I wasn't telling him. He would have been right—how right, he couldn't have guessed.

Moira came in, stirred the stew pot on the range and turned off the gas under it. She carried it to the table and put it down on a trivet. She ladled out bowls of the stew, placed them in front of us with thick slices of bread. Finally she sat down herself. "You two have met by now? Tom Doyle, Byron Wilson . . . Byron, Tom."

I reached across the table to shake his hand, but he just kept spooning the stew into his mouth.

"Byron," Moira said.

"No need to introduce us," Byron said. "We've been talking. I feel I know Mr. Doyle very well."

His eyes bored into me then and I suddenly felt uncomfortable.

I looked away, blew on a spoonful of stew, sipped it. It was a thick, salty Irish broth of carrots and potatoes with fibers of beef and bits of onion. It landed in my grateful stomach like lotion on a burn. "This is very good."

"You see, Byron? A person can say nice things about my cooking."

"You know I like your stew," he said.

"I know it, but not because you say it."

"I'm your brother. I don't have to say it."

"You're not eating?" I said.

She had a bowl in front of her but it was empty. "I will. I just wanted to rest for a moment."

I stood up, uncovered the pot, dug the ladle out. "So rest." I filled her bowl.

They were both watching me. I sat down.

"Thank you, Mr. Doyle."

"No one calls me Mr. Doyle," I said. It was the truth, God knows. "Call me Tom."

"Tom," Byron said, "you planning to stay here for long?"

I hesitated before answering. "Can't say, honestly. I didn't plan to come here at all. I'll stay as long as you want me to and no longer." I turned to Moira. "When you want me to go, say so and I'll go."

Byron leaned forward in his chair. "I will, Tom. That I will."

I SAT IN the tub and let the water stream down over my head, hot enough to be almost painful. The drain was open and the water was running out as fast as it was running in. It was wasteful to use their hot water this way, but I needed it. The rhythm beating against my skull, my shoulders, the warm pool draining away at my feet. From the next room I could hear the radio, whispering its melodies as if it were a hundred miles away.

The world had gone crazy—not just my world, which was bad enough, but the whole world, three years into a war that looked no closer to ending today than it had when it began. The songs on the radio were mostly war songs, and the news bulletins, war updates. By now we'd all forgotten what life was like without a war. I know I had.

Once upon a time I had been a private investigator, licensed by the state of New York, scratching out a living tracing bail jumpers and cheating husbands. Then the war had come and my chance to be a part of it had come too: the OPA, with its gleaming white office, its scientifically planned price ceilings, and its Cracker Jack–prize booklets of ration coupons. I sold myself on the idea that this was my way of fighting the war. All it really was was my way of making a living. I had lived off of it for more than a year. Then the world had caved in.

If I'd never joined the OPA, what would have become of me? I didn't know. But I knew this: I wouldn't have had to suffer every time I shut a garage door. If the war hadn't come, or hadn't lasted this long, I wouldn't have been soaking now in a dead man's tub, or sleeping in his bed, or eating his dinner, or wearing another man's name. But it had and I was, and no amount of water would wash that away.

I stood up in the tub, shut the faucets off, collected my clothing from the floor. There were towels on the rack that I could have wrapped around me, but I didn't feel right walking out like that. So I took one of the robes that were hanging behind the door. It had been his robe, I assumed, judging by how big it was on me. I almost put it back, but there was no use fighting it at this point: I'd be doing his job soon enough, so I might as well wear his robe.

I padded down the hall to the bedroom. Moira was there, collecting Matt's things in a basket. The radio was playing one of those songs you couldn't get away from, "Sentimental Journey," and there were tears in her eyes. When she saw me, she smiled, almost laughed. I looked down at myself to see why.

"You're wearing my robe," she said.

"I'm sorry."

"It's okay, I don't mind." She reached out to turn off the radio but I caught her hand.

"No, leave it. It's nice."

"Okay."

"You didn't have to take his things away. Not on my account."

"I'd have had to eventually. Might as well be now."

"What was he like?" I heard myself say it. I don't know where the words came from.

She bent at the knees and slid slowly to the floor, her back against the dresser. "What was he like? He was good to me, he was bright, he was handsome. He looked like his father, God rest his soul. He was headstrong sometimes, he could be stubborn. He was my son. I'll never have another."

I sat next to her, took the basket out of her hands, put it down on the floor.

"He was just fourteen when we came here. All he knew was that he was coming with his mother to a new country, and he came and he never had one complaint. I did—heaven knows I did. He never did. He just took everything in stride."

"How did his father die?" I said.

"There was a fire in the garage. It was the same fire that took

Byron's legs." She turned to me. "Steven came over before we did, to earn the money to bring us out. He worked here, with my brother. It happened while Matthew and I were on the boat coming over. Steven and Byron were getting the place ready for us, and a fire started in the garage. The whole place nearly came down. Byron was caught when a piece of the wall fell in. The firemen could barely get him out."

"That's terrible," I said.

"It is. And then Matthew—" Her voice caught.

"It's all right."

"Matthew fixed it up again."

"It's okay."

"He finished just before he—"

I put my arm around her shoulders, pulled her head to my chest, let her weep into her robe. The radio hissed, a silence between songs. I stroked Moira's hair gently, said "I'm sorry" again and again. I meant it; maybe she could hear that, or maybe she just heard the pain in my voice. She looked up and when I kissed her forehead she pulled my face down to her lips.

❧

WE LAY UNDER the robe in his bed. She slept. I stayed awake, holding her shoulder, listening to "Deep Purple" on the radio. A floor beneath us, I could hear the wheels of Byron's chair turning as he rolled around his room. I wondered if he needed any help getting into the bed. I wondered if he had heard us. I wondered what I was doing with Moira Kelly in my arms. I didn't think I would, but eventually I fell asleep.

She was gone when I woke up. I dressed in the same clothes I'd worn the day before. I buttoned my shirt at the window, looking out at the gas pumps and the fenced-in meadow across the way. A car pulled in and I saw Moira go out to meet it. After the day I'd put in yesterday, it was no surprise that I'd overslept. Still, I owed Moira a day's work and had already slept through the first few hours of it. I hurried downstairs.

Byron was sitting at the kitchen table, just as I had left him the night before. He was thumbing through a newspaper, taking sips from a mug of tea. He looked at me but didn't say anything as I passed through into the glare of a cloudless morning.

I walked up behind Moira while she was taking money from the customer. She turned to face me when the car drove off.

"Good morning," I said.

"Morning." She walked into the garage. I noticed that she had gotten the garage door open by herself.

"Where do I start?"

She pointed to a rack of tools and a disassembled automobile engine lying on a bench. "You can start by putting that back together."

"You fixed it already?"

"Byron did." She crouched next to the bench. "That much he can still do."

I carried a handful of wrenches to the bench, dropped them on the ground, and settled into a squat. "I think I can handle this."

"Good."

She watched while I put the thing back together, making plenty of mistakes along the way. She pointed them out as I made them, walking away twice to take care of customers, correcting my work when she came back. When I finished, she showed me a couple of auto carcasses she kept for spare parts, a tool cabinet in the corner of the garage, the row of gas cans lined up behind the garage in the shadow of an eave.

Around noon, I took over from Moira at the pump while she went inside. A few people drove in, not too many. I kept the cash in my shirt pocket, put the coupons in a cigar box in the garage. No one asked me to give him more than his fair share of gas. It was a good thing. I don't know what I would have done if someone had.

Moira called me in to eat just after one. Before I went in I looked back at the house, at the window I had dressed in and the one below it. Byron was sitting in the ground-floor window, staring back at me.

We ate quickly, reheated stew and chicory coffee. After wolfing down his food, Byron rolled himself outside. Through the kitchen window I saw him heading toward the garage.

"He's got some things to finish," Moira explained.

"What things?"

"Making sure you put that engine together properly, for one."

"He doesn't trust you to keep an eye on me?"

"No man trusts his little sister with another man."

There were things I wanted to say, things I wanted to ask, but I couldn't say any of them. "When did Byron come to this country?" I asked instead.

"Nineteen twenty-nine."

"Hell of a year to come to the United States."

"Hell of a year in Ireland. Hell of a year anywhere."

"I guess."

"Have you ever been out of the country?"

I closed my eyes. A couple of washed-out memories surfaced, like photographs left out too long in the sun. "My father took me into Mexico once." The scene I remembered best had a woman in it. She spoke Spanish to my father, which he seemed to understand. My mother had died the same year and I remembered wanting to hit my father for the way he was looking at this woman. That's what I remembered of Mexico, that and how hot it was.

"You should see Ireland," Moira said. "Not now, of course. When the war ends."

"If the war ends."

She stood up and walked past me to the door, stopping to kiss me on the forehead first. "What is it that turned you into a cynic?"

I wanted to say, *A woman whose son I killed just kissed me. That's what turned me into a cynic.* "You just never know what's going to happen next in life," I said, and followed her out into the lot.

❧

ONE NIGHT A week later, I left Byron and Moira sitting at the table, the dinner dishes crowding the sink. I told them that I was tired, that I wanted to take a bath, that I needed to rest, all of which was true. But I didn't go upstairs. I walked past the stairs and into Byron's room.

The room was identical to Matt's, down to the gray blanket on the bed, except that there was no radio on the dresser. Instead there was a stack of newspapers, copies of *Life* magazine, issues of *Time* and *Look*. A few newspapers were scattered on the floor. I thumbed through the pile, not really looking for anything, just looking. Then I went to the window and looked out through the blinds.

The land was dark, the grass of the meadow blue-black in the night. Some light shone from the half-moon, and the two gas pumps stood out, looming shadows in the dark. Cars drove past in silence. I knelt by the window and tried to imagine a car driving into the lot. I pictured my car; I pictured what it would have looked like from this window when I stopped at the pumps that morning. I had had the windows open and I'd sat in the driver's seat for a good ten minutes before I'd driven off with Matt Kelly next to me. If Byron had been sitting at this window then, he would have had plenty of time to see me. The window would have given him a perfect view.

Behind me, I heard a wheel squeak.

Byron cleared his throat. "Saying your prayers?"

I turned around. Byron pushed himself toward me, rolling over the papers on the floor. The light in the room was turned off. He was not a big man, but neither am I. In the dark, with me on my knees, he loomed over me, a black shape with no features, no face, just a dark mass with a dark voice.

"I was just looking out."

"That you were. But looking out for what, Mr. Doyle?"

He rolled closer, catching me between his chair and the wall. "Should I call you that? You said you prefer Tom, but since neither is your name I don't know what to say."

I said nothing. We both could hear Moira washing up in the kitchen.

After too long, he spoke again. "Moira doesn't know."

"Why not?"

"I haven't told her."

"I don't understand."

"I wasn't sure at first," Byron said. "I had to get a good look at you. And even after I did I couldn't believe you would come back here."

"It was an accident—"

"Maybe."

"I never meant to come back."

"You didn't mean to kill my nephew either. You do a lot of things you don't mean to."

"Why haven't you told Moira?"

"You idiot," Byron hissed. His voice dropped to a whisper. "Do you think she picks up men from the road every day? Do you think she makes a habit of taking strangers to her bed? Say yes and I'll deck you."

"No, I'm sure she doesn't."

"Mr. Harper, is it? Other than me, Mr. Harper, you're the first person she's so much as talked to in weeks."

"Why me?"

"I don't know why you. But I didn't see her cry once today. That's another first."

"It's been months—"

"Did you ever lose a son, Mr. Harper?"

"I've never had a son."

"A wife?"

I shook my head.

"Well, think about it, then. Look at me. How do you think you would feel if one day your brother got drunk and started a fire that killed your husband?"

"You—"

"And then, years later, when you thought you'd put your life in order again, what would it do to you if you lost your son in another stupid, terrible accident?"

"I had no idea."

"Now you do."

My eyes were getting used to the dark and I could make out his face now. It had been better when I couldn't.

"I don't know why you ended up here again, but you did. She's not going to lose you too." He rolled closer. "But if you ever hurt her, I will tell her who you are and give her a gun to kill you in your sleep."

"I won't hurt her."

"I believe you don't mean to," Byron said. "Just make sure it works out that way."

He rolled backwards and out the door. I got to my feet.

"Thank you."

"Don't thank me. Take your bath, Mr. Doyle, and go to her. Every man deserves a second chance. Even me. Even you."

THAT NIGHT WE slept in her bed and woke together just before dawn. "Byron told me about the fire," I said.

"What about it?"

"That it was his fault."

"It was. And he paid for it."

"You're not angry at him?"

"The man lost his legs. What more am I going to take from him?"

"That's very forgiving."

Moira raised herself on one elbow. "I don't forgive him, Tom. I'll never forgive him. But he's my brother and a cripple and I can't hate him for what happened."

"Other people would."

"Maybe they would. I don't."

What about me? I thought. *Would you hate me, if you knew what I had done?* I got out of bed and dressed quickly. I felt her eyes on my back.

"You understand about Byron, don't you?"

"Yes," I said.

"You resent him, though."

"No," I said. "He's been nothing but kind to me."

"That's not true."

"Kinder than I deserve."

"No."

"Believe me," I said. "Kinder than I deserve."

THE SUMMER DIDN'T last. The days were long, and then suddenly it was getting dark early again; the breeze was warm, and then one day it chilled you when it caught you in short sleeves out by the pumps. Paris was free again. Our troops crossed the Siegfried Line. For the first time in memory, the reports coming over the radio brought hope—everyone felt it. But the war went on, and the days grew colder, and we all held tight to one another when we saw the newsreel footage of snow falling in Malmédy and the Ardennes.

Bing Crosby was on the radio, singing another one of those songs you couldn't get away from, "White Christmas," though it wasn't quite time for it yet, not for a week still. Moira was inside, fixing lunch while I wiped oil from a broken twist of metal I'd pulled out of a car I was fixing. I heard tires on the gravel outside, then the blare of a horn. "I'll be right there," I called out. The horn didn't let up, so I carried the bracket out of the garage with me, laid it down on top of one of the pumps.

The guy in the car let up when he saw me, pulled off his gloves and rolled down the window. He leaned out and held out an A coupon. His breath fogged in the air.

"Hey, mac, be a pal and let me have"—his voice slowed down—"four gallons." He peered out at me. "Holy God. Rory Harper, is that you?"

I stared at him. My own name sounded unfamiliar to me, so much so that I didn't even respond when he said it. I had no idea who he was.

"Don't tell me you don't recognize me. Oh, wait, it's this, isn't it?" He took hold of his hair, lifted it off, and dropped it in a matted heap on the seat next to him. "I wear the rug in this weather. Keeps me warm," he said. "But maybe you never saw me with it."

I knew who he was then.

"Tom Doyle," he said. "You remember?"

I spoke in an undertone. It was all I could manage. "You've confused me with someone else. My name's—" I suddenly realized I couldn't finish the sentence.

He grinned. "You don't know your name?"

"Byron Kelly," I said. "Of course I know my name."

"You're Byron Kelly like I'm Edward G. Robinson. A beard don't make you someone else. Come on, Harper, what's the score? You in some kind of trouble?"

"My name is Byron—"

"You gone off your nut, Harper, or you just putting this on?"

I swallowed what I was about to say. Through the kitchen window I could hear Moira inside, taking a kettle off the stove. I looked in Byron's window, but he wasn't there. He was probably already in the kitchen. At any moment Moira would come out to call me in.

Doyle followed the path of my eyes and when I looked back at him, the grin had returned, splitting his fat face in two. "I follow. They don't know who you are. You on the run? No, don't tell me. I won't spoil anything for you."

I didn't say anything. My palms were wet.

"But be a sport and give a pal some gas." I reached out for the coupon, but he pocketed it. "No one has to know."

"I can't."

"I won't report you, if that's what you're worried about."

"They'll know."

"So what? A few gallons of gas are missing. They'll know much more than that if I don't keep my mouth shut."

"Please," I said.

He raised his voice. "Please what, Harper?"

We stared at each other for a second. "Nothing."

"That's right. So start pumping. Might as well fill it up."

I turned to face the pump. I could hardly breathe. A tank of gas was nothing. But the kind of man Doyle was, once he had you on the hook, he played you for all you were worth.

He'd come back. He wouldn't let up. I could give him the gas, buy him off for today and then run tonight, pack my bag and never come back—but I didn't want to run. Not now. I couldn't let him ruin everything.

I took the iron bracket off the pump.

"Tom," I said softly.

He leaned farther out his window. "What?"

I turned and swung, bringing the bar down across his face, snapping my arm back and striking again, and then again. I couldn't stop. His face crumpled under the blows.

I lifted his head from the windowsill, shoved it back inside, pushed at his shoulder until he tipped toward the passenger seat. I reached inside for the latch and swung the door open, got my hands under him and rolled him out from under the wheel. He groaned then, his ruined face pressed against the passenger-side window.

My heart was racing, my hands shaking. Moira was still in the kitchen. Another minute, maybe two—it was all I needed.

There was blood in the gravel, but only a little; most of it was on the door. I kicked the stones over to cover it. Then I threw the bracket in the backseat and climbed in under the wheel, slamming the door shut. He was still alive, but for how much longer? I would drive him into the woods, find a place to hide him, find a ravine to push the car into—

The front door opened then. Moira stepped through it, a dish towel in one hand. She looked over at the car, took a step forward. "Tom?"

I turned the key in the ignition, heard the engine hungrily turning over, but it didn't catch. I wanted to race away before she could take another step, but the car wouldn't go and she kept coming. I opened the door, put one leg out, reached an arm out toward her across the top of the car. "Don't come any closer! Moira, please, stay back!"

But she didn't. "What's going on, Tom?" Now she had seen Doyle's face in the window, crushed and bloody against the glass, and she ran to the door. "What happened to him? Tom, he's hurt!"

"Go back inside, Moira, please—"

She threw the door open, and Doyle fell forward into her arms, his face smearing her apron. "Tom, we've got to help this man."

Doyle groaned again, turned his head slightly. He spoke then, in a ragged whisper. "I'm Tom Doyle," he said. "Son of a bitch is Rory Harper." And he died in her arms.

She watched me climb the rest of the way out of the car, come around to her side, take the weight of Doyle's body from her hands. She watched me sink to my knees, watched me clasp her bloody hands between mine. She watched it all, but she didn't see any of it. She stared through me and past me. She looked defeated then—for the first time, I looked in her eyes and saw nothing. No rage, no fury, no life.

I SAT IN the gravel until the police came. I made it easy for them to get the cuffs on me, holding my wrists together at the small of my back. They asked me what had happened and I told them: I told them who the dead man was, I told them I had killed him. I didn't tell them why.

Byron watched from his window as they put me into the backseat of the car. I turned away. I couldn't look at him.

They drove, and in a few minutes we reached the spot where

the accident had happened. I looked out the window as we passed it. You couldn't see the blood anymore, but the asphalt was still scorched in a few spots.

When I looked up, a car was coming toward us in the other lane. I thought, *If only that car had stayed in its proper lane then, how much could have been avoided.*

They hadn't locked the door, perhaps because I was such a docile prisoner. I wedged my knee under the latch and forced it up. The door swung open. I launched myself out of the car.

The other driver swerved to miss me, but there wasn't enough room.

If only, I thought.

THE LAST FLIGHT

BRENDAN DUBOIS

O N THIS MAY morning the wind was whipping something awful, and Gus Foss stood on the grass field of the small airport near the Atlantic Ocean in New Hampshire, wondering if the wind would keep him from his scheduled flight this day. The large orange sock on a pylon above the cottage-size office building was filled with air, heading toward the south, but there was a sputtering noise, and he looked out to the grass airstrip, saw a small Cessna move along at a fair clip, its tail now tilting back a bit, as it cleanly broke free of the ground and went up into the air. It soon headed toward the sun, and he would have liked to have shaded his eyes, to follow its progress, but his hands were occupied. They were presently holding a metal container, about the size of a large coffee can, and in that container was the dust and grit and bone that remained of the only woman he had ever loved in his quite long life.

Driving over to the airport earlier that day, Gus had again and again looked at the small container sitting in the passenger's seat next to him. At first it had seemed obscene, that the place

that had always been taken by his wife was now taken by a dull
metal container that held the remaining organic materials of
what had once been the former Miss Trish Cooper. All of those
dreams and laughter and scoldings and cooking and loving and
reading and living . . . reduced to a fistful of stuff. Yes, that was
obscene, but when he kept on glancing at the container, something else started to bubble to the surface: humor. God, how
Trish would have laughed, seeing her remains riding there. No
doubt she was Up There looking down at him, giggling and
wondering why he hadn't seat-belted the remains before he ex-
ited the driveway. Yes, that would have been Trish. Always willing to find the humor in the most stressful of times.

Now, though, they were safe in his hand, ready for their last
flight, and he just stood there, waiting.

A slapping noise reached him and he turned, seeing a man
come out of the airport's office, the screen door bouncing shut
behind him. The man wore oil-stained denim overalls, a white
sweatshirt, and muddy work boots. He had thick black hair and
a beard that reached to his chest, and he nodded a greeting as he
came over.

"Gus?"

"The same."

The man held out a hand, and Gus freed up a hand to shake
it. The man said, "Frank Grissom. I guess I'll be flying you
today."

"I guess so." He quickly dropped his hand, noticing that it
was beginning to shake, and that his knees were trembling as
well. *Easy now,* he thought. *Easy.*

Frank took a step back, looked him up and down. "You
know . . . I've got the oddest feeling I've met you before."

Gus resisted the temptation to rub at his bare upper lip.
"Really? I can honestly say I don't think we've ever met." Which

was true, if you were being legalistic, and Gus was in the mood to be legalistic.

Frank shrugged. "If you say so. Ready to go up?"

"Yep."

"Then let's do it."

Gus followed Frank as they made off to the right, to a small collection of hangars and aircraft parked on the grass, tied down by cables and straps. Most were Cessnas or Cherokees, but a funny tingling sensation started climbing up his back as they went to the aircraft they would be using that day: a small LR-2 Piper Cub, painted dark green and with Army Air Corps markings from World War II on its fuselage and wings. He couldn't help it: he slowed down as he approached the parked airplane, and Frank sensed that he was no longer following him. Frank turned and said, "Everything okay?"

His mouth was dry. "Sure. Everything's fine."

Frank said, "If you say so. You just look . . . funny, that's all."

Gus tried to smile. "Thing is, I used to fly in a plane like that."

"Really? Where?"

"ETO. Back in 1944 and 1945."

"E-T what?"

"ETO. European Theater of Operations."

Frank grinned. "No fooling? You were a pilot?"

Gus shook his head. "Nope. Was an artillery spotter. I let somebody else fly me. We used to take off early in the morning, fly over the German positions, try to spot troop concentrations, tanks, artillery pieces, self-propelled guns . . . anything and everything that our own artillery could fire on."

"Jeez," Frank said. "Bet you pissed off the Germans something awful. Bet they tried to shoot you down."

"All the time."

Gus went forward, Trish's ashes now under his right arm. He reached out and touched the nearest wing, smiled at the memory. Stretched canvas, that's all. Damn aircraft could barely reach ninety knots, and was made of wood and canvas and a bit of metal, besides the engine, but by God, she did the job and did the job right, hovering over enemy positions, catching views of the enemy below, and him in the rear, radioing the coordinates back to the artillery some miles away.

Frank now stood next to him, and Gus could smell mouthwash on his breath. "Bet that's why you asked for me and this plane, right? Because of what you did back in the war. Bring back some memories."

Gus's hand was still on the cool canvas. "You could say that."

"Well, thanks for your service back then, and all that. You still want to go up?"

"Oh, yes, yes I do."

"Okay."

They ducked under the right wing, went to the ridiculously small cockpit, with its two seats not side by side, but front to back, each seat with a control stick in front of it. Frank opened the thin door and said, "Since you're a vet and all, your choice. Rear or front?"

Gus smiled at the pilot. "Since I spent all that time in the war flying in the rear, how about if I try the front this time?"

"Sure. Let me help you in."

Another memory as he climbed into the tight quarters. God, how many times had he climbed into a similar cockpit back in '44 and '45, fueled in the morning with coffee and cold oatmeal or powdered eggs and, if he was lucky, fried slabs of Spam? Flying with Whizzer or Mike or Gray or any other pilot back then. Climbing in the rear with a Thermos of coffee and a bag of sandwiches for the flight home, and the large clipboard with folded-over map and grease pencil, and the radio gear to talk back to the artillery folks so that they could—

"Gus? You okay?"

He realized now that he was stuck, half in and half out, and he forced his old joints and muscles to bend so that he could get up and forward. He was breathing hard when he sat down, the metal container now in his lap, and he struggled a bit with putting on the seat belt. But he was done and there was motion as the light aircraft rocked when Frank clambered into the rear. He took a breath. So far, so good. Frank had been the perfect gentleman ever since he arrived, and he almost felt just a bit— just the tiniest bit!—guilty that in a while he was going to take this aircraft from Frank.

And as he settled back in the stiff seat, Gus also tried to ignore the metallic object in his coat pocket, pressing into his ribs.

❧

THE ENGINE START-UP and takeoff was just as he remembered, with an airport worker coming over and actually turning over the propeller, like with a Sopwith Camel or something from World War I. Frank made some motions to the other guy and the engine roared to life. Frank tapped Gus on the shoulder and yelled, "On the floor! Headset and microphone!"

He reached down with some difficulty and picked up the headset and microphone, which he pulled over his ears. There was a crackle of static and then Frank's voice boomed into his ears.

"You hear me okay?"

"Yes, yes—you don't have to be so loud."

"Oh. Sorry. Let me dial it down a bit." A pause. "This okay?"

"Yep."

"Okay, I just like to talk to my passenger, that's all. Better than yelling back and forth. Bet you had to do that a lot back in the war."

"You know it," Gus said, looking over what was in front of him, feeling a warm sense of nostalgia glancing at the simple dashboard with the handful of dials and gauges and the thick piece of wire that protruded upward from the engine cowl, marking the fuel gauge. The lower the wire sat, the emptier the fuel tank. About as simple as you could get, and simple was a good thing when flying over German territory and dodging the occasional Mauser gunfire sent your way. At his side and feet were cables that ran from the ailerons and rudder and elevators outside the plane, and that connected to the control stick in front of him, and the stick that Frank was using in the rear.

There was a surge of noise from the engine as Frank gave the throttle a goose, and the Piper Cub bounced some as he headed out to the runway. There was a murmur of talk, and in a tiny mirror before him Gus could see Frank speaking into a hand-held radio. Damn. A complication. But then he saw Frank put the radio away in a leather pouch hanging from the fuselage's interior. Frank noticed him and said, "Something up?"

"Not really," Gus said. "I didn't know you had to talk to air traffic control."

Frank laughed. "Oh, hell, no. We're too slow and small to bother much with air traffic control. I was just letting the office know we were getting ready to take off. You okay up there?"

"Yep."

The airplane was now at the south end of the grass airstrip, its whirring propeller facing north. Frank goosed up the throttle and the Piper Cub started heading up the airstrip, and it was magical, just like all the times nearly sixty years ago—it was as if the old plane were just eager to get up in the air. There was no real hard transition from the ground to the air; it was just a gentle lift as they rose up. He had to remember to breathe as the land fell away beneath them and the short seacoast of New Hampshire came into view: plenty of woods and housing developments, and the long strips of asphalt that marked Route 1 and Interstate 95. Frank made a gentle bank to the west and through the earphones Gus heard, "You okay up there?"

"Wonderful."

"Okay, you have me and the Cub for the next fifty minutes. Where to?"

"The ocean."

"You got it."

The aircraft then gently banked to the east, and Gus took another deep breath. He could hear Frank breathing through his earphones, and though he was probably imagining it, he thought he could smell the mouthwash as well.

Frank said, "Ask you a question?"

"Sure."

"What was it like, flying in the war?"

"Different."

"Yeah, I suppose so . . . I mean, the Cub is easy enough to fly, but I don't know how it'd be, flying and worrying about someone shooting your ass off."

"Uh-huh."

They flew on in silence for a few seconds, the rocky coastline coming into view, the slate blue of the ocean almost beneath them. Frank cleared his throat and said, "You still think about it, what it was like?"

What it was like, what it was like, the same damn question asked over and over again, ever since that damn TV newsman wrote his book about the allegedly greatest generation a few years back. Some generation. *We just went in and did our job and kept our mouths shut, and that's supposed to be something magical.* What it was like. It was being thousands of miles from home, most often cold and wet, usually having the runs or trench foot. It was waking up every morning trying not to think that this might be the day that you got killed or got your balls or a leg or an arm blown off. That today might be your last flight. That's what it was like. It was moving east toward Germany knowing those Kraut bastards were going to put up a hell of a fight when they got to their own territory. It was looking down on the terrain and being able to spot the German positions even if they were under camouflage netting, and how powerful you felt, speaking into your radio and seeing the hidden tanks or SP guns explode because of you. It was seeing crumpled piles of canvas and wood and metal at the end of some of the dirt runways, where some of the spotter planes didn't clear the trees at the end of the crude, quickly made runways. It was hoping and praying for bad weather, for you didn't fly in bad weather, and sure, that made it tough for the tanks and soldiers moving forward under German fire, but at least your ass wouldn't be hung over German territory, ready to be shot down by eighty-eight-millimeter antiaircraft fire. It was an LR-2 wobbling back to the ground, piloted by a chum from your own home state, Henry Kasen, yeah, Henry, and the plane wobbled and wobbled and you stood there in the drizzle, trying to will the damn thing to land safely, and it hit and bounced and hit and bounced and then stood on its nose, and when you got there the artillery observer who flew with Henry— Scott something or another—was being dragged out with a broken leg, crying, "I did the best I could, I did the best I could!" and in the front seat, strapped firmly in, was what was left of Henry, the windscreen in front of him splattered with blood and brain and hair . . . That's what it was like.

Frank repeated himself. "Like I said, you still think about it?"

"Sometimes," Gus finally said. "But not that much." And if Frank wanted to know more, to hell with him.

Now they were over the ocean, and he looked down at the swells, leading to waves that broke at the shore. There were a few sailboats down there, with another handful of lobster boats, and he squeezed the metal container, hard. *Just a few more minutes, Trish,* he thought. *Just a few minutes more.*

Frank coughed and said, "Any place in particular?"

"As far east as you can."

"All right. Ocean mean much to you, then?"

He looked down at the water and then the metal container. Remembered the very few times he and Trish had gone to the beach for the day. How Trish always complained about the heat and the strong sun and the sand getting into her bathing suit and food and drink. Not to mention complaining about the slow traffic, the loud music, and the expensive parking. Poor Trish.

"My wife," he said. "She loved the ocean and the beach. That's why."

Frank said, "Not the first time I've heard that."

"You've done this before?"

"Sure. A half dozen times at least. Last wishes . . . people like to see their loved ones' ashes scattered across their favorite place. I guess that's what you have there with you, right? Your wife?"

"Yeah," he said.

Your wife. Two tired old words that couldn't even come close to describing what Trish was like, what their life together had been like. High school boyfriend and girlfriend before he enlisted. Letters arriving almost weekly, as they followed him across France and Germany. Discharged finally and wanting to get back home, get married, and start a new life. Nothing earth-shattering, nothing that made the newspapers. Just a nice job at a bank in Dover, starting off as a teller, working his way up to president of the damn thing before retiring decades later. And Trish was there with him, side by side, tall and slim and blond, aging gracefully as the years slipped by. Oh, God, how he missed her . . . and the memories weren't all wonderful, of course, for how could they be? There were the times they lost their parents over the decades, and in '52, when she miscarried with their first child—a girl—and afterward being told she could never bear children. A couple of times when some pretty thing at the bank had tempted him (and thank all the gods he had done the right thing and had turned those temptations away . . .). They had talked here and there about adoption, but their lives had seemed so full, so rich, as they grew old and traveled and learned more about their world and each other, right up to last fall, when they had been planning one big splurge before they got too old, a cruise around the world, and—

"Gus."

"Yeah."

"We've gone about as far as we should," Frank said. "It's time."

"Sure," he said. "Thanks."

He fumbled for a moment with the window at his side, opening it up, the air now rushing in, and he unscrewed the top to the container and, thinking for a moment, tossed it out into the breeze, the chunk of metal in his coat pocket digging again into his side. He brought the container up to the window and had a horrid thought of the airstream blowing Trish's remains in over his face and arms, and so he tossed it out the window. He had wanted to see the ashes fly through the sky. He wanted to see the container fly down to the ocean. He wanted . . .

He brought his hands up to his face, the tears suddenly blossoming, and he bent forward a bit, the palms of his hands wet.

Oh, Trish, he thought. *Trish.*

AFTER A BIT he wiped at his eyes and saw that they were now heading west, back to shore. He rubbed at his hands, now feeling at peace, now feeling good. It was time.

"Frank?"

"Yes, Gus."

"You want to hear more, what it was like back in Europe?"

"Sure."

He folded his hands in his lap, squeezed his fingers tight. "Flew a lot, day after day. You must fly a lot too."

Frank laughed. "Not as much as I'd like. It's something in your blood, you know?"

"Sure," Gus said. "A tradition, right?"

"That's right."

"Flying and drinking and whoring. Did that as much as we could too, over there in Europe. We were young and we didn't know what tomorrow was going to be like, so that's what we did. Flying and drinking and whoring. The true pilot's creed."

"Yeah, I guess so."

"I know you like to fly, Frank, and I leave the question of whoring for later, but I bet you're a drinker. Right?"

Frank didn't say anything for a moment, and then forced a laugh. "I've been known to hoist a few. What the hell, right?"

"That's right. What the hell. We drank a lot as we moved through France. Mostly stuff we liberated from wine cellars as we chased the Germans. French wines, champagnes, some beers. Sometimes . . . well, we'd wake up, our heads aching, our joints nice and stiff. So what. If we flew with a hangover or if we were still a bit drunk we could still get the job done. Isn't that right?"

Another pause. "Sure. That's right."

"That's where I got the taste for wine. Love wine, especially Bordeaux. What's your favorite drink, Frank?"

"Oh . . . it depends."

He now found that his hands felt curiously empty without the ashes of his wife riding along with him. "Yeah. Depends. I bet it depends on your mood. I guess it depends what you're up to. But I bet your favorite is rum and Coke. Am I right, Frank? Rum and Coke."

No reply. He looked in the little mirror, saw Frank focusing on flying the plane. His face glum. No wonder. Gus took a breath, was pleased his hands weren't shaking, were nice and firm.

"You see, Frank, even in Europe you had to trust your pilot. You had to trust your pilot to get you off the ground, over the enemy positions, and, most important of all, back home in one piece. You soon learned who you could trust. And those pilots who drank too much and screwed the pooch, they would have a hard time finding any artillery observer to go up with them. You have a problem like that, Frank?"

Again, no answer. It seemed as though the engine increased in speed, as if Frank was trying to hurry them back to the airport, and again Gus felt just the tiniest bit of guilt that he was about to take this plane away from him.

"No, I guess not," Gus said. "I bet your problems are mostly on the ground. Drinking and driving. Not as romantic as drinking and flying, is it? But that's your lot in life. Drinking and driving. Two under-the-influence arrests in Massachusetts, one in Maine, and four in New Hampshire. Including one last winter—am I right, Frank? Of course, there was something different with that arrest. It ended with someone's death."

Frank's voice was low through the earphones. "You're . . . you're her husband. You've shaved your mustache. And your name isn't Gus . . ."

"That's the nickname my wife used to call me. My full name is John Augustus Foss. Gus is what Trish called me. What she called me before you killed her."

Frank nearly yelled, "I didn't kill her!"

Gus was stunned at how composed he was, talking to this man. "Sure, not at first, when you struck her. But when you left the Sea and Stein Pub that night, you had five rum and Cokes in your system. You blew through a stop sign and rammed into the side of my wife's Toyota. You refused to take a Breathalyzer test, and through the good graces of your lawyer dad, you plea-bargained everything and didn't serve a day in jail. And my Trish was in a hospital room, hip broken, leg broken, and she was there for weeks and weeks, barely talking, barely alive, and then she died. And the county attorney refused to bring charges. So there you go, Frank. Legally, it wasn't murder. But I'm not concerned with legalities, Frank. I'm concerned with justice."

Frank was studiously ignoring him. Gus knew he had just seconds to go before he had to take care of business. Gus said, "So here you are, flying along, another good thirty or forty years ahead for you. Can you imagine that big stretch of time that's out there waiting for you, Frank? All the way to the midpoint of this new century and beyond. All that golden time, just waiting for you. Trish and me, we didn't have much left. Not at all—just a few years more if we were lucky . . . and you took that time away from her. And from me. Because . . . because those years stretching ahead of me, they aren't a gift for me, Frank. They're now a curse. Thanks to you."

The engine noise revved higher. He reached into his coat pocket, felt the cold metal. "And Frank, one thing I learned in the war is a sense of justice. That things often even themselves out toward the end. And right now I'm going to even out everything. You, me, and Trish. All even."

Frank's voice came through loud and urgent. "Mr. Foss, don't you dare touch that control stick. You understand? Don't you dare touch that stick."

Gus looked at the mirror, saw the fear in that man's eyes. "But I'm just an old man, Frank. Aren't I? How in God's name can you let an old man like me wrestle the controls away from you? Am I right?"

The pilot seemed just a bit calmer. "Yeah, you're right. Look, I'm sorry and everything, about what happened. But it was an accident. Okay? Just an accident."

Gus took a breath. "All right, Frank. You apologized. For that, I promise I won't touch the control stick. You can be sure. But I need to know one thing."

Another pause, and the cautious voice. "Go ahead."

"Why did you wait so long to apologize? It's been months, hasn't it? Why?"

"My . . . my dad, he told me . . ."

Gus shook his head, sure that Frank back there had seen the gesture. "Wrong answer. You're a man, Frank. With man-size responsibilities. And you've skated over your responsibilities, all these years. You're in your thirties, and when I was just barely out of my teens I was defending this country, helping kill its enemies so clowns like you could grow up and kill my wife."

He made a motion with his right hand, inside the coat pocket, now hauling out the worked piece of metal he had brought along, and Frank was practically screeching, "Don't you dare! You promised! Don't you dare touch that control stick!"

And Gus turned with some difficulty in the seat, then undid his belt so he could look back at Frank and hold something up to his face.

"All right, Frank," Gus said. "I promise to keep my promise."

And then he held up the object in front of Frank, wiggled it back and forth so the pilot could get a good view, and then he sat back down in the seat. Time. He thought to himself, *Ah, Trish,* and he bent down and leaned forward.

Frank started yelling, and kept on yelling, as Gus went to the exposed control cables, a set of very sharp wire cutters in his hands.

PART LIGHT, PART MEMORY

BONNIE HEARN HILL

1865
GALVESTON, TEXAS

T HEY ARE NOT all good and not all evil, Little Mary. And neither are we."

My father told me that right before they hanged him. For looking at a white woman, they said. For looking, yes. For looking proud, for looking strong and fearless, even as his lifeless shadow sloped across the dusty ground and his silence shouted down the jeers of those who had come to watch.

"I'll kill her," I promised my final glimpse of his body, dangling from the noose, then turned away from the sight before it broke me.

Alvis frowned me silent with a look that said they'd hang us too if I didn't hush.

He found me later that day, crying in the barn when I was supposed to be fetching water for Miz Bessie's bath. Usually the strength of him beside me could help me bear any misery, but not then.

"Don't, Little Mary," he said. "Don't let them see—'specially don't let Mister see you hurting." In the lingering light, his skin glowed like gold.

"I can't help it," I whispered, as tears choked my vision and blurred him up tall and strong as a man older than his years. "He was my father. It was evil what they did."

"I know that," Alvis said, his eyes offering no hope. "But you're just a girl, barely fifteen."

"A girl who knows the truth," I said. "John William never looked at that white woman. He loved Big Mary."

"Don't start," he said. "It won't do no good."

"He never looked, not even after . . ." I couldn't finish, but Alvis knew.

"Big Mary be sold when?" he asked. "Three years now?"

My brother Henry too. I remembered the day, the spot of sunlight beside the patch of purple ground cherry, where my mother had stood rooted as a tree, how they'd dragged her past that spot, into darkness. I could still hear her screams. *My babies. Please save my babies.*

"'Bout that long," I said. "But I know that Miz Bessie got him killed. And one day, Alvis—I'll kill Miz Bessie too."

"Don't," he said. "You can't live for killing."

I turned away from him and headed back to the house. "I can," I said.

After that I did live for killing, although I didn't talk to Alvis about it. He was my sweet man, but now there was no room for him in my heart or my thoughts. The hate kept growing, pushing out the soft side of me. It reminded me of Big Mary, gone. Of my brother Henry, gone. Of my father, gone, his body still swinging in the shadows of my dreams.

The Monday after the hanging, it stormed that angry, unnatural way it sometimes does in June in Texas. Sheet lightning cut the air, and Mister cursed about the cotton.

I forced myself to lift the silver-handled brush and bring it through Miz Bessie's hair, down her long milky neck, so smooth that it was all I could do to keep from grabbing her by the throat and squeezing the life from her.

She was the woman they said John William, my father, looked at, the reason he got hanged. Miz Bessie, who had pretended to be kind to him in those days after Big Mary was taken. Miz Bessie, half crazy herself after little Chuck, her boy, caught the yellow fever and died. Miz Bessie, who got my father killed. As I brought the brush down through her hair, I promised myself that I would find a way to kill her too.

She watched my face in the mirror that day with the look she got when she thought no one else was noticing. The strands in my dark fingers shone like coins in the sunlight. I wished the brush were a hatchet, an ax with a sharp silver edge. Oh, how I'd rip it through her long white neck.

"'Amazing Grace,'" she said.

I jerked at that. "Ma'am?"

"It's a hymn. When I think I can't take any more, I sing it."

What did she know about hymns, about having to suffer?

"Yes'm," I said, and began braiding those silky strands, hating her even more for the blue eyes that could look gentle when they wanted to, the voice that could sound soft and good if you didn't know about her.

I'd have her hair braided and pinned soon. I'd help her put on the black riding hat with its billed crown and sheer golden drapes that would fly behind her as she rode. And what would I do next? Could I let her leave here for an afternoon of horseback riding, with my father's murder crowding out my every thought?

She caught my eyes in the mirror again. "You don't even have to sing it, Little Mary. Sometimes you can just hum it."

"Yes'm."

She frowned as if to tell me I didn't have to use slave talk with her. "I'm so sorry about what happened to John William," she said. "He was a good man, and he loved your mother very much."

In the mirror I caught what looked like tears in her eyes. Then I saw myself, my eyes as hard as a hangman's, my face as dark as hate, as black as the sky when it was ready to storm down. The clothes she'd given me hung like rags from my narrow shoulders. I looked like the scarecrow man Mister stuck up in the field to frighten the birds away.

"Yes." I paused. "Yes'm," I said again.

"It's going to be over soon, you know."

"What, ma'am? What's going to be over?" It was better to act as if I didn't know, as if I'd never seen a copy of the *Galveston News*. The South had recaptured us last year, but it wasn't any worse or any better than when the North claimed us two years before that. Now nothing that happened would free my father. Nothing but heaven would bring him back to me.

"Everything," Miz Bessie said, and, turning from the mirror, she let her eyes blaze through mine. Then she dropped her head. When she lifted it, her eyes were full of tears. "I lost my son," she said, "my baby."

"And I lost my father." I answered in the language she had given me, forgetting to talk like a slave.

"And John William lost Big Mary," she said. The flow of her tears was steady now. "Loss isn't only a person," she said. "It's a connection. It joins people, the way grief does."

My grief went far too deep to connect me to her. I nodded just the same and said, "It does, ma'am."

"We're just women," Miz Bessie said. "Weak women. We can't change anything. But how do you think John William felt?"

"He felt weak too, ma'am," I said.

And to myself: *Because of you.* Again the need for revenge burned in my fingers and my brain.

Just then Mister burst into the room. He had to be the biggest, blondest man in all of Texas. I wished I could duck out of there before he gave me that look that always made me feel used and dirty. His pants were hitched up above his thick waist, his pale hair slicked down hard around his skull. But what kept me watching, hoping I could find a way out of that room, was the smile on his face that was anything but joyful, the colorless, cruel eyes narrowing on me.

"What's she doing here?" he asked Miz Bessie, looking me up and down in that way of his.

When I glanced up from Miz Bessie's hair again, I knew he was staring at her now and not at me. I wouldn't have wanted that look. Miz Bessie didn't either. I could see that by the way she huddled inside her thin wrap. Then, just as I settled my hands around her shoulders, protective-like, I reminded myself that this was the woman who caused my father to die.

"She's always here at this time," Miz Bessie said.

"You ain't giving her another reading lesson?" Mister asked, the smile twitching as if he had a tic.

I felt my cheeks burn and saw a similar flush on Miz Bessie's cheeks.

"I just taught her enough to read the Bible."

Before she could say anything else, he slapped her across the face. She screamed and crumpled to the floor. I jumped back, glaring at him, realizing that maybe I didn't have to kill this woman anyway. Maybe something else would happen and I wouldn't have to do anything.

"You want the same?" he asked, waving his fist at me.

"No, suh."

Huddled beside her dressing table, Miz Bessie gazed into my

eyes as if saying, yes, it was best to hide my true speech. If he knew she'd taught me to read, he'd kill me right here. He stepped around her and gave me that smile.

"You slaves know everything," he said.

"Suh?"

"Don't pretend with me," he said. "You've heard what's happened. You know it's only a matter of time."

I'd heard, yes, from Alvis, that the war was ending, that even with President Lincoln dead we might be free, but I didn't believe it. I tried to think of something to keep Mister from doing to me what he'd done to Miz Bessie. "I don't care about that," I said.

"Well, I care." He stomped his big muddy boot too close to me. "As long as I'm alive, my slaves will do as I say."

"Charles," Miz Bessie said in a voice stronger than she looked, "leave her alone. She hasn't done anything."

"But her daddy did," he said. "John William did."

"He didn't," I said. I didn't care what happened to me. I couldn't let him speak against my father.

"He looked at Bessie," Mister shouted. "He dared to look at my wife."

"Charles, don't." Miz Bessie pulled herself to her feet. Her face was scarlet, her eyes full of fear. "Not in front of her."

"Go on, then," he said to me, and I dashed out of the room before he could change his mind. Then, as quickly as I'd left, I stopped. Something stronger than fear pulled me back. He was going to hurt her, I knew, but what could I do to stop him? And if I could stop him, why would I want to?

As I stood outside the room, I could hear Miz Bessie sobbing. "I taught him to read the Bible," she said. "That was all."

"Don't lie to me," Mister said. "You're lucky I didn't tell them to hang you too."

"Would you have liked that, Charles?" Her voice went sharp, and I cringed. "One more death to make you feel alive?"

"Don't you ever speak to me like that," he said, and when she cried out I knew he'd hit her again. The sound brought tears to my eyes. "You're my wife," he said. "Understand? I don't want you reading to them, I don't want you touching them. Especially, I don't want you touching them."

"As you wish." Her voice sounded weary with tears. "Before long we'll have no slaves to argue about. It will all be over soon."

"It already is," he said. My skin prickled. "That devil Lincoln. I'm glad he's dead."

"What do you mean?" she asked. "How do you know?"

"Messengers," he said, and the hard laugh that followed chilled my bones. "Lincoln tried to send one down here before he got shot. Now they're trying again."

"What messengers, Charles?" she asked in a strangled voice.

"Dead ones."

"No."

"Lee may have surrendered, but we're fighting for what's ours," he said. "I have to go down to the harbor. A ship is on its way. We're going to make sure those devils never make it here."

I couldn't understand what she was saying through her sobs, but then she cried out again—a sudden shriek of pain—and I realized that I had too.

I took off running, not knowing where I was going, only that I needed to find someone, Alvis, to tell what I'd heard, to keep Mister from carrying out his plan. The rain had stopped, but the sky was heavy and black. A sheet of lightning hit it but I didn't stop, dashing past the ground cherry, the barn. If I could make it to the cotton field, I'd have a chance.

Something heavy butted me from behind and I fell, sprawling in the primroses, my face smashed into their strong, sugary scent, followed by the smell of mud. That's where I was, face-down in mud, trying to find my feet.

"Get up." Mister's boot stabbed my side. I screamed and scrambled up. "Now get in there," he said, pointing at the barn.

To do so would end my life, I knew. I stepped back, ready to run again. Before I could, he reached out and grabbed my arm.

"No," I said. "Please." Tears ran down my face as he dragged me inside. My father hadn't begged. I couldn't beg either, no matter what.

He let go and shoved me onto the dirt floor.

"You know the real reason I had John William hanged?" he asked. "Tell me you know, Little Mary."

"No." I crouched in the dust he'd kicked around, staring up at him. In the barn light, his face was twisted and hungry. I forced myself to slow my speech. "I don't know nothing, suh."

"I caught them together," he said, his voice singsong. "I had to protect my reputation and hers, couldn't let anyone know." He hooked his thumbs into the waist of his pants and looked at me like a little boy getting ready to torture a bug. "I think I owe him one, don't you?"

John William and Miz Bessie? I thought of what she had said about loss, about how it connected people. Nothing my father did could have been bad. I fought to keep the fear from my voice. "What do you mean, you owe him one?" I asked.

"Get up and I'll show you."

"No," I said. He was going to kill me anyway. I wouldn't allow him any other pleasure.

"Your black devil of a father took something from me," he said. "I hope he's watching from hell right now."

"No," I repeated. I couldn't stop myself.

"Did you say *no?*" The boot again. A rush of pain choked out a moan from me. I rolled to my side, cutting my face on something sharp, a rusted tool. "You get up right now, Little Mary," he said, "or I'll fix you so you can't."

Through my tears I focused on the discarded tools I'd rolled onto. Shovel. Hoe. Pitchfork. I would not beg. I would fight, and if he killed me, as he surely would, I could face my father with pride.

I got on my knees as if I were praying. "Yes, suh," I said.

"Good. You're as smart as you are pretty." His hands moved to the front of his pants. "Don't look so scared. You might like it."

I pulled myself up, slowly, leaning on the pitchfork, forcing the fear out of my head. His pants loosened and fell. I gripped the handle, as if for support, learning the feel of it with my fingers.

He smiled and said, "What's the matter, Little Mary? You never seen a real man before?"

In one movement, I swung the pitchfork, drove it into that part of him he'd revealed to me.

Mister let out a scream that will follow me to the grave. Right then, though, lost to rage, I pulled the pitchfork from his jerking body, and when he toppled to the ground I drove it into him again and again.

Then I looked down at what I had done, and tears burned my frozen cheeks. I, who had talked of killing to Alvis as if I knew it well, hadn't begun to understand how it felt to take the life from another person, even in order to save my own.

❧

MISTER AND OTHERS like him would not have been able to stop the messengers who sailed into Galveston that day. Men in blue uniforms filled the streets, they say, and soon they marched down every road under the leaden sky.

Miz Bessie met the soldiers at the gate and brought the news inside the house to me, her face as pale as flour.

"You're free, Little Mary," she said.

"Free?"

The sound of cheering came from outside. I began to tremble.

"Free." She took off the black hat from her dressing table and handed it to me.

I stumbled out my thanks, unable to complete a simple sentence.

Miz Bessie looked at my helpless hands and said, "Sit down."

And there I was, in front of her mirror. She reached for her hairbrush, and lifting the silver handle swept up my hair, smoothing it up to my crown, not speaking, only humming softly. "Amazing Grace." Then, when the hat was secure and I'd gotten up, she sat down at the dressing table and put her head in her hands.

I looked in wonder at myself, my black, free self, and then I ran down the stairs to where Alvis waited. Hymns shouted like thunder, like a storm of joy. Together we rushed out to join the dance.

Jublio, the older slaves called it, that night of our celebration. And later, Juneteenth. Although we didn't know it then, we'd been free for more than two years. My father had been free and hadn't even known it.

Some slaves left that night. The ones with kinder masters dressed up in their clothes, wearing their joy and disbelief in those ridiculous garments, as I wore Miz Bessie's hat. Later we told our children about it, about the way we laughed and sang and cried. One day they will tell their children, so that the future can remember.

Mister ran off, they said, when he heard the news was coming. Said he couldn't bear to stay to witness what he knew would happen—the ending, the beginning. Some even thought he might have taken his own life. The poor missus, they said. Poor Miz Bessie.

We've stayed with her, Alvis and me, our three sons and one daughter, all these years, in our own house right beside hers. She's an old lady now, her eyes a calm blue most of the time, the ghosts gone. Now and again she still hums that hymn. Now and again I hum it too.

The primrose still blooms every spring, filling the air with the smell of grape. The purple ground cherry has spread like a potato vine. Same plants, different flowers. Sometimes, when the sun slants against the side of the barn at dusk the way it's doing right now, and the tangled shadow of the silver maple tree stands there looking back at me, I think about my father.

They are not all good and not all evil, Little Mary. And neither are we.

Alvis comes out and stands beside me. His big hand warms my arm like the sun. "What you looking at?" he asks.

"Nothing much," I say.

"I'll go back inside then."

"You can stay."

In the faint light our eyes meet and I know that he knows I'm carrying a secret, and that it's not one he can ever help me bear. "I'll go on in. Have you tended to Miz Bessie yet?"

"I will."

The moment he takes his hand away, I feel cold.

"You've got that look again," he says, not moving from my side. "I can always tell when you're thinking about those times."

"Sometimes I can't help but think about them," I tell him, "but mostly I don't. You know that."

"Nobody can change what happened," he says, and from his

voice I can tell that he wants this talk of ours to be over. "We're free now. We can't look back."

Free.

"I wouldn't go back for anything," I tell him, and realize how much I mean it.

"It's good how it worked out," he says. "Good you didn't do what you was thinking after they hanged your daddy. I wouldn't have wanted my woman to do something like that."

"No," I say. "I wouldn't have wanted to."

"And it wasn't Miz Bessie's fault. It was that evil man of hers."

"Yes," I say. "It's good how it worked out."

He narrows his eyes as if trying to make out the shape of another person standing here with us, and I can almost guess what he's thinking.

"Mister," he says, shaking his head. "I wonder what happened to Mister."

"No telling." I look down at my hands and see that they are steady. "A lot of them just ran off. Guess we'll never know."

"And that's good too." He touches me briefly again and gives me a smile that's as much sadness as anything else. "Don't be thinking back on those times, Little Mary," he says. "Ain't nothing there but sorrow."

"You're right," I say. "I won't. And now I'd better go tend to Miz Bessie."

I've never told Alvis about those hours before the messenger, when Miz Bessie stepped inside the dim light of the barn and, seeing what I'd done, said, "Come now. We must hurry."

I watch him walk back inside, this large, honest man who thinks he protects me, this man who was afraid I'd kill the woman who may have been the only person who could truly share my father's pain.

I see his shoulders relax as if someone has lifted a weight from them.

And I see something else right then, a reflection from the barn, part light, part memory. Two women, neither one of us very large, but that day with the shovel, the pitchfork, in the mixed scent of hay and blood, we were strong.

BLARNEY

STEVE HOCKENSMITH

D ON'T WRITE A story that starts with a dream. Don't write a story that starts with a storm. Don't write a story about a writer. And never, ever, under any circumstances, write a story about a writer in a bar.

I know the rules. And up to now I haven't had any trouble sticking to them, for all the good it's done me. I write mysteries—or try to—so the problem solves itself: I start with a dead guy. The dead guy could be a writer, even a dead writer in a bar, and I don't think I'd be breaking the rules. He'd be dead, and that trumps everything. He wouldn't be a writer anymore. He'd just be The Dead Guy.

But I'm not starting this story with The Dead Guy. I'm starting it with a writer. A writer in a bar. A writer in a bar with two other writers. So it's not just a cliché. It's a cliché times three.

Sorry. But what's a writer supposed to do when the truth is a cliché? What's a writer supposed to do when *he's* a cliché?

You see, I'm the writer in the bar. Did you see that coming? Is my story hackneyed? Predictable? That's my problem. That's why I'm in the bar: I'm not a very good writer. (Had you guessed *that* already?) I was looking for a mentor, a guru. And if you're a writer looking for a guru, you're going to end up in a bar sooner or later.

I'd been going to mystery conferences and fiction seminars and adult-learning writing classes for years, an apprentice in search of a master. I was on a quest for wisdom, insight, encouragement, truth. And what did I get?

Reams of Xeroxed handouts. Stacks of promotional bookmarks, postcards, pencils, coasters, napkins, matchbooks, finger puppets, crap. Endless sales pitches. ("If you want to learn more about plot and pacing, you should pick up my book, *Giving Wings to the Writer Within*. It's on sale in the lobby.") Notebooks filled with useless scribbled "tips" and "secrets" and "rules."

"Show, don't tell."

"Write what you know."

"Writer stories bad—bar stories worse."

So let me show you. Let me write what I know.

I'm a writer in a bar with two other writers: Russ, writer of Tolkienesque fantasy epics, erotic horror stories, *X-Files* fan fiction, crap; and Daniel, writer of Joycean word jazz, free-form poetry, postmodern metafiction, crap. They're the perfect companions for me, Robert Potts, writer of Jim Thompsonish noir, two-fisted detective stories, post-postmodern hard-boiled crime fiction. All of it unpublished. All of it *crap*.

Russ I know from "The Write Way to Success: A Workshop for Pre-Published Authors." Daniel I know from "Fiction for Dummies: The Seminar" and "So You Want to Be a Novelist?"

The three of us are in a pub called O'Grady's that's about as Irish as a burrito and we're dissecting the way we've squandered our day. Six hours, two hundred bucks, blown on something called "Unlocking the Mysteries of the Storyteller's Craft."

Daniel and I are post-thirty/pre-forty, bloated, tired, cynical. But Russ, older than both of us, is still boyish, exuberant, full of hope. It makes me want to hug him. Like a snake. Squeeze him to death.

"That Susan Tracy lady was interesting," Russ says.

Daniel and I look at each other, become voices in each other's heads.

Interesting how?

Interesting "She's doable in a Mrs. Robinson kind of way"?

Or interesting "I can't believe we spent an hour getting advice about 'the storyteller's craft' from a woman who writes romance novels"?

All without speaking. Cynics are psychic, but only with each other. Contempt's always on the same wavelength.

"Remember when I went to the john? When they were having us write our own obituaries?" Russ continues, my conversation with Daniel passing through him harmlessly, unnoticed, like radio waves through a marshmallow. "I saw Susan in the hallway."

Daniel's eyebrow twitches.

"Susan"?

They're on a first-name basis now?

Screw that—she can stay "Mrs. Tracy" to me.

I smile at a joke never spoken.

"I went up and talked to her, and she was really nice. Look— she even gave me her card."

Russ reaches into his shirt pocket and pulls out a business card, white with gold fleur-de-lis wrapped around cursive script so ornately curved, I can barely read it.

SUSAN TRACY

NOVELIST

A P.O. BOX IN THE SUBURBS

AN AOL E-MAIL ADDRESS

A WEB SITE: WWW.ROMANTRIX.COM

I don't even have to look at Daniel this time.

A card?

We've all got cards.

"Me—Writer."

So what?

"If I sent her a story, do you think she'd critique it?" Russ asks.

"Sure. Send her one of your zombie sex stories," I suggest. "Those are romantic."

"Yeah," Daniel says. "She should know all about zombies. That's her audience, right?"

Daniel and I chuckle, sounding a little like Beavis and Butthead, and I feel a touch of shame as Russ slips the card back into his pocket and mumbles, "My stories are about *vampires.*"

I give him a slap on the back, swatting at my own guilt.

"Oh, come on, man. You don't need advice from someone like her."

"What the hell does she know, anyway? What the hell did any of those clowns know?" Daniel adds, helping me get things back on track: *us* versus *them.* "I mean, I heard only one guy all day who had any clue at all."

Russ smiles, recovering instantly, suddenly all tail-wagging puppy-dog enthusiasm again.

"Jack Beaghan?"

Daniel nods. "He was cool."

"Yeah," Russ says. "I thought so too."

"Wait," I say. "The Irishman?"

Daniel looks at me, his gaze wary. He knows he's taken a gamble here. He's expressed approval of something, faith in someone. He's saying he liked the guy, and I'm saying, "The Irishman?"

Jack Beaghan. The Irishman. Writer of midlist Dublin domestic dramas, obscure award-bait slices of Irish life, Jim Sheridan films that will never be shot. Not crap—as far as I know. I don't read writers like Jack Beaghan. And I usually don't listen to them.

The star of the day had been Patrick Powers, writer of *Imminent Threat, Deadly Force, Morbid Obsession*, Whatever Whatever, Adjective Noun, Crappity Crap. But good crap, well-crafted crap, successful crap. All the other speakers and busywork exercises had just been one long warm-up act for Powers's bestselling Elvis.

So when the Irishman took his turn at the front of the overly refrigerated Hilton Hotel banquet hall in which the suckers du jour had been corralled, I passed the time thinking up a question for Patrick Powers. Not the typical time waster. Not "Where do you get your ideas?" or "How do you build suspense?" or "Who's your agent?" I was going to set myself apart. I was going to be the guy who stands up and asks the question that displays such discernment, such wit, such dazzling *potential,* that it wouldn't just squeeze oohs and aahs out of the wannabes but it would win an appreciative chuckle from Patrick Powers, a wave of the hand when the Q&A was over.

Come here. Talk to me. Yeah, you.

I wrestled with the question for nearly an hour, slowly bending and twisting it toward perfection, glancing up only whenever the Irishman won a big laugh from his audience. There were more than a few glances. Beaghan was a crowd-pleaser, I could tell that much, though I had no idea what was so pleasing. I was always a split second behind the joke, saying "What? What?" to Daniel and Russ, who were laughing too hard to hear me.

I paid attention to the man just long enough to catch one sample of his "wisdom."

"Storytelling doesn't come from here," Beaghan said, tapping a bony finger against the side of his head. "It comes from here." And he gave his lean stomach three quick pats.

"And your advice," I wanted to say, "comes straight from here." And I would stand up, drop my pants, and swat my ass.

But I didn't. I just went back to crafting the perfect question for Patrick Powers, building it slowly, word by painstaking word, on the back of a handout about how to create "Prose Like the Pros."

So cut to three hours later and there we are, three writers in a faux Irish pub, and Daniel says he liked Jack Beaghan, gives him his official endorsement, and I say, "The Irishman?" And a voice behind us says, "Be careful now, lads—speak of the devil, you know!"

We're sitting one-two-three at the bar and we all spin around on our swivel-top stools like kids on the Tilt-A-Whirl, and there he is—a wiry, weathered, white-haired little man, a pint in his hand, a grin on his face, and a twinkle in his eyes.

And I'm not just falling into cliché when I write that. The Irishman's eyes are actually twinkling. I never even knew what that meant—eyes "twinkling"—until I see Jack Beaghan's eyes up close. They're shimmering with a dancing light that doesn't come from anywhere in the room.

"You were here for the fleecing, then?" Beaghan says, and the way we laugh fans his wee twinkle into a flashing, crackling blaze. "Well, come have a pint with me, boyos, and I'll make sure you get your money's worth."

Does he really say "have a pint with me, boyos"? Maybe he says "have a drink with me, boys" or "have a seat with me, gents" or "ketchup mustard applesauce." I don't know. Beaghan's got an accent and a smile and that damn twinkle, and it casts a spell on me, enchants us all. The three of us slip off our stools and follow him to a booth, grinning and dazed, like sailors who've heard the Sirens' song.

Just seconds before, I'd been about to diss Jack Beaghan, write him off as yet another hack kept aloft by nothing more than his own hot air. But meeting him now—all *a-twinkle,* for Christ's sake—changes things. He's magic, this guy. He's wearing a dark plaid shirt and worn jeans, but what I see is a green suit and a bowler hat with a shamrock in the band. I'm at the end of the rainbow, only Beaghan's not offering me a pot of gold or a bowl of Lucky Charms. He's offering much, much more.

The Irishman raises his beer and says "sluncha" or "slawn chair" or something like that, obviously a Gaelic toast, and we bellow "sluncha!" and clink glasses and take long, deep, manly Irish pub drinks. Daniel and I catch each other's eyes over the rims of our beer glasses, exchanging a look that says, "Can you believe this, man? Can you *believe* it?"

I was wrong before. Daniel, Russ, me—we weren't three writers in a bar. We were three "writers" in a "pub." But with the Irishman there with us, I feel the quotation marks evaporating, lifting a weight I'd been only dimly aware of until it was gone.

Now we're four writers in a pub, and to prove it, what are we talking about?

"Writing," Beaghan says. "The 'storyteller's craft.' That's what you came to learn about, did you? Well, let me tell you one thing straight off, lads. What you heard today? Blarney, every word of it—and that includes what *I* said!"

Does he actually use the word "blarney"? Does he really talk like something out of *Darby O'Gill and the Little People*? Now I'm not sure. Maybe he says "bollocks." Maybe it's "bullshit." What matters is, I hear "blarney" and we all laugh.

"I'm Jack Beaghan, by the way," the Irishman says, stretching his long gnarled hand across the table toward Russ.

"Oh, we know! I'm Russ. I write speculative fiction."

Beaghan gives him a neutral "You don't say?" nod as they shake, then turns to Daniel.

"My name's Daniel. I write . . ."

He catches himself before he can say "*literary* fiction."

"Fiction," Daniel says instead.

"Just fiction?" Beaghan asks innocently as they clasp hands. "You don't do any speculating?"

Daniel smirks, jerks his head at Russ.

"Not about the same things he does."

"And you are?" Beaghan asks as he swivels around to face me. I'm to his right, on the same side of the table, sharing his view out at the others, the world.

I try to make my grip forceful but not desperate, my gaze steady but not creepy.

"Robert Potts. Mystery writer."

"Oh," Beaghan says, cocking an eyebrow, seeming to reappraise me without quite judging me. "So you're interested in crime and punishment, then?"

"Well . . . crime, anyway."

Beaghan's soft chuckle sends a tingle across my shoulders.

I made him laugh!

"Then you'll find plenty to write about in this world of ours, Robert. Crimes we've got around us all the time. But punishment . . . at least if you're talking about *justice* . . . that's fookin' *scarce*."

His gaze drifts downward, gets lost in his beer. But before any awkwardness can settle over the table, Beaghan whips his head up and points his long jaw at Russ like the barrel of a pistol.

"So tell me, Russ—what do you think writing's all about?"

Russ stutters, blinks, grins awkwardly, the kid who didn't do his homework.

"Maybe . . . maybe escapism?"

"Oh, it's an escape, is it?" Beaghan says. "For who, then? Your readers . . . or *you?*"

Before Russ can stammer out another answer, the Irishman's swinging his twinkle toward Daniel.

"Maybe you can tell us. What's writing all about?"

Daniel throws a nod at Russ, obviously hoping to one-up him, earn the Irishman's approval.

"It's the opposite of what he said. It's a writer's job to unearth the dark truths of life and report them without flinching."

" 'Unearth the dark truths of life'? Sweet Jesus, lads—we've got a poet in our midst!"

Russ and I laugh, and Daniel flushes pink. Beaghan reaches across the table and gives him a no-hard-feelings slap on the arm.

"Ahhh, I've written a bit of the purple stuff myself. It's nothing you won't get over eventually. I did."

Daniel smiles, then joins in the laughter, obviously deciding to wear the bruise as a badge of honor. We're in a scene from an old chop-socky movie: before you can have killer kung-fu, the master has to kick your ass.

And now it's my turn.

"What about you, then?" Beaghan says to me. "What do you think writing is?"

I'm ready for him.

"Telling lies for fun and profit."

My answer's superficial, glib—stolen from the title of a how-to book. But glib seems to suit the Irishman, and I think maybe I've won the contest.

Beaghan nods and puts down his glass. (He's taking long, gulping swallows each time we speak, I notice now.)

"Well, it is fun, yes it is." Suddenly his nod turns into a shake. "But there's damn little profit in it for most of us, believe me.

Why do you think I was up there whoring myself this afternoon? As for lies . . . no. You can't just tell lies. A story's got to feel utterly and completely true." And he tilts his chin down, drops his voice, and honors me with a conspiratorial wink. "Even if it's shite."

Beaghan finishes his beer as we chuckle, throwing his head back to swallow even the last slug-trail of foam.

"No, you can't write wrongs, ho ho," he says when he's through. "And pardon me if that sounds like *real* blarney, but I happen to believe it. Before you can tell a good lie, you've got to know the Truth."

He capitalizes the word with a hard rap on the table. His beer glass rattles, and he looks down at it, seemingly surprised to find it there before him so heartbreakingly empty.

"Well, now," Beaghan says, pursing his moist, rubbery lips. "If you kind sirs were to stand me to a drink, I'd tell you what writing means to *me*. What storytelling means, anyway. And what's more, I'd tell you in a story—a *true* story."

I expect Russ or even Daniel to hop up and fetch the man his beer—expect it even as I'm coming to my feet, saying, "What do you want?"

"I'll have another touch of the black stuff—Guinness—thanks."

When I come back a few minutes later, two Guinnesses in my hands, I find three writers laughing uproariously. I've missed the joke again—just like at the seminar—but I don't feel left out. Beaghan takes his beer and gives me a "sluncha" and we clink glasses, just the two of us. He takes a drink, and I take a drink, and I don't put down my glass until he does. When I do, a third of my pint is gone.

"How old do you think I am?" Beaghan says to Russ.

Russ stutters, shrugs, on the spot again.

"I . . . I don't know. Maybe . . . sixty?"

"Sixty, he says?" Beaghan shakes his fist at Russ with mock outrage. "You heartless bastard! So I look like a withered old man, do I? Well, I'll have you know, boyo, that ol' Jack Beaghan here isn't a day over forty-five!"

He smiles as he lays out this obvious lie, his grin putting even more lines and creases in his already wrinkled face. But Russ and Daniel don't seem to know how to react. Russ's doughy features flutter between amusement and embarrassment, the urge to laugh and the urge to apologize struggling for dominance. Daniel just nods, either playing it safe or genuinely clueless.

Even before he's really begun his story, Beaghan's spreading on the "shite" with a trowel. He's going to show us what story-telling's all about, all right—show us by whipping up a big pot of blarney right on the spot.

"Wow! Forty-five?" I say, the only one of us who knows how to play along. "Jeez, Jack—what the hell happened to *you?*"

Beaghan sneaks a peek at me, throws me a sly smile.

I'm his accomplice in this now. His second banana.

His student.

"Bangladesh—that's what fookin' happened," the Irishman says, suddenly straight-faced, somber. "Twenty years ago, my mate Dan and me, we set off to have an adventure. Around the world in eighty-plus-ten days, that was the plan. But boyos . . . we didn't see home again for *two years*."

Russ and Daniel are both wide-eyed now, like kids around a campfire hearing "The Man with the Golden Arm" for the first time. I'm amazed at how easily Beaghan draws them in. He doesn't need my help here, he's got these suckers hooked, but I throw out a little bit of business just to show which side of the table I'm on.

"You got lost in Bangladesh?"

"No," Beaghan says, bringing just the right hint of irritation to the curt shake of his head. The guy's an Irish Olivier. "It was a matter of crime and punishment, Robert. Not that there was much crime to it. Not at first. But it was a hell of a lot of punishment. Drunk and disorderly in Dublin—why, that's a given for a couple of young lads. Hell, it's a fookin' rite of passage. But in Bangladesh, have a few too many of these"—he lifts his Guinness and gives it a swirl, the dark liquid sloshing to the lip but not quite spilling over—"and they look at you like you're Charlie bloody Manson. I mean, it's not just illegal to be drunk and disorderly. It's illegal to be a wee bit tipsy. It's illegal to wet your damn whistle. And Dan and me, we got wet. Ohhhhh, boys—we got soaked."

Beaghan's really rolling now, he's not even pausing to drink, so I just settle in and watch him work his magic. Across the table from me, Russ and Daniel stare at the Irishman, slack-jawed, hypnotized, and I have to fight to keep a smirk off my face.

"Now Bangladeshi justice—if you want to call it that—is a swift business, conducted in volume without much worry about niggling details like a man's rights. Before you know it, Dan and I are thrown into the deepest, darkest pit of slime, misery, and degradation you could imagine. In fact, I'd bet you *couldn't* even imagine it, it was so awful. You've seen *Midnight Express*? The movie? Well, a Bangladeshi prison makes that look like fookin' *Bambi*."

I lose it there for a few seconds, break into a chuckle I have to drown in my beer, but it doesn't throw Beaghan off. He plows on, focusing all his attention on Russ and Daniel now, not letting anything break the spell.

"So you want to know why I look a little rough? Well, it's rough surviving a beating each and every day. It's rough fighting off the men who want to steal from you and rape you and wipe their feet on your soul. It's rough having your head jammed into a bucket of your own filth until you think you're going to drown. And it's rough watching your friend go through it all with you—watch him die inch by inch, day by day. And that's just what happened to me and Dan, boyos. We were both dying in that hellhole, and we knew it."

Finally Beaghan stops here for a long pull on his beer. He's picked just the right spot for a pause—a cliffhanger. Daniel glances at me, a look of awe on his face.

Can you believe this shit? he's saying.

But I can't return the look. Instead I fight more giggles, and our psychic link is shattered. Daniel's expression changes, darkens. He still doesn't see the joke, can't smell the blarney. If he did, he'd be giggling too.

"Two things saved us," Beaghan starts up again. "First, half the miserable sods in there with us spoke English. And second, I knew how to tell a good story. Now you've got to know your audience, and I knew these sons of bitches pretty damn well. So I could give them just what they wanted to hear: stories about brutal, heartless, evil bastards doing brutal, heartless, evil things. And my stories all starred the same two bastards."

I can't resist.

"George Bush and Dick Cheney?" I say.

Beaghan manages a soft, good-natured laugh, but Daniel and Russ both glare at me and I quickly realize how close I've come to blowing my mentor's cover. I hide behind my glass for a moment, washing the grin off my face with beer, noticing only when I put the glass down that it's already almost empty.

"No," Beaghan says. "The two bastards were Dan and myself. I told the story about the time we went to work for a bookie and ended up kneecapping the man's own father over a twenty-pound bet. And the one about us kidnapping a barrister's wife and leaving the body on his doorstep in Christmas wrap after we got the ransom. And the one about us shoving an entire Pekingese up a man's arse. Hell, I even told them about the time we shot a man in Reno just to watch him die. All of it a big, steaming pile of shite."

Beaghan smiles, so we have permission to laugh. I laugh a little harder than Russ and Daniel because I've got more to laugh about. I can see what they can't—that Beaghan's toying with them, practically admitting that he's making the whole thing up on the spot. And the more he hints at the Truth, the more the suckers eat up the Shite. It's a lesson in storytelling I'll never forget.

"But you know what, boyos? People started to believe those stories. I told them so many times, *I* started to believe. Only once did a man in that prison call me a liar. Of course he was right, yet still it made me so furious, filled me with such rage that anyone would dare doubt my word, doubt that I was the cold-blooded killer I made myself out to be, I brought one of those stories to life right then and there."

The pub we're in serves food—fish and chips, bangers and mash, all that brick-in-your-stomach British crap. So there are place settings at our table, little napkin-wrapped bundles of silverware. Beaghan casually unravels the one in front of him and slides out something long and gleaming.

"You can kill a man with a fork, you know." And he turns to me and moves his hand up fast, and I feel the cold metal tines tickle the flesh beneath my chin, sending a jolt through me that stiffens my spine. "You just have to get him right here, where a man's soft, and drive straight up. Do that hard enough"—the fork digs a little into my saggy flesh—"and you'll have yourself a brain kabob."

And then the fork's back on the table in front of Beaghan and the Irishman's grinning at me. And when the surprise and fear melt away, I actually feel *honored*. Whether I'm the magician's assistant or his prop, it doesn't matter—he's made me part of the act.

"We were in the cafeteria when I did that," Beaghan says, turning back to our audience. "There were men all around me—but not a one ratted me out. Because they knew then for sure that those stories about me were true. And what's more, *I* knew they were true. And after that, no one so much as said boo to me or Dan. That's the power of storytelling, my friends."

The Irishman eases back, rests against the wood behind him. The tension around the table releases, deflates like a balloon, and it's clear where we're headed next: the epilogue.

"Well, we made it back to Dublin eventually. Dan and me, we're still mates. But we're different men now. Because stories have the power to change you, lads—both in the hearing and in the telling. There are times when I think back on those stories I told, and they seem as real to me as actual memories. And Dan, he lives completely in that world now. He went and became a real criminal—this a man who was in *art school* when we started our trip, for fook's sake! He's been in prison again—in Ireland, in England—three, four more times. And every so often I'll meet a hard-looking man, a man with that scared-angry way about him, and I'll know where he's been before he even asks me what he wants to ask.

" 'Tell me, Jack,' he'll say. 'That story about you and Dan Kelly and a Pekingese . . . is that true?'

"And I'll feel that old fire kindle up in me again, feel that other Jack Beaghan, the one I created through my stories, trying to burn his way back into the world. And I'll look the dumb bastard doing the asking dead in the eye, and do you know what I'll say to him?"

Beaghan leans forward, his hands gripping the edge of the table not far from his knife and fork.

" 'Every . . . fookin' . . . word.' "

His gaze bores into the man across from him—poor, pop-eyed Russ—like a drill into butter.

"So here's the lesson," Beaghan says softly. "Storytelling doesn't come from your head or your heart or even your gut. If it's to be any damn good at all, it has to come from right here."

His right hand disappears beneath the table, and Russ jumps out of his chair squealing, his hands cupping his crotch.

"You've gotta grab 'em by the balls, boyos," Beaghan says, and I just can't keep it in any longer.

I'm roaring with laughter, beating the table, turning heads throughout the pub. There's maybe a five-second pause before Daniel joins in with a few uncertain laughs of his own, and then Russ is giggling along with us as he slides slowly, cautiously, back into his seat.

Beaghan smiles smugly, a Picasso of bullshit who's just put the final brushstroke on his latest masterpiece.

"Damn, you're good!" I say. "You had these suckers going from word one." And I reach over and slap the Irishman on the back.

And what I'll end up asking myself not a minute later is this: When did his smile waver? When did his twinkle start to flicker? Was it when I touched him? Or when I spoke?

"I think you'd best buy me another drink, Richard," Beaghan says.

"No problem, man," I reply cheerfully. "You earned it!"

I'm out of my chair and almost to the bar before it hits me.

Did he call me "Richard"?

It stops me dead, and I stand there for a moment, rewinding and replaying the sound bite in my head.

"I think you'd best buy me another drink, Robert"?

No.

". . . best buy me another drink, Richard"?

Yes.

". . . another drink, Richard."

". . . *Richard.*"

I manage to start moving again, but I'm not through thinking.

Is he calling me . . . a dick?

Do the Irish even use that phrase?

Wouldn't he call me a "wally" or something?

And then the look on Beaghan's face takes shape in my memory, the way his grin soured into something bitter just before he spoke. I make it to the bar, put in my order—two Guinnesses—before letting myself glance back at our booth.

The Irishman's talking, but he's not looking at Russ or Daniel. He's looking at *me*. And that expression is still on his face. He's staring at me like I'm a turd in his soup.

I turn away, dread suddenly pressing down on me, trying to squash me like a bug.

Am I that drunk? Am I that dumb?

Was Beaghan's story *true?*

I feel nauseous with doubt and shame. Again. I'd been in the "pub" with my "writer" friends (the quotes are back in full force) to drown out the memory of my moment in the spotlight—my question for Patrick Powers, bestselling author, guru candidate, asshole. His presentation had been as rote and meaningless as his novels. Practice makes perfect. Believe in yourself. Blah blarney blah. All of it delivered in a monotone by a man who appeared to be in the grip of a boredom so powerful, it was practically narcoleptic.

He wrapped up early, leaving twenty-five minutes for questions, and my hand was the first in the air. I was the third person called, after a redheaded PYT who asked where he got his ideas and an aging, Botoxified beauty trying to land an agent for her unpublished series of dog-grooming mysteries. When it was my turn, I stood and cleared my throat—and felt my mind clear too.

"In *Primal Fear* . . . no . . . [Damn!] . . . *Mortal Fear,* you . . . the protagonist, the character of . . . [What was that name again? Screw it.] . . . the writer you depict is a . . . a writer of thrillers and you . . . he says something like, fear doesn't come from the in—. . . [Shit!] . . . I mean, the *out*side. Fear is always with us. Inside. Inside is where it comes from and certain . . . things, events, let it out. And I'm wondering if . . . if you were to deconstruct your . . . ["Deconstruct"? Shit, I'm lost.] . . . if you have a philosophy that . . ."

I finally gave up, reaching down for the paper on the table in front of me, thinking I'd just read the damn question—I'm a writer, not a performer. But before I got the paper in my fingers, could even finish my question, Powers was giving me an answer.

"Yeah, okay, I think I see where you're going with this," he said, squinting at me as if I were something he couldn't quite pull into focus. A distant cloud, a fuzzy picture, a mirage. Then he looked away, addressing his answer to everyone *but* me. "Actually, that quote comes up all the time. Don't take it too seriously, folks. It's BS."

A hundred soft chuckles rose and fell in unison, sounding like a gentle wave rolling up a beach before retreating back into the sea. Powers called on someone else—a dowdy grandma who launched into a harangue about "nasty words" in modern books—and I sank back into my seat. When the seminar was finally over not long afterward, I left my "perfect question" behind in a thousand pieces, confetti sprinkled around my chair.

I needed a drink, some alcohol to send me home with the buzz Patrick Powers and the rest of the day's charlatans hadn't provided. And then along came Jack Beaghan and I got that buzz. Until it curled up inside me and died.

Had I just laughed and wisecracked my way through the most horrific memory of a man's life? Had Beaghan been teaching me—or merely tolerating me? And what about that fork at my throat? Was that part of an act? Or a genuine act of rage?

What kind of man was Jack Beaghan? What kind of man was *I?*

My beers come, I pay, I head back to our spot. I see the Irishman hunched over the table, his lips moving fast. Russ and Daniel nod, then all three of them turn to look at me as I walk up. Their faces are blank, unreadable, even Beaghan's now.

I hand the Irishman his Guinness.

"Thank you, Richard," he says as I sit down.

No one corrects him. Not Russ, not Daniel. Certainly not me.

If he thinks I'm a dick, I'm a dick. I'm not going to contradict him. I'm just going to finish my beer and get the hell out of there.

Beaghan raises his glass toward me.

"Sluncha."

I clink his pint glass with mine.

"Sluncha," I say, unable to fake cheerful, ignorant bliss.

Beaghan eyes me as he gulps at his beer, his twinkle brighter than ever. Hotter. When he puts his glass down he keeps his hand resting on the table, and his pinky stretches out, comes down on the fork, idly slides the metal back and forth over the smooth lacquered wood.

"Do you remember what I said about lies, Richard?"

I don't, actually. Not then. I feel cornered, and it's hard for me to remember anything. So the Irishman reminds me.

"You can't tell a proper lie unless you can recognize the truth. I really believe that."

He pushes down harder on the fork, two fingers on it now—I can see the red of blood around his nails, the flesh over the joints going white from the pressure.

"So I have to wonder about you, Richard. Because unless I'm seriously mistaken . . ."

The Irishman's words slow down, finally stop, and he lets a beat pass in silence, telling me that what's come before this is just a prologue, a warm-up. When he speaks again, it's with a different voice. It's not the voice of shamrocks and "the little people" and the Blarney Stone anymore. There's no blarney about it. It's the voice of a prisoner, a desperate man. A killer.

"You looked the truth in the face just now—and you spat in it," the voice says. "You didn't believe a word I said. In fact, you think I'm a bloody fookin' liar, don't you? *Don't you?*"

And his fist curled around the fork. I swear it did. I saw it. I can see it now.

So how the fork ended up in my hand, I'm not sure. But I can tell you this: Beaghan wasn't lying when he said you can kill a man with a fork. All you have to do is swing, swing hard, one two three four times into the neck. And hit an artery while you're at it.

Beaghan tilts back off his chair, sprawls across the floor. He presses his hands up under his chin as if he's trying to strangle himself, blood spurting through his fingers anyway. It only takes a few minutes for him to bleed to death, but I don't get to see the twinkle in his eyes go glossy, freeze. I've already been dragged away, beer-fueled action heroes jumping me, prying the fork from my hand, pinning my arms behind my back.

"Let me go!" I hear myself screaming. "It was self-defense!"

And Russ looks at me from across the room, where he's kneeling over the Irishman, uselessly pressing napkins against the man's gaping, gurgling wounds, and he says, "Jesus, Robert! He was joking! He was just *joking!*"

Just joking. Just "taking the piss." Just having a little fun with me. That's what Daniel says too. The detectives told me.

"Your friends say the guy was kidding."

"Your friends say you were drunk."

"Your friends say you were agitated."

Was I drunk? Yes. Was I "agitated"? I suppose so. Was the Irishman kidding?

The cops are checking on Beaghan's story—his Bangladeshi prison saga. But I can tell it doesn't matter to them whether it's true or not. And you know what? It doesn't matter to me. Not what Beaghan's records say, anyway. That might be the truth, but it's not the Truth. Not the one Beaghan created in that bar with nothing but words.

I know what I saw. And I know there's only one way to make everyone else see it too.

So I said to the detectives, "Turn off the video camera. Bring me a pen and a pad of paper. Or better yet, put me in front of a keyboard, if you can. I need to *write* this."

And here it is. I guess some people will say it's my confession, but that's not right. It's not a "confession" or a "statement" or whatever else the cops and lawyers might call it. It's a story. And sitting here now, I'm thinking it's the best one I've ever written. Because you know what?

I believe it.

HEAT LIGHTNING

WILLIAM KENT KRUEGER

IN THE WORST of the heat that afternoon, he'd cleaned his old target pistol, a Browning Buck Mark .22, and put one bullet into the chamber. He'd laid the gun on a shelf just inside the door of the toolshed and, as the day cooled toward night, returned to his preparations.

Now he waited in the yard beside his big farmhouse, patient in the gathering dark, in the stillness after the singsong of the cicadas had died away. He sat on an old cottonwood stump near the rail fence, his feet planted in the brittle grass of a rainless summer. In his hand was an open pocketknife. Occasionally he drove the blade into the rotting wood stump with a soft *thuck* sound. His palms were hard and callused, but he'd scrubbed his knuckles clean and scraped the dirt from under his fingernails. Every so often his eyes flicked toward the lane that led up from the main road.

She came at the time he'd told her, when it was too dark for the distant neighbors to see clearly the make or model of her car. She drove carefully along the dirt lane between Cody's fields of stunted corn. The powdery dust of August rose up thick behind her and hung a long time in the still twilight. She parked her red

Mazda near the toolshed, stepped out, and looked at the farm-house, the barn, the fields.

"So this is it," she said as she walked to him. "The house looks better than you described it."

"Spent the week slapping on some paint, Annie. Nothing to farm these days. Got to keep busy somehow."

She wore a white summer dress, sleeveless, with a wide red belt around her waist. She was so tanned that she seemed to him like a beautiful doll carved of some dark and exquisite wood.

He folded his knife and put it away. "I wasn't sure you'd come." He drew her close and kissed her. The fragrance of her perfume, a scent she'd told him was called Black Cashmere, washed over him, always a profound pleasure. He savored the taste of the camphor and vanilla of the Carmex that moistened her lips.

"Julia?" she said.

He nodded toward the second-floor window. "Asleep in her room. If she wakes, her air conditioner's on. She can't hear a thing."

He took her hand. She held back.

"This feels . . . not right," she said. "Here. Like this."

"You told me you'd like to see my place before you go. Last chance. Come on," he said, urging her gently.

"Where to?"

"Up there." He indicated the hill in the middle of his fields. "You can see everything better."

"I don't know, Cody." She pulled from his grasp.

"I've fixed up something special. You'll see."

"I shouldn't have come." She took a step back. "We said our good-byes already. Why drag this out?"

"It'll be fine, Annie. You'll see."

He reached out, his hand suspended in the air between them, as still as any leaf on his withered cornstalks.

They walked past the rail fence into a field where soybeans were dying in the August heat. She pulled her sandals off and walked barefoot in soil that had become so dry it was as soft as ash. The field rose in the center to a mound from which the horizon in all directions could be clearly seen. Rows of bean plants, as dark as prison stripes, stretched away all around them. In the distance, the two grain elevators in the small town of Dorian stood like the towers of a castle, black against the last feathery blue of twilight. To the south, heat lightning mutely battered the sky. Along I-90, less than a mile from Cody's fields, cars and trucks sped east toward LaCrosse and Chicago, or west toward Sioux Falls. As always, the sound the vehicles made in passing seemed to Cody like a long, painful exhalation.

Annie stopped at the top of the mound and looked down at the clean white cotton blanket Cody had put there. On a linen napkin next to the blanket sat two wineglasses and an old metal bucket with a champagne bottle inside nestled in ice. Beads of condensation trickled down the outside of the bucket, making a dark wet stain on the napkin.

She looked completely surprised. "Dom Perignon?"

"I figured if I was going to try to talk you into making love in the middle of a field, I ought to get you drunk first."

She smiled, a little sadly. "You know me. I'm easy. Something cheap would have done as well."

"Our last time together. I wanted it to be memorable."

He drew her to him, wrapped her in his arms, which were thick-muscled from the years of his labor. He kissed her gently and felt her yield.

She slipped off her summer dress, then looked doubtfully at the small area of the blanket. He took off his own clothes and laid them out in the dust in the shape of a supine man.

"Ménage à trois," he said. "You, me, and the scarecrow. Just put your things on mine."

Annie carefully folded her dress and undergarments, placed them on his clothing. In the airless end of evening, they made love while the topsoil, as light as flour, puffed out around the edges of the blanket beneath them. When they'd finished, he wrote his name on her belly, spelling it out in the layer of dust that, clinging to her sweat, had become dirt again.

"That will never come off," he told her.

"What about when I shower?"

"Uh-uh." He shook his head seriously. "Ten years from now you'll be able to look down and see my name there. I've marked you for life. Just like you've marked me."

She closed her eyes and, after a moment, rolled away from him and sat up.

"And so it goes," he said.

"Vonnegut." She smiled.

"This time last year, I didn't even know who the hell he was. Now you've got me quoting him."

Six months ago, as Julia worsened, he'd looked for an escape and had turned to reading. Annie taught an adult education class on the modern American novel at the community college in Rochester. He'd arranged for friends or family to sit with Julia, and he'd enrolled. It had been a way for him, one evening each week, to slip the yoke of his duty to his dying wife. Over time, it was not just her love of literature that Annie shared with him.

"I bought a first edition of *Slaughterhouse Five*. Signed," he said as he pulled the champagne from the melting ice in the bucket. Vonnegut was her favorite author, and now his.

"No."

"I did. On eBay."

"That must have been expensive."

"All good things come at a high price."

Rare books, he thought. *Land. Love.*

While he opened the champagne, Annie drew idly in the dust, her finger sinking all the way down to her knuckle. "They say rain by the weekend."

"Too late to do any good."

"I'm sorry, Cody." She touched his face. "You look so tired."

"I haven't been sleeping well."

"Worried about the farm?"

"I gave up that worry a long time ago. No, I was trying to think of a way to keep you here."

"There isn't any. Not now."

"You love him?"

He'd known about the doctor in Rochester, a resident at the Mayo Clinic. From the way she'd talked, he'd never believed she would marry him. But they'd become engaged.

"We're a good match," she said.

"You'll have children?"

"I suppose that's what married people do."

He and Julia had wanted children . . . He stopped himself from going there in his thinking. Useless to dwell on what he could not change.

He poured the champagne. "I did think of a way to keep you from leaving."

"Oh?"

"I decided I could kill you."

She laughed, but stopped when she saw that he wasn't even smiling. "Would you really?"

"Why not? It's what crazy men do. And you do drive me crazy."

"I don't mean to."

"You can't help it. It's the way you are. Or the situation. Here." He handed her a glass. "I suppose we should toast."

"I don't feel much like toasting."

"Then I will. To your happiness." He touched her glass.

"Do you mean that?"

"Why wouldn't I?"

He put his back against hers, felt the soft, moist grit between them, felt her skin, her bone, the slow bump of her heart. He picked up a handful of the fine dry dirt and let it slide through his fingers. "All packed?"

"The movers finished this afternoon. I'll leave tomorrow morning. I'm hoping to be off before sunrise."

"He's already there?"

"He started at the hospital yesterday."

"You really think you'll be happy in San Francisco?"

"I'll be happy anywhere I don't have to look around me and see that everything's dying." She caught herself and paused. "I'm sorry, Cody. I didn't mean—"

"That's okay." He sipped from his glass.

"How is Julia?"

"Worse every day. Doctor still says six months, maybe a year. I don't know how that could be. She's so weak she can barely speak. Sometimes the pain's so great it confuses her and she doesn't even recognize me."

"I'm sorry."

"I've been thinking that maybe this drought's a blessing in a way. Gives me time to care for her better."

"You're a good man, Cody."

"Not good enough to keep you here."

"Let's don't go into that."

He felt her tense, heard something sharp in her voice, like a sliver of bone. A slight wind came up, enough to rustle the dry bean plants; then it died and the field was still again. Except for the sigh of the distant cars and Annie's breathing, there was nothing for Cody to hear.

He turned himself, put his heart against her back, and held her tightly.

"Sometimes," he whispered, "driving to Rochester to be with you, I'd spend the whole time imagining what it would be like. You, me, together, for good. I pictured you heading off each morning to do your teaching. Me, I'd do what I love, farm these hills. I tried to make myself believe that somehow it would all work, that somehow it might be possible someday." He tapped the dust lightly with his fist. "But then I'd come home to Julia—"

"Cody, don't."

"She suffers so," he went on. "And that suffering just sucks the life out of those who've loved her. She knows. She begs me sometimes to end it."

"You wouldn't." Annie sounded horrified.

"I've considered it. Thought how it might be. A pillow over her face when she's in one of those deep, painless sleeps the pills put her into. It would be a soft death. Maybe a moment of confusion somewhere deep in her unconsciousness. Then a giving in. She doesn't have the strength to fight it. It would be over in a couple of minutes. An end to everyone's suffering. Hers, mine." He felt her trembling. Or was it him? They were pressed so hard together he couldn't tell where his own skin ended and hers began. "There were moments when I had the pillow in my hands. But I couldn't do it. You know why? The most selfish of reasons. I'm a coward. I'd probably go to jail, and the idea of that, being all locked up, scares the hell out of me."

"Oh, Cody, I'm so glad you couldn't."

He drew away from her a little. "I'm not the husband she deserves. My heart's divided."

"I didn't mean to come between you."

"Couldn't be helped. But Julia, she deserves someone better than me, someone who loves her completely, loves her enough to do what she's asked."

"What's happened to Julia isn't your fault. And ending her suffering isn't your penance."

"You sound like a psychologist. So tell me something, Doctor. How do you think a man would feel after doing something like that? Do you think he'd be full of grief? Or guilt, maybe?"

"Cody, stop. Please."

"I'll tell you what I think. I think it would be like stepping up out of some dark, airless place toward the light."

She turned to him, desperate. "Look at me. Look at me, damn it. Promise me you won't do anything like that. Promise me, Cody."

Beyond her, the heat lightning illuminated the sky and his dead fields and the gray dirt that had once been fertile and now was ash. He said, "I promise."

She leaned her forehead against his shoulder, relieved.

With a slow, deep breath, he drew in the warm summer air. "It's time," he said.

"I know."

She began to gather her things.

"Wait a minute." Cody turned his shirt inside out and handed it to her. "Wipe yourself off so you don't get your dress all dirty."

"Thanks." She brushed the dust off her arms and breasts and belly. He wiped her back and most of her legs. She took the shirt again and carefully dabbed high between her thighs, then looked closely at the fabric. "Oh, shoot, I'm bleeding. I must have started my period. I've ruined your shirt, Cody."

He looked down at himself. Even in the dark, he could see her blood on him. He took the shirt and wiped himself off too.

She slipped into her dress. Cody tugged on his pants. They left the blanket, the champagne, the empty glasses, and walked back to the yard.

"I've got a Tampax in my purse in the car," Annie said, and went on alone.

Cody stepped into his old sneakers and tied the ragged laces. When Annie came back, she handed him the shirt.

"I'll send you a new one from San Francisco."

"No need."

"I want to. I want to send you something special, something—oh, I don't know—frivolous and frilly. All you have are work shirts." She rattled on, as if afraid to stop.

He put a finger on her lips to quiet her. "Whatever." He looked at her carefully, strained to see her face clearly one last time. Mostly, though, he saw only her silhouette against the flash of the heat lightning.

"I have something for you," he said. "I put it in the toolshed earlier."

"What is it?"

"A surprise. The denouement."

She smiled, quizzically. "The what?"

"Isn't that the word? What brings our story to a meaningful ending? Wait here."

He went into the shed. When he came out and she saw what he held, she said, "No, Cody."

"It seemed to me the perfect thing," he said.

"No," she cried again.

He stepped nearer. She lifted her hands as if to stop him.

"Please. Take it." He held out the book to her. "He signed it on the title page, and it's dated. I bought it for you. A book is forever, isn't that what you said? No matter where you are, when you look at it you'll always think of me."

She was crying now. She laid her head against his bare chest and held him tightly.

"Now look what you've done. Gone and got that pretty white dress all dirty." He put his arms around her.

"I'll write," she promised.

"Maybe so. I won't. Never was any good at it. What would I say anyway? Corn's dead. Beans are dead. I love you."

He ran his hand through her hair, memorizing the soft feel of it on his callused palm.

"Good-bye, Cody." She pushed from him, turned, and hurried away, *Slaughterhouse Five* cradled in her hand.

He watched her Mazda pull onto the lane and the headlights bulldoze through the dark between the cornfields. Dust rose up behind her like something momentarily awakened, then gradually settled back.

He felt limp and wilted, as dry of tears as the sky was of rain. He looked up at the window of the room where Julia lay. He went into the house where he'd lived for too long with the smell of his wife's slow dying, climbed the stairs, and entered her bedroom. The lamp was on in the corner. The air conditioner hummed. Julia was asleep. The aide who visited twice each week had washed her hair that morning, and it lay clean and silky on her pillow. She'd been a beautiful woman once. Now she looked like one of the plants in his fields, withered to nothing, sustained by God knew what. He stood above her, leaned down, kissed her lips, which were cracked and dry. Then he slid the pillow gently from under her head and pressed it hard over her face. When the duty was finished, he sat beside her body on the bed. He didn't want to remove the pillow, to have to look at what he'd done, but the end of everything he cared about was already upon him, so what was the use in holding back? He was surprised when he saw that she looked little different, no emptier than she had before. Surprised too that his own emptiness was so complete, he didn't feel the things he'd feared, not guilt or grieving or even relief.

He returned to the toolshed, grabbed his soiled shirt, and lifted a shovel from among the long-handled tools that hung on the wall. He walked past the fence into the bean field, up to the top of the mound where they'd lain. No one knew about Annie. He wanted to be sure no one ever did. Kicking aside the blanket, he dug a deep hole, deeper than the teeth of his plow or the plates of his disc harrow or the roots of any of his crops could ever reach. Into it he dropped the shirt, then he put in the bucket, the blanket, and the glasses, and he filled the hole back up. He spent a moment leaning on the shovel, staring at the freeway, listening to the long, sad exhalation of all that passed there. At last he returned to the yard, put the shovel away, pulled the .22 target pistol from the shelf where he'd laid it that afternoon, and walked back to the old cottonwood stump. He took out his pocketknife and sent the blade into the rotting wood again and again.

Thuck . . . thuck . . . thuck . . .

He thought about the shirt he'd put in the ground, wet with Annie's blood, and he tried to imagine what sort of thing might have grown from a seed like that.

Thuck . . . thuck . . . thuck . . .

He glanced at the heat lightning flaring in the sky far to the south.

Thuck . . . thuck . . . thuck . . .

And with his feet planted in the dead grass of August, he held the open knife in one hand while he stared down at the gun in the other.

TILL DEATH DO US PART

TIM MALEENY

T HE CHEMIST AND the botanist stepped into the dining room at precisely the same moment, entering from opposite doors. They smiled at each other as they took their places at the square table.

"Happy anniversary," said the chemist. His blue eyes were bright and friendly behind wire-frame glasses, but his smile was tentative, the corners of his mouth twitching slightly. He wore an old cardigan she had given him years ago, but he looked vaguely uncomfortable, as if the only piece of clothing that suited him was a white lab coat.

"And to you," replied the botanist, her voice much younger than her steel-colored hair suggested. As she returned his smile, the lines around her eyes radiated outward like the rays of a sun in a child's drawing. Years in the field studying tropical plants had aged her skin like leather.

"Sixty years," said the chemist, shaking his head.

The botanist nodded. "We married young."

"At a time when marriage meant something."

"Indeed."

"There's a reason they call them wedding *vows*," said the chemist solemnly.

"As long as you both shall live," intoned the botanist.

"Till death do us part," replied her husband.

"Just so," they spoke in unison.

They sat quietly for a moment, letting their eyes drift to the table. An elaborate dining set lay before them, half the dishes white and the other half black. Food of every conceivable color, texture, and smell filled the bowls and covered the dishes. Soup tureens bubbled, wineglasses glistened in the late morning light, salads rustled in the breeze from the ceiling fan. Covered dishes, bowls large and small, plates white and black, all overflowing with a feast that would put both Julia Child and Martha Stewart to shame, if the former were not dead and the latter not in jail.

"Such a feast," said the husband, his eyes wide.

"Our best yet," agreed the wife, licking her lips.

"Well, it is a special occasion."

"Anniversaries come only once a year."

"And this is our sixtieth."

"That's a long time . . ."

". . . to be married."

"Sixty years . . ." sighed the wife.

". . . of travel," mused the husband.

"Adventure."

"Discovery."

"Romance."

"Infidelity."

"Dining."

"Drinking."

"Nagging."

"More drinking."

"More nagging."

"Hypocrisy."

"Flatulence."

"Snoring."

"Boring."

"Hungry?" asked the wife, forcing a smile.

"Famished." The husband nodded, the corners of his mouth struggling northward.

The wife spread her arms across the table, palms out in invitation.

"What would you like to try first?" she asked.

"What would you recommend?"

"This soup looks very nice," she said, pushing a bowl across the table. A thick greenish brown broth sent clouds of steam into the air, momentarily obscuring her features.

The chemist leaned forward, waving some of the steam across his face.

He wrinkled his nose. "May I ask where you got the recipe?"

"England," she replied cautiously, looking down at the table.

"Ah . . ." He smiled, nodding. "Lily of the valley. Scientific name, *Convallaria majalis*. Commonly found in eastern Britain, it has white bell-shaped flowers and orange berries."

"Such a fine memory," she replied admiringly.

"Frequently mistaken for wild garlic and made into a soup," he continued, nodding. "Causes hot flashes, headache, skin irritation, dilated pupils, vomiting, nausea, and slowed heartbeat—leading, of course, to coma followed by death."

The botanist frowned as her husband pushed the bowl away with a satisfied smile.

"England," he said. "That was a lovely trip."

"Lovely," she agreed.

"The Tower of London."

"Buckingham Palace."

"The changing of the guard."

"Big Ben."

"Ask not for whom the bell tolls . . ."

". . . It tolls for thee."

"Perhaps I should serve *you*," he suggested.

"You'll have to eat something," she reminded him.

"That is the agreement, isn't it?"

"Every year," she said, nodding.

"Divorce would be unthinkable," he replied.

"Uncivilized," she agreed.

"Immoral."

"Barbaric."

"Try this," he said, pushing a bowl across the table.

"A new recipe?" She eyed the orange and red dish suspiciously.

"Curry chicken," he replied.

"An Indian dish?"

"A taste of nirvana," he suggested.

She frowned. "The dog button plant?"

He shrugged. *"Strychnos nux-vomica."*

"Strychnine," she said, "found in the seeds and fruit of that native plant of India. The blossoms have an odor resembling curry powder."

"Beautiful flowers," he said, nodding.

"Attacks the central nervous system," she continued, "causing agonizing muscle spasms, beginning with the head and neck. Famous for the violent convulsions of the poisoning victim, which increase in intensity until sudden death occurs. Rigor mortis sets in immediately, leaving behind a horrifying facial grimace."

"A bit spicy for some," he admitted.

She pushed the plate away. "That was quite a trip."

"The Taj Mahal," he said, smiling.

"Built as a mausoleum for the sultan's dead wife, you know," she replied.

"A lovely gesture."

"Lovely," she agreed.

"Perhaps an appetizer?" he said hopefully.

"Nuts," she replied.

"I couldn't agree more," he said, pushing a small bowl of mixed nuts to the center of the table.

"You first," she prompted.

"I couldn't."

"You must."

The chemist peered at the bowl for a moment before taking a small handful of nuts and popping them into his mouth.

"Delicious," he said, chewing loudly and smiling.

"Such a variety," she said, looking into the bowl.

"Almonds, hazelnuts, cashews," he said, nodding. "Even macadamia and Brazil nuts. You should try some."

"I think I will," she said, reaching into the bowl. The chemist noticed his wife took only a handful of peanuts, almonds, and cashews, leaving the larger nuts behind.

"You missed some of the best ones," he said.

"That was a lovely trip," she replied.

"Excuse me?"

"Hawaii," she said. "Home to the kukui nut, those larger ones in the bowl there."

The chemist frowned briefly before regaining his composure.

"So observant for your age," he marveled.

"Experienced," she replied.

"They're quite tasty, you know."

"So I hear," she said. "Unlike most poisons, the nuts apparently aren't bitter at all. They do contain jatrophin, however, a violent purgative. Difficulty breathing is followed by a sore throat, dizziness, and vomiting before drowsiness and death ensue."

"The nuts are worn as good-luck charms," he insisted.

She nodded. "A curious culture, Hawaii."

"Warrior kings."

"And queens."

"The hula."

"And Don Ho."

"Tiny bubbles . . ." the husband sang.

"Salad?" asked the wife, proffering a bowl overflowing with mixed greens.

"Recipe?" he asked.

"California," she replied.

"Something domestic," he said appraisingly, arching his eyebrows. "This could be the safe bet, eh? Grown right here on American soil."

"Land of the free," she said, nodding.

"Home of the brave," he muttered, squinting at the bowl.

"Some dressing?" She reached for a bottle next to the salad.

"Hemlock," he replied.

"Pardon?"

"Hemlock," he repeated. "*Conium maculatum,* also known as poison hemlock, lesser hemlock, or muskrat weed. Formerly only native to Europe and Asia—"

"Both faraway lands," she suggested.

"—but naturalized in the United States and found on both the eastern and Pacific coasts."

"The leaves are said to be harmless in spring," she said defensively.

"It's autumn."

"How time flies."

"Life is fleeting," he agreed. "Hemlock weakens the muscles, causing a loss of sight, shallow pulse, and death from paralysis of the lungs. The mind, however, remains lucid until death."

"A blessing," she said.

"Or a curse. The leaves are frequently eaten by quail, by the way, which are immune but pass the poison on through their flesh. So a man could eat a quail that had eaten hemlock and suffer the same effects."

"Something to remember for next year," she said with interest.

The next hour progressed at a similar pace, with dishes being proffered and declined, small plates shared judiciously, tiny sips taken from glasses large and small. Travels were remembered and stories recounted as the clock on the wall measured the passage of time.

"Still hungry?" asked the husband hopefully, his brow sweating.

"Famished." The wife nodded, her bright eyes narrowed.

"Only a few plates left," he observed.

"Your turn," she replied.

"Something new," said the husband, gesturing toward a large covered dish to the right of his wife.

"A surprise?" she asked.

"My own recipe," he answered. "But careful opening the lid. I imagine it's still quite hot." Reaching across the table, he offered her a small pot holder of embroidered fabric.

"How thoughtful," she said, using the pot holder to grasp the cover and expose the dish beneath.

As the lid came free, a noxious cloud enveloped the botanist, causing her to push back violently. As the legs of the chair settled back to the floor she began coughing spasmodically, her nostrils flaring. Leaning against the table, she squinted through watery eyes at her husband, who had pushed back from the table and spread a napkin across his face.

"Cyanide gas," he replied to the unspoken question. "The

container was airtight. Coughing should lead to a shortness of breath, then fainting, followed by convulsions and death."

The botanist pushed herself up in her chair, wheezing.

"You cheated," she said accusingly. "That wasn't a food," she rasped. *"You broke the rules."*

The chemist shrugged. "I'm tired."

His wife nodded her understanding, trying to find her voice. "Of the lying," she said.

"The fighting," he replied.

"The guilt." She struggled to remain conscious, her breath coming in short gasps. Leaning across the table, she smiled weakly and extended her left hand. Her wedding ring glistened in the candlelight.

"You were always so clever," she said warmly.

The chemist came forward in his chair, a smug smile on his wrinkled face.

"And you were always so tenacious," he said admiringly.

"Sixty years," she coughed.

"A long time . . ." he said.

". . . to be married," she answered, opening her hand.

"Sixty years." The husband took his wife's hand, a sudden hint of sadness in his eyes.

As their fingers touched, the botanist clenched her fist around her husband's hand in an iron grip. He tried to pull away but too late felt the barb on her wedding ring cut into his flesh. His eyes widened in horror as he looked across the table at his grinning wife.

"You cut me!" he cried.

"A small needle affixed to my wedding band," she rasped, laughing and coughing at the same time. "Soaked in curare."

"Curare?" he repeated in a voice pitched in fear.

"Strychnos toxifera," she wheezed. "Found in Central and

South America, where it was used by the natives for poison-tipped arrows."

"The flying death," he whispered.

"Exactly." She nodded, blinking and struggling to keep her head erect. "Paralysis starts in the eyes and face, spreading until it reaches the diaphragm and the lungs, at which point the victim dies of asphyxiation."

"*Quickly,*" said the chemist quietly, his breath shallow.

"Within seconds," she said, coughing one last time as she fainted across the table, her left hand still wrapped in a death grip around her husband's.

"That's cheating," he gasped, knocking plates to the floor as he too passed out and died.

EARLY THE NEXT morning the cleaning service found them just like that, their hands clasped together. Their bodies were contorted from the effort of stretching across the table with their dying breath.

Two paramedics arrived half an hour later.

"They look so peaceful," said the rookie, her voice hushed. She was in her late twenties, with black hair framing a face that seemed too young and innocent to be chasing death.

"I'd say determined," said the senior paramedic, his voice gruff and loud in the silent house. He was handsome but weathered, his face deeply tanned and lined, his sandy hair gray around the temples.

"You mean the way they're reaching toward each other," said the rookie. "Like they wanted one final embrace." She smiled sadly, shaking her head.

"You'll see this a lot," he said. "Older couples like this, dying within a few minutes of each other."

"I wonder what the autopsies will show," she said.

"There won't be much of an autopsy."

"How come?"

"They were old," he said simply. "Their hearts stopped, then they stopped breathing. Sure looks like natural causes to me."

"I guess," she said.

"Happens all the time with married couples," he assured her. "There's no medical explanation. One kicks the bucket, the other dies from a broken heart."

"That's so sweet."

"Yeah," he said, rubbing his chin and frowning. "They must have really loved each other."

"The neighbors said it was their anniversary."

"No kidding?" he replied. "It's my anniversary this weekend. You married?"

"No," she replied, adding, "not yet. How long have you been married?"

"Thirty years," he said.

"Wow, that's a long time."

"To be married," he said, nodding.

"Are you getting your wife something special?" she asked.

"Actually, I'm going to cook her dinner," he replied. "It's a surprise."

"How romantic," she said. "Your wife is one lucky woman."

He shrugged. "We'll see."

THE COLD, HARD TRUTH

RICK MCMAHAN

OVER THE YEARS, I've wondered if anything would have been different if I had said something back then. Hindsight is always twenty-twenty and crystal-clear perfect. Still, I've thought that maybe I could have said something to Jesse to prepare him for his role as a jilted lover.

Of course, you can't roll back time.

I met Jesse Brashear more than fifteen years ago, when I was a rookie member of the thin gray line policing the hills and hollers of eastern Kentucky. Eastern Kentucky is the stereotypical setting of feuds between Hatfields and McCoys, but it's also a place of deep poverty. Jobs are scarce, and many abandon the hills for factories in the cities. Those who stay hope hard to get one of the mining jobs . . . and they hope just as hard that they don't die in a cave-in or rot away from black lung. Those that stay and can't find a job are reduced to getting "on the draw" with state handouts. In our remote counties, many fights are handled with knives and guns. When the only thing a person owns is his pride and that's on rent to the state check, the raw nerve is just below the surface, where it's sensitive to careless and hurtful words. Many a person has been buried for bruising a hillbilly's pride.

Jesse lived with his aunt and uncle in a poor excuse of a house at the end of a cracked road. The first time I met Jesse was when I caught him and his buddies drinking Boone's Farm behind an abandoned barn off State Road 130. Though Jesse and his buddies were only a few years younger than I was, at twenty-one I was a new father. I thought I was wiser and more mature. Looking back on it, I'm embarrassed by how I handled the whole thing. Underage drinking's not the crime of the century—hell, it wasn't anything I hadn't done myself—but I was so new that my uniform creases creaked when I walked, so everything was a big deal to me. If I'd had any smarts, I would have had the boys empty the bottle and walk home to sober up. Not then. I thought I had to enforce the law at every turn. I told them all that they were being arrested for underage drinking and public intoxication. I was even foolish enough to add in littering for the empty bottles on the ground.

My mistake was not thinking it through. I got the cuffs on the largest first, a big broad-shouldered buck named Al Earle, who was so drunk he couldn't stand. Jesse was the next closest, and I tossed him to the ground and kneeled on his back, snapping on the cuffs. I should have paid more attention to the last one, Steve Rucker—he was a scrawny kid with rickety teeth and a face pockmarked from acne. To my way of thinking, I was putting down the biggest guy and working my way down, figuring the smaller guy wouldn't be much trouble. I was wrong, and I should have known it, since I'd arrested Rucker for shoplifting at the Wal-Mart a few months before. There I was, kneeling on Jesse's back, trying to get the cuffs on, when I heard a loud click. Glancing over my shoulder, I saw Rucker standing to one side of me, clutching a folding Buck knife, its blade gleaming in the afternoon sunlight.

"What the hell ya doing, Stevie?" Jesse asked calmly. His head was turned toward his buddy. Jesse's long wheat-colored hair shrouded his face like a sheepdog's.

I had made a fatal error. My gun hand was holding on to the cuffs. I knew I'd never reach the .357 Magnum on my belt before the boy gutted me. It felt as though I were facing an eastern diamondback shaking its rattle. If I made a sudden move it might spur the drunk to lunge at me. I stayed still, trying to find my voice. My throat was as dry as sandpaper.

"I ain't going to jail," Rucker slurred, swaying back and forth.

"Steve," Jesse replied. "Put that blade down. We knowed the game when we started. We just got caught. We can't help it this young pup trooper don't know the rules."

"I ain't going to jail," Rucker repeated, the knife moving back and forth. "My old man said if I got locked up again he'd beat me half to death."

"My uncle'll switch me as well," Jesse continued, "but that's on us, not this man. Besides, you don't put that knife down, he'll put a hole in you with that cannon he's carrying."

"I can get him before he clears leather," Steve said in a deadpan voice. I was staring into his eyes, their vacant insanity fueled by alcohol.

"Then we'll bury two," Jesse Brashear said in an even tone. "Put the knife down, Steve. My arms are hurting. You don't want to hurt the trooper. Go on. Put it down."

I'll be damned if Rucker didn't put the knife on the ground and step back. I got the three cuffed and lined up in the back of my cruiser like bowling pins. I kept the knife and just charged the three with public intoxication. Of course, the prosecutor dropped the charges without consulting me. Like I said, it was no big deal.

A few weeks later I came across Jesse walking along one of the main roads in a pouring rain. The radio calls were slow, so I pulled over and offered him a ride. It was the least I could do since he kept me from getting stabbed. Maybe Rucker wouldn't have tried to kill me, but maybe he would have, and Jesse's cool head had helped me.

Jesse climbed into the cruiser and commented, "This is the first time I've been in the front of one of these."

I saw he had a devilish smile, so I laughed as well. That was all it took to break the ice. We talked the whole way up the mountain road. The ride wasn't much, just ten minutes to his muddy lane, but that day a bond was established between Jesse and me. He thanked me for the ride and trotted down the gravel road, leaping between the mud holes, disappearing in the mist. The ride hadn't been much, but Jesse and I saw something in each other we liked. From that day on, we made a point of saying hello to each other when we were out where people gathered to pass time. Mainly the conversations were about things we had in common—Kentucky basketball, where the best fishing hole was, and what mountain thickets hid the biggest bucks during deer season. Jesse was known throughout the county for always catching great crappie, but no one knew where he went to catch the fish. Jesse even trusted me with directions up Fawley Mountain to a small pond. His secret fishing hole. There was one weekend he and I camped out at that small pond, talking about life and fishing under the stars. Jesse was handy with a hatchet, and we made a lean-to. It was almost like some of the summers I'd spent with my brothers growing up.

Other than that one fishing trip, our conversations were short, usually in front of the pop cooler at the filling station. Still, I got to know Jesse. He lived with his aunt and uncle and three cousins. He never knew his father, and no one talked about his mother. While we talked, I also learned the teen had dreams. They weren't exotic or fancy, but they were dreams. He wanted to build a house on a piece of land and have a family. When I asked where he planned to get the money for this, he said, as if it was preordained by God, "My uncle will get me on at the mines. A man can make a good dollar down in those holes." That was that. The way Jesse said his thoughts with such finality, you had no doubt what he wanted would come to be.

Jesse had a determined spirit, and I learned that when he set his mind on something he would make it happen. The next spring he stopped showing up at any of his usual haunts. Well into the summer, when I didn't see Jesse at any of the fishing holes he'd told me about, I began to think he had done like so many people and jumped a Greyhound out of town. Then, just before the Fourth of July, he rumbled into the gas station parking lot with that primer gray Camaro belching smoke and rattling. He'd traded a month of work to a neighbor for a gutted Camaro overgrown with weeds on the man's property. Jesse had hauled the battered car home and spent all his time working on it. His friends told him the thing would never run, but Jesse didn't let that deter him. He worked his heart out on that heap of metal and proved them wrong. The way everyone gathered, you would have thought he was driving something right off the showroom floor instead of a barely road-worthy heap with four bald tires.

And sitting beside Jesse in the passenger seat was Lindsey Calhoun. I wasn't sure which he was prouder of—the car or the pretty girl. Lindsey was a green-eyed blonde with an infectious smile, which she shared with her twin sister, Darla. Her dad was the manager of the A&P, and her mother worked as a teller at the town bank. Jesse and Lindsey made a cute couple.

"I'm going to marry Lindsey," Jesse declared with certainty. "At the end of school. She's the one for me. She'll be mine."

THIS MORNING HAUNTING memories of Jesse Brashear woke me from my fitful sleep. Giving up, I climbed out of bed and started the coffeepot, hoping that the caffeine would steel me for what was coming. While the Mister Coffee percolated, I pushed open the trailer door. Sitting on the cinderblock steps, I looked up through an open space in the trees at the perfect, clear sky, black as oil, with distant stars shining like sharp pinpricks. The air helped push away old memories. The brewed coffee pulled me back inside, where I took my time drinking two cups before rinsing the mug and putting it on the drainer. A long, hard day was ahead of me, and I couldn't put it off any longer. While standing in front of the bathroom mirror, combing my hair after my shower, it hit me again. The knot in my chest had come and gone over the past few weeks since I saw Jesse, but now it settled into the hollow of my heart like a chunk of broken concrete.

Putting on my gray suit, I noticed that the butt of my S&W ten-millimeter had worn a hole through the pocket lining, but it was still the best suit I owned, so I left it on. I figured I owed Jesse my best suit. I didn't want to make the trip. In fact, I dreaded it, but one thing people can say about Bo Stokes is that I keep my word, so I was going to Eddyville. At the end of the day, I'd be back in my Airstream on my little hill, but things wouldn't be the same.

Slipping behind the wheel of my cruiser, I propped a battered metal Thermos on the seat next to me, the paint long flecked off in most places to show the dull steel underneath. I had the rest of the pot of coffee to keep me going. The police radio mounted on the floorboard was quiet, with only the crack and pop of dead air interrupted by the occasional trooper calling in a car tag.

I waited until Dispatch told the trooper that the car had no wants and warrants before I keyed the microphone. "Dispatch, Car 322, ten-eight."

"Ten-four, Car 322," Dispatch replied. There was a slight pause before the voice came back: "Aren't you starting awful early, Sergeant Stokes?"

"Ten-four, Lydia," I replied.

"Long ride to Eddyville," she said. "You be careful and stay awake."

I smiled. Lydia had been watching over third-shift Kentucky state troopers for two decades, and nothing got by her. Thanking her, I fired up the Impala Super Sport and pointed the Chevy toward the interstate. I've always liked driving, whether it was on winding switchback roads in the mountains or pushing the accelerator down on the black ribbon highway with only the headlights and the radio as companions. I slipped a Chris Knight CD into the stereo. The dashboard clock flashed 4:42.

I could have sworn I heard a gunshot echoing across a decade.

❧

THAT SUMMER AFTER he fixed up his Camaro, Jesse and Lindsey were inseparable. The two of them dated that summer and into their senior year of high school. It seemed that where one was, the other was as well. I was low-man on the trooper totem pole, so I got stuck with things like Friday-night duty making sure the local high school football games didn't get out of hand. I remember seeing Jesse and Lindsey sitting close together on the bleachers, more interested in each other than the ball game, just like teenagers will do.

I didn't think much of the young lovers. My hands were full at work. At home, my wife and I were trying to make ends meet and raise a toddler, the first of two girls. Thinking back on it, time sure has flown by. My first girl starts college this year, and my wife is now my ex-wife. Those hard times as a young trooper look more favorable with the rose-colored glasses and distance of time, but the truth was, we had a hard time making ends meet on trooper pay. My mind was occupied, and I lost track of Jesse during winter. Late in the following spring, I heard Lindsey broke up with Jesse right after graduation. The last I heard, Jesse started work at the mine, while Lindsey and her twin sister went off in the fall to college. The whole thing would have ended as an ill-fated teenage romance if Jesse hadn't gone to Richmond after her.

LETTING MY MIND bring up the past had helped me make steady time this morning. At sunup I reached Elizabethtown, and I stopped for gas and to stretch my legs. Plus, I had another promise I had to keep. Winding through town, I circled the courthouse and made my way to the older neighborhood in the center of town where small brick houses were shadowed by gnarled trees and sidewalks.

The woman answered my heavy knock. Though time had etched some harder lines around the eyes and mouth than a pretty woman should have, I could see how Lindsey would have aged.

"Mrs. Calhoun," I said.

"It's Montgomery now," she replied. "Lindsey's father and I divorced six years ago."

I nodded, not because I understood but because I didn't know what else to do. After an awkward few seconds she invited me into the kitchen, where I took a chair at the breakfast nook that looked out on a small flower garden.

As if she had an uncontrollable need to fill the silence, she continued. "It tore us apart. I couldn't stay in the same house with so many memories. And it seemed he and I couldn't stay together. So I got a new job with a bank here."

And a new life, she didn't say but wanted to. I merely nodded.

"Thank you for coming," she said.

"It's the least I could do, ma'am," I replied. She had called me out of the blue six months back with an odd request. I cleared my throat.

She pursed her lips together in a tight line. "I'm not going," she said. "I decided that a long time ago. I wanted to take this day like any other day. Go to work and live my life without thinking about the fuss and what was going to happen. But the news people have started calling, all wanting a sound bite. I can't escape it. It sounds odd, but I want it to just be over."

Her last sentence resonated in my heart. It was almost the exact same line Jesse Brashear had said the last time I saw him.

"Yes, ma'am," I replied, trying to stay focused. "I can imagine it's been a hard time for you, but I still—"

"Trooper Stokes, I just want this to be done," she said, standing in the middle of the kitchen. "You've always been there for me and my family—during the trial and then the appeals. You and Detective Allen."

Hell, I hadn't thought of Bert Allen in five years. He was the post detective who handled the hunt for Jesse in Clement County. Cancer killed Bert less than a year after he retired.

"You've been there," she said, rubbing her hands together. "You know how long this has dragged out. I want it done. I want it over." She put her hands in her lap and looked down at them as if she were embarrassed by something. I learned a long time ago to let people have their time to tell you what's bothering them, so I waited her out. She never looked up, but she started talking again. "The Bible says it's not man's place to take a life. I've searched my heart to accept this. I've prayed a lot on this too, but I can't see it that way. I don't know if it's right or not, but I want it done. That boy robbed me of Lindsey, and what he did surely caused my divorce. It ain't right. He needs to pay." Her voice cracked, and she paused, pulling in a lungful of air as if the oxygen would keep her composure.

"I want you to do two things for me," she said, sliding into the chair across from me.

"I will if I can," I said.

"Just tell me when it's done. When he's gone," she said. "It's taken so long, and I keep having these dreams that they announce it on the news, but in my dreams he turns up at my bank window. It's crazy, I know that. But you always were upfront and honest with us, even about the rough parts. If you tell me he's gone from this earth, I'll know it's the truth."

I clamped my teeth together to keep my own composure as a horde of shared memories came back. I nodded curtly. "I'll do it," I whispered.

"As soon as it's done," she said. "No matter how late it is." I nodded again as she pushed a piece of paper into my hand. I looked down; it was a square piece of pink stationery with lilacs bordering it. In elegant script she had written her name, as if I'd need to be reminded who I'd be calling, and numbers for her house and her cell.

"What's the other thing, ma'am?" I asked as I folded the paper and tucked it into my breast pocket.

"I want you to keep an eye on my girl," she said quietly. A puzzled look must have knotted my brow, because Lindsey Calhoun's mother continued. "Darla, Lindsey's twin. She's going to be there. To witness his death. I tried to talk her out of it, but she wouldn't hear of it. Maybe you've seen her on television?"

I shook my head that I hadn't. Intentionally I avoided the news as Jesse's date had gotten closer.

"She's been on television a lot. She's married and lives in Ohio," she continued. "Both her and her husband, and they are part of a group that works on appeals for people on death row. The newspapers and televisions are eating it up that she's a victim's sister opposing the killer's death."

"Did they take on Jesse's?" I asked before I thought better of it.

She shook her head. "No, not for lack of trying, but the best I understand the situation, it wouldn't look right on appeals if Darla's group handled his case. But she's still trying to get him off death row. Calling people. Writing the governor. It always weighed on Darla's mind that her testimony helped get Jesse the death penalty. You remember what the papers back home all said about her being like a ghost of her sister."

Her eyes drifted up past me to the wall. I didn't follow her gaze, but I knew what she was looking at. I'd noticed it when I came into the room. It was a faded family portrait of a husband and wife and two twin preteen girls grinning at the camera. I wasn't sure that Darla Calhoun's testimony had put the nail in Jesse's coffin, but it sure helped swing the hammer in that courtroom.

"She always felt guilty over that, being so young and all. That's a pretty big burden for anyone, especially a young woman."

"And it swayed her against capital punishment?"

She managed a pale smile. "She and her father haven't spoke since we found out she was opposing Jesse's death sentence and speaking out about it."

I couldn't fathom the turmoil that must be boiling in this woman's heart. One daughter dead in the ground, and another who was working to free killers, including her sister's.

As if reading my mind, she said, "Darla's beliefs caused more than one fight in our home. It probably was part of what split my husband and me up. We couldn't get along. I think looking at each other reminded us of Lindsey, and we fought."

"Over Jesse?"

She smiled sickly. "No, we agreed on that. We both wanted him to pay for murdering Lindsey, but we couldn't agree on anything else. Then he turned on Darla for her beliefs, as if she were betraying him. I don't agree with her, Trooper Stokes, but you can't love one child more than the other. And to turn against Darla would be favoring Lindsey's memory over my living daughter. I can't do that."

I could understand her thinking. I have two daughters of my own. They are a lot different from each other, but I love them both and would die for them.

"Darla is taking one of the family spots to watch Jesse's execution, in protest," she said, sadly. "That's a rough thing, to see a human die. Have you ever seen it, Trooper?"

"Yes, ma'am," I replied. I've seen more than my fair share of death and dying in my job.

"Me too," she whispered. "I was down in Lexington when I was a teenager, and I happened to walk into a gas station right after it had been robbed. They shot the cashier, an old man, and he was lying there bleeding out. I called for the police, and he asked me to hold his hand while we waited. He died. That was hard. I can't imagine how hard it'll be for Darla to watch someone she knows die. Keep an eye on her."

"I'll do that," I promised. "I'll watch her."

"Thank you," she said.

❧

BACK WHEN I first met Mrs. Calhoun, it was the hardest thing I had done in my short career. Being the newest trooper on shift, I got the duty. Standing on the front porch, my

Smokey Bear hat pulled low over my eyes, I could smell the bacon cooking through the open windows when I knocked on the Calhouns' front door. Mrs. Calhoun opened the door and was wiping her hands off on a dishrag when she saw me, the smile fading on her face. Right then I wanted to be anywhere instead of standing in the sun on her front porch. She knew.

"It's not good news that brings you here, is it, Trooper?" she asked.

I shook my head and whispered, "No, ma'am, it's not. In fact, it's bad."

Nothing I told her was easy to say, and I'm sure it was even harder to hear. It's never easy breaking the news to someone that a loved one is dead. Still, the hardest is telling a parent that a child is gone. As hard as it was, I did my job. I took her by the arm and led her back into the house, where I told the truth. Lindsey and her new boyfriend had been murdered down at school.

⤜⟡⤛

"Do you ever think of her?" Jesse asked me a month ago, the only time I spoke to him since his trial. Out of the blue, he sent me a letter asking me to come see him, so I made the drive. His question came suddenly, without warning. We were sitting in the maximum-security visiting room at Eddyville. The room was large and drafty and was ingrained with institutional smells—ammonia and thick decay. We sat on opposite sides of a plastic table.

He wore the jumpsuit and shackles of an inmate. His hair was shorn tight to his skull, and he had bulked up in prison from pumping iron. Dark ink started underneath his handcuffs and wound up underneath his jumpsuit, where I'm sure he had complete sleeve tattoos. On his neck were the twin lightning bolts of one of the Aryan prison gangs. His face and eyes were hard as well. Over a dozen years at Eddyville will do that to a man. A dozen years, waiting.

Gone was the innocence of youth. Jesse was a hardened con. Except when he spoke. For an hour, we talked about years gone by and the fishing holes we had shared or the tracts of land we each had hunted. His eyes became distant, and I knew he was replaying fading memories of his home. At the end, when our talk had petered out, Jesse had popped the question on me.

I didn't respond, so he repeated it. "Do you ever think of Lindsey?"

"I have," I replied.

"Me too," he said. "A lot. I also think about choices I made."

"They weren't smart," I ventured.

"No, they weren't smart," he agreed. He smiled the devilish smile again. "Bo, I wonder if I could ask a favor of you?"

"You can ask," I replied. "I'm not sure I'll do it, but you can ask."

He smiled again. "Fair enough. Bo, the appeals are up. I'm going to die next month. The attorneys still want to fight to keep me alive. But to them I'm not a man—I'm just a cause. I'm another convict that's going to be put to death. I know the court-fighting is through. I know I'm going to be strapped down in the death house and killed. Most of the people on the other side of the witness room window will only know me as a murderer. Nothing else. I'd like to look up and see one face that knows me—knows I'm not all bad."

"How about your aunt or uncle?" I suggested.

He shook his head. "I've tore 'em up with all of this too long. I don't want them here, but I do want to see a friendly face when I die."

I swallowed hard. I told him I'd come to his execution.

A burly guard motioned that the time was up for the visit. I stood, and Jesse joined me. "Do you ever get up to Fawley Mountain?" he asked, as the guard unhooked his shackles from the chair and wound the chain around his ankles.

"Not since I moved out of Clement County," I admitted.

"It was a hell of a fishing hole," Jesse said, his eyes looking beyond the prison walls. "A quiet place. You know, I can close my eyes and see it just like it was. And sometimes I can even smell the way the pond smelled in the summer sun."

"It was a great fishing hole," I admitted. As the guard started to lead him away, I didn't tell him that the last time I went to the county I had driven back up to Fawley Mountain. The company that had put down the logging road finally came through and took most of the trees and cleared out the underbrush. Jesse's secret fishing pond had been filled in, and a fly-by-night developer was looking to put up a trailer park on the mountain.

Suddenly he stopped and called over his shoulder. "You can't go back, but you know one thing I've often wished had happened differently between you and me?"

I shook my head that I didn't, but I was lying. I knew exactly what he was going to say.

"I wish you had killed me," Jesse said.

When the investigators pieced together what had happened, it was a tale cops have seen countless times before. Jesse drove down to Richmond to try to patch things up with Lindsey. Instead, he came across Lindsey with her new boyfriend. Jesse had taken his hatchet with him. And he used it. The crime scene photos were horrific. Blood was everywhere—floor, walls, ceiling. The medical examiner wasn't even sure of the total number of wounds. Neighbors heard the screaming and commotion and called the police. Lindsey's sister lived in the same complex, and she actually saw Jesse's Camaro peel out of the parking lot.

And the clincher was Jesse's bloody palm print on the bathroom door. Lindsey had tried to hide there, but Jesse just broke the door down to get to her.

By the next day, Jesse Brashear was the most wanted man in eastern Kentucky.

Rumors abounded that he was going to make a run for California or Mexico, and some said he was lying low over in West Virginia. Every trooper and county cop across the state had a description of Jesse's rusted-out Camaro, but no one had spotted him. It was as if he had vanished.

When you're chasing radio calls in uniform, either you're so busy running from crisis to crisis that you don't have a free moment to think, or a shift is so quiet that all you have is time tugging at your mind. The night after Lindsey's murder, the radio was quiet. No calls, and I had plenty of time to think. About halfway through my shift, it hit me. I had an idea where Jesse might be hiding. Hindsight is always perfect. If I'd been smart, I would have called for backup before I started up Fawley Mountain. I didn't. If I was wrong, I didn't want to be ridiculed, so I went up the rutted logging road by myself. Jesse's secret fishing spot was a hard-to-find tract, and I missed it on my first run up the road. On the way down the hill, I spotted the turn and pulled down the rutted trail. The hill was thick with underbrush and trees that hung over the road, blocking out the moonlight, but I spotted the Camaro parked at the edge of the fishing pond. It was dark, and my headlights played over the back of the car, lighting up the inside.

I did have the good sense to call Dispatch and ask for backup to start rolling my way. One of the problems about rural policing is that backup can be more than half an hour away. I knew that if anything happened I was on my own. Silently, I prayed that my voice hadn't quaked over the radio.

When I stepped out of the car, I left the headlights on and even had a spotlight aimed on the Camaro, bathing it in light. Nothing moved. Inside the cocoon of the patrol car there had been the hum of the radio, but outside the door of the cruiser there was just the ticking of my engine and the night sounds of animals in the woods.

"State police," I announced without much conviction. I unsnapped the strap on my holster and left my hand gripping the revolver.

The scream came suddenly from my left, and I jumped. It never stopped once the banshee wail started. Turning, I saw Jesse charging up from the reeds near the pond, that hatchet raised up in his hand. His hair had twigs in it, and his shirt and jeans were muddy. He looked like a madman as he rushed up the bank at me. I swear as our eyes locked, we both paused. He stutter-stepped and slowed for a second, the hatchet dropping as he recognized me, but it rose back up. I drew my gun.

When I first came on with the state police they issued us Smith and Wesson 686 revolvers, big old .357 Magnums. I was dead-on with that 686. I've always been a good shot, ever since I was knee-high to my granddad, hunting squirrels, and I rarely miss what I aim for. But, when I tell the story of what happened next, I've always lied. In the official report. And in the retelling to other troopers and family and friends. I say that as I drew my revolver I accidentally pulled the trigger before it was up on target. That was a lie. When I saw Jesse, I didn't want to kill him, so I aimed way low and fired. I wanted to ask him why he had to go murder Lindsey. I wanted him to make me understand. The muzzle blast was like a lightning bolt, and the bullet kicked up dirt right in front of Jesse's feet. Finding my voice, I said, "Jesse, stop," as I thumbed back the hammer. My ears were ringing, and I wasn't sure that Jesse heard me, but I pleaded, "Don't make me shoot you. Don't."

He stopped and stared at me. For a few seconds we stood there, me with that cocked revolver and him a dozen feet away with that bloody hatchet raised. Neither one of us moved, but I felt my heart thumping in my throat. Then, with tears in his eyes, Jesse threw down the hatchet and slumped onto his haunches, exhausted.

I cuffed him, but I didn't put him in my patrol car until I could hear the sirens in the distance. Instead, Jesse and I sat side by side against the rear tire of his Camaro. We stared at the perfect night sky while Jesse cried. We both knew it was the last time he'd ever see his favorite place. He'd never own his own house or have his own family.

"Bo, why didn't you kill me?" he whispered through the tears.

I couldn't answer him. The truth was, I didn't want to shoot him. Even though he'd done an awful deed, I still liked Jesse, and I didn't want to shoot him. In the story I tell after a few beers, I always say that Jesse knew my next bullet would have been in between his eyes. I'm glad I didn't have to find out if that was true. Jesse wanted me to kill him to take away his pain, but he must have seen the look on my face and given up, instead of making me make a hard decision.

⟡

EVERYTHING HAS A price. Nothing is ever easy. And everyone has to pay his or her own way. I knew that this morning when I drove down to the state prison in Eddyville. I never saw Darla Calhoun, and I don't know how she fared watching Jesse die. Neither do I know how she and her folks are doing or whether that divide was ever bridged. I know that I stood in the witness room with a dozen other strangers. I watched as Jesse was strapped to a table and given the injection. The lights were so bright that I'm not sure Jesse could see me, but I think he knew I was there, as much for him as for Lindsey. I believe he had one final thought of Fawley Mountain and wetting a fishing line before his heart stopped beating.

Jesse Brashear wasn't a bad person. I know that he butchered two people with a savagery I've rarely seen, but I also know that the same man had a kind heart. One of the hardest things I've had to reconcile is that good people can do bad, even evil, things. Like Jesse said, we can't change the past or undo deeds we've done. We all have to pay. And that's the cold, hard truth.

ONE SHOT

P. J. PARRISH

THE HOUSE WAS bigger than he remembered it. Not in size, but in sadness. It wasn't the dust-shrouded windows or the scarred wood floors. It wasn't the missing posts in the staircase out in the hall. It wasn't even all the rectangles on the faded blue wallpaper, imprints from the picture frames that used to hang there.

It was a feeling, something radiating from the old place the moment he stuck the key into the lock and the front door opened with a sigh that came from somewhere deep, deep inside.

He was standing in the living room. It was quiet, the November drizzle a steady *tick-tick-tick* against the windows. He let out a long slow breath that gathered in a vapor cloud in the still air. He wasn't used to the cold anymore. Maybe it was because he had been away from Michigan for so long and had the thin blood of a Floridian now. Maybe it was because he was older and things just bothered him more.

His eyes lingered on the rectangles on the walls. He was remembering how the sunlight used to flood this room at certain times of the year, bleaching out the blue wallpaper. Now the spots stared back at him like so many blank-eyed ghosts, and for the life of him he couldn't remember what had once hung here. All he could recall was that the walls had been covered with pictures, like that store back home in Florida that sold prints of leopards, landscapes, and cheesy abstracts.

Leslie had dragged him into the mall store one day to show him a fake oil of a villa in some nondescript country. It was five hundred dollars and she wanted it for the house. He told her he didn't like fake things in the house—plants, paintings, people—and had gone on to Sears to get a replacement for his broken Craftsman saw.

Two days later, Leslie came home with a different painting by a guy named Thomas Kinkade. It was of a small-town street with all the houses sporting Christmas wreaths and glowing gold from within. It was eleven hundred dollars, but it was *real,* Leslie assured him. It came with a letter from the artist himself in which he explained his work: "I find that the places where I feel most comfortable share a sense of neighborhood . . . where people come together in good fellowship, and, above all, brightly lit homes warmed by the light of love . . ."

"I hate it, Leslie," he told her. "It's treacly crap. It makes my teeth hurt to look at it."

"It's just a picture, Stuart. Why are you always so negative?"

He gave up. Leslie hung *Home for the Holidays* in the family room.

He was still staring at the blank spots on the blue-papered wall. Why the hell couldn't he remember even *one* of the pictures that had hung there?

From somewhere outside he could hear the *boom-thucka-boom* of a car's speakers blaring out rap music. He closed his eyes as the sound grew, coming nearer and building to a crescendo, then tapering off. His heart kept time to the dull beat as it died away down the street.

God, how he hated that noise. The awful, soul-numbing monotony of it, digging deep into the chest and brain, pouring through the walls as he tried to watch *The McLaughlin Report* every night until finally he had to go to Ryan's room and pound on the door, demanding he turn it down.

"Why do you listen to that garbage, Ryan?"

"Jesus, Dad, it's just music. Why are you picking on me again?"

The noise was gone. The house was quiet again. He opened his eyes. What was he doing here? What was he looking for in this old wreck of a place?

He turned and walked slowly through the archway, into the empty dining room with its sconces dangling by wires from the walls. He found his way to the kitchen. It was dark in the afternoon dusk. The countertops were the same pale green tile, the walls the same ivy print wallpaper yellowed with the years and nicotine. The green linoleum squares were curling. He wondered if anyone had even lived in the place recently.

A noise, somewhere deep in the house. A creak of a door. Footsteps on old wood. But he might have imagined it. He pulled in a breath, holding it.

"Mr. Bowen?"

He didn't move.

"Yoo-hoo! Anybody here? Mr. Bowen?"

He exhaled and went back to the living room.

A pudgy woman in a fur coat was standing in the middle of the room. She spun quickly when she saw him emerge from the gloom.

"My goodness, you startled me!" She came forward, hand thrust out. "Jane Talley," she said. "I'm sorry I'm late. Traffic was brutal."

He shook her hand, then took a step back to distance himself from her perfume.

"You would think no one would be on the roads the day before Thanksgiving," she said, taking a red silk scarf off her blond hair helmet. "Out gathering those last-minute Butterballs, I guess."

"Thank you for coming out on such short notice," he said.

"No problem. You found the key okay?"

"Yes, it was in the mailbox where you said it would be."

"Good." She smiled. "Well! If you don't mind, we need to make this quick. I have to pick up my daughter at the airport. She's coming in from Dallas with the kids. You know, the usual big turkey day, eating and drinking too much, telling family war stories and watching the Lions lose."

When he didn't smile she looked away, surveying the living room. She couldn't quite hide her grimace. But the bright smile was back on her face as she turned to him again. "So! Have you looked around?"

"Some."

She pulled a leather tote off her shoulder and dug inside. "Here's the sheet," she said, holding out a paper.

He scanned the paper: 989 Strathmore, Detroit, Wayne County, Michigan. 2/2 with 1 bath upstairs. Built in 1945. Property taxes $2300. Asking price $145,000. There was a black-and-white photo of the exterior. The brick of the pseudo-Tudor architecture was hidden behind overgrown evergreens and iron window bars.

Another rap music car was rumbling down the street. He could hear it coming, the music now a dirge for an old house in a dying neighborhood. He waited until the sound was gone before he looked back at the real estate woman.

She was looking at him expectantly, as if she had somewhere

to go. Which she did, of course. He shut his eyes tight, a hand coming up to his temple.

"Mr. Bowen?"

Things were forming in his brain. Images. But they weren't in focus. He knew if he tried he might be able to bring them into focus. But he wasn't sure he was ready to face them.

"Mr. Bowen? Are you okay?"

With great effort he opened his eyes. She seemed relieved.

"How about if we go look upstairs?" she said.

He nodded, pocketing the paper. She led the way, telling him to mind his step because the staircase wasn't in the best of shape but what could you expect since no one had lived in the place for years even though it had been a pretty house in its day before Detroit started going to pot and the mayor who didn't know his butt from a hole in the ground was letting everything go and no matter what anyone said the new casinos down on the river and in Greek Town were *not* going to bring people back downtown but this was 1998 after all and who *didn't* want to live out in the suburbs where at least you could walk the streets at night and your kids didn't have to go through metal detectors at school . . .

His head was pounding by the time they reached the top of the stairs.

"My goodness, it's dark up here," she said, flicking a wall switch to no avail.

He went to the nearest bedroom. It was small and had been painted a bright orange with ugly flower decals on the walls. But he could still see the room as it once was. He was letting the memories come now, and he could see things and he could hear the voices.

The small bed with its tan chenille bedspread. The bookcase

with its stacks of comic books. And the nubby blue rug with the Clue board spread out on it.

Colonel Mustard in the library with the gun! Ha! I won again!

You cheated, Stu.

Did not!

Yes, you did.

Did not. Okay, let's play again.

No . . .

Richie, I didn't cheat. Honest. C'mon, let's play again.

No. I'm tired of this game.

He took off his leather gloves and ran his hand lightly over the door frame, his fingers finding the tiny notches that had measured his and Richie's heights.

"This was my room," he said.

The real estate woman stared at him. "Your . . . ?"

"I grew up in this house," he said, turning away from the bedroom. He could hear her heels on the wood floor as she followed him. He glanced in the master bedroom, and then in the small bathroom.

"Is that why you want to buy this house?" she asked.

He was silent as he turned to her. She had this strange look on her face, and for a moment he was seeing his wife, Leslie, seeing the same look on her face when he first told her he intended to fly to Michigan the day before Thanksgiving so he could go back to see the house.

"Why?" Leslie had asked.

"I have to," he answered.

"But what about our dinner? What about your family? Dammit, Stuart, I don't understand this. Don't do this to me. It's Thanksgiving, for God's sake. We all need to be together."

"That's why I have to go," he said.

He started back down the stairs, ignoring the real estate woman's question. He had no intention of buying the house. He just wanted to see it one more time. Maybe if he saw it he could figure out what had happened.

"So, Mr. Bowen," the woman said, coming up next to him in the living room, "what do you do for a living?

"I teach," he said.

"Really? How nice. What do you teach?"

"Literature."

He moved away, heading toward the kitchen again so she wouldn't ask him anything else. He didn't want to have to explain that he didn't teach "literature." He was a professor of classics at University of Miami, where he taught courses with names like "Ancient Moral Thought and Education." He had full tenure, a house in the Grove, a wife who did volunteer work, a son who didn't do drugs. He had a new Volvo, an aging dachshund, and an unfinished novel in his desk drawer. He had—he would on occasion admit this, but only to himself—a drinking problem.

He was, to everyone who knew him, a success. He knew, in the deepest corners of his heart, that he was a failure. Somewhere along the way, his life had gone off course and he had been stalled—he and Leslie and Ryan. No, not stalled. Wrecked. His life had become derailed and now there they all were, sprawled alone in their pain, disconnected and bloodied, pretending they didn't hear each other's cries.

It was all his fault. He knew he had to make it right somehow. That's why he had come back here. He knew that suddenly. He had come back here, to this house, to try to save himself and his family. To give it one last shot.

He turned and saw the door.

The real estate woman was at his side. "That's just the basement," she said.

"I need to see it," he said.

The woman glanced at her watch and let out a silent sigh that spiraled up in the cold air. He could see in her eyes what was in her head: that he was not a potential buyer but just a weird old man on a nostalgia trip.

"Ah, if you don't mind, Mr. Bowen, it's really getting late, and the airport—"

"I need to see the basement," he said.

She hesitated, then shrugged. "Suit yourself." Now that she knew any hope of a sale was gone, so was her charm. "You don't mind if I wait here, do you?"

The door stuck when he tried to open it, then gave way with a creak. He stood at the top of the stairs, peering down into the darkness. Cold air wafted up, carrying a smell of dampness and decay.

He started down.

It wasn't until he got to the bottom of the wooden stairs that he realized he was holding his breath. He let it out now, slowly, as he looked around. His heart grew smaller in his chest. They had let it go, whoever had lived here after him. They had let the mildew grow, let the dirt and years take over. He could see it, even though the light coming through the small casement windows was thin. He could see that it was all in ruins.

The bar was still there, the one his father had built, but it was heaped with sagging boxes. The knotty pine paneling was still on the walls, but it was dark with grime. The shelves were still there, the ones that used to hold boxes of Christmas decorations and his mother's jams, but they were broken and dusted with rat droppings.

He could hear the steady *splat-splat* of water somewhere. He could hear the voices, like some forgotten broken song.

Stu? Stu, are you down there?

Yeah, Ma!

Get up here. I gotta get to the A&P before it closes.

Ah, Ma, I don't wanna go. I wanna stay here with Richie.

I told you, no staying in the house alone.

Ma, I can stay! I'm almost thirteen. C'mon, Ma! We're doing important stuff!

Stu—

We won't leave the basement, Ma. I promise.

Well . . . okay. I'll be back in an hour and as soon as your father gets home we're going to eat.

Can Richie stay for dinner?

No, not again. Richie needs to go home. I think his mother would like him to come home for a change.

But, Ma—

You heard me, Stuart. Not tonight.

There had been an old sofa in the middle of the basement. He could see it clearly, a lumpy thing with itchy red upholstery and cushions that he and Richie used as building blocks for their forts. There had been a card table where his father had played poker with his friends and where he and Richie had laid out their papers and crayons, where they had conspired, head to head, making their own comic books. They called their superhero Brain Boy, and he had the power to kill someone just by thinking about it. He had made up the stories and Richie had drawn the pictures—beautiful pictures! They were going to publish their own comics when they grew up. They would do it together, just like they had always done things. That was the plan. Grow up and get famous and show everyone. Show Richie's father that drawing wasn't a "homo thing." Show Nate Carson and those dumb boys at school, make them all sorry for what they had done, all the mean things they had said. Grow up and get rich and famous. Grow up and forget about that time

Nate pushed Richie to the asphalt, calling him a dumb Polack, busting his glasses and bloodying his nose. Grow up and forget about those girls watching and laughing. Grow up and forget about telling and then finding his cat hanging dead from a stop sign two nights later. Grow up and make them sorry. That was their plan, Stuart Bowen and Richie Koweski, comic book heroes.

He looked toward the farthest, darkest corner of the basement. He could just make out the door that he knew led to the small room. He closed his eyes and the images went away. But the voices didn't.

Richie? What's the matter with you today?

Nothing.

You wanna go walk down to the party store? I got a quarter. We can—

Nah . . .

You sick, Richie?

No.

Then what's the matter?

I told you, nothing!

How come you weren't at school today?

I dunno.

Okay . . . what you wanna do then?

I dunno.

We could go watch Mr. Wizard.

Uh-uh.

You wanna work on Brain Boy?

Nah.

Cripe, Richie, if you don't want to do anything, maybe you should go home.

I don't want to go home. My dad is home.

So?

He's drinking beer.

Big deal. My dad drinks beer.

Your dad doesn't hit you. I don't want to go home, Stu.

Yeah, but if you're gonna be a puke, then maybe you should!

Silence. He could still hear the silence. The terrible silence that filled the basement as Richie just sat there, slumped on the red sofa. He could still remember what he had thought at that moment, that Richie looked like one of those rubber punching bags, those things with the clown faces, a punching bag that had a leak and was all deflated.

His eyes went again to the door in the corner. He knew he had to go over there and open it, but he couldn't move. He was shivering, and when he wiped his nose his hand was shaking. He had come thousands of miles. He had waited forty years. Just to see what was in that room. If he didn't go in, if he backed away now, there would be no chance. No chance for him and Leslie and Ryan. No chance at all.

His feet moved, carrying him toward the door, as if he were being propelled forward by some outside force. When he reached out to the door, he looked down at his hand, at the blue veins standing out in high relief against the chapped white skin, and he had the odd sensation that it was someone else's hand. The metal knob was icy. The door swung inward with a small groan.

The smell of something rotten filled his nostrils. Gray afternoon light filtering in through a broken window illuminated the tiny room. Sagging shelves dotted with old baby food jars filled with rusted nails. A wooden workbench dark with mold. Puddles of fetid water on the concrete floor. A decomposing rat. The smell—it was just a brew of it all, he knew that.

But there was another smell underneath it, an odd smell, like something metallic. A smell that he had never, ever been able to erase. A smell that had clung to him for decades. A smell that was now pushing its way up over the decay, bringing everything back up with it.

He couldn't stop it. It was all coming out now, and he couldn't stop it.

The metallic smell was everywhere. The blood was everywhere. Richie was lying on the concrete floor.

Richie? Richie? Richie!

Silence. And that metallic smell hanging in the air.

Oh, God, Richie!

Blood. Richie's blood. It was everywhere, splattered on the Chessie train calendar on the wall. And bits of Richie's brains. He saw that too, clinging to the baby food jars and tools.

He saw the gun in his own hand.

Ma! Ma! Oh, no . . . Richie! Ma! Come down here! Ma . . . !

But no one came. Finally he heard a car door slam, heard his mother's footsteps and the sound of her putting away groceries in the kitchen, heard her call his name. But he couldn't answer. Even when he heard her coming down the basement stairs, he couldn't answer. He just stayed there, crouched in the corner, holding the gun in his lap as she screamed and screamed.

The house filled up with strangers. A big man in blue took the gun away and led him upstairs to the kitchen. Another man in blue washed the blood from him. Someone made him put on clean clothes, and then they sat him on a chair in the living room and told him not to move. He heard his mother crying in the kitchen.

He just sat there, not moving, listening to it all, feeling his body turn to stone. The only things that moved were his eyes. His eyes moved over all the pictures on the blue-papered walls, jumping from one to another because he knew that as long as he kept looking at all those pictures he wouldn't see Richie's shattered head. Finally, when his eyes got tired, he let them rest on one picture—the one over the TV of Jesus touching His glowing heart. He stared at Jesus and Jesus stared back.

Then, suddenly, someone was there, kneeling in front of him. His face was white and his eyes were tear-filled. His father? What was his father doing home? How did he get home so fast?

Stuart . . . we need to talk.

I didn't mean it. I just got mad. We weren't really fighting.

I know.

It's just . . . it's just . . . sometimes Richie . . .

Stuart, listen to me.

I didn't think he remembered where it was. We only looked at it once. Honest.

What?

Your gun. We didn't really play with it. I just took it out and showed it to Richie. I didn't think he remembered where it was!

His father looked back over his shoulder. There were other people in the living room now, but he hadn't even seen them come in. Four policemen in blue. A man in a brown suit writing in a pad. The old bald priest from St. Jerome's who smelled of Sen-Sen. And other faces, all just a blur.

His father took him by the shoulders.

Stuey, listen to me . . .

I didn't mean to—

I know.

I think he was sick, Dad. He didn't go to school today and—

Stuey, be quiet.

I don't know . . . I don't know what happened!

He felt his father's hands tighten on his shoulders. Felt the warmth of his breath close to his face.

It was an accident, Stuey Boy.

What?

You were playing with the gun. You were showing Richie the gun and it went off. It was an accident.

But, Richie—

Stuey Boy. Listen to me. That is what happened. It was just an accident. But everything will be all right.

His father's eyes were steady on him, unblinking. But suddenly he couldn't look at him. So he looked over his father's shoulder, over to the priest and the police standing together in the corner. His eyes finally found the picture of Jesus on the wall. He focused on it until it went blurry. Everything after that was blurry too. The only thing he could remember clearly was packing up his comic books when they moved a year later. He found one of Richie's Brain Boy drawings and stuck it inside a *Superman* so he wouldn't ever lose it. It was years later, after he came home from college one Christmas, that he found out his mother had long ago thrown all the old comics out with the trash.

"Mr. Bowen?"

He opened his eyes and the workroom came into slow focus.

"Yoo-hoo! Mr. Bowen, are you still down there?"

"Yes . . ." He cleared his throat. "Yes!"

"I really must get going."

"I want to stay. I'll lock up."

"Mr. Bowen, I don't think—"

"I'll leave the key in the mailbox. Please. Please, just go."

A long pause. "All right. Have a happy Thanksgiving, Mr. Bowen."

He looked up, his eyes following the sound of her footsteps to the front of the house. The thud of the front door closing and then it was quiet, except for the *splat-splat* of water. The workroom felt as dark and close as the confessional at St. Jerome's.

Forgive me, Father, for I have sinned.

Forgive me, Father, I took your gun out of your toolbox.
Forgive me, Mother, I made you cry and you never stopped.
Forgive me, Father, for I have sinned. I shot Richie.

His mother had taken him to church a week after Richie's funeral. He could still see the priest's bald head, glowing white through the screen of the confessional, could smell his Sen-Sen breath, could hear his whispered words: *God loves the sinners among us the most, my son. It was an accident, but everything will be all right. God loves you. For your penance, do . . .*

. . . do forty years. Forty years of waking up sweating at night, forty years of jumping at the sound of cars backfiring, forty years of looking away whenever you saw a blond boy wearing black glasses, forty years of closing down your heart because if you let someone in and they died, it hurt too much.

It was cold in the basement, and he was shivering. He took one last look around the workroom. There was nothing for him here, no absolution, no salvation. There were no answers to the question of what had happened. He backed out of the room, closing the door.

Upstairs, he paused in the living room. It was getting late, the shadows growing into the gloom of the coming winter night. He dug in his pocket for his gloves, but when he pulled them out one was missing. He checked his other pockets, scanned the wood floor, backtracked into the kitchen, but didn't find it. Ryan had given him the leather gloves for Christmas last year. He didn't want to leave without the missing one, but he didn't want to go back down to the basement either.

Then he realized he had taken the gloves off upstairs when he had touched the door frame. Going back upstairs, he spotted the black glove on the floor. As he bent to pick it up, something in his memory shifted. He straightened slowly.

He stared into the bedroom. Suddenly it was as if someone had switched on a lamp, lighting the dark corners. Suddenly he could see himself. He was twelve again, sprawled on his stomach on the chenille bedspread, comic books scattered around him. Then he heard it, heard it clearly, like he had heard it forty years ago. He heard the sharp *pop!* that came from somewhere outside. And he remembered. He remembered what he had thought in that moment—where had someone gotten firecrackers in November?

The memories were coming fast now.

What was it that made him realize the sound *hadn't* come from outside? What was it that made him finally go downstairs, through the kitchen, and back down to the basement? What was it that made him open the door to his father's workroom?

He couldn't remember any of that. But he could remember . . .

Oh, God.

Richie lying there on the concrete floor, the gun inches from his palm.

He could remember screaming. *Richie! Richie! What did you do?*

Suddenly, it was all there in his head, playing like a tape that he had thought was long erased. He could remember calling Richie a puke and telling him to go home. He could remember going up to his room and leaving Richie alone in the basement. Then . . . then. In the basement again, where he picked up the gun because he thought Richie might still be alive and he wanted to get the gun away from him. He could remember staring at Richie's oozing wound and throwing up. He could remember sitting there on the cold cement floor because he didn't want Richie to be alone. He could remember watching the blood as it crawled across the gray floor to the drain. Then . . . then, upstairs in the living room now, watching the gurney with the small lump under the blue covering being wheeled out the front door. The outline of his father's gun in the plastic bag as the policeman carried it away. His mother's sobs in the kitchen and the priest's calm voice. He could hear the priest talking to Richie's father. He could see them all gathered in a tight knot, looking at him and whispering.

Then . . . then, his father's face before him. He could feel the pressure of his hands on his shoulders, and hear his words again: *You were playing with the gun. You were showing Richie the gun and it went off. It was just an accident. But everything will be all right.*

"No."

The sound of his own voice startled him. The empty bedroom came back into focus. Everything was coming into focus.

They knew. They all *knew.*

His mother, Richie's parents, the police, the priest, and his own father. They all knew Richie had shot himself. They all knew what had really happened, and they let him believe that he didn't.

He couldn't breathe. And his heart felt like a dying animal in his chest, heavy with pain, struggling to keep going. Suddenly he had to get out of the house.

He stumbled down the stairs and through the living room. Outside, he stopped on the sidewalk and bent over, feeling sick. He pulled a deep breath of cold air into his lungs, then another. Finally, when he felt steadier, he straightened. He looked back at the house.

The sting of tears came to his eyes, and he wiped a shaking hand over his face. Then, slowly, he walked to his rental car parked at the curb. He got in but just sat there, staring straight ahead. The sleet had caused the windshield to freeze over, giving the black bare trees a wavy, surreal look. He sat perfectly still, his hands on the wheel, his breath pluming in the cold womb of the car.

Why? Why had they done it, this conspiracy of parents, priests, and police? All the people who were supposed to protect him had betrayed him. And his own father had knelt before him and lied, told him it was an accident, let him take the blame and promised him everything would be all right.

But it *wasn't* an accident and everything *wasn't* all right.

The tears fell silently down his face. Slowly, he reached over and popped open the glove compartment. The gun was ice-cold as he pulled it out. He stared at it for a moment, feeling its weight in his hand, thinking how light it felt compared to then.

No one knew he had it. After his father had died in 1972, he had come home to help his mother and he found the gun in a box in the closet. It had been cleaned and oiled and had one bullet in its chamber. He took it back to college, wrapped it in an old sweater and stuck it in a footlocker. The locker was with him when he took the job in Florida and when he and Leslie moved into the house in the Grove. When Ryan was born, he took the gun out to the garage and locked it in a toolbox. For the last seventeen years, it had stayed there. Until last night, when he took it out and carefully packed it in his suitcase for the trip back to Michigan.

He shut his eyes, his fingers closing around the revolver's grip. He didn't have to look; he knew the bullet was still there.

The rain was a steady *tick-tick* on the windshield. His hand was trembling and suddenly the revolver was heavy, too heavy to hold any longer. He let it fall down to his lap and leaned his cheek against the cold glass of the driver's-side window.

How long did he stay like that? Minutes, an hour? But when he finally opened his eyes, he saw a face. He had to squint to see it, but there was someone watching him from a front window of the nearest house. The face was hardly more than a white blur through the icy windshield, but he could tell the eyes were watching him.

It took a couple more seconds before the memory registered: Richie's house . . . that was Richie's house. He quickly rolled down his window to get a better look, but the face had disappeared.

Rolling the window back up, he jumped from the car and started across the street. He realized he still was holding the gun and he quickly slipped it in the pocket of his overcoat. As he approached the porch, a quick memory flashed through his head—Mr. Koweski, out mowing his lawn. It had been the prettiest lawn on the block. But now it was nothing but mud and dead weeds fronting a run-down house with bars on the windows and plastic bags of garbage on the porch.

He rang the bell. There was a dirty blue plastic bin near the door filled with empty booze bottles. He rang the bell again and then opened the sagging screen door and knocked.

After a long time, the door opened just enough for a man to peer out.

"Yeah?"

At first, he didn't recognize him. He had been half expecting to see the big man with the barrel chest and slicked-back black hair, the man he remembered as Richie's father. But this was just an old man, with ashen skin and dirty gray hair. But the eyes . . . he remembered those piercing black eyes.

"Mr. Koweski?"

"I ain't buying anything."

"I'm not sell— Mr. Koweski, it's me, Stuart. Stuart Bowen."

"What?"

"Stuart Bowen . . . I used to live—" He hesitated, then pointed across the street.

The old man's black eyes narrowed. "Bowen . . . Bowen." His eyes shot open. "Stuey? That you, Stuey Boy?"

He cringed at the sound of his old nickname, the one that Mr. Koweski had given him, the one he had always hated because it sounded so little. "Yes, yes . . . it's me. Stuey Boy."

The old man's mouth was hanging open. For a moment he looked as though he might fall over, but his hand gripping the door was like a claw. He pushed the door open.

"Come in, then," he said. "I'm not heating the outdoors here."

He came into the dim interior of the house, closing the door behind him. He had a vague sense of the place as he followed the old man to the kitchen. Dark outlines of old, sagging furniture, piles of yellowed newspapers, overflowing ashtrays. The gloom was undercut with a foul smell—something musty and unclean, as if the place hadn't been opened up to sunlight or other human beings in a long time. He remembered suddenly that about four years after his own family had moved away, his father had discovered Mrs. Koweski's funeral announcement in the *Free Press*. *Heart failure,* his father read. *Broken heart,* his mother had responded.

In the kitchen, the old man moved to the stove, started to pick up a kettle, then let it fall back to the grimy burner. "I'm out of coffee. You want a drink instead?"

"No, thank you."

The old man waved toward the table. "Have a seat."

He slipped into one of the yellow Formica chairs of the dinette set. He had a vague memory of eating baloney sandwiches with Richie at the same table, with Mrs. Koweski hovering nearby, wan and wary-eyed.

The old man came to sit in the chair opposite. He was holding a tumbler of clear liquid and pulled the lapels of his stained bathrobe over his chest.

"Stuey Boy," he said softly, shaking his head.

He didn't respond.

"I heard you moved to Florida," the old man said.

"Yes. A long time ago."

The old man took a drink, running a hand over his unshaved face. "Life been good to you?"

When there was no answer, the old man took another drink. The smell of gin was overpowering.

"Mr. Koweski—"

"Well, you didn't ask, but things aren't so hot for me. You can see that for yourself. Neighborhood's gone to hell and I waited too damn long to sell. The wife wouldn't have it . . . said she wanted to stay here no matter what. Then she died and here I am."

The kitchen was quiet.

"What the hell are you doing back here?" the old man asked suddenly.

"What?"

"Why'd you come back here?"

"Richie. I came back because of Richie."

The old man stared hard at him for a moment. Then he took a drink and looked away.

"I know what happened, Mr. Koweski."

The old man's eyes came back to him. He didn't move, not a muscle, not an eyelash. But something in his eyes seemed to draw inward, as though he was waiting for something he knew was coming, like a punch-drunk fighter waiting for the last blow.

"It wasn't an accident. That day in the basement. I didn't do it."

The black eyes were still waiting.

"Richie killed himself, Mr. Koweski."

Still the old man didn't move. Then, slowly, he brought the

glass up to his lips. His hand was shaking. He finished off the gin and set the glass down on the table, wiping a hand across his mouth. He rose, leaning heavily against the table, and took the empty glass to the counter. He stood at the sink, his back turned, his head down.

"Mr. Koweski?"

No response.

"I *know* what happened. Did you hear me? I know Richie killed himself."

The old man spun around. "Shut up! Don't talk about that!"

For a second he was stunned into silence. Finally when he spoke, it was a struggle to keep his voice calm. "I *need* to talk about it, Mr. Koweski, and you're the only one left to hear me."

The black eyes bored into him. "No! I won't talk about it. I don't want to talk about things like that. Not in my house! This is a good Catholic house, and it's a sin. What you're saying about Richie is a sin!"

The word, spat out in a hiss, hung in the cold air of the dim kitchen, and he could only stare at the old man. Sin? Is that what this was all about? Is that why they had done it? Richie's parents, the priest, his own father—is this why they had let him carry the blame, so the stain of suicide could be wiped clean?

He brought his hands up and covered his face. The only sound was the hum of the refrigerator.

"Stuey?"

The old man's voice was a pleading whisper, but he didn't want to look at him.

"Stuey Boy?"

When he took his hands from his face he was astonished to see tears in the old man's eyes.

"It was just an accident. Can't you see that, Stuey Boy?"

He watched the tears fall down the old man's cheeks. And,

slowly but deliberately, something changed, like the last piece of a jigsaw puzzle slipping into place.

Tears in black eyes. Hands on his shoulders. And that smell . . . the smell of someone's breath so close by, with its stink of beer.

Stuey Boy. Nobody else had ever called him that. It hadn't been his own father who had knelt before him that day. It hadn't been his father who had set the whole thing in motion, made him distrust the truth, all the people he believed in, and himself. In his confused mind, it had all been one huge blur, and he realized now that his father hadn't even been there. It had been Richie's father. He had been the one in the house that day.

Just an accident, Stuey Boy.

He reached into the pocket of his overcoat and pulled out the revolver. The old man's eyes widened when he saw it.

"It was you."

The old man drew back against the counter. "What?"

"I know what you did to me, Mr. Koweski."

The old man's eyes were locked on the revolver.

"But it's over now."

The old man's eyes shot back up. They were watery and wide with fear. But he could see other things in those black eyes now—shame, guilt, loneliness, and fatigue, a fatigue he could see was as long and heavy and as aching as his own.

Stuart Bowen stood up. "I don't need this anymore."

He set the gun on the Formica table.

"Good-bye, Mr. Koweski."

He turned and left the kitchen. He didn't stop as he retraced his steps through the dark house and out to the cold November afternoon. It was only when he was in his car that he allowed himself to pull in a long, slow breath. He could feel his heart beating in his chest, feel the quiet, steady thud of his life. He started the engine and turned on the heater. For a moment he sat there, waiting for the car to warm up as he stared at his old house.

He closed his eyes and exhaled.

The sharp *pop!* made him start. He opened his eyes and looked up at Richie's house. There was no face at the window.

For a moment—just a moment—he thought of going back. But then he put the car in drive and moved forward, without looking back.

CYBERDATE.COM

TOM SAVAGE

WELCOME TO CYBERDATE.COM, WHERE ALL YOUR ROMANTIC DREAMS COME TRUE! MEET, MINGLE, AND GET TO KNOW EACH OTHER IN COMFORT AND SAFETY IN OUR SPECIALLY DESIGNED PRIVATE CHAT ROOMS! FOR JUST $1.25 A MINUTE, YOU CAN FIND LOVE AND HAPPINESS! WE'RE THE FUN CONNECTION FOR YOUNG SINGLES IN THE TRISTATE AREA, SATISFACTION GUARANTEED! (MUST BE 18 OR OVER; SOME RESTRICTIONS APPLY.) WHAT ARE YOU WAITING FOR? SIGN UP AND LOG ON TODAY— LOVE IS JUST A KEYSTROKE AWAY!!! (ALL MAJOR CREDIT CARDS ACCEPTED.)

⤏⤎

SESSION #1
DATE: 10/16
CONNECTED: 9:12 p.m.
TERMINATED: 9:37 p.m.

suzyq@connectme.com: Hi.
littleboyblue@overlink.net: Hi there!

Suzy Q: How are you?

Little Boy Blue: Fine, thanks. I like your picture. You're very pretty.

SQ: Thanks. You're not so bad yourself. Your bio said you're 19, but your picture looks younger. How old are you really?

LBB: 19, just like it says.

SQ: Not hardly! How old are you *really*?

LBB: The truth?

SQ: Please.

LBB: I'm 16. You said you were 21, but your photo looks younger too. You're not really 21, are you?

SQ: Nope. I'm 15—16 next month. Is that okay?

LBB: Sure. I like younger women.

SQ: Very funny.

LBB: I bet everyone on this service is really our age, and we all lie cuz it says we have to be 18.

SQ: Totally. My girlfriend Jane met her boyfriend Biff on this service, and they've been together three whole weeks now.

LBB: Wow. Sounds serious. Your profile says you live in NYC. Where?

SQ: Upper West Side—that's all I'm telling you now, until we know each other better. You like baseball and you're into the Lug Nutz. I think they're really cool.

LBB: Yeah, I got all their albums. "Killer" is my fave song.

SQ: Mine too! I'm also into Rat A Tat Tat. Their early stuff, not that last one!

LBB: Yeah, that last one was a mess. So, we both like gyropunk, and I'm really into blood rap too. Death To White People rules! Those guys are truly awesome. How about you, Suzy Q? You like DTWP?

SQ: They're okay. But my main man is Stephen Sondheim.

LBB: Who?

SQ: The King of Broadway. You know, musical theater? Didn't you read my profile, Blue Boy? Hobbies: cheerleading, clubbing, and community theater. I said community theater cuz I didn't want to say the truth—I'm in my high school drama club. I was afraid it'd give away my age, and the cyberdate.com people would 86 me. I'm really, really, really into Broadway musical theater. Sondheim, Rodgers and Hammerstein, Jerry Herman, Kander and Ebb—you know, *Chicago*, that movie with Renée Z. and Catherine Z.J. That was Kander and Ebb. You like that kind of stuff?

LBB: Zzzzzzz . . .

SQ: Sorry. Never mind. So where do you go to school?

LBB: Trick question, Suzy Q! I'm also in Manhattan, but I'll tell ya where when you tell me where. :-)

SQ: Oh, that's cute. Smiley faces. Honestly! Are you sure you're 16 and not, like, 10? That is soooo sandbox!

LBB: Ouch! Okay, no more graphics.

SQ: Thanks. My nerves can't take it. I'm "Suzy Q" cuz my name is Suzy. What's yours?

LBB: Mike. I use "Little Boy Blue" cuz I'm looking for love. How about you, Suzy Q? Are you looking for love?

SQ: Like, duh. Who isn't? Have you ever done this before, Mike?

LBB: What, cyberdate.com? No. My bud Josh and I got on lovemeup.com once, but it turned out to be porn.

SQ: Yuck. Those sites should be shut down.

LBB: Oh, I don't know. There's nothing wrong with sex, is there?

SQ: No. But people should get to know each other first, shouldn't they?

LBB: RYA!

SQ: What's RYA?

LBB: It means "Right You Are!"

SQ: Let's not go there. I hate all those trendy acronyms.

LBB: "Trendy acronyms"? You sure you're only 15, Suze? You sound like you might be an older woman.

SQ: 15 in my stockinged feet, and don't call me Suze. I hate that. My stepfather calls me that.

LBB: Oh, you got a stepper too? I hate mine. I miss my dad.

SQ: Me too. Mine's in Seattle with a new wife, and she's okay, I guess. My mom flipped out and married this creep who's always trying to put his hands on me. He sells insurance.

LBB: Zzzzzzz . . .

SQ: Totally. So, you have a stepper too. We have a lot in common.

LBB: Yeah. So, you wanna get together?

SQ: I don't know. A girl can't be too careful. I mean, how do I know you're who you say you are? You could be, like, Jack the Raper.

LBB: Jack the Raper? Cute. I'm just a guy, Suzy Q. A nice young guy looking for a nice young woman.

SQ: Girl.

LBB: Yeah, girl. I mean, I got an okay life, and a lot of cool friends, and all that stuff, but there's something missing, you know? Something basic. It's like that Death To White People song "Shoot Me in the Heart," where Rancid goes, "Maybe I puts my gunz away and gets me a bitch." That's how I feel sometimes. Kinda lonely, even with my posse. Your buds can't be there 24/7, and it gets all dark and achey. Is that a word? Achey?

SQ: It's a beautiful word. You sound cool, Mike. Poetic. I think you have the soul of a poet. And I know *exactly* what you mean about being lonely in a crowd. It's like Sondheim says in *Company*, "Make me aware of being alive." I feel that way, like, *all the time*.

LBB: Yeah. Whatever. So, how about it? You wanna meet the soul of a poet, Suzy Q? We could sing our fave songs to each other. I'd like that. Would you like that?

SQ: Let me think about it. How about we meet here tomorrow, same time. 9 p.m. We can chat some more.

LBB: Honest?

SQ: XM♥&HTD!

LBB: Now who's doing acolytes?!!

SQ: Acronyms.

LBB: Whatever. Well, you can cross your heart, but please don't hope to die!

SQ: Okay. Gotta go now. O&O.

LBB: Yeah, over and out, yourself! Tomorrow, 9 p.m. O&O.

SESSION #2
DATE: 10/17
CONNECTED: 9:01 p.m.
TERMINATED: 9:49 p.m.

littleboyblue@overlink.net: You there, Suzy Q?

suzyq@connectme.com: Hi, Little Boy Blue.

LBB: Again.

SQ: Yeah, again. What's up?

LBB: Do you really want me to answer that?

SQ: Very funny. Not! I wasn't sure you'd be here tonight.

LBB: That makes 2 of us. So here we are.

SQ: Yes, here we are. Have you had dinner yet?

LBB: Sure. Mac and cheese, like always. I'm not—my mom's not into cooking, you know?

SQ: Yup. I had meat loaf. Did you go to school today?

LBB: Zzzzzzz. Yeah.

SQ: Ditto. We had an alg. exam. Ugh! I did okay, I think, and so did my girlfriend Jane. Our friend Johnny totally flunked it, but he'll get a good grade anyway. The teacher is hot for him.

LBB: What, she wants to date him?

SQ: It's a him. The teacher, I mean. And yeah, he wants to date him.

LBB: Is Johnny gay?

SQ: Metro.

LBB: Oh. That's cool. Is he gonna get together with the teacher?

SQ: Maybe. Did you ever date a teacher, Mike?

LBB: Nah. How about you?

SQ: I'd have to know you better to answer that. But I'm not from the Virgin Islands, if that's what you mean. I bet you aren't either. You sound like a man of the world. Where is this school of yours, anyway?

LBB: You and your trick questions, Suzy Q! You'll find out soon enough. What else did you do at school today?

SQ: Cheerleading practice. You should see our new uniforms! My mom'll have a hippo when she sees! I hope she lets me wear it.

LBB: I'd sure like to see you in it.

SQ: HYH! We're still chatting, remember?

LBB: Okey-doke, I'll hold my horses. Barely. I think we should meet somewhere.

SQ: Would you like that, Mike?

LBB: Totally, Suzy.

SQ: Hmmm. I told Jane about you at practice today. She says you're probably some DOM, like 40 or something, who wants to hook up with little girls. Is that true? Are you a DOM, Mike?

LBB: Oh, ha ha. I'm a DYM, a Dirty *Young* Man. 16 in my stockinged feet. 6'1" and still growing. In all directions.

SQ: And you're blond. I like the goat.

LBB: It may have to come off. The principal took me aside and said no facial hair. I told him to GFH.

SQ: You did not! I bet you said, "Yes, sir, right away, sir!"

LBB: Yeah, I did. Have to be nice to the authority around here. My stepper's been talkin military school.

SQ: Eek! Are you that big a problem, Michael?

LBB: Not really. But my bud Josh and a couple other guys and me were caught at a club with X last month. So I'm minding my Ps and Qs.

SQ: You still do X?

LBB: Sometimes. When I want to party.

SQ: Cool. It makes me feel sexy.

LBB: I'll bring you some.

SQ: We'll see, Michael.

LBB: I like you calling me that. Michael, I mean. Nobody else calls me that.

SQ: You've had girlfriends before, right?

LBB: A couple.

SQ: What did they call you?

LBB: A-hole. Joke! They called me Cas.

SQ: Cas? Why?

LBB: Casanova.

SQ: Oh, I see. You're the BMOC?

LBB: I'm the *extremely* BMOC.

SQ: Man of the world. Cool. You like girls a lot?

LBB: Oh yeah! And you like boys a lot?

SQ: You could say that. But I've only had one serious relationship.

LBB: How serious?

SQ: Very. I told you, I'm not from the V.I. His name was Brad, he was a JV quarterback. Big guy too. Blond, like you. But we're not an item anymore.

LBB: What happened?

SQ: He liked the showers better than the football field. He came out with the coach.

LBB: Weird.

SQ: Not really. Who knows, Michael? You might have fun with an older man yourself.

LBB: Nah. I'll stick with girls, thanks.

SQ: Any girl in particular?

LBB: Well, that's why we're here, isn't it? Tell me some more about your cheerleading uniform.

SQ: Oh, ha ha. It's very revealing. Tight.

LBB: Ooooooh. My last girlfriend was a cheerleader. And a gymnast. Parallel bars. A real athlete, if you know what I mean.

SQ: I know what you mean. What happened to her?

LBB: She's dating a college guy now.

SQ: So we both lost loves to older people. We do have a lot in common.

LBB: Yeah. But I can understand it, Suzy. Older guys are more experienced. They know what they're doing. You ever date an older guy?

SQ: Once.

LBB: How old?

SQ: He was 17.

LBB: That's not old!

SQ: Well, 2 years older than me!

LBB: Who was he?

SQ: His dad was my doorman.

LBB: Doorman? So, you're rich?

SQ: Not really. But I had a doorman.

LBB: And he had a son.

SQ: Yeah. He was gorgeous. *Big* guy, know what I mean? But we didn't last long together. He was looking for somebody younger, somebody his own age.

LBB: I thought you said you were 15.

SQ: Sorry. Misprint. I meant he was looking for somebody *older*. Besides, I wasn't serious about him like I was with Brad.

LBB: Oh. So are you looking for serious? Or just fun?

SQ: Make me an offer. Joke! I'm looking for whatever comes along.

LBB: Me too. Whatever comes along.

SQ: Oh, that is soooo Metro Man. Is that you, Michael?

LBB: Yup, I'm Metro Man. And you're Metro Woman?

SQ: Metro Girl, anyway. I'm 15, remember?

LBB: Yeah. We should meet, Suzy.

SQ: Well, Halloween is in two weeks. We could wear masks and meet in some dive on the Lower East Side. You dress up like Tarzan and I'll dress up like Jane.

LBB: You mean like your girlfriend Jane, or like Jane in Tarzan?

SQ: Jane in Tarzan, silly! My girlfriend Jane would never be mistaken for Jane in Tarzan. She'd break the vine, know what I mean? Besides, she's too goody2shoes.

LBB: But you're not goody2shoes?

SQ: No, I'm not. I'm a lot more mature than her.

LBB: How much more mature?

SQ: A lot. And you're the BMOC.

LBB: The *extremely* BMOC.

SQ: Right. Are we talking size here, Michael?

LBB: You'll find out.

SQ: Maybe, maybe not. What were you last Halloween?

LBB: Me. I don't do that costume stuff. I like to be myself.

SQ: So do I. I believe in being honest. But last Halloween I went as Marilyn Monroe.

LBB: Well, you're blond, anyway, just like me, and your picture is just as pretty as MM any day of the week.

SQ: Thank you.

LBB: You're welcome. How did you post that picture? I have Scanner X5-11 and PhotoOp. What do you use?

SQ: I have a Mac. I use MacScan and PhotoLab 3.7.

LBB: You got a doorman *and* a Mac? Damn, you *are* rich!

SQ: Okay, so I'm rich. You like the idea of dating an heiress, Michael?

LBB: Well, it's better than not. But I'm not into all that—you know, *stuff*.

SQ: Yeah. Stuff isn't important. People are.

LBB: YSI!

SQ: And what does YSI mean?

LBB: "You said it!"

SQ: Oh. Still, what if somebody offered you a lot of money to get it on with you? What would you do?

LBB: Is this somebody male or female?

SQ: Whatever.

LBB: I guess it would depend how much.

SQ: $1000?

LBB: A grand? I don't know. Maybe. I could score mondo X with that . . .

SQ: You sure could.

LBB: Well, maybe. This is a weird conversation. Would you?

SQ: Would I what?

LBB: Get it on with somebody for a grand?

SQ: Is that your best offer, Mike?

LBB: Har har har! You know what I mean.

SQ: Yes, I know what you mean. Sure, I would. If he was cool, anyway—not some DOM from hell. But if he was nice . . .

LBB: Would you get it on with a woman?

SQ: What, for a grand?

LBB: Yeah.

SQ: No. But you'd get it on with a guy for a grand, right?

LBB: I didn't say that.

SQ: Yes, you did. You said, "Male or female?" and I said, "Whatever," and then you said, "Sure."

LBB: I did not say, "Sure." I said, "Maybe." I don't know. Let's change the subject.

SQ: Okay. Have you ever had sex with a guy?

LBB: That's changing the subject????

SQ: Just curious. You sound so—worldly. I bet you drink martinis and drive a Porsche.

LBB: Not on my budget. Coors Light and the MTA.

SQ: Zzzzzzz.

LBB: Har har har! You know, you're pretty funny, Suzy Q.

SQ: It's the theatrical training.

LBB: Whatever. You're pretty funny—you're pretty and you're funny, get it? I bet you have nice legs.

SQ: Some people think so.

LBB: Truth or dare.

SQ: What?

LBB: You know, you answer a question truthfully and I answer one.

SQ: Okay, shoot.

LBB: Are you wearing panties?

SQ: Yeah.

LBB: What color?

SQ: That's 2 questions. White. White cotton. My turn. Were you a Boy Scout?

LBB: Cub, Boy, and Eagle. Got the patches to prove it.

SQ: Did you go camping?

LBB: Sure, out on LI.

SQ: Did you and the other Scouts ever play dirty games?

LBB: That's 3 questions. Do you wear a bra?

SQ: Of course I wear a bra. Oh, enough of this, Mike. We sound soooo creepy, like those old men in raincoats in the back of the movie theater.

LBB: Hey, some of my best friends are old men in raincoats.

SQ: I'll bet. Do you let them feel you up?

LBB: Now who's being creepy? Enough of this BS. Do you want to meet me or not?

SQ: Hey! Jump back, Michael! Temper, temper!

LBB: Sorry. I just get a little impatient sometimes. How about it, Suzy? Would you like to meet somewhere and get to know each other face2face?

SQ: Maybe. I gotta go now, it's almost 10. Here's what let's do, Blue Boy—you think of a time and place, and meet me here one more time tomorrow at 9. How does that sound?

LBB: Sure. Say, you're not shining me on or anything, are you? I mean, if I think of a cool place to meet, you'll really show up, right?

SQ: XM♥&HTD!

LBB: Word?

SQ: XM♥&HTD!

LBB: Cool! Tomorrow night at 9. Good night, Suzy Q. O&O.

SQ: Good night, Michael. O&O.

SESSION #3

DATE: 10/18

CONNECTED: 8:56 p.m.

TERMINATED: 9:28 p.m.

littleboyblue@overlink.net: Little Boy Blue calling Suzy Q. Come in, please.

suzyq@connectme.com: Oh, ha ha. Hello, Michael.

LBB: Hello, Suzy. Here we are again. S'up?

SQ: Same old same old. You?

LBB: SOSO. SSDD. SOSAD.

SQ: I know the first 2, but what the heck is SOSAD?

LBB: "Same Old Song and Dance." I thought you'd go for that, since you're into Rodgers and Ebbstein and stuff.

SQ: Rodgers and Hammerstein. Kander and Ebb.

LBB: Yeah, them too. Whatever. I rented the DVD of *Chicago* cuz you mentioned you liked it.

SQ: Yeah? That is so sweet! What did you think of it?

LBB: It was okay. But all that singing and dancing—I dunno. Old-people stuff.

SQ: Don't be immature. That movie won the Academy Award for Best Picture. It's art.

LBB: So's Death To White People. Hey, I got their new album. I can bring it when we meet if you like.

SQ: Sure. Okay. Where and when?

LBB: Really?

SQ: Quick, before I change my mind.

LBB: Tomorrow night, 10, 3rd St. & Ave. B. North side, 2 doors in from

B, going toward C. There's this really cool old house. It's empty now and they're gonna build something new there. But there's this little garden in the back that's romantic, specially in the moonlight. Little white flowers everywhere. Wanna see it?

SQ: You want to meet in an abandoned house on 3rd Street?

LBB: Well, yeah. Do you have a better idea?

SQ: No. But isn't it, like, boarded up? How do you get in?

LBB: The front door lock is broken. I go there sometimes when I want to be by myself. Really cool.

SQ: How do you know this place? Do you take all your girls there?

LBB: No, I've never been there with anyone. It's near my house, that's how I know about it. I thought I'd bring my iPod tomorrow night— we can listen to my new DTWP album. Do you like red wine?

SQ: Sure.

LBB: I'll bring a bottle. And some X.

SQ: Listen, Michael, this isn't gonna be one of *those* dates, is it? I don't want to get all the way down to 3rd Street just to, like, fight you off.

LBB: No way! We can dance in the garden in the moonlight. That's all. Promise.

SQ: Hmmm. You'd better be telling the truth.

LBB: Word.

SQ: Okay. But can we make it 9? I've gotta be somewhere by 11.

LBB: Another date, Suzy?

SQ: Oh, ha ha. I mean *home*, of course! I've gotta be home by 11. It's a school night, you know? I'll be there at 9, but promise me one thing, Michael.

LBB: Anything.

SQ: Promise me you'll keep an open mind.

LBB: I knew it! I *knew* you were older than 15!

SQ: That's not what I mean.

LBB: You're not really a cheerleader?

SQ: Oh, I'm really a cheerleader. No, I just mean keep an open mind about us, okay?

LBB: Sure.

SQ: Okay. I'm counting on you to be a gentleman.

LBB: Always, Suzy.

SQ: Promise?

LBB: XM♥&HTD! And you keep an open mind, too. It'll be cool, I promise. Really, really romantic.

SQ: Okay.

LBB: You'll really be there, won't you?

SQ: Yes. I'll be there.

LBB: You're not gonna stand me up, leave me waiting in the moonlit garden?

SQ: I wouldn't do that, Michael. I'm not that kind of girl.

LBB: Great! Tomorrow night, then, at 9. I'll be the guy in the Mets baseball cap.

SQ: Oh, ha ha. Like there's gonna be so many guys to choose from?

LBB: No, just me. Just you and me, Suzy Q. Just us, in the whole world.

SQ: You do have the soul of a poet.

LBB: Yup. And you're my little Suzy Q.

SQ: We'll see. I can't wait to see you face2face.

LBB: Tomorrow night, then.

SQ: Yes, tomorrow night. Sweet dreams, Michael. O&O.

LBB: Good night, my little Suzy Q. O&O.

THE DAILY NEWS
MURDER VICTIM IDENTIFIED

NYC, October 21—The body of a man found in a condemned building on East 3rd Street near Avenue B in the East Village two nights ago has been positively identified as Harold Frobish, 29, of West 74th Street in Manhattan.

Frobish was stabbed multiple times in the face and chest, sometime between nine o'clock and eleven o'clock Thursday night. The body, which was at first mistaken for a woman's, as he was dressed in women's clothing and a blond wig, was discovered by a transient in a ground-floor room of the abandoned building.

Frobish, an actor who performed in drag shows in downtown clubs under the stage name "Suzy Q," was identified today by a friend and fellow performer, Johnny Dillson, 26, a drag artist who performs under the name "Jane Doe." Dillson and others became alarmed when Frobish failed to show up for work two nights in a row at Cheerleaders, a popular drag club in Chelsea.

The victim has no known relatives, but searches of police files produced records indicating that Frobish had been arrested twice on charges of solicitation, public indecency, and endangering the welfare of a minor. Charges were dropped in the first case by the boy's parents, but in the second case Frobish was prosecuted for corrupting the morals of a minor by the boy's father, who was Frobish's doorman. Frobish was convicted and served six months in a state facility.

The transient, who declined to identify himself, told authorities he saw a man running from the building just before he went inside to seek shelter and discovered Frobish's lifeless body. The fleeing man is described as a pale, powerfully built Caucasian, approximately 6'1" and 200 lbs., with dark hair and glasses, 35–40 years of age. The man was wearing jeans, a NY Mets baseball cap, and a bloodstained gray sweatshirt imprinted with the logo of the popular rap group Death To White People.

Anyone with information regarding this case is asked to contact the NYPD . . .

WELCOME TO INTERMEET.COM, WHERE ALL YOUR ROMANTIC
DREAMS COME TRUE! GET TO KNOW EACH OTHER IN COMFORT
AND SAFETY IN OUR PRIVATE CHAT ROOMS! FOR JUST $1.50 A
MINUTE, YOU CAN FIND LOVE AND HAPPINESS! (MUST BE 18 OR
OVER; SOME RESTRICTIONS APPLY.) WHAT ARE YOU WAITING
FOR? (ALL MAJOR CREDIT CARDS ACCEPTED.)

SESSION #1
DATE: 12/04
CONNECTED: 9:15 p.m.
TERMINATED: 9:56 p.m.

younggirl@compuline.com: Hi.
littleboyblue@teklink.net: Hi there!
Young Girl: How are you?
Little Boy Blue: Fine, thanks. I like your picture. You're very pretty. But
    I have to ask you something before we go any further here, Young
    Girl, and it's really, really important that you tell me the truth.
YG: Okay. What's your question?
LBB: It's, like, life-and-death important.
YG: Okay, shoot.
LBB: Young Girl, are you *really* a young girl?
YG: Yes, I am. Really. What's the matter—did you think I was older?
LBB: Something like that.
YG: Well, I know my profile says I'm 22, but I'm really 16. Is that okay?
LBB: That's fine, Young Girl. That's perfect. 16? Yeah, that's just what
    I'm looking for. . . .

HOME COMING

CHARLES TODD

THERE WAS SOMEONE in the house when she walked through the door.

Eleanor could sense it. The very air seemed to have changed.

"Hallo—" she called tentatively, stopping by the stairs. And after a pause, "Maddie?" But it was not Maddie's day to clean. Thursdays were.

She had only been away for an hour, stopping at the green-grocer's, the post office, the bakery. She'd bought scones for tea. Harry loved them . . .

For an instant her heart seemed to skip its normal beat. But Harry was fighting in France; he'd have sent her a telegram if he'd got leave.

One got leave when one was wounded.

She didn't want to think about that.

Uncertain what to do, she said, "Is anyone there?"

And no one answered her.

With a sigh, she scolded herself for nerves and went on through to the kitchen to put away her purchases.

They'd had no children, she and Harry. He'd gone off to war before they could. Sometimes she longed for a child, someone to shower with her love, someone to make the empty house seem livelier. Filled with laughter.

And crying too, she reminded herself. Her sister's baby seemed always to be crying, but Sarah had told her it was the teething.

She put the onions and carrots in the bin, set the scones on a shelf, and took the single piece of mail into the sitting room with her. A letter from her mother. She read it through quickly and found that they were well, a little worn from hearing the guns in France of a night. Kent was too near the raging war for her mother's liking, but her father was always out on the cliffs, watching for zeppelins. He'd never seen an airship; it was almost as if the battle itself drew him, old as he was, crippled as he was. Like an old warhorse remembering the call of the trumpet.

Finishing the letter, she put it away in her desk—and whirled around, startled.

It was as if someone had been sitting in the chair by the window—

She was sure she'd seen something—a snatch of ginger hair, the shape of shoulders—

But there was no one. Still, she'd have *sworn* when she turned that the rocker was moving ever so slightly.

I can't understand, she scolded herself, *why you're jumpy. It's as if you left the house one person and came back another person entirely.*

But nothing had happened in the village to change her. She had gone to do the marketing as she always did, speaking to neighbors and friends, browsing in the tiny bookshop, sometimes buying a few flowers to put on the table for tea. Not that her own garden didn't produce all the flowers she could want. It was the color that drew her, the flaming red of gladioli or the soft fragrance of white lilac, or the yellow of marigolds in a bunch. She'd buy them just to have them, never mind that she had salmon gladioli of her own or lavender lilac, or zinnias in nearly the same color.

It was a lovely afternoon, and she decided to take her tea on the little terrace that Harry had built for her just after they were married. It was only large enough for a table and two chairs, with a view over the gardens. She'd adored it, exclaiming with delight as the two of them had sat there to watch the sun set over the Gloucestershire hills. She couldn't have dreamed of anything more wonderful.

Harry had always had a knack for knowing what she wanted, as if he'd studied her closely enough to guess what it was that would please her. The terrace, the swing under the apple tree, the pair of white stone swans at the end of the garden walk, or the small shelf for books next to her bed, where she could read whenever she couldn't sleep. But with Harry by her side, she'd slept well. It was now, when he was away, that she had come to depend on the books, turning to them in the long dark hours of the night when she missed him most. As if he'd known even that . . .

After making herself a pot of tea and setting the scones on the Worcestershire plate that had been a wedding present from Harry's sister, she carried the tray out to the garden. Behind her she thought she heard something, and she turned quickly.

But there was no one there. Nothing.

Her heart still beating wildly, she hurried out into the garden and set the tray on the table. Pouring a cup, she added milk and sugar and began to stir the tea with her spoon. She should have brought another cup, she thought, for Harry. She did sometimes, just for the companionship of seeing two cups on the tray, the way it used to be.

A little breeze touched her cheek, and she smiled. The way Harry used to touch it, in passing. She missed him so much, had cried for days after he'd gone. She couldn't understand why the murder of an Austrian archduke in some ridiculous Balkan town had touched off this terrible war. It wasn't the English who had shot him, or the English who deserved to be punished for it. Austria should have bombarded Serbia—it made no sense for the English and the Germans to be fighting in France over an obscure princeling.

Harry had explained about the treaties. But men drew up treaties, she'd told him. No wife, no mother, would ever have agreed to go to war just because of a parchment agreement among a handful of states. It made very little sense for her own husband to be taken away simply because a hothead had felt the urge to assassinate someone. Hadn't they shot *him* dead on the spot?

Harry had laughed and said, "There's more to it than you think."

"Not really," she'd told him. "It's just that men prefer to march off in uniforms and do something brave. Any excuse will do when there hasn't been a war for a while."

He'd kissed her then.

She turned quickly, a glimpse of something out of the corner of her eye. A sense of someone there.

But it was only her imagination, conjuring up Harry because she missed him so fiercely. She tried to laugh, but couldn't—

Someone *had* been there. She wasn't losing her mind, and she wasn't a silly girl: she was a married woman who had lived alone here comfortably since October of 1914, and that was almost two years now.

She put down her cup and went to the corner of the house and then looked into the kitchen. Unsatisfied, she walked through the house and, for the first time she could ever remember, locked the hall door.

"Is anyone there?" she called up the stairs. And no one answered.

The neighbor's dog, then. She'd glimpsed the dog among the bushes, a flash of a tail or the quick movement of a head.

Walking back to the terrace, she picked up a scone and began to eat it, savoring the subtle flavor as she sat down again in her chair.

"It's the wrong time of the month," she told herself. "I'm jittery. That's all."

But the garden was haunted now, and as the robin and the sparrow and the chat flew and sang among the plants, she followed them with her eyes, waiting for them to start up into the apple tree, frightened by something.

She didn't linger in the garden, though it was not at all hot for early August and pleasant in the shade of the house. As soon as she finished her tea, she collected the tray and hurried back inside.

The evening was horrible. She could feel a presence, she could sense movement and sometimes glimpse it, but not once could she pin down whatever it was that disturbed her. *My eyes,* she thought, watching the hands of the clock move slowly to ten o'clock, *I shall have to go into town and find someone to test my eyes.*

I mustn't go blind, how shall I ever manage here alone? I don't want my parents here, I don't want Sarah and her child here. I don't want a nurse. This is my home, not theirs, they'd feel uncomfortable and I'd feel pitied . . .

But the book she chose to read sitting up in bed was perfectly clear. She had no problem with the lines of print marching across the page.

Worn out with the strain of trying to feel at ease when she wasn't, she finally fell asleep. The book slipped out of her hands and onto the little rug with a *thunk*.

That brought her sharply awake, and as she tried to think where she was and what had happened, she felt a warmth in the bed beside her. It terrified her, and she flung back the sheet with a wild motion, getting out to stand staring from the floor.

Nothing was there except the indentation on her pillow where her head had rested. She leaned over, certain she'd felt the warmth, running her hand along the sheets. But they were cool except where her body had lain.

Pushing her dark hair back from her face, she said aloud, "I'm losing my mind!"

It was a frightful thought, and it shook her to the core of her being. She'd seen only one madwoman, the aged grandmother of a school friend, who had talked to the chairs in her room and argued with the wardrobe over against the wall, as if it held people and not her coat and dresses and shoes.

Unable to sleep again, Eleanor took her pillow and her blanket downstairs and lay on the couch, her body as stiff as a board and her eyes wide. It wasn't until shortly after dawn, when the summer sun came through the window, that she finally fell into a fitful doze.

The day was a nightmare. She was afraid to go out, afraid she'd make a fool of herself in the village, exclaiming over shadows. Afraid to stay in the house and know that she was not alone. Afraid to look out of the corner of her eye for fear she'd see something terrible, some mad thing that came from the depths of a tormented mind.

By teatime she was unable to eat, and she took the teapot out to the garden without a plate of scones or the thin cucumber sandwiches she relished in the summer. She drank the hot sweet tea as if it were a lifeline that stood between her and drowning. Her throat felt swollen as if she'd swallowed poison. But it was only the tears she was afraid to shed, for fear that she would collapse into madness and never stop crying ever again.

As darkness fell, she was terrified of her bed, terrified of the house, all her peace and serenity broken into dark shards of something she couldn't understand, couldn't quite grasp. She wished everything were safe again, Harry here beside her or busy somewhere about the house, his ginger hair (her sister called it marmalade, but *she* insisted it was guinea gold) glinting as he dug out weeds or bent his head to wind the French clock.

She began a letter to him and tore it up for fear that he would read between the lines and discover she was not herself, that something must be desperately wrong with her. She began another to her mother, to ask if madness ran in the family, and then tore that up as well. Her mother would be headed here on the next train, demanding to know what she was on about.

And still something hovered close by, within reach sometimes, and almost visible. But she couldn't break the barrier of her dementia and come to terms with it.

Early the next morning, she walked barefoot out into the dew wet garden, uncaring what her neighbors might think if they glimpsed her there in her dressing gown. She went all the way to the swans and the bench at the foot of the garden. The chat sat in the apple tree and scolded her. Usually she talked to it, to encourage its song, but this morning she was beyond beguiling, beyond reaching out to anything.

Turning back to look at the house, she said, quite clearly, managing just barely to keep the quaver out of her voice, "Go away. I don't want you here. *Go away and leave me in peace!*"

She could feel the hovering, the sense of something, and she said again, "Truly, I don't want you here! *Go away and leave me alone!* In God's name, go away!"

Tears falling for the first time in the long ordeal, she repeated, "In God's name—"

It was the whistle of her teakettle that finally brought her back to the house, for fear it would run dry and catch on.

She lifted it off the stove and turned to look for the teapot, but she hadn't filled it yet; she'd been in too much of a hurry to run through the garden and defy her own madness.

She drank the first cup there in the kitchen, unwilling to go into the sitting room or out to the terrace. The sharp, strong tea seemed to flow through her, warming the coldness in her heart.

And, listening, she waited. And this time nothing came.

Warily, she moved through the house to the sitting room. And then to the bedroom, and finally out to the terrace in the morning sun.

Nothing.

Madness can't leave like this, her rational mind warned her. *It can't vanish like a bit of autumn smoke.*

But the house was free. She could draw in a deep breath and listen and feel, but there was nothing.

The house was free.

Giddy with laughter, she went up the stairs to her room, flinging open the wardrobe, pulling out a dress she particularly liked and lifting off her nightgown. *A celebration,* she thought. *This calls for a celebration.*

She paused for an instant, certain she heard the front gate. But this was Thursday; it would be Maddie coming through. Hurrying, she pulled the dress over her lingerie and then pulled out a drawer, looking for a pair of stockings.

It was as if a weight had been lifted from her shoulders—

But what if it came back?

She could hear the front door opening and then closing. Maddie.

No, it wouldn't come back. This had been a warning that she'd been too much on her own for too long and needed to bring a little brightness and pleasure into her life again, to combat the darkness that hung on the fringes. Never again. She'd see to that.

She found her shoes and walked out to the landing.

"Maddie? Is that you?"

A sound reached her. A moan.

Suddenly very frightened, she flew down the steps, and at the turning stopped so quickly, she nearly stumbled down the last flight.

Maddie stood by the door, her back against it, her face drawn and swollen, her mouth hanging open in a silent cry, as if her tongue were bereft of words.

Eleanor could feel herself die a little inside as she said, "Maddie—not your son—not *Bill*—"

She came swiftly down the steps and reached out to embrace the middle-aged woman who had cleaned the house from the first day they'd come to live here.

But Maddie held out her hand, the crumpled telegram in her fingers.

"Dear God, no, I don't want to believe it," Eleanor cried, afraid to take it and read the words. Bill was only seventeen, only *seventeen!*

Maddie took a deep breath, tears thick in her voice, charging it with pain. "I said I'd bring it. I said you'd rather I bring it—"

Her hand offered the telegram. It was unopened—

Eleanor took it from the work-roughened fingers and ripped at the sealed envelope, nearly tearing the contents.

Spreading out the sheet, she tried to read the words and failed. They seemed to blur before her eyes.

Maddie mercifully took it from her. "It's Mr. Harry," she said. "He's dead. On the Somme."

Eleanor thought she screamed in pain. But there was no sound. Only the horror beating at her, tearing at her heart.

"No, he's alive—I got a letter from him—it was dated the first of July—"

"There's terrible killing going on. Thousands . . ." The thick voice choked. "Come into here, do." She led her mistress into the sitting room and then was gone. A few minutes later she returned with a cup of tea. It smelled strongly of Harry's whiskey. "Drink up," Maddie said. "You must drink up."

Eleanor tried, her fingers shaking so the cup rattled against her teeth. The first swallow nearly took her breath away. Maddie's hand had been heavy with the whiskey. Harry wouldn't like it—

But Harry was dead.

The house was filled with people soon afterward. The vicar and the postmistress and her neighbors, and even the woman from the bookstore, and James from the pub, and after that she lost track of them and of the dishes that Maddie, face raddled from tears, carried away into the kitchen.

Someone offered to stay the night, but she couldn't bear it. Someone brought her food and she tried to eat, and then thanked them and sent away the plate.

By nine o'clock the house was hers again.

Silent. Empty. She could hear the French clock on the landing ticking. Harry had bought that for her as a wedding gift. "To grow old along with us," he'd said.

But Harry would never hear it again. Harry would never come back—

"Oh, dear God!"

She got to her feet, throwing off the shawl someone had draped over her lap when she'd begun shivering.

"Harry?" she cried into the emptiness. *"Harry, was that you?"* She waited.

"Harry—oh, please come back, Harry—I didn't understand! I didn't know! *Please,* Harry, I never meant to send you away—

"Harry!"

She waited all night long, but there was nothing. No sense of a presence, no sound, no touch on her cheek, no shape just out of her line of sight.

Exhausted, she watched the sun come up. But there was nothing in the house anymore to offer comfort.

Desperate, so hurt and lost that she couldn't abide the emptiness anymore, she went out into the garden and down the path to the bench. Here she'd sent him away—here she might bring him back.

She called his name softly, begging and trying not to cry. She prayed, promising God anything if he'd only bring Harry back again.

And felt nothing. Only isolation—and loneliness so intense it hurt.

I can't live with what I've done, she told herself after a very long time. *I'll find some way to kill myself and join him again. I can't bear it!*

Finally, her legs shaking with weariness and grief and the knowledge of her own foolishness, she walked slowly back up the garden path to the house and into the kitchen. The chat fussed shrilly, and she didn't care. She didn't care about anything anymore.

"Harry, forgive me. God forgive me!" She reached into the drawer for the sharp knife she used to disjoint chicken.

The chat was angrily diving against the light, now a shadow, now a bright bit of feathers just outside the kitchen windows.

Distracted, she watched it for an instant.

The neighbors' dog was barking.

Had the chat fledged its young? She had deserted Harry, she couldn't desert the poor chat as well. The dog would sniff out and kill the little birds. She couldn't shut out the noise it was making—she couldn't simply die and leave it to fend for itself. Not after three years of listening to its song in the garden. Well, then—

Laying down the knife for a moment, she walked to the back door, looking out. She could hear the dog barking, but the sound was coming from the next garden. Where he ought to be. And the chat, seeing her, rushed up into the apple tree and began to complain loudly.

For a moment she stood still.

"Harry?" she asked breathlessly, holding the door open just a bit.

But there was no reply. She'd turned back to the kitchen, then decided to step out on the terrace and calm the little bird. It would be horrible to die with that familiar voice in her ear.

Outside the sun was warm on her face, promising heat by afternoon.

A sound reached her, something she couldn't place.

The baby chat, the one the mother was worried about. Out of its nest prematurely and lost.

She and Harry had never had children. Never would . . .

She searched under the table, where the sound seemed to come from, and heard it again.

A soft, frightened cry.

Pulling out her chair, she saw nothing.

She reached for Harry's and nearly knocked it over in her shock.

A kitten sat hunched on the seat, drawn into itself against the bird's furious attack.

Eyes closed, shivering, it huddled against the sunlight that spilled across it.

A marmalade cat . . . But where had it come from? None of the neighbors had cats; they owned dogs. And this was too far from the village for it to have wandered on its own.

Angry with it for distracting her from what she was committed to do, she was at the point of shooing it out of the garden, if only to soothe the chat. If it had come this far alone, it could find another—

Eleanor felt something twist inside. She fell on her knees by the table, reaching for the kitten and holding its warmth against her breast.

In the sun, its fur was the color of Harry's hair . . .

Getting blindly to her feet as the tears fell unheeded down her cheeks, she exclaimed, "Oh, Harry, Harry—God bless you . . ."

Hurrying, she went inside to find the milk and a saucer.

The house, as she bent to set the kitten down beside her offering, seemed alive again, and full of Harry's spirit.

THE MASSEUSE
A Short Mystery

TIM WOHLFORTH

Teresa hovered over me as I lay on the massage table. Straight black hair almost close enough to touch my chest. Brown eyes wide open in a trance. She emitted a low hum through full naturally colored lips as her long, powerful fingers worked my shoulders. I absorbed her flawless face, the delicate brown of the Filipina. She kneaded deep into my body.

Did I really need a massage? Who cared. I enjoyed my hour with Teresa. Having a beautiful woman devote herself to your body for whatever purpose is damned pleasurable. And then there was the hug she gave me when I left, pressing her firm breasts and thin body against me. My time with Teresa had become a highlight of a rather empty life. Still, this week's massage had been special. The extra-deep probing, the moments when her body gently brushed against mine.

She moved from the shoulders to my head. Her fingers glided over my brow, cheeks, lips. Lifting my head with her two hands, she worked my neck. Her hair brushed over my face. The humming grew more intense, as if she were praying to some spirit of the flesh.

I knew her routine. She was near completion, but I didn't want her to stop. Teresa must have sensed my feelings because she sat on the edge of the platform and continued to go over the outlines of my face. Then she stopped and looked deeply into my half-shut eyes.

"Awake?" she asked me in her accent-free, melodious voice.

"Sort of."

I looked around the little room with its view of Oakland's Lake Merritt. I felt as if I were in a shrine devoted to the flesh. A photo of an Indian woman guru hung on one wall. Sachets of exotic herbs covered a small shelf. Another held moon rocks. Perfume created by a combination of massage lotion and herbs clung to my nostrils.

"We need to talk," she said.

"Wonderful."

I used to talk a lot with her during our visits. I had given her a blow-by-blow description of my divorce. Like a woman in a beauty parlor. And my work. She found my job as a private investigator fascinating. For me most of the time it was boring. I was one half of a two-man agency devoted to corporate security. If I wasn't processing mounds of paper to find out who was stealing what secrets, I sat in a car, sipping cold coffee, watching the door of a high-tech firm, waiting for the thief to emerge with the evidence in his laptop. Usually biotech.

Not boring to Teresa. Or so she insisted. Boring as hell to my wife. So boring she had decided to spend her free nights, while I was snooping, sleeping with my partner. It took me a while to understand why my partner was so keen that I do the nighttime surveillance work. Some PI, huh?

So now I had no wife and no partner. Didn't miss the partner. Traitorous bastard. But the wife was another matter. Not this specific wife. Any wife. I'm not built like Sam Spade, Mike

Hammer, or Philip Marlowe. I needed a woman. And not just for sex. Hated to come home to an empty house. But at least I had Teresa.

She asked questions of me but never said anything about herself. And I never asked her any questions. Too much like work. Recently I had run out of small talk. I preferred to be lost in dreams, serenaded by her musical humming. Most masseuses play new age space music CDs. She performed.

"I have a proposal to make."

"What kind of a proposal?" I asked.

"An unusual one. I want to suggest a mutually beneficial arrangement between you and me."

Sounded strange. Was she going to ask for a loan? Did I know her well enough to trust her? She ran her hand over my face and then my chest.

"Tension. You must learn to avoid becoming tense. What I have to say does not threaten you. And you can turn me down."

"Turn what down?"

"The arrangement." She smiled at me. "Let me explain. I enjoy being a masseuse. But the pay isn't that great. I feel like I'm going nowhere. Always short at the end of the month when I have to scrape up my rent. So I've decided to take up a new career."

"I'll miss these massages."

"I'm offering you far more than a massage. I have to stop working so I can train for a new profession. I will need a place to stay, groceries, pocket change. I thought, since you're single now, you might have some room. It would be a fair arrangement. I'm a marvelous cook. French, Italian, Thai—not just Filipino. I'd help keep the place up. And I'd attend to your sexual needs and you to mine. I promise you will be content."

She reached under the table for her bottle of lotion, squirted some into her hand, and reached under the sheet. She began to massage where she had never gone before. God, it felt wonderful. I couldn't believe this was happening. She fell back into a trance and started again to hum.

"Of course"—she broke out of the trance but continued the massage—"I would expect you to give me fulfillment as well. That shouldn't be a problem. I find you attractive and will train you on just what to do. You should feel free to instruct me as to your needs. How are you feeling now?"

"Fabulous."

"There's no hurry." She slowed the movement of her hand. "We will always take our time. Lovemaking is a fine art, a spiritual activity."

I must say Teresa was proving to be a very convincing lady. I was about ready to hand her the keys to my house right then and there. But they were in my pants in a chair in the corner of the little room.

"There is one very important caveat," she said. She stopped the massaging. "I'm not proposing a relationship. Just an arrangement."

"I'm not sure I understand the distinction."

"This is of critical importance. We're not to get involved emotionally with each other. I don't want to know if you see others, anything about your life outside of what will temporarily be our house. And I don't want you snooping into mine. This is not a matter of love but of mutual satisfaction. Like good cooking. No entanglements. Either one of us can call things off without notice at any time. Do I make myself clear?"

I found myself saying, "Perfectly."

"Then it's a deal?"

"Yes."

This beautiful creature wanted to live with me without commitments. It was a perfect arrangement. What more could a man ask for? But was it too perfect?

"Good." She smiled at me. "I'm not about to leave you like that. Tension isn't good for you." She reached back under the sheet.

◇✕◇

I HELPED TERESA move in the next day. Not much of a job. She wasn't one for possessions. Two suitcases, one garment bag, and a box filled with cosmetics and toiletries. She unpacked immediately, finding places for her few possessions without disturbing any of mine. It was as if she weren't there. And yet she was everywhere. A slight scent in the air. An order that was lacking when I lived alone. I felt her presence in each room. It was a comforting feeling.

Teresa handed me a shopping list. I leaned over to kiss her cheek. She accepted the gesture but didn't reciprocate. Then she gave me a hug. The kind she reserved for her massage customers. Friendly, yet distant.

I returned with exotic fungi, meats, cheeses, and organic produce. She shooed me out of the kitchen. I sat down in the living room and tried to read my paper. It was all so strange, so much to get used to. Soon tantalizing odors floated in from the kitchen.

"Set the table, George," she called out.

Teresa brought out steaming plates from the kitchen. Filet mignon topped with melted Roquefort cheese, porcini mushrooms, and brandy. Scalloped potatoes in a cream and butter sauce. Steamed baby carrots and broccoli. A fine Jordan cabernet. Not a dieter's dinner, but what the hell. Best meal I had had in years.

Teresa turned out to be a perfect dinner companion, asking

polite questions about my work. I was in the middle of a snore-inducing case related to a patent on some genome sequence. I tended to fall asleep in front of my computer. Had a hell of a time explaining the details to her. Yet soon I was chattering away. And she actually seemed interested.

I found tension flowing right out of my body. I was enjoying watching her pretty, animated face, flashes of mischief in her eyes, the slight swinging of her straight black hair, the rhythmic pressing of her nipples against her tight white blouse as she breathed.

She touched my hand. "Leave the dishes for later. I'll take care of them." Then she led me to the bedroom.

☙❧

"TAKE YOUR CLOTHES off," she said, "just as if you were going to get a massage."

I obeyed. Then I approached her.

"Be patient," she said. "We have the whole evening. Sit on the bed."

Standing by the bed, Teresa took off her shoes. She loosened her jeans and peeled them off. She unbuttoned her blouse, revealing a small white transparent lace bra. Erect dark nipples pressed against the fabric. It was as if her breasts fought to free themselves from their restraints. Her cleavage required no uplift. Then she reached behind her back, unhooked and removed the bra. Perfectly smooth, rounded, firm flesh. I could see goose bumps surrounding the nipples. A pink tattoo of a heart decorated her left breast. She stripped off her lace panties and stood in front of me stark naked.

"Now lie down," Teresa commanded. "You'll get the massage I always wanted to give you."

Once again I obeyed without protest. Teresa took those sensitive long fingers of hers, fingers I knew so well from a hundred massages, and slowly stroked my entire body. I responded. Oh, how I responded.

She smiled and said, "Not yet."

Teresa moved up beside me, pressed her body against mine, and placed my hand on her breast. But she didn't kiss me. She rolled over onto her back, directed my head down. She pressed on my head. Then she gently raised my head and guided me up and on top of her.

"Take your time," she whispered into my ear.

Fantastic. No other word for it. I rolled off her and lay on my back. I began to speak. "I—" She cut me off, pressing a delicate finger against my lips.

The rules. Those damn rules.

❦

MY LIFE FELL into a pattern, a pleasurable pattern, a beautiful pattern. Teresa proved to be far more than she promised. A goddess in bed, a no-hassle companion. She furnished the shopping list, cooked each night, tidied up after herself and even a little after me, and made love on demand. Sometimes her demand, sometimes mine. I had never been happier in my life.

We developed our little rituals. Teresa sensed I didn't much like to talk about work at dinner, yet hungered for conversation. Noticing I was an avid newspaper reader, she took up reading the paper as well. I loved politics and international news. She read, as she put it, "only articles beneath the fold." Human interest stories, lost children, exotic animals, the occasional sensational crime story. We reported to each other while eating scampi with basil and lemongrass or grilled skewered swordfish over saffron risotto. She watched little TV, preferring thick hardcover thrillers. Days turned into weeks, and weeks into months.

Teresa had a remarkably even temperament. Never a frown, a scowl, a harsh word. Did she ever have a headache?

She didn't ask for personal expense money during our first month together. She must have been spending past earnings for classes, books, gas money. Then her requests were modest.

"I'm keeping a record. I'll pay you back."

"Don't bother," I said.

"It's a matter of principle with me."

And so it was left.

I wasn't content. It was the rules. Even after months of living together, I knew nothing about her. Each morning she left the house at the same time I left for work. Classes to prepare her for a new career, I assumed. But she didn't say. Once I caught a glance of a book in the backseat of her car when she returned from her day's activities. Chemistry. Was she preparing to be a nurse? I knew I couldn't ask her.

In four months of living together she hadn't kissed me on the lips even once. The ritual hug upon leaving and returning each day. That was all. And, of course, the passionate lovemaking almost every night. But that wasn't affection. It was honest, sweaty, thrilling, satisfying sex. And only sex. Should be enough, damn it, but it left me wanting for more. But more of what? Her. She gave me her body but held back herself.

Who was this woman? Did she have a family? Never mentioned. No phone calls. I had become a PI because I've always been curious, sought answers, wanted to solve puzzles. Now I faced the biggest puzzle of my life—Teresa.

I learned to live with my discontent. The daily rewards were just too damn great to risk tampering.

❧

ONE DAY ALMOST five months to the day Teresa moved in, I entered my house after work and sensed something wrong. A feeling of emptiness. I walked into our bedroom and pulled open her drawers. Nothing. I checked the closet. Her side was empty. The bathroom cabinet had been stripped clear of all her possessions. I ran frantically from room to room, seeking out any sign of her existence. Nothing. Not even a strand of her hair. She must've spent the day packing, cleaning, and polishing. It was as if she had never been there.

I rushed outside to my car and barreled down to her old salon off Lake Merritt. Maybe a colleague of hers would have a phone number, an address, some reference to a relative. I parked by the lake, crossed the street, and approached the two-story stucco building. In the old days, as I walked to my appointment, I could see her standing in front of the large plate-glass window that faced the lake, waiting for me. I saw nothing. I hurried up the street and then climbed the stairs to the studio. A For Rent sign on the door. I knocked. No answer. I pounded on the door. No response. Then I leaned over a banister and peered into a window. The place was empty.

I collapsed in front of the door, as though life itself had drained out of me. Slowly, sanity returned. She had told me the arrangement would end. Suppose I did find her? What then? She wouldn't have taken me back. I had broken the rules by going to look for her. Nothing to do but return home. And hope. Hope for what? That her damn new profession wouldn't pan out. That she'd come back to me tail between her pretty legs. But she had no tail. And Teresa was a person who would succeed if she decided to succeed. I had to face it. It was over. For good.

ONE MONTH LATER I entered my house to find an envelope and her key on the dining room table. I ripped open the envelope. Bills and coins cascaded across the floor. Two hundred seventy-two dollars and thirty-six cents. The money I had given her for personal expenses while she lived with me. Teresa had kept records, just as she promised. I picked up the envelope and looked it over. No address. So anonymous. I fumbled for a chair and collapsed. Contact once more with Teresa brought back the hurt.

I had to find her. Perhaps watch her from a distance. I was good at surveillance. I wouldn't stalk her, but I needed one more look. It might give me closure.

Where to begin? I knew nothing about her. She had left no trace of herself in the house. Her place of work had long since closed down. I had to think back to the time we spent together. She must have made some slip, given me some clue that might help me now to find her.

I remembered something. One morning, as was our routine, I handed her the first section of the *New York Times* when I finished it. She turned the paper over to read below the fold. She spoke to herself, but out loud.

"Yes, this is the place."

"Place for what?" I asked.

"Oh, nothing, George. Just dreaming."

"About where?"

She gave me her no-nonsense look. I had broken the rules. She got up and left the table. She took the newspaper with her. Something she never did. I guess that's why I remembered the incident.

What day was that? The day after Halloween. I remembered because we had spent the previous evening in fear of an invasion of neighborhood kids begging for candy. I had forgotten to stock up. It was my responsibility, so I thought she would be mad at me. Instead Teresa made a game out of our dilemma. She had me turn off the porch light and all the lights in the living room. We hid out in our bedroom. And made passionate love. Not a bad way to spend Halloween.

I had to find that newspaper. The Web would not do, as I needed to see the front page of the *Times*'s print edition. So I huffed it over to Oakland's main library and dug into the microfilm files. And there it was. The below-the-fold area featured an article on Seattle. Halloween revelers had trashed Pioneer Square and broken the front window of a bookstore.

I called Alaska Airlines and made a reservation.

❧

I CHECKED INTO my hotel and the next morning started on my rounds. I had so little to go on. Yet I became convinced that if I persisted I would find her. I am good at what I do. And damn it, I was motivated. I needed to make up for all those months of not investigating when she lived with me. Somehow I had to find her. I would find her.

I toured the hospitals. She had studied chemistry. Maybe she had found some kind of medical technician's job. She hadn't had enough time to become a nurse. No luck. Next I toured the city's medical labs. Then biotech research facilities. I gave up on the medical profession. Perhaps her employment plans had fallen through and she had gone back to her massage work. Or at least practiced a bit on the side. I soon discovered Seattle had almost as many bodywork facilities as it had coffeehouses. Again a blind alley. Then I checked the university. Maybe she had decided to continue her education. Nothing.

Three days later, I got a new idea. Maybe I was misinterpreting the article. It was possible that Pioneer Square per se had some special meaning for her. She could have visited the place on some vacation and fallen in love with it. Everyone has their favorite haunts, where they go to sip coffee, hear music, eat. Pioneer Square could play that role in Teresa's new life. I just had to stake the place out, be patient. Give it a few days.

Situated by the waterfront, the area teemed with crowds of entertainment seekers patronizing jazz clubs, discos, restaurants, and coffee shops. A place to start.

I entered Pioneer Books. Perhaps this was where Teresa came to buy her thrillers. The store featured a large window looking out over the street. It must've been the one smashed during the riot reported in the *Times*. I could easily stand in front of it, pretending to browse the books, and watch the flow of traffic below. And so I spent the next three evenings.

Saturday night came with no results. My eyes began to glaze over as I glanced out the window into the light rain. Had to force myself to keep looking. Hardly anyone out. The trip had been a failure. I was just guessing she had gone to Seattle. I decided I would head back to the Bay Area in the morning. At least there would be sun.

I saw a man and a woman walking very slowly down the street. They passed under a streetlamp. The woman was Teresa. I'd recognize her anywhere: the hair, the shape of the body, the legs. In my mind I saw her naked, walking in the rain, water dripping from erect nipples and down her breasts, shapely legs striding confidently forward, hair bouncing on her smooth light-coffee shoulders.

She sauntered by, fully clothed, clinging to the arm of some man. Some damn man, not me. I ran out the door of the bookstore. I knew I shouldn't, but I had to follow her, find out who this man was, learn about her life now. Her life without me.

I rolled up my jacket collar against the rain, hunched my shoulders, and, sticking to the shadows from the buildings, followed. The two figures were almost out of sight. Then the light of a streetlamp silhouetted them. I quickened my pace. I could hear strains of music wafting through the air. Dixieland. "When the saints go marchin' in . . ." I shivered. My jacket soaked in moisture like a sponge.

I was gaining on them. I passed the entrance to the New Orleans Jazz Club. Trumpets roared, a clarinet soared, a trombone growled. "I want to be in that number . . ." So far she hadn't glanced back. Good.

Teresa pulled her companion to the right. Where was she taking him? There was no doorway, no coffee shop, no restaurant. An alley. Why was she maneuvering him into an alley? For a kiss? Maybe more?

Don't follow, I told myself. *You'll just torture yourself by watching.* But I didn't listen. I had to see.

I reached the alley, entered, and pressed myself against the cold wet brick, hoping the shadow would cover me. Teresa and her friend were now halfway down the alley. As my eyes accustomed themselves to the darkness, I could see her kissing him. On the lips, damn her. So she *could* be intimate.

She pressed him to her with one hand while the other reached into her brown leather shoulder bag. What was she going to do? Hand him a condom and do it right there in that alley?

Headlights from a car passing on the main street sent a shaft of light momentarily down the alley. Shiny steel. A gun. It was small yet had a long barrel. A silencer. She placed the gun against her companion's temple. I heard a pop. Kind of like the slap of a book closing. The man crumpled to the ground. She leaned over, placed the gun directly against his forehead, and fired again. Then she looked up. She saw me.

"You shouldn't have followed me," she said in an emotionless, neutral voice. She walked toward me. "You have broken all the rules. Why?"

"I . . . I couldn't help myself."

"So now you know."

"Know what?"

"What I trained myself for when I lived with you."

"You're serious?"

"Pays better than massages, much better. I learned that the main qualification for this profession is to possess a certain detachment. My strength. Our arrangement gave me an opportunity to read up on weapons, train at a firing range, study forensics at the university, the latest techniques in DNA analysis, fabric fragments, dust."

"My house. You left it so clean."

"Not a fingerprint, not a strand of hair, not a fiber."

I didn't like the look in her eyes. The coldness. Completely disengaged. She hadn't changed. I had imposed upon her a romantic image of my own creation.

"I made one mistake," she said. "I misjudged you. I thought you could be as detached as I was. Men always claim that they want sex without complications. That's exactly what I offered you. But you wanted more. This does cause a complication now."

"What are you going to do?"

"I'm a professional."

Teresa pointed her gun at my head and began to pull the trigger.

Rage overcame fear. Damn it! She was going to kill me for loving her. But not without a fight. I had been an MP in the army, then a city cop. I knew guns. Hers was a .22-caliber tar-get pistol. Subsonic velocity. Good for close-up assassinations, but it had a slow trigger movement. I had less than a second.

I bashed her hand to the side and ducked. She fired. Missed. She had made two mistakes. I bent her arm back until the gun fell to the ground. Then I smashed her across the face with my fist and knocked her down. I picked up her gun and pressed it to her temple.

"How does that feel?"

"Exhilarating."

The first sign of real feeling I had seen in this lady. I shook my head, got up off her, and walked away. When I reached the end of the alley, I turned. She wasn't there. I knew I should re-port the murder to the police, turn her in. That's what she would have done if it suited her purposes. She was detached. I wasn't. We were different inside.

I crossed the road, walked to the shore, wiped off the gun's grip, and tossed it into Puget Sound.

A FEW SMALL REPAIRS

JEFF ABBOTT

FRANK KNEW HE wasn't a good son. His father wasn't a good father. But here he stood, in the old man's hospital room, ready to say hello and good-bye. The disinfectant, the soft rose-scented soap the nurse used, and the reek of the old man dying were all strong in the air. He leaned his face into the flower arrangement his sister insisted he bring and breathed in the scent of the roses, because he suddenly felt dizzy.

"Look who's here!" the nurse said in a voice of pretended gusto and Frank knew he had been discussed. Or complained about. She hurried to the CD player, clicked off the soft trill of a classical violin. Frank had no idea who wrote the music, but he was sure it was his brother, Greg, playing the strings.

"Hello, Trouble," Daddy said. Using Frank's old nickname, as though it hadn't been five long years.

"Hey, Daddy." Frank put the flowers on the table, took off his baseball cap, clenched it in his hands.

"Good God," Daddy said. "I ain't in the funeral home yet. Put your cap back on." He offered his hand for a shake.

Frank shook hands, the old man's palm cool and dry, and stuck the cap back on.

"I'll give you some peace and quiet, Roger, so y'all can talk," the nurse said to Daddy. She patted Frank's arm as she left.

"Thank you, Therese," Daddy said. Frank folded his hands behind his back, crossed his arms, then stuck his hands in his jeans' front pockets.

Daddy glanced at the cap. "Thank God you're still a Cowboys fan."

"Yeah. Still. Always. That Greg playing?" Frank jerked his head toward the silent CD player. "I don't think I've heard that piece."

"You don't keep up with his career?"

"He doesn't keep up with mine," Frank said.

"It's Mozart's Concerto Number Three. Sydney Philharmonic. Why he couldn't play it with a good old American orchestra, I don't know. Pay the musicians here. The CD gets released next December. God, help me hang on, I say to him, so I'll see it in stores, but I've heard it now—I don't have to see all the fancy-ass packaging."

"I know you're very proud of him." He was careful to keep any bitterness from his voice. "I'm proud of him too." *Offer the first olive branch,* he told himself.

"Prouder if he got to play at a NASCAR rally or the Super Bowl halftime." Daddy gave a twitchy cough of a laugh. "Play bluegrass or western swing instead of music by European guys who wore wigs. I tell him that for the entertainment value of watching him smile and squirm all at once." He frowned. "You're standing there staring at me like I'm lying in the coffin."

Frank sat in the chair in the room's corner.

"You can pull it closer," Daddy said. "What I got ain't catching."

Frank raised his butt, dragged the chair to the side of the bed, the legs shrieking against the tile, and sat back down.

"How you been?" Daddy asked.

Frank wanted to say, *Well, the past five years have been chock-full of surprises, Daddy, but what have you ever cared?* "Everything's great," he said.

"You still with Michelle?"

"Yeah. She's good," he added, before Daddy could forget to ask.

"Y'all gonna have kids before I die?"

"No. Sorry. We like it just being us for right now."

"Too bad," Daddy said. "Children are such a blessing."

Frank said nothing. An olive branch from Daddy, but one whipping across his face.

"I'm dying, Frank. Being mad at each other, it seems a little pointless now, son."

Son. "I didn't know I was suddenly a blessing."

"You are. Jesus, Frank. I was mad at you, I didn't stop loving you."

"I don't think you've ever told me that you loved me."

"Words don't matter. I clothed you and fed you and raised you right, didn't I?" Daddy closed his eyes. He looked, literally, to Frank like half the man he used to be, sunken into the bed, his eyes bleary, his flesh sagging off his bones, his skin the color of a peeled apple.

"Being mad at me for marrying Michelle is what was pointless, Dad."

"True enough. You're still married to her, you'll be married to her when I'm dead. But I was mad at you for plenty more. Dropping out of college, getting into drugs, stealing my money. I made a list once of all your crimes against me. In case I got Alzheimer's and started to forget."

Frank ignored the jab. "Michelle and I are clean. Have been for two years now. We're both working. She got a telemarketing job. I work for a couple of lawn services." Frank said all this in a rush, as if Daddy might close his eyes and die on him before the words were spoken. "And I do temp work, and I'm trying to go back to school. For graphics production."

"I won't apologize for cutting you off when you was high, I won't, but about Michelle, I was wrong. She looks like she agrees with you. I'm sorry." He folded his hands on top of the sheet.

"Thanks. I guess."

"Sorry is sorry, Frank," Daddy said. "I said it first. Sometimes all you need to talk and get past the pain is to make a few small repairs to your relationship. I made the first one, asking you to come see me."

"Have you been watching those shrinks on TV?"

"No. A limited amount of time gives you an unlimited perspective," Daddy said.

"Okay. I'm sorry I . . . didn't talk to you."

"No one much likes talking to me these days." Daddy gave a scarecrow smile. He was smiling a lot. It wasn't from happiness, Frank thought. It made him nervous.

"Well, I'm here now."

"You sure are. I need help from you, Frank. I can't ask no one else." He pulled himself up from the bed. "Shut the door, would you? Therese got big ears."

Frank shut the door.

"I'm dying, you know that."

"Yeah."

"I got maybe a year. Maybe six months."

"Yeah."

"I'm hoping for the six months. The pain's gonna be hell. I can't take it. I need your help."

"You want me to get you a different doctor?"

"No," Daddy said. "I want you to . . . help me out of the pain."

Frank's knees went weak. "That's a nice welcome back."

"I can't ask Greg or Laura," Daddy said. "They won't do it."

"And I would help you kill yourself. That's a fine compliment."

"It's a fine reality. You could get whatever pills I needed. Enough to be sure to do the job." He coughed.

"I don't do drugs anymore."

"You know how to get them, Frank. I imagine the process is like riding a bike: you never quite forget."

"I could just shoot you in your bed. Or pull the pillow over your face."

Daddy smiled. "Well, the pillow's here and my gun's under the bed, where it always was. I'll get you a house key."

"You're serious."

"I am."

"I can't kill you."

"All those years, Frankie, you never wished once that I was dead? C'mon, I don't believe you."

"We make peace, Dad, and now you ask me to kill you? What the hell is that?"

"I told you, I can't ask Greg or Laura."

"Because they're the ones you loved. The ones you cared about, when I needed you, when I was on the streets—"

"You made the choices that put yourself in trouble," Daddy said. "Don't blame me. I never stuck a damn needle in your arm. I never shoved the coke up your nose."

"I didn't smoke all those cigarettes that gave you inoperable cancer," Frank said.

"If you could sneak a pack in here with the pills, I'd sure appreciate it," Daddy said.

"I won't do it."

"The one time I've needed you and you say no. I suppose it's sweet revenge."

"I suppose it is."

"Listen. They give me OxyContin. You get enough pills for me, they gonna think I hoarded them. I need a lot because I've built up a tolerance. But I crush them up instead of swallowing them whole, it hits all at once, no time release, I'm good and done."

"No."

"There's no danger to you."

Frank saw it then, as clear as day. "That's why you won't ask Greg or Laura. They're precious to you. I'm just a druggie embarrassment."

"Greg has a career he can't risk," Daddy said. "Laura has three kids. But it's no problem for you."

"Or to you—you're dead and I'm in bad trouble with the police. No. Forget it."

"I never asked anything of you. Not even that you be a decent human being. But I'm asking this, Frank. Help me. Please help me."

Frank stood. "I'm sorry you're dying. I'm even sorrier you want me to help you along."

"Don't leave."

"I think I better."

Daddy reached for Frank's hand, but it was too far away and Frank didn't reach out. The hand fell back to the sheet. "You better go, then. My show comes on now anyway."

"Your show."

"*The Price Is Right*. Therese got me hooked."

"I'm glad you're making the most of your time."

"Yeah, looks like I got a whole 'nother year of time. Thanks, Frank, for coming by. And for the flowers too."

Frank stood there, silent for a minute, watching his dad not look at him. *A few small repairs,* his dad had said, but he could not fix this. No. "I'll see you later if that's okay."

"Door's always open." Daddy watched a screaming contestant run from the cheering audience down to the stage.

Frank left without a backwards glance, hurrying past the smile of Therese, out into the eye-aching morning brightness of the hospital parking lot.

✦

"How did it go?" His sister, Laura, sat down at the table across from Frank in the Starbucks café, shot a warning look at her three boys wriggling at a corner table, sipping Italian sodas and coloring a book of battling ninjas.

Frank pushed a four-dollar coffee toward her. He had never been in one of these fancy coffee places before, full at ten-thirty in the morning with folks pecking at laptops, and he wondered, *What exactly do all these people do?*

"It went just fine," he said.

"Don't lie. I can tell it went badly. I told you I should have gone with you."

"No. He apologized. Sort of." He took a sip of his coffee.

"That's a step, Frank. A big step for Daddy." Laura pushed a lock of newly blond hair from her forehead, gave her oldest a pointed finger that indicated he should share his crayons.

"I guess."

"A big step for you too. Because you're equally stubborn."

"He wants to . . ." He wanted to share the awful secret of what his father had asked of him. Instead, he closed his mouth. Laura would have Daddy bound to the mattress with restraints. Or have him in a mental ward. He sipped again at the coffee.

"What?"

"I think he wants to die sooner rather than later. He's afraid of the pain. Or afraid of waiting to die. You know patience is not among his virtues."

"He'll fight to the bitter end," Laura said. "He won't let go of life easily." Her eyes widened. "Hunter! Give Tyler that blue crayon. Don't make Mama come over there."

The feud over blue ended.

"I don't think he will fight, Laura. He'll give up." He wondered now what his father would do. Enlist another ally in his own murder. Not Laura. He saw clearly as he watched her watch her kids that Daddy had moved to the edge of her life. He no longer mattered to her. He was just a process she was waiting to finish.

Laura frowned and sipped at her foam-covered coffee concoction. "He's never been a quitter."

"This might be a good time for him to start," Frank said.

"Your father called," Michelle said as soon as he came in the door from work. She was getting dressed, heading off to the beginning of her shift to call people during their meat loaf and sell mortgage refinancing packages. She had gained weight since they went clean, but it looked good on her. Watching her, he thought of them sleeping in an alley one night two years ago, the smell of spoiling kung pao chicken thick from the trash bin they rested against, desperate for fixes, his arm around her and him thinking, *She is truly nothing but bone now, there's nothing left of us, we made ourselves go away.* Thank God those days were long over.

"Did you talk to him?" Frank asked.

"Well, sure, I answered the phone."

"I mean, did you have a conversation with him?"

"Yes. He apologized for disapproving of me." She dabbed on lipstick.

"What did you say to him?"

"Thank you and I was sorry he was so sick. I was sweet as sugar. Even though he's treated you like dirt."

"We *were* dirt."

"We haven't been for a long time," she said. "He doesn't fool me, Frank. Your dad's never made an effort to make peace till now, now when everyone can feel sorry for him and say nothing but good words about him."

Frank said, "He just wanted to say he was sorry."

"Did you accept his apology?"

"Yeah. He asked me to help him die," Frank said. "To get him an overdose of painkillers."

She stared.

"I told him no," he said.

"He has some nerve," she said after a long moment of studying Frank's frown. "Or maybe he's just out of his mind with pain."

"You don't think he wants to set me up, do you? To get me in trouble if I got him the drugs?"

Michelle glanced at him. "What an insane thing to say."

"He never loved me the way he did Laura and Greg."

"No, not the same way, but I suppose he loves you in some other way."

"He needs me. I'm just taken aback by it."

"Or consider that this is just one more thing to guilt you with before he dies. He can't control death, but he can still try to control his kids."

He took her in his arms and she tilted her face to keep her makeup off his shirt. He put his face in the clean shampooed smell of her thick hair. "I told him hell no. Put it out of your mind."

❦

MICHELLE WAS AT work, interrupting dinners on the East Coast, and Frank didn't feel like watching TV. He got up from the threadbare couch, stood at the window. He pictured Laura, eating with her shiny family in the suburbs, her little boys scowling at their broccoli. Imagined Greg, asleep in Berlin or London or Oslo, spending his days thinking about songs by dead people instead of his still-living father. Thought of his father, waiting for death in that cold bed, beckoning him to bring the chair closer. Asking his son for the one and only favor he had ever asked.

Frank knew he should stay home. Heading for old haunts meant trouble, they told you that in the group meetings. But he reached for his car keys and the old stirrings and fears in his heart took hold. He drove, in a slow, teasing orbit, past the places he shadowed when he was high: a narrow street off Guadalupe near the University of Texas campus, a neighborhood in northeast Austin where a house at the far end of a circle was a pill popper's paradise, an upscale condo in West Lake Hills where a bored former beauty queen he knew as Gillian the Pillian dispensed pharmaceuticals.

I shouldn't be here, he thought as he turned into the narrow street of Gillian's condo.

It's a bad idea, he thought as he clicked off the car engine.

He has asked you to do this for every wrong reason, he thought as he rang the doorbell.

Gillian was in; she opened the door and he used an old all-clear phrase, "I forgot my cell phone."

"Long time no see, no call, so no buy. I don't think I know you anymore."

"I need your help."

"Who doesn't?" She opened the door and he walked inside. "Everybody staggers back to Gillian when life turns ugly." She spoke with the calm, assured superiority he suspected she'd learned as a high school social queen.

He decided not to say that the drugs weren't for him.

"You want a drink?" Gillian asked. She held a miniature bottle of champagne with a straw sticking up from its neck.

"No, thanks. You look great."

"Do I? You're so sweet. I cut out caffeine. I have a modicum of self-control." She laughed, played with the straw in her champagne bottle.

"Congratulations."

"So what's your poison?" she asked, and her words shook him.

"OxyContin. Say about twenty pills. How much can you get and how much would it cost?"

Gillian frowned, sipped her champagne. "The forty-mil pills, they're about thirty bucks."

Six hundred, he thought. "Okay."

"Let me make a couple of calls. Can you wait?"

"I don't need them until tomorrow. I don't have the cash with me. I just needed to know if you could get it."

Gillian frowned. "I'm not a price list, Frankie."

"I'm buying. Just tomorrow."

She jabbed her straw at the bottom of the miniature bottle. "Here's the deal. You haven't been a regular customer, and I want to be sure you're showing up here tomorrow after I've laid out the money for the shinies." She never said *pills;* it was always *shinies* or *apples* or *candies,* a child's delight.

"I'm good for it. I never stiffed you."

"You haven't done much for me lately," she said.

He slipped off his wedding ring, held it out. "Here. But I swear to you, I'm good for it."

She took the ring. "Be back here tomorrow afternoon at one. I got a dinner party for tomorrow night and I'm doing nothing but napping during the afternoon."

❧

VISITING HOURS WERE over, but Therese was not hobbled by rules, not for a son who hadn't seen his father in five years. She checked with Daddy and let Frank in; Daddy was watching an *NYPD Blue* rerun.

"Hello, Trouble," Daddy said.

Frank switched off the TV. "I thought you'd be listening to Greg's new CD."

"A man can only take so much Mozart," Daddy said.

"I reconsidered your request."

Daddy switched the television back on. "I don't want anyone to overhear."

"You're supposed to be the parent. You're supposed to be the one who takes care of me, not the other way around. But when I needed you, you turned your back on me. I never want to forgive you for that, but I guess I have to, because then I'm no better than you. And I have to be better than you. That means helping you even if you never helped me."

"You're not better than me," Daddy said. "You're exactly like me."

"Do you want my help or not? Don't insult me, Dad."

"I don't want you to kill me if you're going to take pleasure in it," Daddy said with a thin smile. "That's just wrong."

"You finally speak to me again after five years of silence, and it's to ask if I'll help you die. Tell me: how did you think that would make me feel?"

"Loved," said Daddy.

Frank sank into the chair.

"I can't ask Laura or Greg. Well, Greg's never here. I gave up buying beer for all those music lessons, and what did it get me? A boy who thinks more of the rest of the world than he does his own dad. Laura's not a doer. She talks you to death. You see her with those boys? They'll walk all over her when they're older, and she'll be grateful for even that lousy scrap of attention from them. It makes me sick." Daddy opened his eyes. "But you. You understand me."

"I don't think I do. I don't think I could." Frank's voice was hoarse. "Can I sit here and watch TV with you? For just a while?"

"Sure," Daddy said. "Move the chair closer."

❧

HE GOT THE six hundred from Laura by telling her he wanted to spring for presents for Daddy.

"You gave him a present by going to see him, hon," Laura said. Her husband, Brad, nodded, which seemed his response to any statement of Laura's.

"I missed five years of birthdays and Father's Days and Christmases," he said. "I just want to get him a nice gift. I'll pay you back. I promise. I just got on with another lawn service. It starts on Monday." And he had; that was truth. The job was temp only, but he could pay Laura back in dribbles of cash. Michelle might never notice.

"I know you're good for it," Laura said. Brad nodded.

"Hunter! Put that stick down!" she yelled over Frank's shoul-

der. "You do not pretend to kill your brother. Mommy doesn't
like that!" She smiled at Frank. "Do you need to know Daddy's
sizes? They're not far off from Brad's."

Brad nodded and Frank said, "Yeah, Laura, that sounds fine."

"'Shiny . . . happy . . . people,'" Gillian sang as she
plinked the OxyContins, a few at a time, into a cup of foil. She
topped the pills with a blueberry muffin, closed the wrap over the
pastry and his father's overdose, and said, "You're good to go."

"Thanks." He handed her the money; she counted it twice,
fast, with a tongue-wet finger. She tucked it into the back
pocket of her designer jeans.

"Can I ask you a question?" she said, her voice suddenly low,
suddenly shy.

"Yeah."

"You were Mr. Clean for a long while. Why'd you give it up?"

He knew he should lie; Daddy's death would be on the news
simply because of his brother's fame, and his last name was
Montgomery, not an unusual name. But she wouldn't make the
connection between him and an old dead man named Roger
Montgomery.

"What you think your life should be is never all it's cracked
up to be," he said, remembering his father's words. "Sometimes
you need"—he shook the bag—"a few small repairs."

He stopped by the store; he bought cigarettes and a six-pack
of chocolate pudding. He knew his father liked butterscotch
better, but he thought the crushed powder of the pills would be
easier to see in the lighter-colored pudding. He put the pills in

his right blue jeans pocket, and he carried the pudding and the cigarettes in a paper grocery bag.

Daddy was reading the newspaper and listening to Greg play Vivaldi on last year's CD. He closed the paper when Frank walked in.

"Let's go for a walk," Frank said.

"Okay," Daddy said.

He eased his father into the wheelchair and headed outside. The sun flirted with the thin wisps of clouds. It was cool and Daddy shivered under his burnt orange Windbreaker.

"I got your few small repairs," Frank said.

"Ah. That's one way of looking at them. Thank you."

"Cigarettes too."

"I'm not sure which to be more grateful for. Fire me up, would you, son?"

Frank lit a smoke, handed it to his father.

"Therese isn't here today," Daddy said. "They got an ex-Nazi up there named Bernice. She'll shoot us both if she sees me smoking."

"Another solution to your problem."

Daddy exhaled, coughed, his eyes watered. "Sweet Jesus, that's a-okay." He spat in the grass. "I want you to know I liked you best of all three of my kids. I love you all equally. But I liked you the best."

"You never told me."

"It's not a truth you can announce. Being terminally ill gives you a free pass."

"Dad. Why didn't you ever come help me?"

Daddy blew out a feather of smoke. "You had to decide to save your own ass. Nothing I said would have pulled you from the gutter."

"We'll never know." But the bitterness he felt was gone, burned away like a cloud on a summer day.

"You see me lying in that bed, knowing it's the spot where I die, and you pity me. You don't want to see me suffer, because it hurts. Well, I couldn't watch you destroying yourself. I'm weak."

"When will you take the pills?"

"Tonight. After midnight. Nazi Bernice slinks back to her cave."

"They might suspect I helped you."

"I'll leave a note. Make it clear this was my doing. No one will blame you."

"Don't do this," Frank said.

"You lose me sooner or later, and later hurts a lot more."

"But later's more time. More time together." He touched his father's shoulder. He didn't know what else to do.

"All right, Trouble," Daddy said. He reached up, closed his hand over Frank's wrist. He blinked up at the sky. "I'll wait. I'll wait a while for your sake."

They ate the chocolate pudding in the plaza and smoked another cigarette, then he wheeled his father back into the hospital. Frank went home with the pills in his pocket.

Six weeks later the pain won. It was pain that felt like it snapped bone and boiled blood and short-circuited brains, and one night Frank came back with pudding and pills.

He sat next to his father and he crushed the pills into the thick pudding.

"Chocolate as a last meal," Daddy said. "I could do worse." He closed his eyes. "If anyone asks, I asked you to bring the pudding. You didn't know about the pills."

"I know," Frank said. He powdered a pill into the glop, stirred it into the plastic cup. The smell of the chocolate made him queasy.

Daddy's voice sounded like a hoarse whisper coming from a crack in stone. "Tell everyone I was happy when you saw me last."

"Sure."

Daddy closed his eyes. "If you'll just leave it all on the tray, son." Like it was just a dessert he wasn't ready to finish.

"Sure. Can you do this? Yourself?"

Daddy opened his eyes. "You gonna give me a little shove? That's nice of you."

"I just . . ." Frank stopped. He wanted to be selfish, to say, *Please don't, please don't, please don't do this.*

Daddy handed him two pills. "I palmed these this week. Tuck them in my sock drawer. Therese and the docs'll think I collected the overdose over time."

Frank slid two pills under the heap of his father's socks. It made him think of laying flowers on a grave, and his hand shook. He sat back in his chair.

"Okay, then," Daddy said. "I'm ready for my snack. You better go."

"Okay," Frank said. He didn't get up.

Daddy reached over and took his hand. "Be a brave boy now."

Frank stood, unsteady. He leaned down and kissed his father's forehead, then his cheek. The skin was already cooler than it should be.

"Frank."

"Yes."

"You're a mighty fine son."

"Dad . . ."

"Don't say it. We'll both get sad and it just makes going that much harder."

"Okay."

"You better go, Trouble." He let go of Frank's hand and Frank stood and walked out the door, down the corridor past the farewell smile of Therese and out into the cool, living wet of the night.

❦

FRANK WENT HOME and waited. Tonight Michelle worked the dial-during-dinner shift, calling the Pacific coast. He expected a phone call from the hospice, especially if Therese had tucked into his father's room and seen him swallowing a personal pharmacy. But the phone remained silent.

The ten o'clock news came on and the lead was about Gillian the Pillian. It showed her being arrested, led out of the rich-girl condo in handcuffs, her head averted. The reporter's voice-over announced that Gillian Burke, a former Miss Texas finalist, had been arrested and accused of dealing illicit narcotics, mostly painkillers. She was said to be cooperating completely with authorities, and it was suspected that Ms. Burke could provide evidence against a large number of prescription-pill abusers, including well-known people in Austin. She was a friend of the governor's wife; they had been in pageants together ten years back.

Frank sat down, his bones feeling as loose as water. Gillian would talk. She'd scream out every entry in her little black book because she was still the high school goddess—her customers were the losers, not her. He sat on the edge of the bed, wondering what he would tell Michelle. Why had he done it? Because love was not just support. Love was sacrifice. Love was making a few small repairs when they were needed.

Two hours later, the knock on the door came at the same time the phone rang. He stood up. Knock. Ring. Knock. Ring.

Frank reached for the phone, clicked it on as he walked toward the screen door, seeing the policemen waiting on the other side of the plastic, and heard his sister sobbing on the other end of the line as he reached for the doorknob.

CHELLINI'S SOLUTION

JIM FUSILLI

CHELLINI WAS MUCH younger than he seemed. A Sicilian wife, bubbly six-year-old twin daughters, and perpetually aching feet conspired to deprive him of the swagger customary to men from the Puglia region of Italy. So too did a rotund frame, legs that were slightly bowed, and a floppy gray mustache he grew shortly after his discharge from the U.S. Army Air Force in '46. At the time, just seven years ago, the mustache was a deep brown.

Chellini did his best to meet life with a shrug, as would befit a man from a sunny southern province, though life in postwar America was maybe a bit hectic for his tastes, what with his sharp-tongued Lydia, their mischievous daughters, and his job as a waiter in an Italian restaurant near the National Broadcasting Company in Rockefeller Center. Despite the hubbub, he himself kept quiet and sought what he would call uneventfulness. He had no ambitions, save a desire for abundant happiness for his daughters and for Lydia to love him as she once did.

Chellini had a pet bulldog, Ambrose, with whom he shared a slow, labored gait. Each night, after a clattering dinner during which Ava and Rita amused each other and Lydia reminded him of the dreary life he provided, Chellini would wander the cobblestone streets of his mile-square New Jersey town in search of serenity and equilibrium. With Ambrose at his side, he would drift into his own agreeable fantasies, which consisted of little more than sitting under an olive tree in Bovino, straw between his teeth, a manageable herd of goats feeding nearby, white almond blossoms blooming at the lip of the field, and his little family enjoying the stone house in which he was raised.

Chellini would often lose track of time during his nightly sojourns and return home as Lydia slept, her back to his side of their bed. While Ambrose slurped his water, Chellini would tiptoe toward his daughters' bed in the living room and kiss them on the palm of the hand, which he would then close to a fist so they would have a token of his devotion as soon as they awoke. Then he would retire to his room and hope for streams of moonlight and tranquil dreams of Lydia as the bright-eyed girl from Ragusa who had shyly accepted his invitation to dance.

One night not long ago, Chellini found he had returned to the Italian quarter much sooner than he had intended, and he passed Tartuffo's, the cigar store where a group of neighborhood men congregated. On such a pleasant, summerlike evening, the crowd of hardscrabble brown-skinned thugs of one sort or another sat outside the store and played penny-a-point gin and smoked cheroots. Unlike Chellini, most of these dubious men had emigrated to the United States after the war; some had served in Mussolini's army and others remained at home and willingly suffered the indignity of the German occupation.

Chellini preferred to avoid them, as they were not merely argumentative but bitter. He considered them lazy malcontents who pronounced big schemes but took no action when action was needed, thus allowing the Nazis to steal their homes, their women, and their pride.

A voice reached Chellini on the other side of the narrow street.

"Chellini, *dove andate?*"

Of course, it was the man he respected least who had addressed him.

"Chellini, I'm speaking to you," said Emilio Marzano, whose accent revealed him to be from the Liguria region, though he sought to portray a Sicilian tough. "What do you think? I want to talk to your dog?"

The other men laughed with a dark, superior tone.

Under the streetlamp's dull violet light, Chellini stopped, tipped his fedora, and continued walking, Ambrose chugging along at his side.

The men whispered to each other as if sharing a secret. Tartuffo, the impossibly fat store owner and chief of the local numbers racket, flicked his thumb dismissively at Chellini, shaking his mammoth head.

"Hey, war hero," Marzano said with an air of derision. "Wait."

Marzano climbed out of his chair and, though he was built as if cut from the same stubby, thickset mold as Chellini, he tried to affect a strut. On Marzano's skull was a brown cap festooned with colorful buttons of various trade unions and social organizations with which he was associated. He ran a carting business, and what needed removal ended up in his rattling truck for a trip to the city dump. This was said to include Mrs. Feduza's rabid dog, Benny, and the thieving iceman, Stucchi.

"Chellini, what's with you? You can't be a friend?"

As Ambrose sniffed disapprovingly at Marzano's soiled shoes, Chellini shrugged.

"Listen to me. It's about Lydia. Your wife."

Chellini scratched the underside of his chin. Lydia, he knew, bought her many movie magazines at the candy store, and her Chesterfields. With a nature as outgoing as Chellini's was not, she was bound to be known by Tartuffo, Marzano, and the others.

Marzano shifted to give his associates a better view. "I have to say it's not pleasant."

Chellini began to walk away, Ambrose in his wake.

Said Marzano, a snicker in his voice, "Don't you want to know his name?"

THE FOLLOWING MORNING, after dropping his daughters at St. Francis, Chellini returned to the Italian quarter and sat in Columbus Park rather than taking the tubes to his job. As pigeons pecked at the dog biscuit he'd crumpled for their pleasure, he stared at the tattered brownstone in which he lived, and he considered a strategy.

To his mind, there was no doubt Marzano was telling the truth. Chellini knew a few small-minded sharpies in the Sixty-fourth Fighter Wing, and they took a wicked pleasure from others' misfortunes—far more than from a practical joke. These minor-league mafiosi sitting on their old kitchen chairs outside Tartuffo's seemed no different than those wise guys, and surely they were no better, even if they were Italian.

At a few minutes short of ten o'clock, the man who would turn out to be Hans Koppel arrived, and he kicked up the steps with a confidence that suggested he had been there before. A moment later, perhaps two, Lydia, still in the snug housedress she wore during their typically rancorous breakfast, pulled the shades on the third-floor window that faced the vest-pocket park. When she reappeared after thirty minutes had passed, she was wearing a slip Chellini didn't recognize, the kind that barely contained her ample breasts. Lydia's curly black hair was thoroughly disheveled, and Chellini thought he detected, beneath the veneer of caution, a hint of nefarious satisfaction that perhaps spoke of revenge.

As the pigeons happily fed, Chellini concluded that action was required—action of a kind that would provide a thorough solution to his unexpected dilemma. By the time his rival had departed the brownstone, Chellini had devised his plan.

Leaving the park, Chellini fell in behind Koppel, a thin man with blond, slicked-back hair who wore wire-rimmed glasses, an expertly cut brown double-breasted suit, and an apple red silk tie. Before flagging a bus to return him to the Port Authority in Manhattan, Koppel stopped briefly in a storefront with a State Farm sticker in the window and a ding bell on the door frame. Chellini watched as he was greeted warmly by a similarly dressed man, the proprietor, Aichberger, no doubt, who gave Koppel an accordion folder stout with papers. Their conversation ended with the proprietor's joke, and both men laughed as the blond secretary in kelly green tittered and blushed.

When Koppel took his seat on the New York–bound bus, Chellini was several rows behind him. When Koppel rode the subway uptown, Chellini was in the same car.

❧

WHEN KOPPEL LEFT the IRT station, Chellini listened as he paused for a brief conversation with an elderly couple, conducted entirely in German. Crossing 86th Street, Koppel greeted, in German also, the milky-eyed counterman at the Ideal Diner and took for lunch two eggs sunny-side up, a bauernwurst, and red cabbage, which he washed down with a Schlitz and a black coffee while Chellini waited, hidden by the hood of a '49 Buick Super, baby blue.

Now, as Koppel paid his tab, Chellini nodded knowingly and departed, calculating his return to the tubes at Herald Square so as to guarantee that he would arrive home as always, via the same route and unlocking the door at the same time, lifting Ava and Rita as they leaped into his arms, screaming, "Papa, Papa," one louder than the next.

❧

LYDIA SAID, "WHAT? No tips?"

Three seconds in the door, and Chellini had already made his first mistake. The roll of bills and the loose coins he dropped into the cookie jar were no greater than they had been this morning, and in fact were short the cost of the bus, the hot dog and orangeade Chellini consumed at Nedicks on 34th, and a few pennies spent here and there.

The twins' cheery stampede relieved Chellini of constructing a lie.

"I know you don't gamble, Chellini," Lydia said in Italian, hands on her generous hips, bare feet clutching the linoleum. "You couldn't tolerate the excitement."

"Papa, Papa," yelled the gleeful twins.

Chellini went off to examine the drawings they'd made at school.

"That's right," Lydia squealed. "Go, go, why don't you? Why should you talk to me? I'm only your wife. Mother of those two . . . Those two! Go, Chellini. Just go."

The breaded pork chops she dropped before him that evening were especially leatherlike, and the chianti was moments away from completing its conversion to vinegar. Fortunately, the bread was fresh and still had its two heels, so both girls were satisfied.

Lydia, not so.

"Chellini, I want to go to the Avalon on Friday night," she announced.

Chellini had put on a fresh undershirt and had applied a balm to the wounds from the strafing he'd suffered over the Adriatic.

"Kirk Douglas, Lana Turner, Gloria Grahame, Gilbert Roland. Dick Powell. *The Bad and the Beautiful.* Chellini."

Chellini shrugged. Perhaps now was not the time to tell his wife that the actor Powell sauntered over from NBC to eat at one of his tables at least twice a week. Powell tipped like he'd just won the sweepstakes. The fist-size meatballs and bland sausages made him smile.

"Chellini. I am twenty-four years old, and I was not born to slave in this kitchen. I need to live, Chellini. To live!"

Her voice made the glasses ring, and when she shouted the veins in her neck threatened to burst.

Meanwhile, Rita frowned severely, comically, and mocked her mother's diatribe by bobbing her head and silently flapping her jaw. Ava put her hands over her eyes to prevent an outburst of laughter.

"Chellini, if you don't give to me a life, I am going to show you something you won't forget!"

Lydia had a skillet in her hand. Burnt clumps of breading clung to its surface.

"Chellini. Speak to me!"

Chellini shrugged. He had nothing to say. New knowledge had put him in a weak position.

Resigned, Lydia resumed her chores, sprinkling soap powder onto the rushing water. Chellini pushed back his plate and threw down the last of the tart wine.

As if on cue, Ambrose rose up, shook himself awake, and waddled off to retrieve his leash.

⤳⤜⤛

WAITING IN THE shadows under the viaduct, Chellini watched as Marzano leaped from behind the driver's wheel to unlock and open the garage doors, then climbed back up to manipulate his empty truck until it was snug inside the bay.

As Chellini approached, Ambrose toddling too, he wondered if the blood of the missing Stucchi had once stained the concrete floor.

Marzano was more than surprised to find a visitor in the darkness. "Mother of God!" he shouted in Italian. "Chellini, you put a fright in me!"

Ambrose growled from his belly.

"And that dog of yours! What a disposition! Miserable!"

Marzano turned his back on Chellini as he secured the lock and yanked on the knob for good measure.

Not exactly Fort Knox, Chellini thought.

Adjusting his cap and hitching up his floppy slacks, Marzano shoved his hands in his pockets and started his walk south to the Italian quarter some six blocks away.

Chellini stood still, as did Ambrose.

Marzano stopped. "You want to talk, Chellini?"

Chellini looked at the rubbish beneath his feet.

Marzano tilted his head as he returned. "Has this to do with Lydia?"

Chellini nodded.

Marzano wiped his brown lips with the back of his grimy hand. "Well?"

Chellini said, *"Grupo Azione Patrioti."*

Marzano frowned. *"Grupo Azione Patrioti,"* he repeated. "The GAP?"

As he nodded, Chellini saw that Marzano had begun to understand.

"You're saying to me this motherless bastard is a Nazi?" Marzano asked, as he stepped into the black space Chellini and Ambrose now occupied. The smell of urine and gasoline surrounded them.

Chellini shrugged.

If the light had permitted, Chellini would have seen that Marzano's neck and ears were now bright red. His heart was racing inside his chest.

"The Nazis," he said, "they raped my sister."

Chellini thought this unlikely, though it was a tale Marzano repeated often in the neighborhood. His sister had no doubt taken a Nazi lover, if only for the food and security he could provide. Regrettably, many confused young women had, and not only in San Remo, Marzano's birthplace and former home.

"They made a mockery of us," he continued, jabbing himself in the chest with a stiff finger, which he then pointed toward the sky.

Ambrose was sniffing the dirt, exhuming messages from countless dogs who had preceded him to this spot.

Marzano put his right hand over his heart. "I pledged myself to the GAP," he said, adding, "even though I was too young to participate."

Also not true. Marzano was at least thirty-five years old, perhaps forty. The GAP, a unit of the marginally organized partisan movement in Italy, had recruited teenage boys when necessary to resist the Nazi occupation. Marzano would have been well into his twenties when the Nazis arrived.

"And now this godless pig is here! Taking our women again! And who knows how many?"

Chellini shrugged, though now the gesture suggested Marzano had summarized the situation with admirable insight.

"Leave everything to me," Marzano said, tapping Chellini on the shoulder. "It will be a pleasure. Hell, I do it for free."

Chellini nodded, but as Marzano began to walk away, he called to him.

Again, Marzano stopped and peered into the darkness.

Chellini said, *"Avrete bisogno di una lama splendida."*

Marzano stroked his chin. "A superb knife, eh?" He smiled knowingly. "Revenge with a twist, Chellini. Clever man!"

THE FOLLOWING MORNING, Chellini took the tubes to Christopher Street in Greenwich Village and zigzagged until he arrived at Canal Street, avoiding Little Italy in case someone might recognize him as the bombardier who had returned to Puglia to dispatch the Germans.

The barber who shaved off his mustache was a Chinaman, and Chellini could not understand a single word he said. But the man knew his craft and Chellini left satisfied, a mysterious Oriental astringent causing the naked skin above his lip to tingle.

At an army surplus shop off Baxter Street, he bought a bayonet that had belonged to one of Mussolini's fascist troops. A restaurant supply store on the Bowery willingly sharpened it to a razor's edge for a modest fee that did not include a dizzying conversation with a Polish Jew who tried to sell Chellini an enormous refrigerator. Defeated by silence, the insistent salesman then pressed Chellini on the origins of the brown cap the Italian had placed on the counter and the meaning of its array of colorful buttons.

Escaping without comment, Chellini tossed his old hat under a beat-up Oldsmobile on Delancey Street, and the nonsensical buttons he'd purchased at Herald Square the day before went down a subway grate to rest among gum wrappers, beer bottle tops, and what seemed to be thousands of cigarette butts.

The IRT and a crosstown bus delivered Chellini to the restaurant a few minutes later than usual, but his missing mustache seemed to provide an excuse, especially when some gentle ribbing from his colleagues ensued, and so his accordion-playing boss said nothing. With the bayonet hidden in his locker, Chellini went to work and soon his section was crowded with visitors from Wisconsin, Pennsylvania, and even California, none of whom seemed to know that what they happily consumed bore no resemblance to what was served in any region of Italy.

Close to the end of his shift, the actor Powell arrived. He complimented Chellini on his altered appearance. In a voice familiar to millions of moviegoers and, these days, fans of radio's *Richard Diamond, Private Detective,* Powell told Chellini he looked like a new, younger man.

Powell's customary generous tip more than covered the cost of the shave, the bayonet, the sharpening, and the additional transportation.

❦

"Papa, Pa—"

Ava and Rita stopped as if suddenly frozen. They glared at their father's face. Never before had they seen him without his mustache.

Lydia, meanwhile, looked at Chellini and was impressed. He seemed almost handsome, and certainly younger. But she would not admit it.

"Big experiment," she muttered in Italian.

Ambrose opened one eye and, unmoved, immediately shut it.

CHELLINI DROPPED THE money in the cookie jar and went to his knees so his daughters could examine his new face. They did so with warm, curious fingers.

A moment later, Chellini stood. "Going out," he said, as he went toward the bedroom.

Lydia's voice followed him as he reached into his tool chest, stored at the rear of his clothes closet.

"Such an outburst, Chellini! A new face and now you are a talking man! But Chellini, the door is the other way if you're going to go."

Now he had in his jacket a screwdriver, a bayonet, and a few slips of paper, and he was grateful his daughters didn't ask if they could accompany him. They were busy discussing his appearance. Rita seemed in favor, Ava opposed.

"Go, Chellini. Go before you change your mind!" added Lydia.

And Chellini went.

CHELLINI RARELY RECALLED his years in the Army Air Force, though he served in the war with a valor he saw as customary among the men of the Sixty-fourth stationed in San Severo. His bombs struck harbors, submarine pens, bridges and trains and fuel dumps—entirely a team effort, of course—and a strafing by a Messerschmitt BF 109 had ripped open his shoulder. But his wounds were minimal, and he did not consider himself a hero. Their copilot was killed on that fateful run: a convivial boy from Iowa named Leonard McMillan with whom Chellini had taken coffee before the mission began. Chellini considered the redheaded McMillan a hero: he suffered the night sweats and was terrified at takeoff, and yet he fought with courage and ferocity for his country and family back home.

Once the men and women in Puglia learned that Chellini, one of their own, was serving to protect them and give them back their homeland, the legend of the Hero of San Severo was born. The army heard of it, and while Chellini recovered from his wounds, his mother was brought from Bovino to his bedside, where she served him chicken with turnip tops, his boyhood favorite. A photo, provided by Army Public Relations, appeared in the *Journal-American* and soon the gaunt Chellini, swaddled in bandages, was famous stateside too, if only among natives of Italy who lived in or near New York City.

Now, as he approached Marzano's garage, Chellini recalled that Lydia had put the newspaper clipping in her hope chest. It had been given to her by Father Gregorio, who introduced them at the dance at St. Francis. Removing the Phillips head screwdriver from his pocket, Chellini wondered if the yellowing newspaper clipping was still there, tucked among her linens and the white lace of her secondhand wedding dress.

Following a few twists of the wrist, Chellini stepped inside the darkened bay. Calculating where the truck's headlights would shine, he affixed the bayonet to the wall—also an easy task since a protruding nail allowed him to hang it at eye level. The scent of motor oil and the rumble of traffic on the viaduct enveloping him, Chellini then buried in a crowded trash can the receipts from the army surplus and restaurant supply stores. Returning to the twilight, he put the lock plate back in its place and he departed, dusting his hands. Despite his aching feet, he walked at a pace that would have taxed Ambrose had he accompanied Chellini on his task.

THEY FOUND HANS Koppel with his throat slashed—"ear to ear," according to a grisly story on page five of the morning edition of the *Daily News*—in his apartment on 89th Street, between First and York avenues. The German's blood had oozed through the floorboards and saturated the ceiling of the apartment below. The New York City Police were notified after Koppel's downstairs neighbor found vivid red stains on the white fur of her Turkish Angora cat, Geli.

That very same evening, the tabloid carried the headline "Italian Resistance Fighter Nabbed," and made note of an anonymous tip received by police. The receipts were located at Marzano's garage, and the countermen at the army surplus and restaurant supply stores remembered a squat, clean-shaven Italian man with a brown cap festooned with buttons.

Marzano's fingerprints were found on the bayonet, which he foolishly kept at his apartment. Koppel's blood had splattered onto his already soiled shoes.

Marzano told the cops he had no regrets. He killed the German, the *Daily News* reported, to restore the honor of all Italian women. Marzano declared that he had been a passionate partisan in San Remo, where the Nazis raped and defiled women, and his taste for revenge did not end with the armistice.

This seemed to explain, at least to the satisfaction of the *Daily News,* why Marzano carved the letters "GAP" into Koppel's forehead.

Toward the end of its article, the newspaper speculated that there would be a faction among New York City's Italian community that would declare Marzano a hero for his bold determination, and suggested Hans Koppel was active in the movement to revive the Bund in the neighborhood where the Brownshirts had once paraded.

The Hero of Yorkville, Chellini mused. *Emilio Marzano.*

The man had served his purpose. *Let him be a champion, as long as he remains behind bars.*

Later that night, as magenta clouds streaked the starless sky, Chellini, with Ambrose in tow, concluded his walk by passing the cigar store. As he peered across the street at the rabble playing cards, sipping jug wine, and avoiding conversation about Marzano, the man all of them now would claim never to have met, Chellini allowed his tired eyes to find the fat crook Tartuffo.

After a moment's consideration, Tartuffo bowed his enormous head.

Chellini silently accepted the gesture, and he and Ambrose moved on, man and bulldog with an almost imperceptible bounce of pride in their step.

❧

ANY ILLUSION LYDIA harbored that the murder of Koppel by Marzano had been a coincidence was dispatched by the time Chellini returned.

Though it was after eleven o'clock, espresso brewed on the stove, and fried bowties dusted with powdered sugar sat in a dish at the center of the kitchen table. The frilly tablecloth was one Chellini had not seen in years.

"Chellini?" said Lydia, hopefully.

While Ambrose glugged his water, Chellini visited his daughters, gently closing their fingers around his kiss. For a moment, he allowed himself the pleasure attendant in the thought that he had saved his family.

By the time he returned, a tiny cup of the rich, aromatic coffee sat in front of his seat.

Chellini took his place. With a sweep of his hand, he gestured for his wife to join him.

She did so, humbly.

"Chellini."

He took no satisfaction from her fear—in Chellini's mind, love could not exist where trepidation reigned—but he did not immediately reply.

The circular lamp overhead flickered unevenly, and soon they both could hear its buzz.

Chellini took a sip of the espresso.

He nodded his approval and gestured for his bride to take some coffee for herself.

"*Grazie*, Chellini," she said as she filled her cup, all the while keeping her eyes on his.

Chellini waited.

"Lydia," he said finally, as he reached into his vest pocket.

He withdrew a slip of paper and he slid it toward his wife, whose solemnity dominated the little room.

She unfolded the sheet.

"*Lydia,*" it read, "*your husband loves you.*"

Chellini watched as she read the salutation and signature.

"*Your friend, Dick Powell.*"

Chellini reached for a cookie.

"Your Friday movie," he said. "At what time do we go?"

Stunned, Lydia could not respond.

As she stared at the note, young Chellini dropped his hand under the table.

Ambrose happily licked the sugar from his fingertips.

ONE TRUE LOVE

LAURA LIPPMAN

HIS FACE DIDN'T register at first. Probably hers didn't either. It wasn't a face-oriented business, strange to say. In the early days, on the streets, she had made a point of studying the men's faces as a means of protection. Not because she thought she'd ever be downtown, picking someone out of a lineup. Quite the opposite. If she wasn't careful, if she didn't size them up beforehand, she'd be on a gurney in the morgue and no one would give a shit. Certainly not Val, although he'd be pissed in principle at being deprived of anything he considered his property. And though Brad thought he loved her, dead was dead. Who needed postmortem devotion?

So she had learned to look closely at her potential customers. Sometimes just the act of that intense scrutiny was enough to fluster a man and he moved on, which was the paradoxical proof that he was okay. Others stared back, welcoming her gaze, inviting it. That kind really creeped her out. You wanted nervous, but not *too* nervous; any trace of self-loathing was a big tip. In the end, she had probably walked away from more harmless ones than not, guys whose problems were noth-

ing more than a losing card in the great genetics lottery—dry
lips, a dead eye, or that bad skin that always seemed to signal
villainy, perhaps because of all the acne-pitted bad guys in bad
movies. Goes to show what filmmakers knew; Val's face
couldn't be smoother. Still, she never regretted her vigilance,
although she had paid for it in the short run, taking the beat-
ings that were her due when she didn't meet Val's quotas. But
she was alive and no one raised a hand to her anymore, not unless they paid handsomely for that privilege. She had come a
long way.

Twenty-seven miles, to be precise, for that was the distance
from where her son had been conceived in a motel that charged
by the hour and the suburban soccer field where he was now
playing forward for the Sherwood Forest Robin Hoods. He was
good, and not just motherly pride good, but truly skilled, fleet
and lithe. Over the years she had convinced herself that he bore
no resemblance to his father, an illusion that allowed her to
enjoy unqualified delight in his long limbs, his bright red hair
and freckles. Scott was Scott, hers alone. Not in a smothering
way, far from it. But when he was present no one else mattered
to her. At these weekend games, she stayed tightly focused on
him. It was appalling, in her private opinion, that some other
mothers and fathers barely followed the game, chatting on their
cell phones or to one another. And during the breaks, when she
did try to make conversation, it was unbearably shallow. She
wanted to talk about the things she read in the *Economist* or
heard on NPR, things she had to know to keep up with her
clientele. They wanted to talk about aphids and restaurants. It
was a relief when the game resumed and she no longer had to
make the effort.

She never would have noticed the father on the other side of
the field if his son hadn't collided with Scott, one of those heart-

stopping, freeze-frame moments in which one part of your brain insists it's okay even as another part helpfully supplies all the worst-case scenarios. Stitches, concussion, paralysis. Play was suspended and she went flying across the still-dewy grass. Adrenaline seemed to heighten all her senses, taking her out of herself, so she was aware of how she looked. She was equally aware of the frumpy, overweight blond mother who commented to a washed-out redhead: "Can you believe she's wearing Tods and Prada slacks to a kids' soccer game?" But she wasn't the kind to go around in yoga pants and track suits, although she actually practiced yoga and ran every morning.

Scott was all right, thank God. So was the other boy. Their egos were more bruised than their bodies, so they staggered around a bit, exaggerating their injuries for the benefit of their teammates. It was only polite to introduce herself to the father, to stick out her hand and say: "Heloise Lewis."

"Bill Carroll," he said. "Eloise?"

"Heloise. As in 'hints from.'"

He shook her hand. She had recognized him the moment he said his name, for he was a credit card customer, William F. Carroll. He had needed a second more, but then he knew her as Jane Smith. Not terribly original, but it did the job. Someone had to be named Jane Smith, and it was so bogusly fake that it seemed more real as a result.

"Heloise," he repeated. "Well, it's very nice to meet you, Heloise. Your boy go to Dunwood?"

His vowels were round with fake sincerity, a bad sign. Most of her regulars were adequate liars; they had to be to juggle the compartmentalized lives they had created for themselves. And she was a superb liar. Bill Carroll wasn't even adequate.

"We live in Hamilton Point, but he goes to private school. Do you live—"

"Divorced," he said briefly. "Weekend warrior, driving up from D.C. every other Saturday, expressly for this tedium."

That explained everything. She hadn't screwed up. Her system simply wasn't as foolproof as she thought. Before Heloise's company took on a new client, she always did a thorough background check, looking up vehicle registrations, tracking down the home addresses. (And if no home address could be found, she refused the job.) A man who lived in her zip code, or even a contiguous one, was rejected out of hand, although she might assign him to one of her associates.

She hadn't factored in divorce. Perhaps that was an oversight that only the never married could make.

"Nice to meet you," she said.

"Nice to *meet* you," he replied, smirking.

This was trouble. What kind of trouble, she wasn't sure yet, but definitely trouble.

❧

WHEN HELOISE DECIDED to move to the suburbs shortly after Scott was born, it had seemed practical and smart, even mainstream. Wasn't that what every parent did? She hadn't anticipated how odd it was for a single woman to buy a house on one of the best cul-de-sacs in one of the best subdivisions in Anne Arundel County, the kind of house that a newly single mother usually sold post-divorce because she couldn't afford to buy out the husband's 50 percent stake in the equity. Heloise had chosen the house for the land, almost an acre, which afforded the most privacy, never thinking of the price. Then she enrolled Scott in private school, another flag: what was the point of moving here if one could afford private school? The neighbors had begun to gossip almost immediately, and their speculation inspired the backstory she needed. A widow—*yes*. A terrible accident, one of which she still could not speak. She was grateful for her late husband's pragmatism and foresight when it came to insurance, but—she'd rather have him. Of course.

Of course, her new confidantes echoed back, although some seemed less than convinced. She could almost see their brains working it through: *If I could lose the husband and keep the house, it wouldn't be so bad.* It was the brass ring of divorced life in this cul-de-sac, losing the husband and keeping the house. (The Dunwood school district was less desirable and therefore less pricy, which explained how Bill Carroll's ex maintained her life there.) Heloise simply hadn't counted on the scrutiny her personal life would attract.

She *had* counted on her ability to construct a story about her work that would quickly stupefy anyone who asked, not that many of these stay-at-home mothers seemed curious about work. "I'm a lobbyist," she said. "The Women's Full Employment Network. I work in Annapolis, Baltimore, and D.C. as necessary, advocating parity and full benefits for what is traditionally considered women's work. So-called pink-collar jobs."

"How about pay and benefits for what we do?" her neighbors inevitably asked. "Is there anyone who works harder than a stay-at-home mom?"

Ditch-diggers, she thought. Janitors and custodians. Gardeners. Meter readers. The girl who stands on her feet all day next to a fryer, all for the glory of minimum wage. Day laborers, men who line up on street corners and take whatever is offered. Hundreds of people you stare past every day, barely recognizing them as human. Prostitutes.

"No one works harder than a mother," she always replied with an open, honest smile. "I wish there was some way I could organize us, establish our value to society in a true dollars-and-cents way. Maybe one day."

Parenting actually was harder than the brand of prostitution that she now practiced. She made her own hours. She made top-notch wages. She was her own boss and an excellent manager. With the help of an exceptionally nonjudgmental nanny, she had been able to arrange her life so she never missed a soccer game or a school concert. If sleeping with other women's husbands was what it took, so be it. She could not imagine a better line of work for a single mother.

For eight years, it had worked like a charm, her two lives never overlapping.

And then Scott ran into Bill Carroll's son at the soccer game. And while no bones cracked and no wounds opened up, it was clear to her that she would bear the impact of this collision for some time to come.

"WE HAVE TO talk," said the message on her cell phone, a number that she never answered, a phone on which she never spoke. It was strictly for incoming messages, which gave her plausible deniability if a message was ever intercepted. His voice was clipped, imperious, as if she had annoyed him deliberately. "We have to talk ASAP."

No, we don't, she thought. *Let it go. I know and you know. I know you know I know. You know I know you know. Talking is the one thing we don't have to do.*

But she called him back.

"There's a Starbucks near my office," he said. "Let's meet accidentally there in about an hour. You know—*Aren't you Scott's mom? Aren't you Billy Jr.'s dad?* Blah, blah, blah, yadda, yadda, yadda."

"I don't think we really need to speak."

"I do." He was surprisingly bossy in his public life, given his preferences in his private one. "We need to straighten a few things out. And, who knows, if we settle everything, maybe I'll throw a little business your way."

"That's not how I work," she said. "You know that. I don't take referrals from clients. It's not healthy, clients knowing each other."

"Yeah, well, that's one of the things we're going to talk about. How you work. And how you're going to work from now on."

HE WASN'T THE first bully in her life. That honor belonged to her father, who had beat her when he got tired of beating her mother. "How do you stay with him?" she had asked her mother more than once. "You only have one true love in your life," her mother responded, never making it clear if her true love was Heloise's father or some long-gone man who had consigned her to this joyless fate.

Then there was Heloise's high school boyfriend, the one who persuaded her to drop out of college and come to Baltimore with him, where he promptly dumped her. She had landed a job as a dancer at one of the Block's nicer clubs, but she had gotten in over her head with debt, trying to balance work and college. That had brought Val into her life. She had worked for him for almost ten years before she had been able to strike out on her own, and there had been a lot of luck in that. A lot of luck and not a little deceit.

People who thought they knew stuff, people on talk shows, quack doctors with fake credentials, had lots of advice about bullies. *Bullies back down if you stand up to them. Bullies are scared inside.*

Bully-shit. If Val was scared inside, then his outside masked it pretty well. He sent her to the hospital twice, and she was pretty sure she would be out on the third strike if she ever made the mistake of standing up to him again. Confronting Val hadn't accomplished anything. Being sneaky, however, going behind his back while smiling to his face, had worked beautifully. That had been her first double life—Val's smiling consort, Brad's confidential informant. What she was doing now was kid stuff, compared to all that.

"Chai latte," she told the counterwoman at the Starbucks in Dupont Circle. The girl was beautiful, with tawny skin and green eyes. She could do much better for herself than a job at a coffee shop, even one that paid health insurance. Heloise offered health insurance to the girls who were willing to be on the books of the Women's Full Employment Network. She paid toward their health plans and Social Security benefits, everything she was required to do by law.

"Would you like a muffin with that?" Suggestive selling, a good technique. She used it in her business.

"No, thanks. Just the chai, tall."

"Heloise! Heloise Lewis! *Fancy* seeing you here."

His acting had not improved in the seventy-two hours since they had met on the soccer field. He inspected her with a smirk, much too proud of himself, his expression all but announcing, *I know what you look like naked.*

She knew the same about him, of course, but it wasn't an image she wanted to hold on to.

Heloise hadn't changed her clothes for this meeting. Neither had she put on makeup, or taken her hair out of its daytime ponytail. She was hoping that her Heloise garb might remind Bill Carroll that she was a mother, another parent, someone like him. She did not know him well, outside the list of preferences she had cataloged on a carefully coded index card. Despite his tough talk on the phone, he might be nicer than he seemed.

"The way I see it," he said, settling in an overstuffed chair and leaving her a plain wooden one, "you have more to lose than I do."

"Neither one of us has to lose anything. I've never exposed a client and I never will. It makes no sense as a business practice."

He looked around, but the Starbucks was relatively empty, and in any event he didn't seem the type capable of pitching his voice low.

"You're a whore," he announced.

"I'm aware of how I make my living."

"It's illegal."

"Yes—for both of us. Whether you pay or are paid, you've broken the law."

"Well, you've just lost one paying customer."

Was that all he wanted to establish? Maybe he wasn't as big a dick as he seemed. "I understand. If you'd like to work with one of my associates—"

"You don't get it. I'm not paying anymore. Now that I know who you are and where you live, I think you ought to take care of me for free."

"Why would I do that?"

"Because if you don't, I'm going to tell everyone you're a whore."

"Which would expose you as my client."

"Who cares? I'm divorced. Besides, how are you going to prove I was a customer? I can out you without exposing myself."

"There are your credit card charges." American Express Business Platinum, the kind that accrued airline miles. She was better at remembering the cards than the men themselves. The cards were tangible, concrete. The cards were individual in a way the men were not.

"Business expenses. Consulting fees, right? That's what it says on the bill."

"Why would a personal injury lawyer need to consult with the Women's Full Employment Network?"

"To figure out how to value the lifelong earning power of women injured in traditional pink-collar jobs." His smile was triumphant, ugly and triumphant. He had clearly put a lot of thought into his answer and was thrilled at the chance to deliver it so readily. But then he frowned, which made his small eyes even smaller. It would be fair to describe his face as piggish, with those eyes and the pinkish nose, which was very broad at the base and more than a little upturned. "How did you know I was a personal injury lawyer?"

"I research my clients pretty carefully."

"Well, maybe it's time that someone researched *you* pretty carefully. Cops. A prosecutor hungry for a high-profile case. The call girl on the cul-de-sac. It would make a juicy headline."

"Bill, I assure you, I have no intention of telling anyone about our business relationship, if that's what you're worried about."

"What I'm worried about is that you're expensive and I wouldn't mind culling you from my overhead. You bill more per hour than I do. Where do you get off, charging that much?"

"I get off," she said, "where you get off. You know, right at that moment I take my little finger—"

"Shut up." His voice was so loud that it broke through the dreamy demeanor of the counter girl, who started and exchanged a worried look with Heloise. A moment ago, Heloise had been pitying her, and now the girl was concerned about Heloise. That was how quickly things could change. "Look, this is the option. I get free rides for life or I make sure that everyone knows what you are. Everyone. Including your cute little boy."

He was shrewd, bringing Scott into the conversation. Scott was her soft spot, her only vulnerability. Before she got pregnant, when she was the only person she had to care for, she had done a pretty shitty job of it. But Scott had changed all that, even before he was a flesh-and-blood reality. She would do anything to protect Scott, anything. Ask Brad for a favor, if need be, although she hated leaning on Brad.

She might even go to Scott's father, not that he had any idea he was Scott's father, and not that she was ever going to inform him of that fact. But she didn't like asking him for favors under any circumstances. Scott's father thought he was in her debt. She needed to maintain the equilibrium afforded by that lie.

"I can't afford to work for free."

"It won't be every week. And I understand I won't have bumping rights over the paying customers. I'm just saying that we'll go on as before, once or twice a month, but I don't pay for it anymore. It will be like dating, without all the boring socializing. What do the kids call it? A booty call."

"I have to think about this," she said.

"No, you don't. See you next Wednesday."

He hadn't even offered to pay for her chai, or buy her a muffin.

SHE CALLED BRAD first, but the moment she saw him, waiting in the old luncheonette on Eastern Avenue, she realized it had been a mistake. Brad had taken an oath to serve and protect, but the oath had been for those who obeyed the laws, not those who lived in flagrant disregard of them. He had already done more for her than she had any right to expect. He owed her nothing.

Still, it was hard for a woman, any woman, not to exploit a man's enduring love, not to go back to that well and see if you could still draw on it. Brad knew her and he loved her. Well, he thought he knew her, and he loved the person he thought he knew. Close enough.

"You look great," he said, and she knew he wasn't being polite. Brad preferred daytime Heloise to the nighttime version, always had.

"Thanks."

"Why did you want to see me?"

I need advice on how to get a shameless, grasping parasite out of my life. But she didn't want to plunge right in. It was crass.

"It's been too long."

He placed his hands over hers, held them on the cool Formica tabletop, indifferent to the coffee he had ordered. The coffee here was awful, had always been awful. She was not one to romanticize these old diners. Starbucks was taking over the world by offering a superior product, changing people's perceptions about what they deserved and what they could afford. In her private daydreams, she would like to be the Starbucks of sex-for-hire, delivering guaranteed quality to business travelers everywhere. No, she wouldn't call it Starfucks, although she had seen that joke on the Internet. For one thing, it would sound like one of those celebrity impersonator services. Besides, it wasn't elegant. She wanted to take a word or reference that had no meaning in the culture and make it come to mean good, no-strings, quid pro quo sex. Like . . . *zephyr.* Only not *zephyr,* because it denoted quickness and she wanted to market sex as a spa service for men, a day or night of pampering with a long list of services and options. So not *zephyr,* but a word like it, one that sounded cool and elegant, but with a real meaning that was virtually unknown and therefore malleable in the public imagination. Amazon.com was another good example. Or eBay. Familiar yet new.

But that fantasy seemed more out of reach than ever. Now she would settle for keeping the life she already had.

"Seriously, Heloise. What's up?"

"I missed you," she said lamely, yet not inaccurately. She missed Brad's adoration, which never seemed to dim. For a long time she had expected him to marry someone else, to pursue the average family he claimed he wanted to have with her. But now that they were both pushing forty with a very short stick, she was beginning to think that Brad liked things just the way they were. As long as he carried a torch for a woman he could never have, he didn't have to marry or have kids. Back when Scott was born, Brad had dared to believe he was the father, had even hopefully volunteered to take a DNA test. She had to break it to him very gently that he wasn't, and that she didn't want him to be part of Scott's life under any circumstances, even as an uncle or Mommy's "friend." She couldn't afford for Scott to have any contact with her old life, no matter how remote or innocuous.

"Everyone okay? You, Scott? Melina?" Melina was her nanny, the single most important person in her employ. The girls could come and go, but Heloise could never make things work without Melina.

"We're all fine."

"So what's this meeting about?"

"Like I said, I missed you." She sounded more persuasive this time.

"Weezie, Weezie, Weezie," he said, using the pet name that only he was allowed, given its horrible associations with that old sitcom. "Why didn't things work out between us?"

"I always felt it was because I wanted to continue working after marriage."

"Well, yeah, but . . . it's not like I was opposed to you working on principle. It was just—a cop can't be married to a prostitute, Weezie."

"It's my career," she said. It was her career and her excuse. No matter what she had chosen as her vocation, Brad would never have been the right man for her. He had taken care of her on the streets, asking nothing in return, and she had taken him to bed a time or two, grateful for all he did. But it had never been a big passion for her. It had, in fact, been more like a free sample, the kind of thing a corporation does to build up community goodwill. A free sample to someone she genuinely liked, but a freebie nonetheless, like one of those little boxes of detergent left in the mailbox. You might wash your clothes in it, but it probably didn't change your preferences in the long run.

They held hands, staring out at Eastern Avenue. They had been sweeping this area lately, Brad said, and the trade had dried up. But they both knew that was only temporary. Eventually, the girls and the boys came back, and the men were never far behind. They all came back, springing up like mushrooms after a rain.

⤜⤛

HER MEETING WITH Scott's dad, in the visiting room at SuperMax, was even briefer than her coffee date with Brad. Scott's father was not particularly surprised to see her; she had made a point of coming every few months or so, to keep up the charade that she had nothing to do with him being here. His red hair seemed duller after so many years inside, but maybe it was just the contrast with the orange DOC uniform. She willed herself not to see her boy in this man, to acknowledge no resemblance. Because if Scott was like his father on the outside, he might be like his father on the inside, and that she could not bear.

"Faithful Heloise," Val said, mocking her.

"I'm sorry. I know I should come more often."

"It takes a long time to put a man to death in Maryland, but they do get around to it eventually. Bet you'll miss me when I'm gone."

"I don't want you to be killed." *Just locked up forever and forever. Please, God, whatever happens, he must never get out. One look at Scott and he'd know. He was hard enough to get rid of as a pimp. Imagine what he'd be like as a parent. He'd take Scott just because he can, because Val never willingly gave up anything that was his.*

"Well, you know how it is when you work for yourself. You're always hustling, always taking on more work than you can handle."

"How are things? How many girls have you brought in?"

Unlike Brad, Val was interested in her business, perhaps because he felt she had gained her acumen from him. Then again, if he hadn't been locked up, she never would have been allowed to go into business for herself. That's what happened when your loan shark became your pimp. You never got out from under. Figuratively and literally.

But now that Val couldn't control her, he was okay with her controlling herself. It was better than another man doing it.

"Things are okay. I figure I have five years to make the transition to full-time management."

"Ten—you continue taking care of yourself. You look pretty good for your age."

"Thanks." She fluttered her eyelashes automatically, long in the habit of using flirtation as a form of appeasement with him. "Here's the thing . . . there's a guy who's making trouble for me. Trying to extort me. We ran into each other in real life and now he says he'll expose me if I don't start doing him for free."

"It's a bluff. It's fuckin' cold war shit."

"What?"

"The guy has as much to lose as you do. He's all talk. It's like he's the USSR and you're the USA back in the 1980s. No matter who strikes first, you both go sky high."

"He's divorced. And he's a personal injury lawyer, so I don't know how much he cares about his reputation. He might even welcome the publicity."

"Naw. Trust me on this. He's just fucking with you."

Val didn't know about Scott, of course, and never would if she could help it. The problem was, it was harder to make the case for how panicky she was if she couldn't mention Scott.

"I've got a bad feeling about this," she insisted. "He's a loose cannon. I always assumed that guys who came to me had to have a certain measure of built-in shame about what they did. He doesn't."

"Then give me his name and I'll arrange for things to happen."

"You can do that from in here?"

He shrugged. "I'm on death row. What have I got to lose?"

It was what she wanted, what she had come for. She would never ask for such a favor, but if Val volunteered—well, would that be so wrong? Yet the moment she heard him make the offer, she couldn't take it. She had tested herself, walked right up to the edge of the abyss that was Val, allowed him to tempt her with the worst part of himself.

Besides, if Val could have some nameless, faceless client killed from here, then he could—she didn't want to think about it.

"No. No. I'll think of something."

Not my son's face, she told herself as she bent to kiss his cheek. *Not my son's freckles. Not my son's father.* But he was—she could never change that fact. And though she visited Val in part to convince him that she had nothing to do with the successful prosecution that had been brought against him when the undercover narc Brad Stone somehow found the gun used to kill a young man, she also came because she was grateful to him for the gift of Scott. She hated him with every fiber of her being, but she wouldn't have Scotty if it weren't for him. She wouldn't have Scott if it weren't for Val.

Maybe she did know something about divorce, after all.

FIVE DAYS WENT by, days full of work. Congress was back in session, which always meant an uptick in business. She was beginning to resign herself to the idea of doing things Bill Carroll's way. He was not the USSR and she was not the USA. The time for cold wars was long past. He was a terrorist in a breakaway republic, determined to have the status he sought at any cost. He was a man of his word and his words were ugly, inflammatory, dangerous. She met with him at a D.C. hotel as he insisted, picking up the cost of the room, which was usually covered by her clients. He left two dollars on the dresser, then said, "For housekeeping, not for you," with a cruel laugh. Oh, he cracked himself up.

She treated herself to room service, then drove home in a funk, flipping on WTOP to check traffic, not that it was usually a problem this late. A body had just been discovered in Rock Creek Park, a young woman. Heloise could tell from the flatness of the report that it was a person who didn't matter, a homeless woman or a prostitute. She grieved for the young woman, for she sensed automatically that the death would never be solved. It could have been one of hers. It could have been her. You tried to be careful, but nothing was foolproof. Look at the situation she was in with Bill Carroll. You couldn't prepare for every contingency. That was her mistake, thinking she could control everything.

Bill Carroll.

Once at home, she called her smartest girl, Trini, a George Washington University coed who took her money under the table and didn't ask a lot of questions. Trini learned her part quickly and well, and within an hour she was persuading police that she had seen a blue Mercedes stop in the park and roll the body out of the car. Yes, it was dark, but she had seen the man's face lighted by the car's interior dome and it wasn't a face one would forget, given the circumstances. Trini gave a partial plate—a full one wouldn't have worked, not in the long run—and it took police only a day to track down Bill Carroll and bring him in for questioning. By then, Heloise had Googled him, found a photo on the Internet, and e-mailed it to Trini, who subsequently had no problem picking him out of a lineup.

From the first, Bill Carroll insisted that Heloise Lewis would establish his alibi, but he didn't mention that their assignation was anything more than two adults meeting for a romantic encounter. Which it technically was, after all. No money had exchanged hands, at his insistence. Perhaps he thought it would be a bad idea, confessing to a relationship with one prostitute while being investigated in the murder of another. At any rate, Heloise corroborated his version. She told police that they had a date in a local hotel. No, the reservation was in her name. Well, not her name, but the name of "Jane Smith." She was a single mother, trying to be careful. Didn't Dr. Laura always say that single parents needed to keep their kids at a safe distance from their relationships? True, hers was the only name on the hotel register. He had wanted it that way. No, she wasn't sure why. No, she didn't think anyone on the staff had seen him come and go; she had ordered a cup of tea from room service after he left, which was why she was alone in the room at eleven p.m. She spoke with many a hesitation and pause, always telling the truth yet never sounding truthful. That's how good a liar Heloise was. She could make the truth sound like a lie, a lie sound like the truth.

Still, her version was strong enough to keep police from charging him. After all, there was no physical evidence in his car and they had only two letters from the plate. Witnesses did make mistakes, even witnesses as articulate and positive as the wholesome young GW student. That was when Heloise told Bill she was prepared to recant everything, go to the police and confess that she had lied to cover up for a longtime client.

"I'll go to them and tell them it was all made up, that I did it as a favor to you, unless you promise to leave me alone from now on." They were meeting in the Starbucks on Dupont Circle again, but the beautiful girl had the day off. That, or she had moved on.

"But then they'll know you're a whore."

"A whore who can provide your alibi."

"I didn't *do* anything." His voice was whiny, put-upon. Then again, he was being framed for a crime he didn't commit, so his petulance was earned.

"I heard there's a police witness who picked you out of the lineup, put you at the scene. And once I out myself as a whore— well, then it's an established fact that you traffic in whores. That's not going to play very well for you. In fact, I'll tell the police that you wanted me to do something that I didn't want to do, an act so degrading and hideous I can't even speak of it, and we argued and you went slamming out of the room, angry and frustrated. Maybe that poor dead girl paid the price for your aggression and hostility."

He very quickly came to see it her way. He muttered and complained, but once he left the Starbucks she was sure she would never see him again. Not even back in the suburbs, for she had signed Scott up for travel soccer, having ascertained that Bill Carroll's son was not skilled enough to make the more competitive league. It was a lot more time, but then, she had always had time for Scott. She had set up her life so she was always there for her son. If there was a better gig for a single mother, she had yet to figure it out.

Her only regret was the dead girl. Heloise's debts to the dead seemed like bad karma, mounting up in a way that would have to be rectified one day. There had been that boy Val had killed for a crime no greater than laughing at his given name—Valery. She had told the boy, a drug dealer, Val's big secret and the boy had let it slip, so Val killed him. Had killed him, then driven off in the boy's car, just because it was there and he could, but it was the theft of the car that made it a death penalty crime in Maryland. And even as Heloise had soothed Val and carted shoeboxes of money to various lawyers, skimming as much as she had dared, she was giving Brad the information they needed to lock him up forever. She had used a dead boy to create a new life for herself, and she had never looked back.

And now there was this anonymous girl, someone not much different from herself, whose death remained unsolved. If it had been Baltimore, Heloise could have leaned on Brad a little, pressed to know what leads the department had. But it was D.C. and she had no connections there, not in law enforcement, and Congress's relationship with the city was notoriously rocky. The Women's Full Employment Network offered a reward for any information leading to an arrest in the case, but nothing came of it.

Finally, there were all those little deaths, as the French called them, all those sighing, depleted men slumping back against the bed—or the carpet, or the chair, or the bathtub—temporarily sated, briefly safe, for there was no one more harmless than a man who had just orgasmed. Even Val had been safe for a few minutes in the aftermath. How many men had there been now, after eight years with Val and nine years on her own? She did not want to count. She left her work at the office, and when she came home she stood in her son's doorway and watched him sleep, grateful to have found her one true love.

WIFEY

R. L. STINE

EVERYONE KNEW THAT Frank cared more about Ruby than anyone else in his life. He was so into that dog, I always called her Wifey. It was really like they were married or something.

To tell the truth, I'm a cat person. I don't like big dogs. And Ruby is a big dog—some kind of black Lab–shepherd mix, tall and barrel-chested with a meaty head and long bushy tail. The dog barks a lot and likes to bump you with her head, and if she spies you in your yard she'll come racing over and take a running jump and knock you backwards and get mud all over your suit with her elephant paws. Then she'll lick you and slobber sticky stuff all over your face.

So no, I didn't like Ruby.

But when Frank left her to me in his will, I almost wept.

Face facts, I'm an emotional guy. Mom always said, "Jake, you're wound tighter than a midget's yo-yo." Does that make any sense? I don't think so. Mom had a million of those, mostly designed to put me down.

Too intense. That's what she always said about me. She didn't understand that intense is what gets you places in this world. "Jake, go jump in the blender and turn it on." She said that when I'd be bouncing off the walls. Maybe she meant it to be funny.

A lot of women have accused me of not having a sense of humor. Like that's a big put-down. I always tell them if I'm not a laugh a minute, it's just cuz I care too much. Try to explain that to some women.

Try to explain that to Sonya Gordon. Sonya made her choice. She preferred easygoing Frank.

Easygoing . . . going . . . gone.

I didn't spill any tears over Sonya, believe me. But when the letter came from Frank's lawyers, and I saw the somber embossed letterhead—Dunville, Mahoney, and Berg—and gazed down to the third or fourth paragraph of legal bullshit until I read the part where I was mentioned in Frank's will . . . Well, I got real emotional.

Frank and I were buddies, after all. I mean, we lived three houses from each other in this Suburban Hell we both admitted we liked. And we worked together. Rising young architects, although neither of us seemed to be rising. Our buildings went up, but we seemed to stay on ground level. But, hey, the money wasn't bad. We were lucky enough not to own the firm. And we were doing what we loved.

At least, I was. I got in on planning sessions and did a lot of drawing. Frank got stuck with securing clearances and bribing the right guys to get the building permits and standing in long lines at municipal buildings to pick up licenses and legal stuff. That's all part of being a rising young architect, you know. That's the Dark Side.

But we were thrown together a lot, Frank and I. We shared the drive into the city most every morning. And, a lot of days, we shared our lunchtime. And of course we shared Sonya, in a manner of speaking.

So I got a little teary when I learned I'd been included in Frank's will. A few days later, I sat in a very attractive conference room—polished oak table, Knoll chairs, and mahogany floor-to-ceiling bookshelves, dark green plush carpet. Rich but not pretentious. I'd have given them something a little brighter, maybe. Newer. But no one was asking me.

It didn't take long for the lawyer to appear. A seven-foot-tall dude with Conan O'Brien red hair standing straight up on his needle-like head, although I have to say he wore a great pin-striped Italian suit. He introduced himself. I immediately forgot his name.

He tsk-tsked about Frank. Then he opened a folder and searched through a bunch of papers. When he told me Frank had left Ruby to me, I got choked up and thought I might ac-tually spill a few tears on the polished oak.

Everyone knew how much Frank adored that dog. So you see, his leaving Ruby to me told everyone that I had to be Frank's best friend, that I had to be the most trustworthy, dependable, straight-arrow, nicest guy in the world.

My heart was still pitty-pattying as I shook hands with the lawyer and turned to leave. I was still thinking about Frank's kindness as I took the elevator down to the lobby, and who should be waiting there, handkerchief raised to her sniffly face, but La Sonya herself.

How did she look? Not too shabby. Sonya knew how to put herself together, even in her grief. Only Sonya could get away with that short haircut. With those high cheekbones and the big, round green eyes, she didn't need hair. She had plastic rings on her fingers and red dangling earrings, and that tiny diamond on one side of her pointy little nose.

What was she wearing? I didn't get to see, cuz she threw herself on me like a middle linebacker and hugged me, pressing her hot wet face against mine. I guess the bobbing up and down meant she was sobbing or something.

After a minute or so, I peeled her off and told her how sorry I was about Frank: "He was my best friend, after all."

"Mine too," she said, and the tears started to flow again.

She asked if I wanted to have lunch. "Would it help you to talk about it, Jake?" She was squeezing the sleeve of my suit jacket, knotting it with her wet hand.

No, I didn't want to talk about it. I told her I had to go pick up Ruby. The poor dog was locked up at some kennel in Scarsdale. I said how deeply touched I was that Frank left Wifey to me. I started to escape. Sonya raised a hand to her ear, made that two-fingered telephone sign with her pointer and pinky, and mouthed the words "Call me?"

"Sure." I waved and trotted off, gazing at the wet spot on my jacket sleeve. Did Sonya think she was going to jump right back to me? Interesting . . .

I picked up my car at the garage across the street and headed north on the Henry Hudson. It was one o'clock in the afternoon, but the highway was jammed. You'd think it was afternoon rush hour. As I inched along, I had plenty of time to think.

No, I didn't think about the dog. It hadn't hit me yet that taking on a big dog like Ruby was a major, life-changing responsibility. I still felt grateful to my old buddy Frank for remembering what a good friend I'd always been.

When I murdered Frank, I never dreamed he'd leave Ruby to me. Who'd believe he'd help me out by making me look like such a good guy? I mean, you don't leave your precious dog to the guy who murdered you—do you?

Face facts, I *had* to murder Frank. It wasn't even personal. It was business.

Yes, I was in a rage. The kind of fury that used to drive me to all those smash-the-walls, tear-my-clothes, scream-till-I-turned-blue tantrums when I was a kid.

"Jake, hold your breath," Mom would say. "Hold your breath and count to a million. Then you'll be calm."

Good advice, Mom. A little hostile, maybe. Holding my breath and counting to a million? I don't think that would have saved Frank.

Listen, steal my girl? Okay. I can handle it. I *did* handle it. Maybe there was a little resentment bubbling around below the surface. But I handled it.

Steal Sonya? Fine. But steal my *drawings?*

Whoa. And believe me, there was no doubt about it. Sure, Frank and I had talked about the Tucson apartment building project. Casual talks at lunch and across our desks. And yes, we even sketched out a few rough ideas together.

But the drawings he presented to Graver and Robinson were mine. He saw his moment to rush in and show them, and he took it. Yes, they loved the style and the clean lines. And they were blown away by the elevated parking garage.

All mine!

Frank had even signed each drawing on the bottom with that fruit-loopy signature he thought was so distinctive. Signed *my* drawings!

What was he *thinking?* He knew he couldn't get away with it, didn't he? We both knew this was a big opportunity to show off our stuff. Was he so desperate for a little recognition that he had to climb over the back of his best friend? *Screw Jake. It's my move, and I'm taking it.*

Well, I have a good vocabulary. And I know the word *betrayed.*

When Graver came running into my office to show me "Frank's" fabulous drawings, I held myself in. I didn't let him see how shocked I was. I gripped my desktop so hard, I actually broke my little finger. Yeah, the pain was intense, shooting down my arm, but it was nothing like the pain I felt in my heart.

Graver stood there, waiting for my reaction. I nonchalanted it, although I could feel my face burning. And I held my grip on the desk so he wouldn't see my hands shaking. I said something about being impressed and wanting to see more. And as I said it, I knew I had to kill Frank.

What choice did I have? I'm twenty-eight, too old to throw a big blue-faced tantrum.

Was it premeditated murder? Call it what you want. I knew I was going to kill him, but I didn't really plan how I was going to do it. I had about half a quart of Johnny Red for dinner, so I wasn't as clearheaded as I should have been. As I crossed through the backyard toward Frank's house that night, I figured I'd pick up something like a lamp or a vase and beat him to death with it.

It's pretty easy to kill someone if you're so angry, you can barely breathe. I stepped along the path in front of Heimer's tomato garden and glanced at Heimer's house. The house was dark, which was good. It meant Heimer and his wife weren't home, so they couldn't come to the rescue or call the cops in case Frank screamed a lot.

Heimer owns the house between Frank's and mine. He's a grumpy middle-aged guy who escapes his grumpy middle-aged wife by drinking many six-packs of Budweiser and spending all his time on his tomatoes in the backyard.

Heimer always acts very suspicious around Frank and me. Two single guys living in the suburbs. I know he thinks we're gay. And he's always complaining to Frank about Ruby and threatening to call the cops because sometimes Ruby likes to dig in his tomato garden.

Frank has a garden, too. A small flower garden—mostly gladioli, petunias, and a few rosebushes. I stepped onto Frank's back stoop and heard music inside, the Grateful Dead, I think, or maybe one of those boring, endless Phish numbers he loved.

Of course, I wasn't thinking about his taste in music. I was thinking about the pewter lamp next to his reading chair. It was slender and heavy and kinda perfect for bashing his head to a nice pulpy consistency.

My head throbbed. The liquid dinner was a bad idea. I squinted through the window. Beyond the dark kitchen, I could see Frank in the living room, slouched in the reading chair, Ruby stretched out at his feet like a dark shadow.

Just seeing him sitting there so comfortable set me off. Like a volcano erupting in my gut. I almost punched my fist through the glass storm door. Somehow I stopped myself, looked down, and saw a pair of gloves on the ground. Heavy, rough-textured gardening gloves, white with green and brown stains.

I slipped them on. They fit okay. And yes, the rest is history.

I ran into the living room. Ruby looked up, saw it was me, then lowered her head to the floor. Frank dropped his magazine and stood up to greet me. "Hey, Jake—" Those were the only words he got out. I didn't bother with the lamp. I just wrapped the gloves around his throat and pressed the thumbs real hard into his larynx.

He didn't have a chance to look surprised, and he didn't struggle much. He didn't even wake Ruby. I squeezed hard and I heard a cracking sound inside his neck. All the color drained from his face, and he made like an "Ucch, ucch" sound for a short while. Then his eyes closed and his body slumped, and I was holding him up by his head.

Frank died an untimely death, and I set him down in his reading chair and put the magazine back on his lap. I spun away from him and saw Ruby sitting up now, head lowered, eyes wide, glaring at me, not moving or anything, just glaring at me, panting softly, lips pulled back a little so I could see a flash of teeth.

Did she plan to attack? Feeling dizzy, I stumbled backwards and plopped down into Frank's lap. His head dropped forward and bumped me in the back. I found myself gripping his limp, lifeless hands, but I didn't move. It must've looked kinda comical. Us sitting together like that.

Ruby glared at me for a few more seconds, then rose to her feet and moved to the corner next to the bookshelves, tail between her legs. I started to feel a little better, calm enough to stand up. I crossed the room and turned off the CD player. No way I wanted Heimer to come over to complain about the loud music.

The Johnny Red made it hard to clear my mind. But I had this flash that I should make it look like a break-in. I figured the dog would go crazy if I smashed a window, so I just raised the den window as far as it could go. And I messed up a lot of stuff in the den, quietly so Ruby wouldn't get riled. I knocked over a shelf of CDs and pulled open a lot of drawers. Maybe I should have actually stolen something, but I didn't think of that.

I just made a mess, then closed the kitchen door quietly behind me and hurried home across the backyards. I grabbed the back door—and saw I was still wearing the gardening gloves. *Okay,* I thought, *I'll take them to the city when I go to work. I'll drop them in a trash can. No problem.*

Fritzi, my cat, was waiting for me in the kitchen. Fritzi is thirteen, the poor old dear, and she's losing her eyesight and her memory. But she always remembers her dinner, and so there she was, scolding me for being late. "Sorry, Fritzi," I said, pulling off the gardening gloves. "I've been bad. I know I have."

A week later, as I entered the kennel to pick up Ruby, I wondered how Fritzi would adjust to having a new member of the family. Probably curl up and go back to sleep, I figured. That's how Fritzi spent most of her time these days. She'd been a sweet pet, and I really cared about her and felt sorry that she was slipping away like that. You get so attached to these animals.

The waiting room walls were covered with snapshots of dogs and cats. I felt a little tense. I didn't know what to expect. When the attendant brought Ruby out, she ran right past me to the glass door in front. Panting excitedly, she glanced all around, tail wagging furiously. I knew what she was doing. She was looking for Frank.

"It's okay, girl," I said, bending down to wrap my arms around her neck. "It's okay. I'm here now. I'll take good care of you." The attendant smiled, but Ruby didn't react to me at all. She stood there kinda stiffly, head down, ears back, staring at me with mournful dark eyes.

I leashed her and walked her to my car, my new silver Beamer, only the second month of my lease. The dog seemed pretty calm and jumped into the backseat without hesitating. I talked to her as I drove, soothing words, trying to reassure her. My plan was to stop at a supermarket and buy a bag of dog food and some biscuit treats. But I'd only driven a few miles when I glanced into my mirror and saw her squatting on the leather seat. "Hey! Stop! Ruby! Damn it!" The dog took an enormous dump on the backseat of my car.

I guessed she'd been holding it in for days at the kennel. Christ. I have a weak stomach when it comes to bad odors, and opening the car windows didn't help at all. Let's just say Wifey was not my favorite family member that afternoon.

I figured she'd be starved after a week in the kennel, but Ruby wouldn't eat the bowl of Iam's Chunks I set down for her. Fritzi was hiding somewhere. I hadn't seen the cat since Ruby arrived. "Go ahead, eat," I urged. "Ruby. Hungry."

But the dog stared up at me with a mournful expression, her tail tucked tight between her legs. To look at her, you'd think she was almost intelligent. She looked like she wanted to say something to me.

It didn't dawn on me till later what Ruby wanted to say.

I'd been sleeping like a baby ever since Frank died that tragic death. But that night I couldn't get to sleep. I had a problem with the Tucson apartment design I kept trying to work out in my head. And I kept thinking about Sonya Gordon, wondering how long I should wait before calling her.

I heard footsteps. Out in the hall. My head shot up from the pillow. Heavy thuds on the carpet. I reached for the chain on the bedtable lamp. Couldn't find it. My bedroom door swung open and crashed against the wall. I struggled to sit up. Running footsteps, and—ouch!—someone grabbed my chest and shoved me back down.

Squirming away, I saw a dull glow, two eyes staring down at me. My hand fumbled for the lamp chain. Tugged it. And yes, there was Ruby, paws on my chest, staring at me with those black marble eyes, panting loudly, tongue hanging down, staring . . . staring.

Oh, Christ. It took me a while, but I finally realized what was up with this dog.

The police had been so thorough. They had questioned me for hours, and everyone at the office, and Frank's family, and all his friends. But they hadn't talked to the one witness, the one who had seen the crime from *inside the room.*

Ruby. She watched me do it. She saw it all. And now she was letting me know. I could read those eyes. I could see her expression. Suddenly, I got what she was trying to tell me. She knew everything. She saw everything. And she wasn't going to let me forget it.

I felt a tingling at the back of my neck. I reached out and wrapped my hand around the dog's snout. "Hey, Ruby," I said softly. "It's me and you now. Just me and you. So drop it." I gave her snout a little squeeze, not enough to hurt her, just enough to show her who was in control.

She whimpered and I felt like a fool. I suddenly remembered a dog trainer we had for our springer when I was a kid. A guy named Pete something. He told me dogs have an attention span of ten seconds. Every ten seconds, their mind is wiped and they're on to something else.

So what was I getting all itchy about? Ruby had what they call a vacant stare. She didn't have a thought in her tiny brain. I shoved her off me, slid back under the covers, and shut my eyes.

The next morning, a Saturday, I was finishing my coffee, reading the *Times,* and a knock at the front door started Ruby barking and jumping around. I opened the door to a young girl, maybe eighteen or twenty, a looker with frizzy streaked blond hair over a broad forehead and pale blue eyes. She wore these low-riding jeans, and I could see a couple inches of smooth skin to where her silky purple top began. Nice.

I was about to ask her what she wanted when Ruby bumped me out of the way and leaped on the girl, whimpering, her tail whipping back and forth. Such excitement. The dog jumped all over the girl, licking her face frantically.

The girl dropped to her knees and hugged Ruby. "You're okay, girl? You're happy to see me? I was so worried about you." When she bent down, I glimpsed a tattoo of a flower over her right breast. She petted Ruby and smiled at me. "She seems to be okay. I'm Cindy. The dog walker."

I stared at her. The *what?*

She climbed to her feet, brushing her hair off her forehead. "I walked Ruby every afternoon for Frank while he was at work. I thought maybe you might want to hire me too."

"Uh, yeah," I said. I hadn't thought about Ruby being walked in the afternoon. I realized I hadn't planned this out at all. "That's great, Cindy. You're hired."

"Frank was such an awesome guy," she said. "He was so kind. I . . . I got to know him a little. We had some really good talks. We got pretty close."

I wondered if Frank was banging her. I bet he was. "The dog seems to really like you," I said.

Cindy smiled at Ruby. It was a toothy smile, kinda sexy. "Ruby and I have a special relationship. It's weird. We really communicate. It's like . . . well, it's like she *talks* to me."

Ruby talks to her? *No way* I wanted Ruby talking to her.

Cindy bent down so I could see the flower tattoo again and put her hands on the sides of Ruby's head. The dog didn't move, just stared up at her with those big cow eyes.

"She's feeling sad," Cindy told me. "That's natural, right? And . . . very tense. She's very tense and worried about something, maybe about moving to a new home."

"Maybe," I said.

"I'm totally psychic," Cindy said. "I can read animals' thoughts. For real."

I knew the girl was just Looney Tunes, but this was making me uncomfortable. I told her I was kinda busy. I gave her a key to the front door and paid her a week in advance, twenty bucks a walk.

She hugged Ruby again on her way out. "Bye, Ruby. Don't be sad. We'll have a nice long talk on Monday." As soon as the door closed behind Cindy, Ruby lowered her head and her tail and sank back to her old personality, flashing me sullen looks.

I pointed a finger at her. "You'd better not talk to her," I said. Imagine that? Me warning a stupid dog? Anyway, I finally found Fritzi hiding behind a couch upstairs in my workroom. I carried her downstairs and fed her. Later, I saw Ruby furiously licking the cat's food bowl. Face it, dogs are animals.

Sunday afternoon I planned to get some exercise, hit some balls at the driving range, when two cops showed up. I recognized them from another visit. They said they had more questions for me. We sat in the living room, and Ruby stared at them the whole while. Again, I felt uncomfortable. Like the dog wanted to burst out talking and rat me out.

But the two cops took it in that Frank had left his beloved pet to me. It gave me a chance to gush about how close Frank and I were and how Ruby and I both missed him. I thought they bought it. I really did.

I gave Ruby an extra biscuit that night. But the next morning I wished I hadn't. The alarm went off at seven. I struggled out of bed and came down to the kitchen to get the coffee brewing. I was still blinking and yawning. I stepped on something cold and hard.

Jeez, my heart skipped. It was Fritzi, stretched out dead on the floor. Poor old cat. I let out a sigh. I'd been expecting this for a long time. I squatted down to be closer to her. Her heart must have given out, I decided.

I picked her up, cradled her in my arms—and felt the wet, sticky fur at her throat. "Hey—!" I gently pushed back the cat's head and saw the thick gob of saliva clinging to her fur.

I didn't have to think about it. I knew what had happened. And yes, Ruby stood a few feet across the kitchen floor, on her haunches with her head lowered, giving me that cold stare. The damned dog was talking to me, okay? And I could read her loud and clear.

Jake, you killed Frank, so I killed Fritzi. In exactly the same way.

I set Fritzi down carefully on the floor. Then I walked up to the dog and gave her a hard backhand smack across the head. She didn't howl. She knew she was guilty. She just whimpered softly, turned, and walked out, tail tucked between her legs.

"You're history!" I shouted after her. "You're dead meat. Hear me? You're worm food!" I shouted for a long time, till I calmed down. I didn't think about Heimer hearing me from next door. I had to get my anger out.

Every time I pictured Fritzi dead on the floor, strangled by that dog, a fresh wave of rage burned my chest. I picked up the phone. I needed to call information and find out the nearest dog pound. But I stopped myself.

Ruby was the only witness to Frank's tragic death, and she wanted me to know it. She was taking the Wifey thing seriously. But face facts, I had to hold on to her for at least a few more weeks, till the investigation was over. She was helping me with the police. I knew she was.

I dragged a shovel from the garage and buried Fritzi under the big sassafras tree at the back of my yard. I could see Ruby watching me from the kitchen window, and it made me furious all over again.

That night I had a ridiculous dream that woke me with the

cold sweats. I dreamed Ruby was on TV on some kind of talk show, and she was sitting on a couch talking, in a high-pitched little girl's voice, telling about how I murdered Frank.

I woke up shaking. No, wait. It wasn't a high-pitched little girl's voice. It was Cindy the dog walker's voice. I turned on the lamp. My throat felt like I'd swallowed razor blades. Sure enough, there was Wifey, her head inches from my face, giving me the accusing stare.

"Get out! Damn it! Get out!" I shooed her out the bedroom door and slammed it. I couldn't stop the shivers. I wasn't safe in my own room. In my own *dreams!*

The next day I couldn't concentrate at work. I kept drawing dog bones. I went home early and pulled up the drive, and there was Cindy bringing Ruby back from the afternoon walk. She was wearing these faded vintage jeans torn at the knees and a tight yellow T-shirt. She really had a go-for-it bod.

"Ruby's been talking to me," she said as I climbed out of the car. "She's still very sad and totally tense."

She's making me *sad and tense,* I thought.

Cindy petted Ruby's side. "I guess you still need time. Is that it, girl?"

Ruby nodded her head. I swear she did. She really was talking to this girl. My heart pounded like crazy now. I knew it was only a matter of time . . .

I didn't sleep at all the next couple of nights. I locked my bedroom door, but that didn't help. I could hear Ruby padding around, pacing the hall, and I knew what she was thinking. I pictured the accusing stare. And I pictured her nodding her head, talking to Cindy.

I started leaving her outside at night. But that didn't help me sleep.

All week I was worthless at work. I think Graver noticed. He kept popping out of his corner office and walking by my cubicle. I leaned over the monitor, hiding the bare screen.

I drove home early again, nearly getting in two accidents because I needed sleep and I couldn't think straight. I didn't see Ruby at first. She never came running to greet me like a normal dog. Finally, I found her in the spare bedroom. She sat stiffly next to the mattress I'd put down for her. And resting on the mattress, I saw a dark object.

I took a few steps closer, picked it up, and opened it. Frank's wallet. Fat with cash. His driver's license photo stared out at me. *"Where did you get it?"* I screamed, waving it in front of the dog. She stared up at me and didn't flinch or back away.

"Where did you get it? You didn't go in Frank's house, did you? You couldn't get into Frank's house. *Could* you?" Ohmigod. I was talking to her as though she were a person. And what was I going to do with the damn wallet?

Wifey was trying to rat me out, and I knew I had to keep one step ahead of her. I raced around the house, searching for a place to hide the wallet. Just holding it made me sick. I couldn't think straight. I ran into the bedroom and started to shove it into my underwear drawer—and saw the gloves.

The gardening gloves. I'd forgotten. They were supposed to be tossed in the city. How could I have left them here? "Jake, get it together, dude," I scolded myself. I grabbed the gloves, carried them downstairs, and put them on the bench by the front door so I wouldn't forget them when I went to work the next morning.

Then I poured myself a tall Johnny Red and tried to think clearly. Ruby had to go no matter what. That was a no-brainer. On Saturday I'd check her into the nearest dog pound, and good-bye and good luck.

That decision should've calmed me down. With the dog gone

I knew I'd be safe. But I still couldn't sleep that night. Was this the fourth night in a row?

Friday morning I could barely drag myself out of bed. My head felt as heavy as a rock, my throat ached, and my ears rang. I thought about bagging it and climbing back into bed. But I remembered my ten o'clock meeting to pitch two new houses in the Hamptons. No way Graver would excuse me from that.

A shower helped a little. I drank two mugs of black coffee as I got dressed. I grabbed the keys to the Beamer, started out the back door—and remembered the gardening gloves. "Front bench," I reminded myself. With the gloves gone today and the dog gone tomorrow, the future for Jake looked as bright as the morning sky.

I trotted to the bench in the front entryway and picked up a glove. One glove. I stared at it, then at the empty bench. The other glove? Where was the other glove?

I dropped to my knees and searched under the bench. No glove. I jumped up and spun around, squinting at the floor. No. Not there. I could feel the blood pulsing at my temples as I took the stairs two at a time. I pulled open the dresser drawer and started pulling everything out, heaving it onto the floor. Did I leave one of the gloves in the drawer?

No. No glove. I glanced at the clock. *Okay, okay. I'll go to my meeting. Then I'll come home and find the other glove. No problem.*

I kept the glove on the seat beside me as I drove to work. I had a lot of time to think, and I concentrated on Ruby. I'd left her outside all night, and I hadn't seen her in the morning. Had she taken the glove with her? Three guesses. I pictured her going from door to door with the thing in her teeth, showing the neighbors what I used to murder Frank.

I parked my car in the garage on 42nd Street, tossed the glove into the first trash can I saw, and hurried to my meeting. It went very well. The clients—a middle-aged guy who had just taken over his father's clothing business, and his bubbly trophy wife—seemed to like me and most of my ideas. Graver actually smiled at me. Wish I had my camera.

After lunch, I told my assistant I had important business at home, which was true, and left early. When I pulled up the driveway little more than an hour later, I found Ruby waiting for me on the back stoop. I closed the car door behind me and walked up to her slowly. She didn't wag her tail or act glad to see me. Big surprise.

"Where is it, Ruby?" I asked in a soft, calm voice. "Good girl. Show me the glove. Where is it?"

She stared at me. I knew she understood. But that's the way she was going to play it.

"Where is it?" I tugged at her collar. "Get up. Show me. Where's the glove, girl? Where did you hide it?"

To my surprise she took off, loping across my backyard toward Frank's house, her head down, tail raised behind her, waving like a pennant. Frank's house. Of course. I knew I'd find the glove there. I should have guessed.

But halfway across Heimer's yard, I stopped. And stared at the low mound of loosely packed dirt at the side of the tomato garden. The dog stopped too. She stared at the fresh dirt pile. She trotted over to it and sniffed it, pushing at the dirt with her snout.

She buried the glove.

No way I could leave it there. In plain sight. Where Heimer could find it easily. Is that what Wifey had planned?

Too bad. I had to dig it up. I glanced to the house. No sign of Heimer. I made my way to his little garden shed and crept inside. Yes. He had a shovel propped against the wall. I dragged the shovel out to the tomato patch, lowered it to the soft dirt mound, leaned into it, and started to dig.

It didn't take more than a minute to unearth the glove. I turned and searched for Ruby, but I didn't see her. I wanted to gloat. Her plan was definitely ruined. I let the shovel drop to the ground, bent and picked up the glove.

I'd started to brush the dirt off it when I heard a shout behind me. "There you are! I couldn't find you!" And Cindy came running up with Ruby at her side. (Was Ruby leading her to me?) "I came to walk Ruby," Cindy said. She didn't finish her sentence. I saw she was staring at the glove in my hand.

"The glove," she said, pointing. "The local paper this morning . . . The police said Frank was strangled with gardening gloves. They . . . they found fibers on his throat, and—and—You're *burying* it, aren't you!"

"No. I'm not," I started. But I realized I couldn't explain.

"You . . . you're *burying* it!" Cindy cried. "You killed him!"

I didn't think. I didn't hesitate. I stood up, grabbed the shovel, and swung it at Cindy's head. A lucky shot. It slammed into her cheek and her temple, made a surprisingly solid *thunk* sound. Her eyes bulged, she opened her mouth and let out a low grunt, her knees buckled, and she went down. Her head hit the dirt hard, and she kinda folded in on herself.

Now what? No time to figure this out. I heard the dog barking. I turned and saw two police officers trotting behind her across the grass. "Your neighbor called us about half an hour ago," one of them said. "He complained your dog was digging up his tomato plants."

That's the way it went down. The cops saw the girl on the ground, the murder glove in my hand, the shovel beside me— all thanks to Ruby. Ruby the talking dog.

It was all the dog's fault, right? I'm not making any of this up. The dog did it all. It was the damn dog.

My lawyer says I'll never have to stand trial. He says to just keep on talking nonstop about Ruby. He says he has the perfect defense for me. That's why I'm in this hospital, not in a prison cell.

I'm wound tighter than a midget's yo-yo. But I'm not sure what the lawyer plans. I only know one thing. When I get out of here, I'm going to give that dog something to talk about.

PUSHED OR WAS FELL

JAY BRANDON

> ⁴fell: fierce; terrible; cruel
> —*Webster's New World Dictionary*

A s soon as they were married, everything went to hell.

Every morning of the cruise, Walt woke confused, wondering where he was and why there was another person in his bed. Walt was not a person who adjusted easily to change, and Sharon didn't help, throwing changes at him continually.

Anyone could have been confused; his life had changed so much so quickly. Walter should have been at work today at his desk, inside his cubicle on the twenty-third floor of the enormous, featureless skyscraper in downtown Dallas, in the comforting confines of the insurance company where he had worked since he'd graduated from college four years earlier. Walter's routine was such that he could find himself working at his desk of a midmorning without clearly remembering waking up that day. It was nice to live on such a track—shower, coffee, drive, desk—but he must have felt at least a trace of dissatisfaction or he would never have gone to the PAL picnic two months ago.

Walter didn't belong to PAL—the Paralegals and Associates League—but he'd received an invitation. The picnic was partly a recruitment drive. Walter wasn't a paralegal, though he did do legal research for the insurance company. "So you'd be an associate," the smiling hostess had informed him as she'd pinned a visitor's badge on his shirt at the picnic. "We love our associates." Maybe so, although Walter suspected that they'd added that membership category just to give themselves a good acronym.

The picnic had been on the last day of May, after work. Memorial Day was already past, and Dallasites were more dismayed than delighted at the prospect of the long summer about to get its grip on them. They'd already had three hundred-degree days. But twilight stealing over the park brought an illusion of relief. Walter strolled around, loosening and then removing his tie, sipping a beer. There were maybe fifty people spread over the acre of the picnic. The men looked like Walter: shy, quiet, youth wasted on them because they'd already developed middle-aged routines. The women were more open in their hopefulness, smiling at strangers. Walter smiled back but walked on because he wasn't good at starting conversation.

The picnic was at a large public park, beside the swimming pool. A few people had brought their suits and joined the swimmers in the pool. Walter walked that way and looked wistfully at the cool water. There were only a few bodies in the pool, mostly floating, a few languidly swimming. Walter was turning away when he heard a splash and saw that a young woman had dived into the pool. She surfaced a fourth of the way across, lifted one white arm, then another, swimming so fast that she created a miniature wake. Walter watched her reach the end, do a flip turn, and start back. Without thinking, he walked slowly toward the end of the pool where she'd started her swim, toward which she was heading again. So Walter was there when she climbed out of the water. Unthinking, he offered her his cup of lukewarm beer.

"No, thanks," she said, but not in an unfriendly way. She sat on the edge of the pool, hardly breathing hard, took off her swimming cap, and shook out her medium-length light brown hair. Then she lifted her feet out of the water to reveal that she was wearing flippers; that was how she'd moved so fast through the water.

"You're a professional," Walter said.

The young woman glanced at him sharply, then smiled a little when she saw his expression. "I just wanted a dip. It's so hot."

Walter nodded. He stayed beside her when she stood up. Her eyes came to the level of his. She was an ordinary-looking girl, her best feature a small cute nose, but my goodness, what legs she had. Walter stayed where he was to watch her walk away so he could admire those long, tapered legs. He stared so unabashedly that when the young woman glanced back at him she looked a little nervous.

That was the first hint Walter had that maybe he wasn't exactly the way he'd always thought of himself: mild as milk, so much the perfect gentleman that he hardly ever dated. The young woman in the bathing suit saw something else in his face, something that startled her. Walter even startled himself. He saw her hook her fingers under the back of her bathing suit and pull it down over her bottom, and he envied those fingers.

He came across her again half an hour later. She was wearing shorts and a sleeveless top, neither garment damp, so she wasn't wearing her bathing suit under them; she had found someplace at the park to change. The image of her briefly naked in a parked car or a ladies' room flitted through his mind, but he must have kept it out of his face this time because the young woman smiled. "Oh, you're here for the picnic too."

"Yes," Walter answered urbanely. "I'm thinking of becoming a PAL."

"You should. We need fresh blood. All right, this time I will." She took his beer cup from him and sipped it. Walter hadn't realized he'd extended the cup again.

"It's Sharon," she said.

"What?"

"Sharon. You were trying to read my name badge, weren't you?"

"Oh. Yes, thanks."

"And you're—" It was dark by then, and she peered at his badge with the scrawl the hostess had put on it.

"Walt—"

"Walt, how nice," Sharon said. As simply as that, she changed him again.

"You're a paralegal?" he asked.

"Yes, I work for Jim Thornton. The lawyer?"

Walt knew the name. At insurance companies such as the one where he worked, the names of well-known plaintiffs' lawyers were invoked in the same tones as the name of Satan at a tent revival.

He and Sharon didn't talk long at the picnic, but long enough that Walt thought he would join PAL. He saw her at the next meeting. She was friendly enough but still glanced at him with just a trace of anxiety, which made Walt feel manly and dominant, enough to ask her out.

❧

THEY'D HAD TWO dates, only two, when Walt came to Sharon's office one day to pick her up for lunch. They'd been ordinary dates, dinner for telling each other the mundane stories of their lives, a movie for sitting close in the dark. Both dates had ended with good-night kisses at the door of Sharon's apartment, the first kiss awkward and brief, the second longer, ending when she put a hand on Walt's chest as if she had to stop him.

Then they were going to have lunch, and Walt picked her up at the office of Jim Thornton, the plaintiffs' lawyer, Walt feeling rather like a spy in the enemy camp. He found Sharon in a large office, twice the size of his cubicle, but with a lot of the space taken up by filing cabinets and bookshelves. Sharon smiled happily at seeing him, but otherwise seemed a little distracted. "Let's get out of here," she said, but then stopped in her doorway and glanced out. "Oh, God—just a minute."

Then she did a most surprising thing. She pulled Walt back into the office and close to her. Sharon's arm went around his back and her mouth fastened on his. Her thigh pressed against him. In the space of two seconds they'd entered a passion zone of such intensity, Walt felt lost. But he put his arms around Sharon's back, feeling how thin she was, how he encompassed her. Her lips were soft. His molded hers. She was so pliable. Her thigh seemed to reshape itself against his. He could make her into anything.

They broke apart. Sharon sighed, looked at him dreamily, but then the anxiety returned to her face. She stepped to the doorway and looked out both ways. "It's okay, he's gone."

"Who?" Walt asked, but Sharon only shook her head mutely. She wouldn't answer until they were in Walt's car.

"My boss," she said then.

"Mr. Thornton? What's the matter? Does he—"

Sharon shrugged one shoulder. "He—bothers me sometimes. It's nothing, really." She put her hand on Walt's forearm as if he'd suddenly looked murderous, and she had to hold him back.

"It's something all working women have to learn to deal with," Sharon said with another sigh. "I thought if he saw me with another man he might get the idea—I'm sorry, Walt. I used you."

He had been used by a woman. Wow. Walt felt great. It had been the best kiss of his life. Maybe it was the suddenness, when he hadn't been prepared for it, but in those few seconds a darkness had enfolded them, lifted them out of the ordinary world—so much so that Walt hadn't even heard the lawyer walk by and then depart. The memory of the kiss stayed with him all through lunch. He thought it stayed with Sharon too, because she'd catch him looking at her and she'd look away, but with her smile matching his. He felt so intimate with her that he hated letting her go back to work. Walt insisted on walking her back through the old mansion that served as Thornton's law office, all the way to Sharon's office. Walter felt swelled, his chest expanded and the muscles of his arms tight. By contrast, Sharon seemed to shrink as they went inside the building. She ducked her head, barely answered greetings, and her shoulders hunched inward as she approached her own office. She opened the door and looked into it carefully before turning back to Walt.

"Thanks, Walt. Thanks for everything."

Only her eyes hadn't shrunk. They were large and brown, fastened on him. Maybe it was unshed tears that made her eyes so big. She clamped her lips together.

"I'll stay here," Walt said. "Maybe I should talk to him."

"Oh, no!" Sharon almost cried. "Don't do that, Walt. I'll be all right. After all, I have to work."

"No, you don't."

Sharon stared at him. "Of course I do. What else—"

"Come with me," Walt said, putting his arm around her. He

was suddenly more excited than he'd ever been in his life. He realized the building around them was just a shell, a paper movie set. He and Sharon could walk right out through the walls. Only he and she were real. He remembered her thigh against his, reminding him of her extraordinary legs. He hadn't seen them since the day of the picnic.

Breathless, Sharon said, "What are you saying, Walt? Are you asking me to—"

"Marry me," he finished her sentence. He was as startled as she. Walt felt his heart swell. Another change. Walt had never been impulsive. But he loved impulsiveness in that moment.

Sharon smiled at him. But her smile still held a trace of fear, as if she wondered what Walt were changing into.

✑✎

Two weeks later they were on the cruise. The wedding had been amazingly easy to arrange, since neither of them had close friends. Walt's confused-looking parents and a friend of Sharon's from work were the only witnesses to the union in a judge's chambers at the courthouse. Sharon had been beautiful in a white outfit that was more a suit than a gown. While she hugged her friend, Walt's mother had whispered, "Are you sure?" Walt had felt forceful and decisive. Everyone else was so unsure. Only he and Sharon were positive.

They'd spent their wedding night in a fancy hotel in Dallas, with so much champagne that Walt didn't remember it very clearly afterward, except Sharon's legs wrapped around him. The next day she'd looked shy but wicked, and he'd had a headache that the flight to Miami didn't help. "I've always wanted to go on a cruise, haven't you?" Sharon had said, a secret desire Walt hadn't known he'd possessed until she said it. Water, the sea, foreign climes, a shipload of strangers, and a beautiful new wife.

IT WASN'T FAIR to say that Sharon changed after the wedding; he hadn't known her well enough to say she was different now. But daily living with someone was a difficult adjustment. She spent so long in the bathroom at night that he was half asleep, lulled by the ship's roll, by the time she came to bed. One morning he found his toothbrush on the floor of the bathroom. Probably the ship's motions had tossed it there, but Walt felt unreasonably violated. "Is something wrong?" Sharon asked, and he only shook his head, annoyed by her anxious tone.

Sharon turned out to be an early riser. He was too, normally, but he'd expected life to be more languid on a cruise. Probably he had habits that irritated her too. Certainly Sharon was cool to him sometimes when he sought her out after waking grumpily alone.

One morning he found her in the ship's pool. Sharon was underwater when he came upon the scene. Her arms at her sides, she took long strokes with her legs. After a week of seeing her first thing in the morning, Walt had reverted to his opinion that Sharon was of no special prettiness, but in the water she was striking. Two men stood watching her, talking low to each other. Another man slipped into the water and swam toward her path. Walt's face reddened.

Sharon climbed out and pushed water and hair back from her face, eyes closed. She had gotten a new two-piece swimsuit for the trip. It wasn't a daring cut, but in that moment Walt thought it showed more skin than a woman should reveal to anyone except her new husband. Sharon wasn't heavily laden in the bust, but when she stood her legs seemed to rise and rise, the suit showing her thighs up almost to her waist. As she walked toward Walt her hands went behind her, straightening the suit. The men across the pool watched.

"Hello, darling," she said, patting his chest as she walked by, toward a chair beside which she had a glass of orange juice. Walt grabbed her arm and pulled her close. "Good morning," he said significantly, and kissed her.

"Goodness," she said after a minute.

"Come back to the cabin."

She didn't pretend she didn't know what he meant. "Darling, I'm all wet," she protested mildly.

"That's okay, I can get wet. I haven't showered yet."

"I noticed." She ran her palm over his rough cheek.

"I came looking for you as soon as I woke up. You're always gone."

"I waited"—she shrugged—"but you stayed asleep so long . . ."

"Come on back," he insisted, pulling her close again and slipping his fingers inside the waistband of her suit. Sharon jerked away, almost revealing herself to everyone at the pool. "Walt!" she gasped.

"It's a honeymoon!" he said, too loud. He felt watched.

Blushing, Sharon grabbed up her robe and hurried away. Walt turned and saw the two men watching, wearing knowing smiles.

THEN WHEN SHE would snuggle against him at night, he was so sleepy that he found her touch more irritating than arousing. Much as he was annoyed when she disappeared on ship, having her around all the time got on his nerves too, after his years of living alone. Walt continued to surprise himself. He'd expected to blend more easily into marriage.

"Do we have to get dressed up?"

"Walt," Sharon said reprovingly. She was wearing a long black dress with a webwork of straps that left her shoulders mostly bare, and with a modest slit up the side to halfway up her thigh. He hated that tone of voice. "If you wanted to spend all your time in T-shirts and cutoffs, we should have just gone to a beach. Cruises are for adventure too."

"Okay," he gave in. Sharon stood in front of the mirror. He went behind her and helped her clasp her necklace of fake pearls. Then he kissed the nape of her neck and put his arm around her, pressing against her. Sharon pressed back for a moment, putting a hand on his cheek, then neatly extricated herself and walked away. In that moment he wanted to kill her. The feeling increased when she turned an inquiring smile on him.

There were, in fact, customers of the Freeport casino wearing shorts and Hawaiian shirts. Walt felt overdressed, though there were other dressed-up couples, even a couple of old geeks in tuxedos. Sharon gravitated toward them, pulling Walt along. When she smiled eagerly back at him, she looked sixteen years old. He couldn't help but fall in love with her again.

But she aged considerably, into a fake sophistication that put his teeth on edge, as she chatted with the elegant couples then languidly asked Walt to get them some chips.

"That's all right, my dear," said one of the men, who was well dressed but not as old as the others, and didn't have a woman with him, at least at the moment. "Let me place a bet for you."

"That's okay," Walt said, "I'll get chips."

"Just one," the well-tanned man insisted suavely. As far as Walt was concerned, the intruder might have been asking, "Just one quick feel," but Sharon looked at Walt hopefully for permission and Walt half shrugged, half nodded, then stood with his hands in his pockets while Sharon and Tan Face huddled over what color or number to choose.

He hated the evening. He had never felt suave in his life, but he had never felt as out of place as he did that night in the casino. Rather than try to match the casual sophistication of the elegant crowd, he felt pushed toward the oafish opposite extreme. He kept balling his fists. The fact that Sharon fit in easily with the others made it worse.

He tried to kiss her once, behind a pillar but in sight of a few people. She held him away. In the cab going back to the ship, not even mindful of whether the driver spoke English, he almost screamed at her. Red-faced, the too many drinks he'd had coursing through him, he gestured at her and shouted, "You wear all these, these clothes, and that swimsuit, in front of everybody, then you don't want me to touch you!"

Sharon stared at him, aghast. Her expression deflated Walt. He wasn't being himself. He was turning into some monster.

Abashed, looking away from him, Sharon said, "I bought these clothes because I wanted to be seductive for the first time in my life. And I want to be—courted too."

"Great," Walt said, his bad mood having a momentum of its own. So he was expected continually to court his own wife, to try subtly to seduce her over and over.

He didn't have it in him. He knew he should apologize, but he didn't have that in him either. He looked across the narrow backseat of the cab, knowing that this was what he would remember of their glorious cruise, saw Sharon needing consoling, and felt nothing for her. She was too different, too complicated. He didn't feel like delving through layers to find her. Walt wanted his life back more than he wanted her. In that moment he decided he would get an annulment.

That was all he was thinking, he would swear later: annulment.

THE NEXT DAY, having slept back-to-back with her, Walt felt more sad than angry. He was absorbed in self-pity and wanted to stay withdrawn, but she kept picking at him. "Walt," she said beguilingly, sensing the secret he hid from her.

She followed him when he went out on deck, Walt wanting nothing but to be alone. It seemed like a long time since he hadn't been surrounded by people. "Nothing," he kept saying, and when she finally held his arm he jerked it away from her. He whirled on her, ready to fight her off. He didn't realize until he saw her shocked face that his fist was clenched again.

Later he saw her in a deck chair, talking to one of the older women, Sharon almost tearful. Walt wanted to go to her, but then the two women raised their eyes toward him. Their gaze was a wall.

It was their last day aboard ship; they would dock back in Miami late that afternoon. The ship bustled with preparations. Lots of people stayed on deck, anticipating. Walt was one of them. Sharon came to him at the railing late in the afternoon. She carried a handbag the size of a small suitcase, as if already ready to debark. "Tell me what you're thinking," she insisted.

"I just want to go home," he said.

"It's harder work than we thought, isn't it?"

He looked at her face, her cute little nose, her dark eyes drawn close together with worry. She would not age well, he saw. He decided to be brutally honest. "Sharon, we just made a mistake."

She looked shocked. "And I have to be the one to pay for it," she said bitterly.

"What are you talking about? We just both go back—"

She spoke low and venomously. It was Walt's turn to be

shocked. Sharon poured out a torrent of rage against men in general and Walt in particular. "I thought you were my rescuer, my hero. I can't believe you turned out to be such a coward."

"I'm not," he said, more certain than ever that he'd made a mistake in getting involved with her.

"I'll take everything you have," she said bitterly. "You'll be paying me for years."

Walt stepped back, baffled. "I'm just going to walk away."

"No, you're not." She grabbed him. Walt tried to jerk away, but she held his arms tightly at the biceps. This was ludicrous, no contest. But Sharon's grip was strong, pinching him. He raised his arms sharply, breaking her hold. He saw her gasp, then she reached for him again. He wouldn't let that happen. All the rage Walt had felt toward her returned in an instant. He put his hands on her chest and pushed.

Sharon screamed. She fell back against the waist-high railing, then over it. Her purse went sailing. She wasn't gone, she managed to grab the rail with one hand as she went over it, then she was hanging outside the railing, barely holding on. Walt rushed toward her, thinking there was still time, and managed to touch her hand just as Sharon let go. She screamed again as she fell.

Walt turned, horrified, looking for help but instead seeing everyone watching him. A few men rushed toward the railing, but most of the passengers just stood frozen, staring. When Walt took a step they drew back from him, as if a beast had suddenly dropped into their midst.

◦───◦

THE BIG POLICEMAN in the rumpled brown suit said, "Witnesses said your wife almost saved herself, she had hold of the railing, but then you ran over and hit or clawed her hand until she let go."

"No," Walt said, "no. I tried to save her."

"So you had second thoughts," the policeman said.

Walt's face opened in surprise, but before he could issue a shocked denial he realized it was one of those questions: *Have you stopped beating your wife?* Walt looked more closely at the police officer, who had a big, open all-American face—but there was thought behind it. After all, he was a detective, not a simple patrolman.

The two of them were alone in a small lounge on the second floor of the shipyard passenger terminal. Outside was a small balcony, with a view of the cruise ship. The ship had been close to port when Sharon had gone over the rail. Walt had been confined to his cabin by the crew until Miami police officers had come aboard and taken him off the ship, but not far. Police wanted to get the names of the passenger witnesses and question them before they took off for addresses across the country. The detective had decided to keep Walt handy in order to confront him with what these witnesses said. The officer saw a scared little man who'd done something terrible in a bad moment and would start crying about it at any minute. The detective expected a confession before they left the lounge.

"I didn't kill her," Walt said.

The detective looked puzzled. "You're saying she committed suicide?"

"No." Walt tried to keep his voice calm. "I mean, I didn't mean to hurt her and I didn't push her hard." He found himself demonstrating, his hand outward at chest level. The policeman watched the gesture impassively.

"Do you recognize this?" he asked, handing Walt a document.

Walt almost didn't answer, seeing what was coming. Then, "It's an insurance policy," he said tonelessly.

"On your wife."

"On both of us. This was Sharon's idea. Like a wedding present. She said she didn't have much money, but she'd make herself valuable to me." Walt tried to smile. The paper was crumpling in his hand. The policeman watched.

"You signed it," he said.

"Yes."

"Isn't this the insurance company you work for?"

"Yes, but—"

"But your wife arranged it?"

Walt stopped talking, and after a while the detective dropped his amiable pose. Little worthless wife-beater who collapsed like a dish towel when confronted by a man. The detective decided somebody else could finish this interrogation. He walked toward the door of the lounge.

Walt grabbed one of the flimsy wooden chairs, lifted it more easily than he'd expected, and crashed it down on the policeman's head. The detective went down to his knees. In a moment the doorway would fill with more cops. Walt turned the other way. He ran out onto the balcony and, as he heard shouts behind him, went the way Sharon had gone, over the rail.

❧

AT A BRANCH of his nationwide bank, Walt gutted his checking account. Every time he turned around he expected to see police filling the room. He tried to stay outdoors as much as possible, and was enormously grateful when night fell. He decided he couldn't risk the airport or a car rental place, and after a fearful few hours he did something he'd never done before, hitchhiked. He was rather surprised anyone would pick him up, and even more so that it was a woman who did.

She was a long-haul trucker, a little heavy, but with a lovely voice, little used. She gave Walt a sharp study when he first climbed up into the cab, then for several miles she let her left hand hang down beside her seat, where she probably carried protection. She was right to be nervous about him.

But she was also lonely. She was willing to compromise her safety for companionship. Walt kept his answers short and colorless. Ever since he'd seen her he'd been almost trembling with fear. Not of her recognizing him as a fugitive. He was afraid of himself.

What if he liked the trucker? What if they fell into easy chat, then became attracted? He had enough imagination to play out at least a weekend of happily ever after. Lust and love and the chance of happiness.

Then what if she did something to make him mad?

"I didn't kill her!"

"What?" She looked more puzzled than alarmed. Walt realized he'd muttered aloud.

"Sorry. Nothing. I said I'm out of kilter."

The truck driver's hand fell beside her seat again. It was black night outside, the interstate only sharply visible in the brief islands created by her headlights. They were high off the road in the cab of her truck. When Walt looked down they seemed to teeter on a height. He put out his hands to steady himself. His hands hit the dashboard hard, making the ashtray rattle.

❧

THE TRUCKER DROPPED him off in New Orleans, which he pretended was his destination. He was halfway home. But what did that matter? He didn't have a home anymore.

Walt bought a Miami newspaper and found a small story about a honeymoon that ended in tragedy. The story seemed remote from him. Sharon's body hadn't been recovered. That was the one fact he gleaned.

He smelled like a street person, so he bought a colorful new shirt in a drugstore. In the old shirt's pocket was the copy of the insurance policy with which the Miami cop had confronted him. He stuffed it in his back pocket. From the big city he felt safe in taking a bus, paying cash for a ticket. He couldn't return to Dallas, but he headed into Texas anyway. Texas was big; he could lose himself.

But what good would it do? Even if he managed to escape the consequences of his crime and start over, he could never make a real life.

On the bus he fell asleep and dreamed of her murder. In the dream his hands were huge—they almost covered Sharon's body as they swept her over the railing. His vision followed her down as she screamed in fright, then everything went silent as she plunged into the water. He saw her continue to fall, but slowly, shedding her clothes, turning gracefully, as smooth as she'd been.

Walt jerked awake in darkness and the smell of his own sweat. He fumbled the insurance policy out of his pocket, snapped on the reading light, and skimmed the policy with a practiced eye. Quickly he found his own name, but that wasn't what he was seeking. In the next paragraph he found another name, one he'd never heard before.

The policy shook in his hands. Walt hadn't known himself very well, but he hadn't known Sharon at all. What if she had been the one who was so different? Walt was an avid reader. In the dark, still haunted by his dream, he was taken by a phrase he'd read once: "pursued by a fell power." It seemed very apt now that he was a fugitive. He'd had to look up the adjective. *Fierce*, it meant; *terrible, willing to do anything.* Had Sharon been more fell than he could have suspected?

At the next stop he got off the bus and changed direction.

FROM ACROSS THE small-town street, Walt watched her and smiled. The fear stopped. He felt his self-image reassemble itself.

He was in the pleasant town of Fredericksburg, a farm town / tourist trap nestled in the Texas hill country. This was where the alternative beneficiary to Sharon's life insurance policy lived—a supposed sister named Karen of whom Walt had never heard. Sharon had told him she was all alone in the world. Walt watched "Karen" go into an old-fashioned drugstore. She was an ordinary-looking young woman, though it was hard to tell that under her hat, behind her large round sunglasses. Walt could see, though, that she had a cute little nose.

As he waited for her to emerge Walt carried on an imaginary conversation with the Miami police detective. "I knew I didn't push her hard enough for her to go over that rail. She went over on purpose. It was how she could fake her death. You haven't found that handbag she had, have you? I know what was in it— flippers and a float. Karen could have swum ashore, believe me. Leaving a lot of witnesses to her 'death' but her still alive to collect the insurance payment."

This was in answer to an imaginary question from the detective: "So she picked you out of every man in Dallas to go after. She lured you in."

"Don't you see, that's the beauty of it," Walt muttered. "It didn't have to be me, it could be anybody. Anybody who was attracted to her, anybody she could draw in with that helpless act of hers. Maybe she'd tried it before and hadn't gotten far enough. It could be anybody, because she wasn't going after some rich man's money, she was going after an insurance payoff that would be paid to this imaginary sister of hers—who was really Sharon herself."

That's what Walt insisted on thinking. Not that he'd harbored a hidden rage powerful enough to make him kill. He remembered instead how protective he'd felt toward Sharon at first. During the disastrous honeymoon she'd carefully goaded him into the one hateful act of his life. But it had been his kindness she'd counted on.

⁂

HIS THEORY FALTERED a little when he questioned the cashier in the drugstore. "Excuse me, I thought I saw somebody I know walk out of here. Was that Karen Miller?"

The cashier, barely out of her teens, didn't even glance at him suspiciously. "That was her, all right."

"I met her in Dallas when she was visiting her sister Sharon," Walt took a shot. But this query did make the cashier look at him more intently.

"I don't know about any sister," she said. "And Karen's lived here for the last few years. I remember her substitute teaching when I was in high school."

Walt walked more slowly along the sidewalk, the way the young woman had gone. The woman who really was Karen Miller.

⁂

HE FOLLOWED HER the rest of the day, and in the evening to the cottage on the outskirts of town where she lived alone. It was a quiet life Karen Miller had, a subsistence existence in every way: the bare minimum of money, of shelter, of people. Walt studied her, afraid to approach close enough for her to spot him. She was the same size as Sharon; it could have been Sharon's face as well as he could tell. Her walk was different—he would have liked to see her legs in all their glory, that would have settled

it—but she had the same habit of ducking her head when someone spoke to her.

Walt found a bed and breakfast to spend the night in, during
the middle of which he woke with his theory restored.

❧

HE SPENT THE next morning watching her again. The young
woman spent half the morning at a table behind a bright front
window of her cottage, sewing the little dolls she sold to the
cute-as-hell gift shops that lined the main street of Fredericksburg. Once in a while Karen would close her eyes and stretch
her neck, leaning back. Walt imagined standing behind her,
massaging her shoulders. She needed someone. The little cottage, what he could see of it, was so plain. There were curtains
around the window where she sat, but they had been washed so
often that he could see through them. The front yard was so
narrow, it held only a small bed of flowers the girl must have
planted herself.

Then Walt remembered who she was and stopped feeling
sorry for her. He imagined his hands around her neck in a different way.

Later she went out on her rounds and stopped in a tea shop
for just that, tea. It was lunchtime, but the young woman
couldn't afford lunch out, so she had only a cup of tea. *Of course,*
Walt thought, *she has to be seen, she has to establish herself in
town.* The tea shop was large, including a gift store. From across
the big room Walt saw her lean her head sideways and back.
She'd removed her sunglasses but still wore her hat, covering half
her face. As she listened to the conversations around her, her
mouth was pursed wistfully. Walt had had lunches like that
himself, treating strangers as if they were actors hired for his
amusement, to fend off his loneliness.

Walt steeled himself. That was how Sharon had sucked him in: play a lonely woman to lure a lonely man. With sudden decision he strode across the tea shop and sat down across the table from her. The chair was so quaint it almost collapsed under him. She gasped.

Walt reached across the table and swept off her hat. Light brown hair he remembered so well fell down her neck.

But the startled eyes that stared into his were an unfamiliar blue. Sharon's had been brown.

"I'm sorry," he said. "I thought—"

He stared. There was a resemblance—it was clear they were sisters—but Karen was younger and softer than Walt's wife had been. Her lower lip trembled. It was amazing she didn't scream, the way he'd scared her.

"I'm sorry," he said again. "I thought you were someone else. Someone I knew in—" He almost said Miami. ". . . in Dallas." He didn't know why he risked saying more. Possibly it was the way Karen stared at him, her eyes growing less alarmed the more he explained. She kept watching Walt until he added, "Her name was Sharon Miller."

She smiled. "My sister."

"I read about her. I'm sorry."

Pain condensed her features. "Thank you," she said.

He couldn't leave then—remind her of her tragedy and then walk away. He stayed at the table and when the harried waitress appeared he ordered lunch for both of them, over Karen's protest, and watched to make sure she ate her soup and half sandwich. Walt kept studying her for signs of Sharon, but it became more and more obvious that Karen was a different person. As his theory dissolved his fear returned, as well as a new feeling. He recognized Karen's quietness and the contradictory feelings behind her shy smile. He recognized her whole life.

He made up an imaginary connection to Sharon in order to ask Karen about her life. They'd been orphaned as teenagers, and Sharon had been as much a mother as a big sister to her, though they were only three years apart. Then Sharon had gone to Dallas to find work. She'd asked Karen to join her, but Karen had had the sense to prefer Fredericksburg to Dallas.

"Why didn't you get a teaching degree instead of just substituting?" Walt asked. Karen looked at him strangely, and he realized she hadn't volunteered the information that she was an occasional substitute teacher. But she answered anyway.

"I just never . . . settled on what I wanted to do, you know?"

Yes, he did. He knew exactly. "I'm still trying to decide . . ." he began, then realized she was saying the exact same thing. They laughed.

He paid the bill and walked out with her, then continued along the sidewalk. Karen didn't object. He felt the nearness of her shoulder. He knew when he looked at her she'd be glancing sidelong at him. Her cheek colored. Karen's shyness didn't make him feel dominant the way Sharon's had. It made him want to take her hand like Hansel and Gretel in the woods, finding their way out into the world together.

But the thought of taking her hand reminded him of his own hands. They felt heavy. Walt could never find his way out. Even if some miracle occurred to give him a life with Karen, he couldn't take the chance. Her late sister had taught him that he harbored a beast that might come snarling out at any moment.

If only he'd met Karen first.

People jostled them, smiled at them, occasionally one murmured a condolence to Karen. They turned off onto an unpeopled side street and walked toward Karen's cottage. Her steps slowed. Walt looked at her curiously. Karen looked sad, but not deeply mournful the way someone who'd just had news of a beloved sister's death should be.

They reached her cottage and went up the sidewalk onto the porch, but Karen stopped there, not inviting him in. She put her back to the door and looked at him very forthrightly. "You're him, aren't you? Sharon's husband."

It hardly crossed his mind to deny it. Since Walt had seen that Karen was not Sharon, as he'd imagined, he had known his life was over. It didn't matter whether police caught him or he went back into hiding.

"Can I explain? We can stay out here. I don't have any reason to hurt you."

"I know," she surprised him by saying. He looked into her eyes and saw that some of Karen's sadness was for him.

He told her the story quickly, emphasizing how early he'd known he'd made a mistake. He'd gotten mad at Sharon, yes, but—

"I know how she could be," Karen said very quietly. So that was why she looked at him the way she did. Amazed, Walt met her eyes. He found sympathy there.

He told her about his theory that Sharon had survived, and that she'd invented an imaginary sister to be the alternative beneficiary to her life insurance—after Walt couldn't collect because he'd caused Sharon's death. He didn't have to explain why that theory had failed.

"But then I thought, maybe it wasn't the sister who was imaginary, maybe it was Sharon herself. Maybe she'd had this life as Karen here all along, while she was off in Dallas looking for someone . . ." Looking for a victim for her scheme. It had made sense. Karen's life was so marginal, she could be gone for days or even weeks at a time and no one would notice. He had sat down at her tea table convinced that when he removed the hat he'd be looking into Sharon's eyes—a Sharon who had figured out how to be her own beneficiary.

Instead he'd met eyes he felt he knew at once. By this time he was bold enough that when his heart leaped with hope Walt acted on it. He took Karen's hand, suddenly short of breath. "Karen, come with me. I'm so sorry. If I could undo everything I would. Everything, from the first day I met your sister. If I could somehow have met you instead—I know it's crazy, but if you feel it too . . ."

She did. From the way she looked at him he thought sure she did. But it *was* crazy. How could he ask her to run away with her sister's murderer? How could she—or he—forget what he was?

They both had so little life to give up that for a moment it seemed possible. But it wasn't. As Karen stared sadly at him, Walt heard the sound of tires. It was almost a relief to turn and see the police car pulling up to the curb.

Walt didn't make a fuss, and the arrest was quickly accomplished. "I'm sorry," he called as the one cop eased Walt's head below the door frame and settled him in the backseat of the cruiser. The other one finished questioning Karen, then joined his partner. The two uniformed police officers stood talking quietly beside their car as Karen went into the cottage.

She was sorry too. Sorry for Walt. She was the only person on earth who knew what he'd been through. Karen almost felt she'd been following his progress from afar as he'd made his way toward her, thinking her someone else. She too had felt the connection when their eyes met.

Karen dropped her hat on a chair. She didn't turn on a light. The small cottage was dim in the afternoon. It held a secret, cloistered coolness that emanated from the two bedrooms in the back. Karen stood indecisively, feeling that coolness come stealing over her, almost as tangible as the hands that gripped her shoulders a moment later.

"He almost got it," Sharon said. "But not quite." Still holding her shy sister in place, Sharon licked her earlobe playfully.

Karen looked out at the bright sunlit street, where the police car no longer sat. Her heart shriveled.

ENTRAPPED

HARLAN COBEN

MY HUSBAND IS missing," I said.

I waited for Sergeant Harding's reaction, but he seemed preoccupied—if not enamored—with the half-eaten croissant in his right hand.

He was fiftyish, I guessed. His suit looked like it'd been stored in a laundry hamper since the Watergate hearings. So, actually, did he.

With a sigh, Harding put down the croissant and picked up a pencil. He flashed me a smile with teeth the yellow of a Ticonderoga pencil. "Well now!"

I tried my best not to swoon.

"How long has your husband been missing, Mrs. . . . ?"

"Kimball," I said. "Jennifer Kimball. My husband's name is Edward and he's been missing for two days."

He wrote it down, barely looking at the notepad. "Address?"

"Three Markham Lane."

"Markham Lane?" he repeated. "Isn't that where those ritzy new mansions were just built?"

I nodded, adjusting the gold bracelet on my hand—a gift from Edward—and crossed my legs. His eyes brightened and followed, slithering along my flesh like earthworms.

"My husband and I just moved to New Jersey last week," I explained. "From Arizona, outside Phoenix."

He looked surprised. "You from this area originally, honey?"

Aside from perhaps "babe" or "sweet buns," there are few things I enjoy more than being called "honey" by a charismatic hunk who possesses that rare combination of boss threads and top-drawer dental hygiene. "Why on earth would you need—"

"Look, Mrs. Kimball, I'm on your side." He spoke in that patronizing tone some men get around me. "I want to find out what happened too, okay? But put yourself in my position. You move out here from Phoenix and a day or two later your husband disappears. I have to consider the possibility that there may have been a lovers' tiff, or—"

"There was no lovers' tiff," I interrupted. "My husband is missing. His car is gone."

"What kind of car?"

"A 1997 blue Mercedes 500," I said. "Burgundy interior. Brand-new."

He whistled low. "A 500, huh? Jersey plates or Arizona?"

"New Jersey. AYB 783."

He jotted it down. "What does your husband do, Mrs. Kimball?"

"Edward is an international trader," I said vaguely. "But he hasn't had time to rent an office here yet."

"Does he have any friends or family in the area?"

"None."

"Do you have a photograph of him?"

I reached into my purse with fumbling fingers and plucked out a small photograph of Edward.

"Nice-looking man," Harding commented.

I said nothing.

"How long you been married?" he asked.

"Six months."

His phone rang. "Harding," he answered. "What? Oh, good. Fine." He replaced the receiver and rose. "Well, Mrs. Kimball, we'll do a little checking and see what we come up with."

I was dismissed.

⚬⚬⚬

I CONFESS TO having expensive taste. So sue me.

The car—my cuddly baby—is a Jag. She is a powerful, sexy machine. Edward wanted me to get a Mercedes like his—more reliable, he claimed—but I was not to be dissuaded.

I drove up our circular driveway and parked by the front door. But when I put my key in the lock, the door was already unlocked.

Strange.

I eased it open. If I had been trying to do it quietly, I had failed miserably. The door squeaked like a dog toy. I stepped inside, my heels clacking loudly against the marble floor. Then I looked around. Nothing. I meant that almost literally. Very little of our personal belongings had been delivered yet. The large foyer was almost bare.

Then I heard footsteps coming from the other room.

I shivered and backed toward the door, preparing to sprint.

"Jen? Is that you?"

He burst in the foyer, smiling at me. "Hi, hon. Where were you?" He was about six feet tall with wavy dark hair. Fairly run-of-the-mill in the looks department—not bad, not great. He was also a complete stranger. I had never laid eyes on the man in my entire life.

Logic would probably have dictated that I run, but fleeing had never been my style. "Who are you?" I snapped.

The man looked at me, puzzled. "Are you joking?"

"I am two seconds away from screaming," I said. "Who are you?"

"Are you feeling okay, Jen?"

"Who are you?"

His puzzled look gave way to a weary smile. "Okay, Jen, let's have it."

"What?"

"Why are you still mad? I thought we had this all straightened out."

"I'm calling the police."

He watched me walk toward the phone but did nothing to stop me. "You're serious."

"Of course I'm serious. Who are you?"

He looked at me with what appeared to be genuine concern. "Jen, I think you'd better sit down."

Should I run? To hell with it. I would call Sergeant Harding and see how this guy reacted. I picked up the phone, keeping my eyes on him. He continued to watch with a mix of confusion and concern on his face. I'd started to dial when I glanced down at the table and gasped.

"Honey, what is it?"

I barely heard him. My hand reached down and picked up a silver key chain—Edward's key chain.

"They're just my keys, Jen," the man said.

I whirled toward him. "Where did you get these?"

"Will you stop it already? Stop pretending you don't know your own husband."

My husband?

I dropped the key chain and dashed outside. So much for my

no-fleeing style. The impostor followed, calling my name in a gentle, pleading voice. I veered left and headed toward the garage. When I peered inside, I felt something in my brain stretch taut.

A 1997 blue Mercedes 500. Brand-new. I checked out the license plate. New Jersey. AYB 783.

The man came up behind me. "It's just my car."

I spun toward him. "I don't know who you are or what you're trying to pull—"

"'Pull'? What the hell are you talking about?"

"How did you get his car?"

"Whose car?"

"Edward's!"

"Please stop it, Jen. You're scaring me."

"I'm calling the police."

He shook his head in what appeared to be resignation. "Fine. Call them. Maybe they can tell me what alien scrambled my wife's brain."

I strode back into the house with the man a few paces behind me. I kept glancing back, wondering when he was going to attack, preparing for his imminent pounce. But none came. Surely he would never allow me to place the call. Once I spoke to the police, the gig, as they say, would be up.

I picked up, my hand trembling as though the receiver were a jackhammer. The man moved closer to me. I stepped away, and to my surprise he raised both hands in a surrender salute and backed off. "Whatever I did, Jen, I'm sorry. You have to believe me."

The phone on the other end was picked up. "Livingston police."

"Sergeant Harding, please. This is Jennifer Kimball."

"Hold on a moment." I heard the phone ring again. Then: "Harding."

"Sergeant Harding, this is Jennifer Kimball."

"Well, hello, Mrs. Kimball. Find your husband?"

I felt oddly like a tattletale who just yelled for the teacher. I expected the bully to run away now that an adult was coming. But the Edward impostor kept as still as a Rodin.

"No," I said slowly. "But a strange man broke into my house."

"Is he still there?"

"He's standing right in front of me. He says he is Edward."

"Your husband? I don't get it."

"Neither do I, Sergeant. He has Edward's keys and Edward's car, and he claims he is my husband."

Pause. "Well, what is he doing?"

"Doing?"

"Is he trying to escape?"

"No." I imagined how crazy this must have sounded to Harding, so I could not really blame him in the least. But of course I did anyway.

"Mrs. Kimball, would you mind putting him on the phone?"

"If you want."

I handed the phone to the mystery man. "He wants to speak with you."

"Fine," he said, taking the receiver. "Okay, joke's over now," he said into the phone. "Who is this?"

I could barely hear the tinny sound of Harding's voice through the receiver; the impostor's words, however, were quite clear: "What police force? Oh, come on now. The joke has gone too far." Pause. "Fine, I'll put you on hold." He pushed down the hold button and pressed for the other line.

"What are you doing?" I asked.

The impostor's face remained set. "Your friend on the phone," he began while dialing the phone, "claims that he is a

Sergeant Ronald Harding of the Livingston police. I'm calling the police department myself, to end this little charade once and for all."

I was stunned. How far was this guy going to take this?

He said nothing while waiting for the connection to go through.

Then: "I would like to speak with Sergeant Harding." Pause. "What? So you are a police officer. My God. I apologize, Sergeant, but something very odd . . . Yes, of course I am Edward Kimball. No, I do not know what this is all about. My wife left this morning and . . . She said I was what?" He turned and looked at me tenderly. I returned his tenderness with my best hell-spawned glare. "Sergeant, I do not know what is going on here . . . Yes, we had a little fight but . . . Fine, that's a good idea. Jen, he wants to speak to you." He handed me the receiver.

"Yes, Sergeant?"

"I'm coming out there right now," Harding replied. "Do you want to stay on the line with another officer until I arrive?"

"I'll put it on speakerphone," I said. I hit the button and replaced the receiver. "Just hurry."

"On my way."

"He'll be here in a few minutes, Jen," the impostor said. "Try not to upset yourself, okay?"

"Give it a rest already," I said with a sigh. "And stop calling me that."

"What?"

"Jen. That's what Edward calls me."

"Now, honey, I know this move has been stressful, but—"

As he rambled on, an idea came to me. You see, most of our belongings had not yet arrived from Arizona, but a few had— including a box of Edward's personal belongings. And what had

Edward immediately unpacked from the box and put on the night table next to his bed? Our wedding photo.

That would be my indisputable proof that this guy was an impostor. Case dismissed. Lock him up for breaking and entering and maybe something much worse.

"Jen?"

I tried to smile. "I'm going to go upstairs for a few minutes, uh, darling." Play along, get along—that was my new credo.

"Good," he replied. "Why don't you splash some water on your face? Maybe it'll help clear your mind."

"I'll do that."

❧

MY LEGS FELT like spaghetti strands as I made my way up the grand staircase. This man could not possibly imagine he could get away with taking Edward's place. *He must be insane,* I thought. *An escaped mental patient . . .*

Oh, God, maybe that's it! Maybe he really believes he is Edward. Maybe he stole Edward's wallet and because of some short circuit in his brain he now thinks he is my husband.

Stay cool, I told myself. *Don't upset him. If he really is unstable, who knows how he'll react if I continue to confront him? Sergeant Harding will be here soon. Just stay calm.*

"Jen, are you all right?"

His voice made me jump. "Much better," I singsonged, doing my best June Cleaver on happy pills. "I'll be down in a minute."

I tiptoed toward Edward's night table in the bedroom. Relief washed over me when I spotted the familiar silver picture frame. But when I picked up the wedding photograph, my heart slammed into my throat. I closed my eyes and opened them again. But nothing changed.

There I was, wearing white and lace, looking the way a man

dreams about his bride looking on his wedding day. And standing next to me, with a tan face and bright smile, wearing a black tuxedo with a white tie and cummerbund, was the impostor.

"Jen?"

I dropped the picture and heard it crash. He was leaning against the door frame, his arms crossed like the casual guy in a Sunday circular. "Get away from me," I said.

"It's okay, Jen. Sergeant Harding is here."

Harding rounded the corner as if he'd just been introduced on Leno. "Hello, Mrs. Kimball," he said, spreading his hands. "So what seems to be the trouble?"

"This man is claiming to be Edward," I said.

"Oh, stop it," the man countered. "This has gone far enough."

Harding turned to the impostor. "Where have you been the past two hours?"

"Right here, for crying out loud. Jen and I were unpacking. We just moved from Arizona. Look, Sergeant, I am sorry about all this. We had a little disagreement this morning, but I thought it was all settled. Here"—he walked over to the shattered frame—"this is our wedding picture."

Harding examined the photograph. "Is this your wedding picture, Mrs. Kimball?"

I shook my head. "He must have done something to it," I said. "Trick photography or something. He's about the same height as Edward, but aside from that, they look nothing alike."

The phony Edward stepped forward. "You have to face reality, Jen," he said in a soothing tone. "Did I fake all of these IDs too?" He handed Harding a Fendi wallet—Edward's Fendi wallet. I gave it to him for his birthday. There were three picture IDs. All read Edward Elaine Kimball. All had the mystery man's picture on them.

Harding examined the items carefully and then looked at me. "They're fake," I said. "All of them."

Harding nodded, but he was humoring me now. "Mr. Kimball, do you mind if I talk to your wife alone for a minute?" In other words: *I'll straighten out the hysterical bimbo for you, bub. Part of the job.*

My voice was strong and measured. "He's not Mr. Kimball, and I am not his wife."

Harding ignored my outburst and kept his eyes on "Edward," who nodded his consent and left the room. Once we were alone, Harding closed the door, took a deep breath, and rubbed his face. "You know how this looks, don't you, Mrs. Kimball?"

"Like I'm raving mad," I replied evenly. "But I'm not. He is not Edward. He has fake IDs and he tampered with our wedding photo. He must be a lunatic of some kind. He must . . ."

Harding held something in front of my face and my words drifted off. Reality, something that was always so firmly planted for me, was being ripped up by the roots. "No . . ."

"This is the photograph of Edward you gave me no more than an hour ago," Harding said. "Take a look at it."

I shook my head.

"Take a look, Mrs. Kimball."

I looked. It was a picture of the impostor.

My head spun. I felt faint, though I had never fainted in my life. It couldn't be, it just could not be . . .

"There are two explanations," he continued, "for what's going on here. One, you are not a well woman, Mrs. Kimball. Two, you are a spoiled brat who craves attention—and let me tell you, lady, I don't appreciate your involving the police in your little minidrama." He flipped the photograph onto the bed in undisguised disgust. "Get professional help, Mrs. Kimball. I'm a busy man."

He stormed out of the room. I could not move. Somewhere in the distance, I heard a door close and then: "Jen? Are you all right, honey?"

My head did not stop spinning until, mercifully, I passed out.

～✦～

I HAVE ALWAYS dreamed a lot. Since I was a little girl, my sleep has taken me on vivid nocturnal voyages that do not fade away when I am awake. I remember everything, which is not always good. I do not claim to be a prophet, and I do not believe we see the future in dreams, but, well, let me tell you what I saw.

I could see myself standing in an alley. I was watching from afar, like Jimmy Stewart in *Rear Window*, helpless to prevent whatever horror might befall my other self. The stench of spoiled garbage was overwhelming. Broken cinder blocks, overturned trash cans, and shattered glass lay sprawled like the wounded. A single lightbulb at the end of the alley cast the only illumination. I stepped forward.

Up ahead, I could see Edward's Mercedes. I took another step, and suddenly I could see a whole lot more. Resting on the steering wheel was Edward's head—or, at least, what was left of it. Blood covered his shoulders and dripped over the dashboard, forming a murky puddle on the floor near his feet.

Now I could see that someone was in the car next to him. But who? I squinted and then saw who it was. No surprise, really. It was the Edward impostor. He reached into the pocket of Edward's custom-made English suit and took out his wallet. He pocketed the money, checked the ID, and then turned and looked at me—looked straight into my eyes—and smiled.

I sat up in the bed, gulping down deep breaths. A light film of perspiration coated my skin.

"Feeling better?" The impostor stood in the doorway, that horrid dream smile still pinning his lips.

I stood and stumbled a few feet in his direction. "Please," I said, angry with myself for sounding so weak. "Tell me what you want. I'll do anything you say. Just stop . . ."

He started toward me but when I backed away again, he sighed and shook his head. "I have work to do," he said in a tone of surrender. "I'll be downstairs in the study."

And then it dawned on me. I suddenly knew how I could prove he was an impostor: Edward's aunt.

Rose Kimball was Edward's only living relative. The old goat was over seventy and lived in Boston, but she would know this guy was a fake in two seconds. Rose and I, to be honest, had never been very close. To be precise, the old goat hated me. Like many people I have come across, she equated beauty with gold digging and thus took an immediate dislike to me.

But now Rose would be my salvation. She knew Edward better than anyone and would be able to tell just by the voice that this man was an impostor. I reached for the phone next to the bed and quickly dialed her number. After four rings, someone answered: "Hello?"

"Hello, Rose."

"Hello, Jennifer." Her tone could frost a wedding cake. "What can I do for you?"

For once her snootiness did not bother me. The important thing was that she had recognized my voice right away. "Someone wants to talk to you," I said. I put my hand over the mouthpiece. "Edward! Your aunt is on the phone."

The impostor picked up the extension downstairs. "Rose? Is that you?"

He knew her name.

"Oh, Edward, I'm so glad you called."

The hope soaring inside me took a nosedive. "That's not Edward!" I shouted.

"What are you talking about?" Rose snapped.

"It's all right, Aunt Rose," the impostor said in a maddeningly calm tone. "Jen has been under a little strain lately."

"I'm not under any strain! You're not Edward! Tell him, Rose. Tell him you know he's a phony."

"I most certainly will not," Rose huffed. "I warned you about her, Edward."

"She'll be fine, Aunt Rose. I think it's the move. How are you feeling?"

They chitchatted for several minutes before saying their heartfelt good-byes. I sat there with the phone in my hand, my mouth agape. The impostor did not even sound like Edward.

My head felt like it was splitting in two; nothing made sense to me anymore. Before my call to Rose, I could see how the whole thing could be possible, if not rational. You see, my dream earlier had provided a possible explanation for this whole thing: the impostor had simply pushed Edward's body out of the car and decided to take his place. He had somehow tampered with the wedding photograph and might have even paid Harding off to switch the wallet pictures. I'm not suggesting that this made sense, mind you, but at least it was within the realm of possibility.

But not now. Aunt Rose would never go along with such a scheme. She could not be bought (the old goat had more money than God) and, more important, she loved Edward unconditionally. There was no way she would go along with such a stunt, no way at all, unless . . .

But no, that was impossible—impossible and irrational and utterly ridiculous. Better not to think of it . . . which left me with only one other possibility, a possibility that kept poking me with a long finger: maybe I had indeed lost my mind.

Maybe I was going through some sort of nervous breakdown. It's not the kind of thing you can look at very objectively, but only someone completely insane would not begin to question their own sanity after all this.

"Edward?" I called down sweetly. Donna Reed on saccharin.

"Yes, darling?"

"I'm going to take a long hot bath. Can we talk after that?"

"I'd love that. Don't worry, darling. You're going to be all right. I'll take care of you."

Oh, right, sure. I went into the bathroom and turned the water on. I had no intention, however, of taking a bath. I tip-toed down the stairs, passed the study door, and headed into the yard. A minute later I was in the garage, standing over Edward's car. I am not sure what I was looking for—bloodstains, perhaps. A clue of some kind. But I found nothing. The front seat was spotless, just as Edward himself had always kept it. There was just one little problem.

The interior color was not the same.

Edward had a specially designed burgundy interior. This car—the impostor's car—was gray.

I almost cried out. This was not Edward's car, and I was not insane. The man in my house was not Edward. Part of me felt relief. Part of me felt mounting terror. It brought me back to an earlier fear, a fear that swept through me when Rose insisted that the impostor was indeed her nephew. There was only one way Rose would go along with such a lie: if Edward told her to.

There, I said it. I knew, of course, that this was not possible. I would sooner believe that Rose could be bought off than believe that Edward was somehow behind all this. Yet, the more I thought about it, the more bothersome it became. Eliminate the impossible and what do you have left?

I quietly opened the door of my Jag and slid into the seat. As

I pulled out of the driveway, I glanced behind me. Through the study window, I saw the impostor talking on the phone, watching me.

≈≈

IT TOOK ME half an hour to find the alley—mostly because I had to make sure I wasn't being followed. When I got there, everything was exactly as I had seen in the dream—the darkness, the bare lightbulb, the stench that could paralyze a zebra.

Holding my breath, I hurried toward the Dumpster. It would have been quite a spectacle to those who know me to see Jennifer Kimball down on all fours in a filthy alley, reaching through the buzzing flies for something under a Dumpster. But those people did not know what Jennifer Kimball had gone through in the past. But not anymore. Not ever again.

I felt around until my hand hit metal and pulled it into view. A gun—a .38, actually, Smith and Wesson. I checked the chamber. I was sure there was going to be blanks. It was the only explanation for everything that was going on. I emptied the five chambers that were left intact. The bullets were real. No blanks.

I dropped the gun as though it were on fire. Yet again, nothing made sense, absolutely nothing. It was as though I had woken up one morning and all the laws of nature had been changed. E did not equal MC squared. The Atlantic Ocean was a landmass. The earth was flat. And the clear line between life and death was suddenly very blurry.

I turned the corner and was greeted with yet another surprise that tore at my sanity with sharpened claws: a 1997 blue Mercedes 500, brand-new, New Jersey plates AYB 783. Just where it had been in the dream.

I moved closer to the car and peered through the back window. There was a body slumped across the front seat, the head resting on the steering wheel.

With something past horror, I realized that my hand was grasping the handle. The car door swung open slowly. I swallowed and reached in to pull the head back. At the last moment, as I stared at the dried blood on the burgundy interior, I had a second to wonder why, if Edward was behind all of this, he had not let the impostor use his own car. And in that split second, the answer came to me: Edward's Mercedes was state evidence and needed in another scheme.

The head on the steering shot upright and smiled at me. "Hello, Mrs. Kimball."

I jumped back, tripping over a can and falling to the ground. I clambered back up as he got out of the car and faced me. Suddenly everything made sense. All the pieces were coming together. And it wasn't a pretty picture.

"It can't be," I shouted, though in truth I knew it had to be. It was the only thing that fit. You see, Edward was not behind all this. Edward was indeed dead.

"It's over, Mrs. Kimball."

Sergeant Harding stepped out of the Mercedes as a police car pulled in behind us. Two men got out and pointed guns at me. One was the Edward impostor.

I swung my head back toward Harding. "I don't . . ."

"Understand?" he finished for me. "I think you do. We found your husband's body here the night he was murdered."

Time to play Dumb Dora. "Murdered?"

"You killed him, Mrs. Kimball, just like you killed your first husband."

Time to play Grieving Widow. I produced a tear in my eye. "Gary died in a car accident."

"His car went over a cliff and into a ravine," Harding agreed, "but you pushed it. You also collected a half-million-dollar insurance policy on him."

Shocked. Insulted. Confused. "What are you trying to say?"

"When we found Edward Kimball's body," he began, "his ID still had your Arizona address. The only emergency number listed was for Mrs. Rose Kimball, an aunt who lived in Boston. When we told her what had happened, she immediately suspected you. Now, I've listened to a lot of weird old ladies, so I did not pay much attention until I did a little background check. Edward Kimball had recently purchased almost three million dollars' worth of life insurance. Imagine that."

I'd been conned. Me. "This proves nothing."

"Right again," he continued. "You were very smart about it. You knew your husband the international trader was actually a drug dealer and, as a result, his murder would look like a hit. But like Rose Kimball, I suspected otherwise. So we came up with the idea of creating another Edward."

"I still don't—"

"You were right, of course. The wedding photo was a little bit of trick photography. The IDs were police forgeries. We picked up another Mercedes, but we couldn't get one with the burgundy interior so we used a gray one."

"So you wanted me to think Edward was alive?"

He shrugged. "We were playing a little mind game, that's all. You knew *you* shot him in the head. But after all of this, you began to have doubts. You began to wonder if Edward had somehow survived, if he had somehow discovered your plan and pulled a fast one on you—switched your real bullets for blanks, used a little ketchup to make everything look nice and bloody. And now maybe he was wreaking revenge on you with this impostor. That was what you thought, wasn't it?"

I was too busy looking for a way out to respond.

His face was so damn smug. "So you came back here to check the gun for blanks and prove to yourself that Edward was alive," he continued. "And once you turned that corner, Mrs. Kimball, you gave it all away. There was only one way you could have known where the gun was, or about this alley. Because you killed him."

I spotted a sliver of light. "Can I borrow a cigarette, Sergeant?"

He tossed me a pack of Marlboros. I took one out and lit it. I expected to choke and start coughing hysterically—I have never tried a cigarette before—but I found it rather pleasant and somewhat comforting. "Suppose I had not thought Edward was behind it?" I asked.

"Excuse me?"

"Suppose," I continued, "that instead of doubting Edward's death I began to doubt my own sanity. Suppose my already fragile mind was pushed to the brink by your heartless scheme?"

Harding looked at me, a little lost now.

I turned toward the impostor. "Edward, will you take me home now?"

"Huh?"

Yes, it was time to play Ms. Insanity Plea. Paint myself as Victim of Overzealous Police. Juries loved that. I threaded my arm in the impostor's. "Sergeant Harding wants to lock me up, Edward. He thinks I killed you. But here you are, alive and well. You know I would never harm you. I love you. You're my husband. They think I've done something awful to you. Well, we'll just have to hire the best lawyer in all the land . . ."

ABOUT THE AUTHORS

With twenty novels under his belt, the bestselling author **Ridley Pearson** has earned a reputation for stories that grip the imagination, emphasize high-tech crime and forensic detail, and, all too often, imitate life. In 1991, Ridley was the first American to be awarded the Raymond Chandler Fulbright fellowship at Oxford University. Raised in Riverside, Connecticut, Ridley, with his wife, Marcelle, and their two daughters, Paige and Storey, divides his time between the Northern Rockies and the Midwest.

Lee Child was born in 1954 in Coventry, England, but spent his formative years in the nearby city of Birmingham. He went to law school in Sheffield, England, and after part-time work in the theater he joined Granada Television in Manchester for what turned out to be an eighteen-year career as a presentation director during British TV's "golden age." During his tenure his company made *Brideshead Revisited, The Jewel in the Crown, Prime Suspect,* and *Cracker.* But he was fired in 1995 at the age of forty as a result of corporate restructuring. Always a voracious reader, he decided to see an opportunity where others might have seen a crisis and bought six dollars' worth of paper and pencils and sat down to write a book, *Killing Floor,* the first in the

Jack Reacher series. The novel was an immediate success and launched the series, which has grown in sales and impact with every new installment. Lee spends his spare time reading, listening to music, and watching the Yankees, Aston Villa, or Marseilles soccer. He is married with a grown-up daughter. He is tall and slim, despite an appalling diet and a refusal to exercise.

Charles Ardai is an entrepreneur, writer, and editor. He is best known as the founder and CEO of Juno, an Internet company, and more recently as the founder and editor of Hard Case Crime, a line of pulp-style paperback crime novels. His writing has appeared in mystery magazines such as *Ellery Queen's Mystery Magazine* and *Alfred Hitchcock's Mystery Magazine,* gaming magazines such as *Computer Gaming World* and *Electronic Games,* and anthologies such as *Best Mysteries of the Year* and *The Year's Best Horror Stories.* He has also edited numerous short story collections such as *The Return of the Black Widowers, Great Tales of Madness and the Macabre,* and *Futurecrime.* His first novel, *Little Girl Lost,* was published in 2004 and was nominated for both the Edgar Allan Poe Award by the Mystery Writers of America and the Shamus Award by the Private Eye Writers of America. He previously received a Shamus nomination for the short story "Nobody Wins."

The award-winning mystery and suspense author **Brendan DuBois** is a former newspaper reporter and a lifelong resident of New Hampshire, where he lives with his wife, Mona, their overactive cat, Roscoe, and one happy English springer spaniel named Tucker. DuBois's first novel, *Dead Sand,* a murder mystery set in his home state, was published in 1994. It was followed by *Black Tide, Shattered Shell, Killer Waves,* and, most recently, *Buried Dreams.* The mystery series features Lewis Cole, a magazine writer and former Department of Defense research analyst who investigates things mysterious on and around the New Hampshire seacoast. In addition, he is the author of the thrillers *Resurrection Day, Six Days, Betrayed, Final Winter,* and the upcoming

Twilight. He has had more than seventy short stories published in such magazines as *Playboy, Mary Higgins Clark Mystery Magazine, Ellery Queen's Mystery Magazine,* and *Alfred Hitchcock's Mystery Magazine,* as well as in numerous original short fiction anthologies. In 1995, one of his short stories, "The Necessary Brother," won the Shamus Award for Best Short Story of the Year from the Private Eye Writers of America, and the PWA also awarded him the Shamus in 2001 for his short story "The Road's End." DuBois has also been nominated three times—most recently in 1997—for an Edgar Allan Poe Award from the Mystery Writers of America for his short fiction. One of his short stories in 1997 was also nominated for the Anthony Award for Best Mystery Short Story of the Year.

Bonnie Hearn Hill's novel *Intern* was published by MIRA Books in 2003. Her next novel, *Killer Body,* was published in hardcover in 2004, followed by *If It Bleeds,* the first of a series of mass-market newspaper thrillers. A national conference speaker and contest judge, Bonnie leads a private writers' workshop in Fresno and teaches online fiction classes for the Writer's Digest School.

Steve Hockensmith's debut novel, *Holmes on the Range,* was published by St. Martin's Minotaur in early 2006. The book stars Sherlock Holmes–worshipping cowboys (and *Ellery Queen's Mystery Magazine* perennials) Big Red and Old Red Amlingmeyer. A sequel is slated for release in 2007. A freelance journalist, Hockensmith has written about the entertainment industry for the *Hollywood Reporter,* the *Chicago Tribune, Cinescape,* and other publications. His column about mystery TV shows and movies, *Reel Crime,* appears in *Alfred Hitchcock's Mystery Magazine,* and his musings about pop culture and other inanities can be found at www.stevehockensmith.com.

Kicked out of Stanford University because of his radical activism, **William Kent Krueger** tried his hand at a number of professions— logging, construction, freelance journalism, academic research—

before finally settling on writing full-time. He is the author of the Cork O'Connor mystery series, set in Minnesota's great Northwoods. His work has received a number of awards, including the Anthony Award, the Barry Award, the Loft-McKnight Fiction Award, and the Minnesota Book Award. He lives in St. Paul, a city he dearly loves, with his wife and two children.

The son of an organic chemist and a registered nurse, **Tim Maleeny** suspects his love of poisons began at age five, when he conducted a failed experiment involving everything he could find under the kitchen sink, a paper cup, and some Drano. (Looking back, he readily admits the paper cup was a bad idea.) His novel *Stealing the Dragon* is coming in February 2007 from Midnight Ink, the first in an ongoing series featuring detective Cape Weathers. He lives in San Francisco with his wife and two lovely daughters.

In his "day job," **Rick McMahan** is a special agent with a federal law enforcement agency in the U.S. Department of Justice, and in his spare time he writes mysteries. Rick's writing has appeared in *Over My Dead Body, Hardboiled, DAW's Year's Best Horror Anthology,* and other publications. He has stories slated to appear in the forthcoming mystery anthologies *Derby Rotten Scoundrels 2, Fedora,* and *High Tech Noire.*

Kristy Montee, writing as **P. J. Parrish**, is the author of the critically acclaimed Louis Kincaid mystery series. The series is coauthored by her sister, Kelly Nichols. Their books have been on the bestseller lists of the *New York Times* and *USA Today,* and have been nominated for the Edgar Award, given by the Mystery Writers of America. They are also multi-nominees for the Anthony Award and the Shamus Award, given by the Private Eye Writers of America. Before turning to fiction, Kristy was a journalist, first with newspapers in her native Michigan, and then in Fort Lauderdale, as a reporter, columnist, dance critic, and editor. She began her fiction career in the 1980s and had four women's fiction books published, all set in the newspaper industry. "One Shot" is the first short story she has written since eighth grade.

Tom Savage is the author of four suspense novels: *Precipice, The Inheritance, Scavenger,* and *Valentine,* which was made into a Warner Bros. film starring David Boreanaz and Denise Richards. As "T. J. Phillips" he has written two detective novels, *Dance of the Mongoose* and *Woman in the Dark.* His previous short stories have appeared in *Alfred Hitchcock's Mystery Magazine* and in anthologies edited by Lawrence Block and Michael Connelly. He lives in New York City, where he works at Murder Ink, the world's oldest mystery bookstore.

Charles Todd is a mother-and-son team writing about Britain just after the Great War. The latest in their Inspector Ian Rutledge series is *A Long Shadow,* from Bantam. *False Mirror,* from Morrow, follows in winter 2007. Their Web site is www.charlestodd.com. The authors live on the East Coast, where Charles has been secretary of Mystery Writers of America and a member of the national board. He was also president of the Southeast Chapter. Caroline is well-known for her photography, her interest in foreign affairs, and her travels to out-of-the-way places. The unheralded member of their family is John, chief of the exchequer, who does the proofreading, the driving on the left-hand side in Britain, and even the baking of chocolate cake when deadlines loom.

Tim Wohlforth has had more than sixty-five short stories published in print magazines, e-zines, and anthologies. He is a 2003 Pushcart Prize nominee. He has received a Certificate of Excellence from the Dana Literary Society and lives in Oakland, California, where he is a full-time writer. A contemporary noir novel, *No Time to Mourn,* featuring the private eye Jim Wolf, was published in 2004. Lee Child, a *New York Times* bestselling author, writes of that book, "Like a great twelve-bar blues—the comfort of a familiar form jazzed by a fresh key and an exciting new voice." He is the coauthor of the nonfiction book *On the Edge: Political Cults Right and Left.* His Web site is www. timwohlforth.com.

In **Jeff Abbott**'s new stand-alone thriller, *Panic* (Dutton, August 2005), a young filmmaker discovers that everything he knows—his family, his lover, his life—is all a deadly lie. Jeff is the bestselling, award-winning author of eight novels of mystery and suspense, including his Whit Mosley novels: *A Kiss Gone Bad, Black Jack Point,* and *Cut and Run.* He is a three-time nominee for the Edgar Allan Poe Award and a two-time nominee for the Anthony Award. His short fiction was featured in *The Best American Mystery Stories 2004.* His first novel, *Do Unto Others,* a more traditional mystery, won both the Agatha and Macavity Awards for Best First Novel. He lives in Austin with his family.

Jim Fusilli is the author of the New York City–based Terry Orr series, which includes "Closing Time," "A Well-Known Secret," "Tribeca Blues," and "Hard, Hard City," which won Mystery Ink's Gumshoe Award for Best Novel of 2004. Jim also writes for the *Wall Street Journal,* for whom he has served as a rock and pop music critic since 1983, and is a contributor to National Public Radio's *All Things Considered.* His book on Brian Wilson and the Beach Boys' album *Pet Sounds* was published in 2005 by Continuum.

Laura Lippman is the author of the Tess Monaghan series, which has won the Edgar, Anthony, Agatha, Shamus, and Nero Wolfe awards. She also has written two stand-alone crime novels, *Every Secret Thing* and *To the Power of Three,* and has published short stories in *Dangerous Women, Murderers' Row, Tart Noir, The Cocaine Chronicles,* and *Murder and All That Jazz.* Her short story "The Shoeshine Man Regrets" was chosen for *The Best American Mystery Stories of 2005.* A former journalist, she lives in Baltimore.

R. L. Stine's Goosebumps and Fear Street series have made him one of the bestselling children's authors of all time. He has written more than three hundred books of horror and humor for young people. His latest adult thrillers are *The Sitter* and *Eye Candy,* published by Ballantine Books.

Jay Brandon balances two successful careers; on one hand, he is an attorney in San Antonio, Texas, on the other, a mystery novelist. With a master's degree in writing from Johns Hopkins University and experience as an attorney with the district attorney's office in Bexar County and with the Fourth Court of Appeals, Jay knows his settings. Each of his novels takes aspects of people, places, and happenings in the world of law and adds Jay's own brand of gripping suspense and excellent writing. A native Texan, he now devotes his time to writing and his law practice in San Antonio, where he lives with his wife and three children.

Winner of the Edgar, Shamus, and Anthony awards—the first author to win all three—the *New York Times* bestselling author **Harlan Coben** has had his critically acclaimed novels called "ingenious" (*New York Times*), "poignant and insightful" (*Los Angeles Times*), "consistently entertaining" (*Houston Chronicle*), "superb" (*Chicago Tribune*) and "must reading" (*Philadelphia Inquirer*). His most recent novels, *Just One Look, No Second Chance, Tell No One,* and *Gone for Good,* are international bestsellers, appearing on the *New York Times, London Times, Le Monde, Publishers Weekly, Los Angeles Times,* and *San Francisco Chronicle* bestseller lists, as well as on many others throughout the world. His books are published in more than twenty-eight languages in more than thirty countries. He was born in Newark, New Jersey, and, after graduating from Amherst College a political science major, worked in the travel industry. He now lives in New Jersey with his wife, Anne Armstrong-Coben, a pediatrician, and their four children.

COPYRIGHT INFORMATION